KITTY NEALE

A Daughter's Courage

avon.

This novel is entirely a work of fiction.
The names, characters and incidents portrayed in it are the work of the author's imagination. Any resemblance to actual persons, living or dead, events or localities is entirely coincidental.

Avon
A division of HarperCollins*Publishers*
1 London Bridge Street,
London SE1 9GF

www.harpercollins.co.uk

This Paperback Edition 2018
1

A catalogue record for this book is available from the British Library

ISBN-13: 978-0-00-819170-2

Typeset in Minion by Palimpsest Book Production Ltd, Falkirk, Stirlingshire

Printed and bound in Great Britain by
CPI Group (UK) Ltd, Croydon CR0 4YY

MIX
Paper from responsible sources
FSC C007454

This book is produced from independently certified FSC™ paper to ensure responsible forest management.

For more information visit: www.harpercollins.co.uk/green

For my dad, the first man I ever truly respected.

You've always been there for me offering quiet strength, dependability and security.

Thank you for everything you have done for me, and for your continued support.

We rarely share soppy sentiments, but I know you love me very much and you're proud of me. I love you dearly too, and am so proud to call you my dad xxx

Chapter 1

Battersea, London, 1956

Crimson nail polish was the only splash of colour in the dank kitchen as Dorothy Butler painted her nails in preparation for her date with Robbie Ferguson. It was mid-September and she was sitting at the battered kitchen table. While waiting for the varnish to dry, she watched as her mother, Alice, flicked soapy suds from her hands before wiping them down the front of her washed-out apron.

Now twenty-two years old, Dorothy had been a child when her father returned from fighting in France, a broken man, unable to resume his work as a groundsman in Battersea Park. Since then, with only a small army disability pension to live on, her mother had taken in washing, which helped to pay the rent and buy the coal needed to warm the house during the long winter months. It was all Alice could manage as her fear of going outside kept her a prisoner in her own home. However, constantly leaning over the sink and scrubbing clothes had damaged her back, and Dorothy saw her grimace as she stirred the three cups of tea she'd just made.

Dorothy winced at the sight of her mum's hands. They looked blistered, red raw, and she wished she could do more to ease her burdens. Her own job as a baker's assistant didn't pay well and, though they had sufficient to eat, there was only just enough money left to pay the bills.

'Dottie, be a love and take this cuppa through to your father, will you?' Alice asked.

Dottie blew on her freshly polished nails, hoping they were dry, as she obligingly took the weak tea which had seen the leaves stewed three times. She carried it through to the sparsely furnished front room. She wasn't surprised to find her father Bill in his usual place, sat on a faded brown wing-backed armchair, staring up at the bare light-bulb hanging from the ceiling rose. Dorothy knew that her mother didn't believe in luxuries, neither could she afford them. If it wasn't practical or didn't serve a purpose, then it wasn't needed, and lampshades came under the latter heading.

'Here you are, Dad,' Dorothy said gently as she knelt next to her father's chair. 'I've brought you a nice cuppa.'

She studied her father's pale face. His skin was almost translucent and etched with lines. He had an especially deep furrow across his brow which Dorothy thought had been caused by a constant frown. He looked in a permanent state of anguish and rarely spoke or acknowledged anyone. She wondered if her father even knew who she was. It had broken Dorothy's heart when she had first seen him in this state, but it was something she'd now become accustomed to.

Having got no response from her father, she returned to the kitchen, where her mother was putting some freshly washed clothes through the mangle. For the umpteenth time she tried again to challenge her.

'Mum, why won't you let Dr Stubbs get some treatment for Dad? He's not getting any better and this has been going on for over eleven years now. It's pretty obvious that he's out of his mind.'

Alice wiped her forehead with the back of a ravaged hand as she turned to look at her daughter. Her greying hair was held in a loose bun with thin strands hanging scraggily down. Though only in her forties, the hard life she'd been forced to live had prematurely aged her, and she said wearily, 'I've been through this with you before, Dottie. I won't have your father put in one of them places 'cos you know what they do to them in there. They electrocute them! He just needs lots of love and patience from his family. You'll see, one day we'll have your dad back to how he was, but if he goes into that nuthouse, that'll be the last we ever see of him.'

'What if you're wrong, Mum? What if he never gets better?'

'He will, love. You know that Mrs Brigade, the woman from up Lavender Hill with the nine boys all with ginger hair, well, I saw her the other day in the haberdashery shop. She told me that three of her sons had come home from the war as very changed young men and it took years to get back to normal. The point is, they did eventually, and remember they're a lot younger than your father, so of course they would get better quicker. But mark my words, gal, your father will be back to his silly old self soon enough.'

Dorothy wasn't convinced and would rather have put her trust in modern medicine but she didn't want to push her mother any further. 'If you say so, Mum. I reckon it's a bloody travesty though. The army should never have sent him home like that. They should have sent him to one of those centres first, you know, the ones where they have special head doctors to sort out soldiers with that combat stress thing.'

'Perhaps you're right, love, but at the end of the day they washed their hands of him. Many years ago I did apply to have his pension increased, but they turned the application down.'

'You could try again.'

'No, love, your dad isn't physically disabled and, as they sort of hinted that he could be putting it on, it would just be a waste of time.'

'Of course he isn't putting it on,' Dottie said indignantly.

'You know that and I know that, but I'm not going to put him through one of those medicals again. Now come on, go and do something with your hair before that lovely young man of yours arrives. Is he taking you dancing tonight?'

Dorothy couldn't help but smile at the mention of Robbie, even though she knew her mother was changing the subject, which she always did whenever Dorothy brought up her father's health or his pension. 'He is, and tonight there's a band on who sound just like Bill Haley and His Comets. I've made myself a smashing pencil skirt to wear, but I'm not sure I'll be able to dance very well in it.'

'I don't know, you youngsters and your funny fashions. Don't get me wrong, Robbie's a lovely lad, but those trousers he wears are so blinking tight they're nearing indecency, and as for his daft floppy hair . . .'

'His hair is just like that film star Tony Curtis, and I don't hear you knocking him. And as for his trousers, well . . . I think he looks dishy in them!'

'Dishy? What sort of word is that?' Alice asked, laughing.

Dorothy joined in and then left her mother at the mangle as she skipped up the stairs to her bedroom to change her clothes and plait her long blonde hair.

Alice was so pleased to see the joy Robbie had brought to her daughter's life over the past few months. After all, the girl didn't have it easy. She worked long hours in the bakery and deserved a bit of fun.

A pang of guilt struck Alice again, the same feeling she'd harboured since Dottie first started work aged fifteen. Her daughter was such a beautiful girl and could easily have been a model, but instead she'd had to take the job with Bertie Epstein, the baker in town. Dorothy never failed to hand over most of her wages and she never complained about it. Alice tried hard to contribute herself, but couldn't earn enough to cover all the household expenses from taking in washing.

She was grateful to her neighbours for helping her out. It wasn't as if most of them could afford the privilege of someone to do their dirty laundry, but still they rallied around, paying a few pennies where they could for Alice to wash their clothes and sheets. She had a couple of clients from the posh houses facing the park, but they were proper skinflints and didn't pay much. She wanted to ask for more, but was too scared of losing the work. She paid a lad threepence to pick up the laundry and return it, and though it ate into her earnings, she was reluctant to add to her daughter's load by asking her to take on the task.

It was a hard life, but Alice wouldn't grumble. Bill couldn't help being how he was. He was all right physically. He could walk and with a push from her he would wash, dress and feed himself, but she knew that left to his own devices he would just sit in his own muck.

Alice sighed. It wasn't as if he'd deliberately sent himself mad, and when she tried to imagine what her husband must have witnessed to send him over the edge, a shudder went down her spine. He'd always been such a good provider, but when war broke out, being loyal to King and country, he had immediately put himself forward to 'do his bit'. Yet look at him now, rocking backwards and forwards in his chair, mumbling to himself and still screaming out in bed when the nightmares haunted him.

Alice yearned to help him recover but Dorothy's questions still rang in her ears. *What if he never gets better?* Alice stiffened with resolve. In sickness and in health, that's what she had vowed on her wedding day, and come what may she would stick to her promise to Bill.

Chapter 2

Dorothy's heart was beating nineteen to the dozen as seven o'clock approached. Robbie would be calling for her and butterflies fluttered in her stomach as she checked her reflection in the cracked mirror on her small oak dressing table. She applied a slick of red lipstick, using it as blusher too to rosy her cheeks. Her blue eyes were framed with jet-black mascara and a red satin bow held her long plait in place. She was strikingly pretty, with long legs that put her three or four inches taller than most of her friends, yet she was a humble girl who didn't realise how attractive she was to men.

Satisfied with her appearance, Dottie went over to the window and saw Robbie walking along the street, his hands tucked firmly into his trouser pockets and a roll-up hanging from the corner of his mouth. With a clap of glee, she grabbed a cardigan before racing down the stairs to open the front door.

'Hello, Dottie,' Robbie greeted her, flashing a wide smile. 'You're a sight for sore eyes! You look ravishing as always. Come here and give me a kiss.'

Dorothy giggled and pulled away from Robbie's tightening clinch on her. 'Pack it in, will you, my mum's just round the door,' she said, indicating with her head at the front room. 'She'll hear you.'

'Well, I don't mind if she does. I'll tell her what a gorgeous daughter she has and how I can't keep my hands off her lovely bum.'

Hoping her mother hadn't heard Robbie's remark, Dorothy yelled a hasty goodbye, grabbed her coat and quickly closed the front door behind her as she heard her mother call back a warning. 'Don't be late and behave yourself!'

Robbie and Dorothy both held their breath until they got safely out of earshot, but then burst out laughing. 'Behave yourself,' Robbie parroted as he pulled her into his arms again. 'I hope there's no chance of that.'

Dorothy tingled as Robbie lowered his head to kiss her passionately on the lips, and she squirmed with excitement as his tongue explored her mouth. Breathless, she untangled herself from his arms, aware and embarrassed that the neighbours might see them cavorting in the street. 'Let's get a move on,' she urged. 'We don't want to miss the best dances.'

Robbie threw his arm over her shoulder and led her down the street. She felt so proud to be with him. He was different, well spoken and from a nicer part of the borough than where she lived. She admired him, though she'd heard rumours about Robbie seeing other women. She quickly quashed her niggling doubts, looking forward to meeting up with their friends in the local church hall.

As they got closer to the dance venue, the sound of rock 'n' roll floated through the air. Dorothy felt her excitement increase and was eager to dance with Robbie, but then she heard shouting over the sound of the music and recognised the raised voice of her friend Jimmy. It sounded like he was having an argument with Kimberley, his old school sweetheart who was now his wife.

Robbie and Dorothy rounded a corner and came face to face with the quarrelling couple. She noticed that Kimberley quickly hung her head.

'Talk of the devil,' Jimmy spat.

'It sounds like you two are having a bit of a tiff,' Robbie said.

'I wonder why that might be,' Jimmy answered sarcastically. 'Care to shed any light on it?'

Robbie shrugged. 'I don't know what you're talking about.'

'Don't play the innocent with me, Rob. I've heard all about you sneaking round to mine when I've been out and getting up to all sorts with my missus.'

'I haven't been getting up to anything,' answered Robbie as he took Dorothy's hand and pulled her towards the entrance of the church hall, 'and if your missus says any differently, then she's a lying bitch.'

Jimmy arched his shoulders back. 'Don't talk about my Kimberley like that.'

'Huh, one minute you're accusing her of doing the dirty on you and now you're defending her. Get your facts straight, Jimmy. I popped round last week to help her out with a leaky tap which it seems you couldn't fix. I was just doing you a favour, *mate.*'

There were a few moments' silence and Dorothy looked again at Kimberley, who, with her head still hung low, quickly flashed her a sideways glance. In that split second Dorothy was sure she had seen something in Kimberley's eyes . . . something she couldn't quite put her finger on.

Jimmy broke the silence. 'Is that true, Kim? Was that all he was doing?'

'Yes,' Kimberley answered quietly, her head still low.

'Then why didn't you just say so?'

It was Robbie who answered. 'She never said anything because she didn't want to hurt your pride. Come on, Jimmy, get a grip.'

'All right, all right. Just don't keep stupid secrets from me again, either of you,' said Jimmy, looking back and forth between Robbie and Kimberley.

Tensions seemed to lower and the two couples made their way through to the filled hall, but those niggling doubts that had bothered Dorothy earlier were in her head again. She didn't want to spoil the evening, but she had to know the truth.

Half an hour later, Dorothy was finding it difficult to be heard over the loud music in the small hall as she repeated for the third time, 'I said, tell me the truth, Robbie. Have you been seeing any other girls behind my back?'

'I can't hear you properly,' Robbie answered close to her ear. 'Come outside.'

Dorothy followed him out and then he led her down an alley between the hall and the church. 'Now, what were you saying to me?' he asked as he gently pushed her against the brick wall.

The alley was dark, the moon being the only illumination, and it wasn't the sort of place Dorothy would venture alone, though she felt safe with Robbie. 'I feel silly now, but I need to know. Have you been seeing any girls behind my back?'

Robbie pressed his firm body up against hers as he

cupped her face in his large hands. 'Don't be daft, woman. You're the only girl for me.'

He kissed her in the way that always made her tingle and slowly slipped his hand up inside her sweater to gently cup one of her small breasts.

'Robbie, stop,' Dorothy forced herself to say. 'You know I'm saving myself.'

'Marry me then, Dottie. Be my wife,' Robbie said breathlessly.

Dorothy was astounded and could feel Robbie's excitement rising in his tight drainpipe trousers.

'What?' she asked. 'Did you just ask me to marry you?'

Robbie kissed her harder. 'Yes, marry me,' he said, between necking her and rubbing her erect nipple.

Dorothy tried to answer, but Robbie's mouth was firmly on hers and his other hand was yanking her skirt up to her hips. Her head was giddy but eventually she managed to whisper, 'Yes, yes, I'll marry you, but, Robbie . . . stop, we're not married yet.'

'Oh, Dottie, please, why wait? I love you and I'm going to be your husband. Let me get inside you.' Robbie had his hand at the top of her thigh and was sliding it inside her knickers.

'No, Robbie, we can't. I don't want to get pregnant.'

'You can't get pregnant the first time,' he husked, while doing things to her that made her gasp.

She had been dating him for five months and had held out against his advances until now, but he had never mentioned marriage before. Now, Dorothy couldn't believe she was going to be his wife. It wasn't the most romantic of venues for a proposal, but she found her body responding to Robbie's caresses and, with her head spinning, she wrapped her legs around his waist.

As he pounded her against the wall, she buried her head in his neck, enjoying the pleasure of feeling him pushing into her. He began to move faster, harder, and then threw his head back, letting out a long groan.

'Dottie, yes, yes,' he quietly moaned and then with a final thrust he finished, leaving her feeling thrilled yet strangely dissatisfied. It hadn't been like she thought it would, but who cares, she thought, as her head filled with images of herself in a wedding dress.

He pulled away from her, took a roll-up from his pocket and drew a long breath as Dorothy adjusted her clothing. 'I can't wait to get back inside and tell everyone about us getting married,' she said enthusiastically.

'Whoa, hold up,' Robbie answered quickly as he blew smoke up into the air.

Alarm bells rang in Dorothy's head and she suddenly feared she might have been duped into losing her virginity. 'What do you mean? You are still going to marry me, aren't you?'

'Yes, yes, of course. But before you go announcing it to the world, don't you think I should get you a ring first?'

Dorothy felt her panic subside and was relieved to hear that Robbie's reluctance to announce their engagement was only because he wanted to ensure it was done correctly. 'OK, but you had better get me one soon 'cos I can hardly contain myself. I'm going to be Mrs Ferguson. Mrs Dorothy Ferguson.' Yet, as she spoke, Dorothy noticed that Robbie's expression didn't seem to be as blissful as hers.

Robbie threw his roll-up to the floor before slinking back inside the hall with Dorothy. He couldn't believe he'd asked her to marry him, but in the heat of the moment he knew it would persuade her to give in to his lust.

He liked her, quite a lot in fact, but she was so prim and proper, unlike the other women he visited around here who were only too happy to open their legs to him. Robbie knew he was good-looking, and he easily charmed women, but usually if they weren't forthcoming he'd just drop them and move on. It was easy, too easy, and maybe that's what attracted him to Dottie. She was a stunner, and the fact that he had to try harder made her more of a challenge.

Then a thought struck him. Dorothy wanted a ring and he was totally broke. He'd only been paid yesterday, but already most of his week's wages had been blown in a card game. He was in debt to a couple of loan sharks, and he also owed money to his brother Adrian. If he was going to buy Dorothy any sort of ring, he would have to come up with a plan to get his hands on some cash, or be forced to go cap in hand to his brother yet again.

Dorothy had made a run for the ladies' toilets when Kimberley sauntered up to him with a knowing look on her face. He glanced around to make sure that Jimmy hadn't noticed.

'Keep your mouth shut, Kim, and make sure you stick to our story. I don't want Jimmy or Dottie finding out about us. What happened earlier was a bit too close for comfort.'

'Don't worry. I don't want Jimmy to know about us any more than you do, but someone up our street saw you leaving our house and had a word in his ear. He'll be going out on Tuesday night to darts, but best you come round to the back door. If it's all clear I'll leave my bedroom curtains closed, but if they ain't drawn, you'll have to scarper.'

Robbie wasn't sure if he still wanted to risk it with Kimberley, but then again she did things for him that very few of the others would. She liked to take control and would lead the way in the bedroom, which Robbie found was a real turn-on for him.

'OK, I'll see you then, and make sure you've got that little black lacy number on, the one you told me you wore on honeymoon with Jimmy.'

When Dorothy quietly closed her front door that night, Alice was waiting in the kitchen for her. She never went to bed before she was sure her daughter was home safely.

'Did you have a nice time? Judging by that big grin on your face, I'm guessing you did,' Alice asked, pleased to see Dorothy looking so happy.

'Oh, Mum, you won't believe it. I'm not meant to say anything until it's official but I'll burst if I don't tell you. Robbie asked me to marry him and I said yes!'

Alice was genuinely pleased for her daughter, but had been secretly fearing that this day would come. Her heart sank. She could help to make Dorothy's wedding dress, but, suffering from agoraphobia, she doubted she'd be able to get to the church to see her walking down the aisle. These damn stupid fears, she thought, cursing the affliction that would cause her to miss her only child's wedding day.

Not only that, but Alice didn't know how she'd cope without Dorothy. She hadn't left the house since before the Blitz, not even to take shelter as bombs had dropped around her, razing houses to the ground. Thankfully Dorothy had been evacuated to Devon and Alice's neighbours had rallied round, getting her shopping and anything else she needed. She had missed her daughter so much, but when the war ended and Dorothy was old enough, the young girl had taken over any outside tasks that Alice had been unable to do.

She had tried to step over the threshold of her front door on many occasions, but her phobia had always beaten her and she had retreated back into the safety of her home. Though she knew it was selfish, Alice worried how she would manage without Dorothy's wage. She felt sure that Robbie wouldn't want to live with his in-laws, especially in this part of Battersea. Their house didn't have any of the modern conveniences like an inside toilet, and, from what Dorothy had told her, Robbie lived in the posh part of the borough. Apart from anything else Alice knew that they would want to start a family soon, and then Dorothy wouldn't be able to work.

As if sensing her qualms, Dorothy quickly spoke.

'It's all right, Mum, you won't have anything to worry about. Me and Robbie will make sure you and Dad are well looked after. We'll have two salaries coming in, and I reckon he must earn a good one working as a mechanic. Whatever happens, I'll still get your shopping in, and as for my wedding day, we'll sort something out, even if it means I have to get married in the back yard.'

Guilt flared again at her daughter's words, but Alice was so proud of Dorothy. What a thoughtful girl to be thinking about her mum and dad! Robbie was a lucky man, and she hoped he realised it.

Dorothy was far too excited to sleep that night, tossing and turning as she began trying to plan her wedding dress down to every fine detail. She pulled the thin blankets up under her chin and shivered. She wasn't sure if the tremble was down to the chilly night or the memory of Robbie's touch and what had happened in the alley. All her good intentions of losing her virginity on her wedding night had gone out of the window, but at least the man who had taken it was destined to be her husband. It hadn't hurt like she'd heard it would. Actually, looking back she'd found it very enjoyable and couldn't wait to be living with Robbie, sharing a bed with him every night.

But that was something to ponder on, and, though she had reassured her mother, Dorothy wondered what she was going to do about her parents. She couldn't just abandon them. With her mother too afraid to leave the house, her father mentally unstable and no other family to share the burden, it would be down to her to ensure their security. Yet Dorothy was sure that Robbie would be understanding and supportive. He was fully aware of her situation so she wondered if he might consider moving into their home. It was an idea, but when she thought about the house that Robbie shared with his older brother Adrian she feared he wouldn't agree. It was much larger and grander than this place, and in a better area too. She'd been surprised when she'd first seen the house and met Adrian. He was very different from his brother. Whereas Robbie was tall and good-looking,

Adrian was short, tubby and balding, though his face was nice to look at.

Her mind drifted back to where they would live. If she could persuade Robbie to move in here it would be the perfect solution, at least until they were ready to start a family. They would have to rethink the situation then as there was nothing she wanted more than a child of her own, lots of them in fact – a house filled with little Robbies. Dorothy thought about how gorgeous they would look if they took after their father with his dark hair and big brown eyes.

She remembered how her dad used to play with her when she was a child. He was always so attentive and such fun to be with. Now, though, her dad's illness was the only shadow in her landscape, but maybe holding a grandchild in his arms would bring him back to them.

Dorothy smiled, hoping her dreams would all come true as she pictured her future with the man she was going to marry and loved with all her heart.

Chapter 3

Adrian replaced the telephone receiver and turned his attention to Robbie, who was looking agitated as he paced the office floor. Adrian knew they would never be taken for brothers. Robbie was tall, slim and dark with swarthy good looks, whereas Adrian knew his weight detracted from his pleasant face – and they were poles apart in character too.

Before his younger brother had a chance to speak, Adrian guessed that Robbie would be asking for money again. He took a deep breath, resolving that this time would be different; he wouldn't be a pushover. He would stand his ground and be firm. It was about time he gave the young man a few home truths. He knew it would be difficult but it needed doing as Robbie's finances appeared to be spiralling out of control.

'Hello, Rob. Why aren't you at work?'

'It's a bit slow today. We haven't got any vehicles in so Roger sent me off early, not that I'm complaining. He doesn't dock my wages and I bloody hate working in that greasy pit.'

Adrian sighed. 'I told you to continue your education, Rob, but would you listen? No. You insisted on leaving school and in fact you're lucky to be in your position. Lots of people would love to be a mechanic and earn the money you do. So stop complaining.'

'Yes, but I wish I'd listened to you now.'

Adrian narrowed his eyes. That remark was enough for him to know that his brother wanted something and he could guess what it was. 'So what brings you here?'

'You couldn't see me straight for a few bob, could you?'

Adrian looked at his brother's confident stance and couldn't believe his audacity. He didn't even look sheepish about asking. He just came straight out with it.

'I'm sorry, Rob, but no. You still haven't paid me back from last time, or the time before that. I suppose you've been gambling again, but it's about time you knocked that card playing on the head and took responsibility for yourself. I'm fed up with bailing you out all the time. You're twenty-six years old, a grown man, and it's time you acted like one.'

Adrian spoke firmly. He didn't like being so harsh, but knew it was the right thing to do. Since their parents had died of influenza when Robbie was thirteen, Adrian had become very protective of his younger brother. However, Robbie was trying to take advantage of his generosity one time too many and his patience was wearing thin.

'Don't be like that, it's not like you can't afford it. This business of yours makes you a fair packet.'

'Whether I can afford it or not is irrelevant. I've worked hard to build Ferguson Haulage up to what it is today, and to be honest, Rob, it's not just about the money.'

'What are you on about?'

'I'm always clearing up the mess you leave behind with your reckless behaviour. Christ, man, I've lost count of the number of times I've had to console an upset woman because you've led her a merry dance with your lies and philandering. Not to mention the many times I've reimbursed the money you've swindled out of them. I've had it up to here with you.'

'But that's just it . . . I'm getting married! I'm going to change, I swear, and that's why I need some money. I want to buy Dottie a ring.'

Adrian pushed his chair back from his desk, his thoughts turning. Could it be true? Was his brother really going to settle down? He doubted it, which could only mean one thing. 'Oh, God, please tell me you haven't got Dottie in the family way?'

'What do you think I am, stupid? Of course I haven't, but now I've asked her to marry me, I'll need to get her an engagement ring. So if you lend me the money I promise I'll pay you back this time.'

'I've heard it all now. Does she have any idea about your debts? Just how on earth do you think you are going to support Dottie and her parents? Because from what you've told me about them before, they will need looking after too.'

'Don't you worry about that,' Robbie answered slowly with a wry grin. 'It's going to be a very, very long engagement.'

Adrian's blood began to boil. He couldn't believe how unprincipled his brother could be, and though he'd only met her a couple of times, Dottie seemed such a lovely young girl. It wasn't as if Robbie had been brought up this way. Their parents had worked hard in instilling in them the difference between right and wrong and, after they had passed away, the boys' elder sister Myra had taken up the reins. She had cared well for Robbie until her move to Scotland, back to their family roots.

'I don't suppose Dottie knows that she'll be waiting a long time before she's walked up the aisle? No, I suspect not. Another one who's had the wool pulled over her eyes. Why do you do it, Rob? What are you getting out of her? Because I know it can't be money.'

There was a silent pause but the lascivious look on Robbie's face told Adrian all he needed to know. 'You can be such a ruthless bastard.'

Robbie just laughed. 'So are you going to lend me the money or not?' he asked.

'Not,' said Adrian.

Robbie approached Adrian and leaned forward, resting his hands on the desk. 'Honestly, I'll never ask you again if you just do this one thing for me.'

'The subject is not open for debate. I won't be any part of this. If you want to mislead that girl, then you will have to do it without my help. For goodness' sake, Rob, our mother would be so ashamed of you.'

Adrian saw a black look come over his brother's face, the same expression he had seen when Robbie was a teenager and would fly into an uncontrollable rage. Myra had always been able to calm him and he seemed to have grown out of his outbursts, but, seeing that same look now, Adrian braced himself. He was right to do so because without hesitation Robbie swept his arm across Adrian's desk, sending paperwork and pens flying.

'How dare you bring our mum into this!' he screeched as he brought his fist down heavily on the wooden desk.

Adrian sat transfixed in his chair, waiting for his brother's next move. He knew he'd gone too far with his last remark and instantly regretted it, but it was too late to retract it now. He watched as Robbie kicked a wastepaper bin, sending it soaring into the air, and then pushed over a shelving unit with such force that it skidded across the wooden floor. Then without a glance back his brother stormed out of the office, slamming the door behind him. Adrian was left shaken – but glad that Robbie had gone.

As he surveyed the mess around him, the door opened again, filling him with dread. Much to his relief it was only Joe, one of his drivers, though it was customary for his employees to knock before entering.

Joe was a burly looking chap yet even he looked shocked at the state of the office. 'Are you all right, guv? Only I saw that bloke just leave and he didn't 'alf bang that door.'

'Yes, everything's fine, Joe. He's my brother, nothing to worry about,' Adrian said hurriedly as he scanned the paperwork on the floor, picked up a piece and handed it to Joe. 'Here you go, this is the ticket for your next collection. You'll have to get a move on if you're going to be at the drop-off on time.'

Joe looked at him for a moment with narrowed eyes, but said nothing. He took the ticket, stepped over the scattered furniture and strewn papers, then left quietly. Adrian sat down at his desk again, still shaken, and struggled to pull himself together.

It had unsettled him to see Rob's anger. He'd thought his brother had learned to control his temper, but now he found himself anxious about living with a grown man who could be prone to such violent eruptions.

After leaving Adrian's office in a rage, Robbie decided that, though he didn't have the money for a ring, he had enough in his pocket to call in to the Union Arms on Battersea Bridge Road to have a pint or two and calm down. Adrian had always been a pompous git, but he shouldn't have brought their mother into the conversation. Though, if he was honest, his anger was mainly at his brother's refusal to lend him any money.

Robbie supped on his ale, savouring the smooth liquid. Two scruffy-looking men stood further along the bar and, as Robbie caught some of their conversation, all thoughts of Adrian and his condescending manner went out of his mind. The men were huddled quite close together, obviously hoping that no one could hear what they were saying, but as they swayed on their feet it appeared the pair were pretty full of beer and didn't realise how loudly they were talking.

Robbie listened intently as he heard the smaller man in a flat cap say, 'I'm telling you, George, it'll be a piece of cake. My cousin said that it's all about the timing. As long as we get it right we'll be home and dry, and we'll be at least a couple of hundred quid or more better off.'

'Run it by me again,' George slurred, 'and slowly this time.'

The man in the flat cap leaned against the bar. 'It's easy. You know my cousin works in Leonardo's, that posh jeweller's over in Knightsbridge? Yeah, well, she's gone and got herself up the duff so she'll be out of a job soon, but in need of some quick bucks. She said she watched old Leonardo put money in the safe and clocked the combination. We had a right laugh when she told me. The old boy must be losing the plot 'cos you'll never guess what it is.'

George scratched his head, 'I ain't got a clue. Go on, tell me . . .'

'It's only left four, right three, left two, right one. He must have set it up like that so he doesn't forget it, but neither will we,' the man in the flat cap said and laughed. 'She reckons he puts the day's takings in the safe on Saturday when they close, and it just sits there 'til Monday when he banks it. So all we've got to do is break in on a Sunday and Bob's your uncle.'

George nodded but then asked, 'What about alarms and all that? He must have a place like that belled up so how are we gonna break in? If we smash a window, or jemmy the door, the Old Bill will be straight on to us.'

'Don't you worry about that, I've got it all covered. My cousin said there's a small attic skylight on the roof. It's not alarmed so we just need to lever it open, drop down inside and then head for the safe. We'll grab the cash and then leave the same way. No one will know we've been in there until Monday morning when Leonardo goes to his safe and finds it empty.'

'Bloody hell, it's genius! When we gonna do it? This Sunday?' asked George.

'Well, we could, but I've already promised my mum that I'll bring Ginny and the kids over this weekend, and you know my life won't be worth living if I let either of the battle-axes down.'

George groaned. 'Yeah, I know what you mean. Next weekend it is then.'

The two men shook hands as Robbie inwardly smiled. This was the answer to his worries. Lady Luck must be smiling on him because it had been handed to him on a plate. All he had to do was get in there this weekend to beat the two old drunks to the stash of cash. It sounded fail-safe and he would never have to go to his brother again for money. He'd be able to pay back all that he had borrowed and that would get Adrian, along with others, off his back.

Grinning, Robbie ordered another pint, well chuffed that all his money problems would soon be over.

Chapter 4

Dorothy gave her mother a quick peck on the cheek before she dashed out of the door to meet Robbie. He was taking her to the cinema and she was really hoping that tonight would be the night when he would present her with the engagement ring she was so eagerly anticipating. After all, it had been over a week since he'd asked her to marry him.

As she walked along the street of small terraced houses, she caught sight of her reflection in the window of the newsagent shop on the corner. Her dress was homemade, as were most of her clothes, but she was pleased with her creations and was always up to date with the latest trends. Her long jacket was finished with a velvet collar, and though she would have preferred to be wearing a pair of high heels, she couldn't afford to buy any. Still, she'd made an extra special effort with her hair so was relieved that it was a dry evening, meaning her curls wouldn't be washed out. It was important that she looked her very best as she was sure that at some point during the evening Robbie would get down on one knee and formally propose.

As Dorothy quickened her pace and got closer to the

bus stop, she could see that Robbie was already there, but her heart sank as she saw he was talking to a group of three young women. He looked a little too close to them, particularly one of them. Dorothy could see the woman placing a cigarette in her mouth, looking up into Robbie's eyes as he lit it for her.

'Hello, Robbie,' Dorothy called. She was trying her best to sound unfazed and cheerful, but in reality she was feeling very insecure and self-conscious in her homemade clothes, which couldn't compare with the sophisticated appearance of the women. They cast their eyes over her as though they were looking down their noses, making Dorothy squirm inside. She saw Robbie wink at the woman with the cigarette before he sauntered towards Dorothy and kissed her on the cheek.

'Hello, darling. These ladies are heading for the Junction too, but their car has broken down so I've told them to join us on the bus.'

Dorothy feigned a smile. She was irritated and a little jealous of the woman with the cigarette. Along with the elegant outfit, she was wearing high heels and appeared to have grabbed Robbie's attention, but before Dorothy had time to dwell on it the bus arrived and all five of them clambered on board.

Robbie, being the gentleman he always was, paid for all their fares and entertained the three ladies for the length of the journey. Dorothy did try to join in their conversation, but the topic was politics, which she knew nothing about, and though Robbie's knowledge normally impressed her, this time she felt left out and sat pouting in silence.

Once they arrived at the Junction, Robbie said farewell

to his new-found friends but Dorothy was vexed when the cigarette lady gave Robbie a flirty smile and said, 'I'll see you tomorrow then, Robert.'

Dorothy quickly alighted from the bus and stomped along the pavement, but Robbie soon caught up with her and marched in time at her side.

'Hey, slow down, Dottie. What's got into you?'

'What was all that about, "I'll see you tomorrow, Robert"? Since when has anyone called you *Robert*?' she said, seething.

'Calm down. I'm a mechanic, her car's broken down and I'm going round tomorrow to fix it. You want a nice ring, don't you, so I need the extra cash. And she called me Robert because I told her my given name as it sounds more professional.'

Dorothy suddenly felt very embarrassed about her little sulk. Robbie had only been thinking about her and, even though she obviously wouldn't be getting her ring tonight, it warmed her inside to think that Robbie was willing to work on a Sunday to buy her one. That proved how much he must really love her.

'I'm sorry, Robbie,' she said. 'I don't mean to act like a spoilt brat. It's just that I love you so much and can't stand the thought of losing you to another woman.'

'That's never going to happen. I've told you before, you're the only girl for me. Now put a smile on those sexy red lips, and don't be expecting to see much of this film tonight as we're going to be busy in the back row.'

Dorothy knew that this meant lots of kissing and that was fine with her. She would much prefer smooching with Robbie to watching a film. Of course they could only kiss and cuddle. There could be no funny business, not in public, but the thought of his touch made her shiver with delight.

Robbie was glad to see there wasn't much of a queue for tickets. He'd been paid and so far he still had a full wage packet, which meant that, once inside the cinema, he could go to the kiosk and buy Dottie some chocolates to soften her up.

Pleased to see her smile at his gift, Robbie then avoided the usherette and gently pulled Dorothy to a back row in the far corner of the cinema. He had sat in these seats before with Martha Jones and knew it was a dark spot. He could get away with being frisky without worrying about being caught.

The auditorium only half filled and the film began to flicker on the big screen. Robbie wasted no time and as Dorothy stared wide-eyed at the glamorous film stars, he began to run his hand up her leg.

'Robbie, no,' Dorothy protested.

'Come on, Dottie. I'm not really here to watch *The Green Man*.'

'We can't do anything, someone will see us.'

Her naïvety annoyed him sometimes, but he put up with it because she was such a stunner. 'Look around you, there's loads of couples having a snog, so stop worrying,' he urged and kissed her in the way he knew she liked.

Dorothy responded, but when he took her hand and placed it on his unzipped trousers where his manhood was bulging through his pants, she just left it where it rested. It added to his annoyance. He'd been hoping that she would at least give him a rub, so he tried again to get his hand up her skirt, and though she didn't brush him away this time, she kept her legs clamped tightly together. 'Come on, Dottie, relax, will you,' he urged.

'It doesn't feel right, doing this in here,' she whispered. 'I don't like it with all these people around. It'll be different when we're married and living together.'

Robbie's frustration was bursting. He jumped up, zipped up his trousers and pulled Dorothy to her feet. 'Come on, let's get out of here,' he barked, ignoring the hurt look on her face.

Once outside, his mind raced as he tried to think of an excuse to get rid of her. She was a beautiful woman, there was no question about that, but he had a big job to do in the early hours and before he set out to do it he had to relieve some of his tension. It was obvious that Dottie wasn't going to be the woman to do that for him tonight.

'I'm not feeling all that clever,' he lied. 'My stomach is churning something rotten. I think it would be best if I drop you back home and then get myself off to bed. I'm sorry, sweetheart, I'll make it up to you next week.'

'Is that why you suddenly dragged me out? It wasn't because I didn't want to do *it* in there?'

'Yes, it just suddenly came over me and I felt all hot and sweaty. I bet it was that ham I had earlier. I thought it smelt a bit iffy.' Robbie couldn't believe how easy this girl was to manipulate. She didn't seem too upset, which made his life much easier.

They sat in silence holding hands on the bus ride home, but Robbie could feel his jaw clenching as he mulled over his plans for later. He was like a wound-up coil and decided that, once Dottie was safely deposited back at home, he would call in to see Cynthia. She was quite a bit older than Robbie, but always made him very welcome. Cynthia wasn't much to look at, but she was good with her hands and he knew he would get a tantalising all-over massage. Just the ticket, Robbie thought, and afterwards he'd make his way over to Knightsbridge. He'd decided that if he waited until well after midnight there'd be fewer people about. He'd never attempted a burglary before and had to admit to himself that he was more than a little nervous about the whole thing. From what he'd heard, though, it was going be straightforward enough, and boy, did he need the money.

Of course he could have put off paying Adrian back, but the loan sharks were after him for what he owed and it wouldn't be long before his excuses wore thin with them. He didn't want to end up taking a pasting, so stealing what he hoped would be at least two hundred pounds would easily sort out all his debts. If there was more in the safe he might even be able to buy a decent second-hand car. A nice motor would impress the birds too, and Dottie would more than likely be up for a bit of fun on the back seat.

Robbie's jaw relaxed as he thought about what else he would spend his stolen money on. Any fears he had about the prospect of getting caught and ending up behind bars in a stinking prison were quickly pushed to the back of his mind.

Alice sat quietly in the dim living room listening to *The Archers* on the radio. It was the omnibus edition and Alice was looking forward to the rare hour of relaxation. With Bill being the way he was and sitting in silence, the characters on the radio were all she really had for company on a Saturday night.

She heard a key turn in the front door and was surprised to see Dorothy walk into the front room. She hadn't been expecting her home for a while yet.

'Hello, love, you're early. Did you have a nice time with Robbie?'

'Not really. He wasn't feeling too well. No official proposal tonight but he did talk about doing some extra work to buy me a nice ring.'

'Oh, well, that'll be something nice to look forward to then. There's some warm milk on the stove if you fancy a hot mug of cocoa. You can come and sit with me and listen to my programme if you like?'

Dorothy smiled. 'Thanks, Mum, but I think I'll pass on that and finish off hemming the dress I'm making.'

With that, Dorothy left the room like a whirlwind. Alice wished she had the same energy as her daughter, but years of toiling over the kitchen sink had left her spine bent and the constant pain had been really wearing her down lately. Oh, well, she thought, trying to be positive, it wouldn't be much longer until Bill recovered and then things would be back to where they were before the war. Alice reached across to pat the back of Bill's hand. She just hoped he would be well enough to see his daughter get married.

Chapter 5

Robbie decided to case the area first, but his heart was thumping so loudly in his chest that he was sure the posh-looking people in Knightsbridge could hear it as they walked past him. He was trying his best not to look guilty, fearful that the expression on his face would give the game away and raise suspicion.

Rounding a corner he saw a pub and decided a stiff drink would be in order to calm his rattled nerves. It had been nice with Cynthia: she had more than relaxed him for a while, and he'd managed to pinch a large screwdriver from her, one that he thought would do the job. Now, though, his tension had risen again and for a fleeting moment he considered calling the whole thing off.

He just caught the pub before closing time and once inside, with a large brandy down his neck and another in his hand, he felt his courage returning. Of course, the thought that soon he'd have stacks of money in his pockets was the driving force, especially as earlier in the week one of his debtors, Brian, had threatened him. He'd managed to hold him off with the promise of full payment, and now that promise was soon to become a reality.

It wasn't just clearing his debts that drove Robbie. He wanted stuff, nice things like his brother owned, and, though he was reluctant to admit it, he was jealous of Adrian. Yes, he knew he was much better looking than his brother, but Adrian, who was ten years his senior, had money and his own business. Adrian didn't have to sweat over oily engines all day or be at the beck and call of a whinging governor. Adrian was his own boss and Robbie wished he could be too. This will be one in the eye for him, thought Robbie, imagining the look on Adrian's face when he turned up in a newly bought car.

Robbie knocked back the second large brandy as time was called, and feeling more resolved he took a deep breath and headed for the jeweller's. Not being familiar with the area, he had no idea how to access the shop's rooftop and hoped it would be obvious when he got there.

With the strong drink coursing through his veins, Robbie felt more assured than he had earlier. He reached Leonardo's and had a quick look around, but then carried on by. There were still too many people about so he killed more time by casually walking around until the area thinned of pedestrians. Once he felt it would be safe, he made his way back to the jeweller's and looked over his shoulder to check that no one spotted him as he darted down a narrow alley next to the shop. To his pleasant surprise Robbie saw there was an old metal ladder, attached to a wall, that looked as though it went straight to the roof. He assumed it was a fire escape, but it didn't look very secure so he tugged hard on it, ready to scarper if his action set off an alarm. Nothing happened and, hoping it was firmly fixed, he gingerly climbed up to the roof.

Once on top, he squinted in the darkness, and, just as he'd heard the two drunken men describing it, he saw the skylight directly above the jewellery shop. Robbie scurried across to it and levered it fully open so that he could peer down inside. It was too dark to see anything, and, unsure how big the drop would be, he hesitated, but there was no time to fear injury. This was it. There was no turning back, so, bracing himself, he lowered his body in until he was just clinging on to the edge of the skylight frame. For a moment he hung there, but then, gathering his nerve, Robbie let himself drop.

He landed in a heap, with a loud thud which he prayed had gone unnoticed. He lay in the silence for a while, but didn't hear a sound. When he felt confident that the premises were empty, he scrambled to his feet, straining his eyes to look for a way down to the shop.

It was no good; even though his vision had adjusted to the darkness it was too black to see anything and he cursed himself for not having had the sense to bring a torch. He at least had matches so he lit one, and in the dim light of the flame spotted a door. He opened it, but before he could go any further the flame burned his finger. Quickly dropping the match, he swore under his breath and lit another, which revealed a wooden staircase twisting downwards. Unsure if there were any windows in the stairwell, he carefully felt the walls to guide his way down the stairs – he didn't want to risk anyone seeing the light of a match.

At last he was at the bottom. Slowly, Robbie pushed open another unlocked door. He sensed it was a small room and, judging by how dark it was, he guessed there were no windows. He lit another match, and seeing he was right he switched on the light. Despite being taut with tension, Robbie smiled. He was in the back office of the shop; this was where he'd find his treasure.

It didn't take him long to locate the safe. He turned the combination lock and laughed out loud when the safe door sprang open. This all seemed so easy, almost too easy. He stuffed his pockets with the notes, taking a gleeful moment to hold a handful of money in the air and kiss it, grinning to himself as he thought of the flashy car he would soon own. He'd never seen this amount of money before, let alone touched it, and wished he had thought to bring a bag to put it in. His pockets were bulging and he even had money stuffed into his socks.

When the safe was empty Robbie went to the door that led to the main shop. Why not, he thought? He was here now so he might as well get Dottie a ring. It would save him having to waste any of his newly acquired wealth on buying one. Robbie paused for a moment. This was going to be more risky. When he'd clocked the shop from outside he'd noted the windows were protected by pull-down metal grilles, but they didn't completely obscure the interior. Sod it, he thought, he was dressed in black so hard to spot, and if he was stealthy enough he felt sure he could pull it off.

Cautiously Robbie pulled down the handle and pushed the door slightly open. He peeped through the small gap, his wide eyes scanning the street in front. It looked clear. There wasn't anyone visible so, feeling more confident, he pushed the door fully open.

Alarm bells pierced the air. The clanging was so loud that it startled Robbie into a frozen stance. He panicked, looking all around him as his mind went into a frenzied state. Should he go to the street door and make a run for it out the front? No, the door would be locked. He would have to go back onto the roof and climb down the ladder, but the police might arrive before he was able to get away.

Hide? He could hide. Wait for them to search the place then sneak out. Where could he hide though? In the attic? No, they would find him there. He had no choice. He would have to get out the way he'd come in.

Robbie made a dash for the stairs and fell up them in his haste. The adrenalin pumping through his body stopped him feeling the pain in his shins, and, gathering himself together, with the alarm bells still piercing his ears, he reached the dark attic. Fear gripped him as he suddenly realised he couldn't reach the skylight, yet he still jumped up in vain, trying again and again to grasp the window frame but failing each time. He searched for his matches as twenty, ten and five pound notes dropped from his pockets.

Robbie wasn't concerned about the money right now. He had to strike a match to light the room – had to find something to stand on so that he could reach the skylight and make his escape.

Chapter 6

On Wednesday, when her early shift finished, Dorothy collected her purse from her locker at the bakery and turned to her best friend, Nelly Jackson. They were completely different in looks, Nelly being short and stout with broad features and mousy brown hair, but they had been firm friends for many years.

'Nelly, I won't be walking home with you today,' Dorothy said. 'I haven't heard from Robbie since the weekend and, as he was feeling poorly, I want to check that he's OK.'

Nelly scowled. 'You know my thoughts on that man . . . you're mad to chase him.'

'I'm not chasing him, I'm worried about him,' Dorothy replied curtly.

'Well, I doubt he'd be so worried about you, but it's your lookout. I'll see you tomorrow.'

Dorothy knew how Nelly felt about Robbie, and though it irritated her she chose to ignore her churlishness. She suspected that Nelly was jealous, but right now she was too worried about Robbie to care. There was an awful stomach bug going around, and, as he'd felt sick in the cinema last Saturday, she hoped he hadn't succumbed to it. Robbie would normally have called round on Tuesday to see her, but he hadn't shown up so she assumed he must still be unwell.

Dorothy decided her first port of call would be the garage where he worked. She felt sure that now she was his unofficial fiancée he wouldn't mind her popping in, especially as she had some fresh ginger biscuits for him and ginger was supposed to be good for an upset tummy. They were the broken ones from work that Mr Epstein had said were in too many bits to sell in the bakery. Though Mr Epstein allowed this small concession, in all other ways he was a mean, strict boss and a stickler for punctuality who was known for sacking girls at a moment's notice. Still, the unsold or slightly stale bread and cakes had always been a godsend for Dorothy to take home, and in exchange her mother washed Bertie's shirts and overalls for him. Dorothy smiled as she thought what a proud woman her mum was – never one to accept charity.

The garage door was open when she arrived and, as Dorothy looked around the greasy workroom, she spied Robbie's boss with his head under the bonnet of a very ostentatious-looking black car.

'Hello, sorry to bother you, Mr Thomas,' Dorothy called nervously.

She made the man jump and he almost bumped his head on the bonnet. He walked towards her, wiping his hands on an oily rag. 'What can I do for you, young lady?'

'I'm Dorothy, Robbie's girlfriend. I wondered if I could have a very quick word with him.'

The smile disappeared from Mr Thomas's face and

was replaced with a scowl. 'You could if he was here but he ain't, and if you catch up with the lazy so-and-so, tell him from me that I'd like to have a word with him too.'

Dorothy was convinced that Robbie must be really sick if he wasn't at work. 'Oh . . . I'm sorry, he must be ill at home. I'll call round there.'

'He hasn't shown his face so far this week, nor has he sent word to me that he's ill. You tell him he'll be lucky if he's still got a job when he can be bothered to turn up.'

'But, Mr Thomas, there must be something dreadfully wrong if Robbie hasn't shown up for work. Please, give him a chance to explain. He needs this job. We're getting married, you know.'

Roger Thomas shook his head and returned to the car he had been working on, muttering under his breath, 'Good luck to you, you're gonna need it.'

Dorothy decided the man had only said that because he was angry with Robbie, and dismissed his rude comment as she made her way through the streets to the other side of Battersea and Robbie's house.

When she finally reached the impressive terraced house where Robbie lived with his brother, Dorothy knocked on the door, but there was no answer. Worried, she banged harder and then called through the letterbox, 'Robbie! Robbie!'

A short, rosy-faced woman appeared from the house next door. 'Goodness, what's all this noise? You won't find the Fergusons in at this time of day. They'll be at work.'

'I know, thank you, but my fiancé Robbie Ferguson

hasn't been at work this week so I wondered if he was at home sick.'

The woman cocked her head to one side and said, 'Now I come to think about it, I haven't seen Robbie this week either, or heard any of his music blaring on that gramophone of his.'

Dorothy was becoming seriously concerned now. Robbie wasn't at work or at home. Had something really awful happened? Was he in hospital?

'Thank you,' she called to the woman as she dashed along the street, heading for Adrian's office, her anxiety reaching fever pitch. Please let Adrian be there, and please let my Robbie be OK, her mind chanted over and over again as she hoped for the best, yet feared the worst.

When his office door flew open, Adrian wasn't surprised to see Dorothy standing there. He had been half expecting this, though when he saw the ashen look on her face his heart sank as once again he knew he had been left to pick up the pieces of Robbie's irresponsibility.

'Adrian, I'm so sorry to barge in on you like this but it's Robbie . . . I'm really worried about him. Is he OK?'

Though he'd only met Dorothy a few times whilst she'd been seeing Robbie, Adrian's impression was that she was a nice girl, and he dreaded what he had to say.

'I don't know what to tell you. That brother of mine is the bane of my life,' he said reluctantly as he lit his pipe while gathering his thoughts. Smoke billowed as he puffed hard on the stem to get it going. The pungent aroma of tobacco began to fill the office.

'What do you mean? Where's Robbie? Is he all right?' Dorothy begged.

The poor girl, thought Adrian, she has no idea, and the least he could do was try to protect her. Robbie was in Scotland, staying with their sister Myra, but he'd keep that bit of information to himself. 'As far as I know he's perfectly well,' he told Dorothy.

'So . . . so he's not ill?'

Adrian didn't know the full story. Robbie had just told Myra that he was fed up with London, and when they'd spoken on the telephone he'd been evasive. 'I received a bit of a garbled phone call from him yesterday. It appears he's up north, but I don't know exactly where, and from what I can make out he has no plans to return,' he told her in a rush. There, he had told it as it was. No sugar-coating it, but he immediately started looking for his handkerchief in anticipation of the tears that were bound to come next from Dorothy.

'But I don't understand. He . . . he never said anything to me . . . and . . . and we're supposed to be getting married. Why has he gone up north?'

'I have no idea. I'm so sorry, my dear, but that's our Rob for you. He's never had any consideration for anyone except himself and you'll never change him.'

'No, no, this can't be right. What about our wedding?

Adrian stood up and walked round his desk to place his arm gently over Dorothy's shoulder. It obviously hadn't sunk in yet and he said gently, 'I think you had better forget any ideas about weddings. We won't be seeing Rob for a very long time. If ever.'

The handle on the mangle felt extra heavy today, and as Alice turned it she was surprised to hear the front door slam shut, followed by heavy footsteps running up the bare stairs, then the sound of Dorothy's bedroom door slamming shut too.

Alice hurried upstairs and opened Dorothy's door to find her daughter strewn across the bed, sobbing her eyes out. 'Whatever's the matter, love?' she asked as she rushed to her daughter's side.

'Oh, Mum . . . he's left me,' Dorothy answered, hair streaked across her face and sticking to her tears.

'What do you mean? Who's left you?'

'Robbie! Robbie has gone up north and his brother said he might never come back.'

'What? But you two are engaged to be married. What's he doing up north?'

'I don't know. He just left without a word to me or nothing. Oh, Mum, what am I going to do? I love him so much and I can't live without him.'

It broke her heart to see her daughter so distressed, and instantly Alice wanted to wring the bloody young man's neck. However, the last thing her daughter needed in this situation was sympathy, so pulling back her shoulders she said sternly, 'Now you listen to me. You managed perfectly well before he came along and you'll get on well enough without him. Look at you, you're beautiful and can have your pick of any man around here.'

'But I don't want any man . . . I want Robbie. How could he do this to me? I thought he loved me.'

When Alice moved to sit on the bed Dorothy instantly clung to her, and Alice could feel her shaking with grief. The bastard, she seethed, upsetting my girl like this. If she ever got her hands on Robbie Ferguson, she knew she would quite happily swing for him.

Chapter 7

The next morning, when it was time for Dorothy to get up for work, she turned over in bed and then all at once remembered. Robbie was gone. She felt her eyes prick with tears again and rubbed them, feeling how sore and puffy they were.

Dorothy didn't know what time she'd eventually cried herself to sleep but her body and mind felt exhausted. The last thing she wanted was to go to work, and worst of all she would have to tell people about Robbie whilst the pain was so raw.

Alice quietly tapped on the door and pushed it open. 'I thought you might like a cup of tea.'

'Thanks,' said Dorothy, taking the chipped cup and saucer, but the last thing she wanted was anything to eat or drink. Her stomach was in such a knot that she was bound to throw it straight back up.

'Oh, Dottie, look at the state of your eyes. You can't go to work looking like that. I'll get you a cold flannel to put on them.'

'All right, but I'd best get a move on or I'll be late and you know what old Epstein is like if any of us are even a minute overdue,' Dorothy said. Then she paused. 'Truth is, I really don't know if I can face going in today. Can I stay home, please, Mum?'

'No, I'm sorry, love, we can't afford for you to lose a day's pay. I know you're upset about Robbie, but at the end of the day he's just a man. Maybe he'll write to you with some sort of explanation, but if he doesn't you've got to get over him. Weeping about at home won't do you any good, so buck yourself up and get yourself off to work.'

Dorothy flopped back on the bed. She knew her mum was right, but that didn't change the fact that she really didn't want to go in.

Alice came back to the bedroom with a cold flannel. 'You're still not dressed?'

'I can't do it, Mum. I can't face it.'

'You can and you will. Now get yourself up and sorted. Anyhow, Nelly will be there and it'll be good for you to talk to a friend.'

When Dorothy thought about it she decided that maybe Nelly could shed some light on Robbie's disappearance. Affectionately known as Nelly the News, her friend always seemed to know about everything that was going on in Battersea.

Soon after, with a heavy heart and swollen eyes, Dorothy traipsed to work and, though she managed to hold herself together, the moment she saw Nelly the hurt within rose again and she broke down. Dorothy felt Nelly's large arms engulf her, yet they brought little comfort, and the look of sympathy in her friend's eyes just added to her pain.

'Dottie, oh, sugar, I've heard about Robbie.'

Dorothy pulled away from her friend's embrace and looked at her imploringly, hoping Nelly would have the answers she so desperately needed. 'I don't understand. We were planning on getting married, so why has he run off like this?'

Nelly bit her bottom lip, and as she lowered her eyes Dorothy got the distinct impression that the woman was hiding something. 'Nelly, you're supposed to be my friend, so whatever it is you know, please, you have to tell me.'

'I've been hearing things over the last few days, but Dottie, it's because I'm your friend that I don't want to tell you. I don't want to see you hurt.'

'It's too late for that,' Dorothy pleaded. 'Look at the state of me. I need to know.'

Nelly led Dorothy to a bench at the back of the bakery, her fat sausage fingers wrapped around Dorothy's hand as she began to speak. 'There's been a lot of talk around about Robbie, things you obviously haven't heard, and to be honest, now he's gone, I think it's best you hear the truth. I should have told you ages ago, but you were so happy and I thought that maybe there was a chance he might change his ways.'

Dorothy's heart was pounding so hard that she thought it might burst out of her chest. Her stomach was in knots again and she held her breath as she waited for Nelly to continue.

'The thing is, Dot, he's a womaniser. He's been putting it about with all and sundry and he's led you a right merry dance. You know I've never liked him and now you know why.'

In her heart Dorothy wasn't totally surprised as she'd had her suspicions. Yet when she had asked Robbie he'd denied it. What a fool she'd been, falling for his lies. Her mind churned. Or maybe he loved her and had changed, just like Nelly thought he might. Confused, she ran her hands over her face. It was all too much; she couldn't think straight.

'Robbie asked me to marry him,' she said slowly, 'and though I did wonder if he'd been seeing anyone else, he swore that I'm the only one. Maybe he was a womaniser at first, but not now. He loves me. I'm sure he does.'

Nelly was shaking her head. 'Dottie, I'm sorry, but there's more and it's worse. I saw Cynthia yesterday and she told me that Robbie was knocking on her door in the early hours on Sunday morning. She said he was in a right old state, sweating and panting. Once she got him inside he said he was on the run from the coppers 'cos he'd just done a big job, and asked her to hide him for a while. He paid her well, so she put him up until a decent hour, then she went and borrowed her brother's car to drop him at the train station.'

Dorothy couldn't believe what she was hearing. Robbie doing a 'big job'? Puzzled, she said, 'I don't understand. What was this job?'

'He robbed some posh jeweller's over the river.'

Dorothy was finding this all very difficult to take in, but then an idea struck and it suddenly made sense to her. 'I know why he did it, Nelly. It was to get me a ring. Robbie's not a bad person and he's no thief. This is all my fault for putting pressure on him to get me that engagement ring. He did it for me! Oh, Nelly, what have I done?'

Nelly sucked in her breath. 'But what about spending the night with Cynthia? She's only got one room and one bed so we know where he slept. Is that your fault too?'

'Well, if he needed somewhere to hide, everyone knows she'll do just about anything for money and maybe he was desperate. He must have been so scared.'

'Dottie, you can be so bloody naïve sometimes. I'm telling you, you're well rid of that man. He's a blinkin' criminal who can't keep his trousers zipped up.'

Dorothy felt a surge of strength and stood up defiantly. 'You're wrong, Nelly. You know what your problem is, don't you? You always want to see the bad in people, to give you something to gossip about. You won't have it that Robbie did this for me because he loves me and wants the best for me. Well, I'm sorry, but if you refuse to accept that my fiancé is a good, decent man, then you can go to hell!'

With that Dorothy stormed from the room, in no doubt that she'd left Nelly gobsmacked. She cared a lot for her friend, but if Nelly wanted to say such malicious things about Robbie, then she had no regrets about calling her a gossip.

She rubbed both hands across her face as her mind reeled. Her mother had been right to make her come to work, and now at least she knew the truth. Robbie had been forced to go on the run, and it was all her fault. Oh, Robbie, her mind cried. When will I ever see you again?

Chapter 8

It was the same thing every day and had been going on since Robbie had left. Dorothy would rush home from work, run straight to the kitchen and ask if there was any post for her. Alice knew that her daughter was desperately waiting on news from Robbie, but there were no letters. Each day she saw the disappointed look on her daughter's face, yet Dorothy still held out hope, which was more than Alice did. Though Dorothy had kept it to herself, gossip had reached Alice that Robbie had been involved in some sort of robbery, and if that was true her daughter was better off without him. It also explained why he'd done a runner and she doubted they'd see him in these parts again. Of course, eventually Dorothy would have to accept the fact that Robbie had gone for good and wasn't coming back to marry her, but she was dreading the day when the truth finally sank in and she would be left to pick up the pieces of her daughter's broken heart.

Though it was a cold November day, Alice was wet with perspiration as she heaved out the next load of washing. Mrs Pierce had given her a large bag of dirty bedding and, as Alice sorted through the laundry, she noticed bloodstains on one of the sheets. It didn't faze her – she was used to dealing with women's menstrual mishaps – but all of a sudden reality hit. Alice gasped and dropped the dirty sheet. She felt giddy and reached out to the kitchen table to steady herself, just as the door flew open and Dorothy walked in.

'Hello, Mum. Anything for me from the postman?'

Alice couldn't bring herself to look up at her daughter, let alone answer her.

'Mum . . . are you all right?'

She drew in a long breath. Maybe she was mistaken. Perhaps she had just missed the signs but there was only one way to find out. Her voice was grave, slow and steady as she stood as tall as her bent back would allow and asked, 'Dottie, when did you last have a period?'

The colour drained from Dorothy's face as she looked at her mother, her mouth opening and closing like a fish out of water.

'I thought as much,' Alice said scathingly. 'You've gone and got yourself in the family way.'

'No . . . Mum. I can't be . . . but . . . but . . .'

'But? What's that supposed to mean, Dorothy Butler? Don't you "but" me, young lady! Are you pregnant or not?'

'I don't think so . . . but . . . oh, Mum, I think I may have missed a period. No, no, I can't be pregnant . . . I just can't be!'

'Did you give yourself to that Robbie?'

Dorothy didn't answer.

'Well, did you?' Alice shouted and saw Dottie's body flinch. She wasn't usually one to raise her voice, but the thought of her daughter being an unmarried mother . . . oh, the shame of it.

'Yes,' Dorothy answered quietly, her head lowered.

'Then of course you could be pregnant, you silly girl. Oh, Dorothy, I thought you knew better. How could you do this to me? That's it, you've ruined your life, and how will we manage? You'll lose your job, and once the street hear about this they'll stop giving me their washing.'

'I . . . I'm sorry.'

Alice pulled out a rickety chair from the table, slumped onto it and buried her face in her hands. She thought she might burst into tears but found that she was too angry to cry. Instead, her head snapped up as she said, 'Sorry? Huh! What's the good of saying sorry? No man will want you now . . . a woman with a child out of wedlock. You'll have a terrible reputation round here. You'll be shunned and no doubt I will be too.'

Dorothy turned and fled the room whilst Alice shook her head in disgust at the thought of the child in her daughter's stomach. Robbie had run off so he wouldn't be doing the right thing, nor would he be any sort of a father to his baby. What were they going to do? Alice knew she would have to think fast before her daughter began to show any signs of her pregnancy.

Dorothy studied her stomach in the cracked mirror on her dressing table. Could she be pregnant? She reached under her bed and grabbed her diary before frantically flicking through the pages.

In mid-September, she had lost her virginity. She hadn't had a period in October . . . and now it was November. Her mother was right, she was pregnant. But they had only made love on the one occasion and it was her first time. Robbie had said that you couldn't get pregnant the first time . . .

There were no tears as Dorothy sat on her bed in disbelief. She had never seen her mother look at her like that before, but she could make everything all right if only she could get word to Robbie. If he knew she was going to have his baby, he would come back to marry her, just as he'd promised he would.

It was dark outside at 6.30 that evening and bitterly cold. Adrian had no plans for going anywhere, so he settled down in front of the telly with a whisky mixed with water and a large slice of fruit cake that his neighbour had kindly made for him, though it would inevitably add to his paunchy belly.

There was a knock on the front door. With a sigh, Adrian got up and opened the door, and was surprised to find Dorothy on the step. She was visibly shaking, and it didn't look like it was due to the cold weather. 'Dottie, what's the matter?'

'Can . . . can I come in, please?'

'Yes, yes, of course,' said Adrian as he pulled the door open wide and ushered Dorothy through to the lounge. 'Here, take a seat by the fire. Can I get you a drink or anything?'

'No, thank you. I'm sorry to disturb you, but it's really important I get in touch with Robbie. Have you heard from him?'

Adrian should have known this would have something to do with his brother. 'No, I haven't. I don't know where he is and you're not the only one looking for the scoundrel.'

'Who else is looking for him? Is it the police?'

'No, not that I know of. If Robbie wasn't seen when he robbed the jeweller's, the police won't have him down as a suspect. It seems he's got away with it, which surprises me considering the gossip.'

'Gossip isn't proof and anyway, people round here aren't grasses,' Dottie said with a sniff.

'He's been lucky then, but he's still in trouble because the men looking for him aren't the sort you'd want to pull a Christmas cracker with. It's just as well he's out of their reach.'

'But, Adrian, it's *really* important that Robbie knows something . . . something that's happened. I *have* to speak to him.'

'As I said, I honestly don't know where he is now, but if he does get in touch, I promise I'll let you know.'

Dorothy's bottom lip began to quiver and Adrian could tell that she was about to cry. His heart went out to her and he said soothingly, 'Don't get upset. Robbie's not worth crying over.'

'But you don't understand. I . . . I'm pregnant . . . and . . . and Robbie is the father.'

Taken aback, Adrian picked up his glass and downed his whisky. Yet more mess his brother had left behind, and as Robbie had moved on from Myra's he really had no idea where he was now. But poor Dorothy, this was a terrible situation for her to be in, and as usual he would have to step in to sort out Robbie's chaos. 'Here,' he said, feeling ineffectual as he offered Dorothy a handkerchief.

'What am I going to do? I can't be an unmarried mother. My mum is so ashamed of me and how will I support my child without a father?'

‘What has your mother suggested?’

‘Nothing yet, but I won’t give up my baby or go and see any backstreet murderer.’

Adrian could see that Dorothy was verging on hysteria. The girl was right to be worried though. It was going to be very difficult for her to raise a child alone. Then he had a thought.

‘Dottie, this child will be my blood too. I’ll be its uncle and, though Robbie may not be around to help, I am. I can help financially, make sure that you and your family are looked after, so please, calm down and we’ll work this out.’

Dorothy drew in juddering breaths and appeared to settle down a little, but then her tears resumed flowing and her nose started running, ‘I’ll still be labelled as a tart . . . and . . . and my child will be born a bastard!’

There wasn’t much Adrian could say to console Dorothy. It was true that she’d be labelled, yet if people knew what his brother was really like they would see that the pregnancy wasn’t this poor girl’s fault. As far as he was concerned, Robbie was the only bastard.

Chapter 9

It was a cold December morning and Robbie's head was banging. There were no curtains at the window and the sunlight streaming in was hurting his eyes. His mouth felt furry and he rolled over on the thin mattress as he tried to recall what had happened last night.

He had vague recollections of getting involved in some sort of drinking game with three miners, but couldn't remember leaving the pub or getting home to the house he shared with two other families. At least he had a room to himself, not like the poor buggers with several kids between them, all crammed into one room per family. He was also thankful that he hadn't woken to the sound of screaming babies again. His head was pounding enough without all that screeching adding to it.

He had moved out of his sister's large house, glad to get away from noisy broods. Her place had been all right at first, but he was peeved when, to make money, his sister let two sets of Irish immigrant families move in without even consulting him first. Annoyed, he'd packed his stuff and left, but now it looked like he was no better off, because this boarding house was just as noisy.

Robbie had a sudden flashback to the night before.

The miners had set a table up for cards. He had no memory of playing but thought he would have joined in. After all, it wasn't like him to turn down a game. Suddenly he sat bolt upright in the bed, swore and scrambled for his trousers that were lying in a heap on the floor. He anxiously searched his pockets, turning them inside out. There was nothing in them, not a single penny. He couldn't even remember it happening, but with a cold sense of dread he realised he'd lost all his money.

Had he lost it fair and square at the card table? Or did those miners rob him? Robbie couldn't be sure, but either way he was in dire straits. The rent on this room was paid up for another two weeks, but he had nothing, no money for food or tobacco. He couldn't even go back to Myra's as he didn't have the fare to get there.

Robbie sank to his knees, feeling hopeless. All the money he'd stolen had gone through his hands like water and he had nothing to show for it, just a sore head and a crappy room in a squalid house with no heating or hot water.

He needed money and fast. There was no way he would go back to working for someone else, slogging his guts out for them to reap the profits. It was a mug's game. He'd have to do another robbery, and though it would mean more risk, this next one would be bigger and better than his last.

Alice put a few more lumps of precious coal on the fire before she sat in the armchair next to her husband. She'd heard Dorothy vomiting again that morning, but her daughter was never one to moan; instead she'd simply got ready and gone to work quietly. The whole business still worried Alice. It was a relief to know that Robbie's brother had promised to help them out financially, but that didn't take away the fact that Dorothy was unmarried.

'Oh, Bill, the shame of it,' she said softly to her husband. 'Dottie won't be able to hide her bump for much longer and then the tongues will start wagging.'

Alice didn't expect any reaction from Bill, but it didn't stop her talking to him. Every afternoon at one-thirty she would pour them both a cup of tea, and then sit and chat to him about the weather, or the neighbours, or whatever sprang to mind. Recently, the main topic of conversation was Dorothy's unwanted pregnancy.

In some ways, Alice was pleased that Bill was apparently unaware of the situation. It saved him the pain of knowing what a terrible mistake his beloved daughter had made. He would have been devastated, she thought to herself, but at least this way he was oblivious to it. But at the same time she missed having her husband to share her worries and woes.

'I know we've always been so proud of our girl, Bill, and don't get me wrong, I will always love her, along with that unborn grandchild of ours, but if only she'd had a bit more sense. I mean, fancy getting herself in the family way. I thought I'd taught her better than that.'

She looked at her husband's blank face. There had been a time when he would have loved to have a new baby bouncing on his knee, especially if it was a boy. Bill had always wanted a son, but after Dorothy was born Alice had never conceived again. Now a grandchild was in the picture and she could just imagine it: Bill kicking a ball around with his grandson in the back yard, making little boats to float on the lake in the park, or building a go-kart from a wooden crate together.

As she rose to her feet and went back to the kitchen and the next load of washing, Alice hoped against all odds that if one good thing was to come out of Dorothy having a baby, it would be that Bill's lost mind would find its way back from whatever murky place it had wandered to.

The bell in the bakery chimed for lunch break and Dorothy was so grateful to hear it. Her stomach was completely empty, most of its contents down the toilet. She was beginning to feel a little weak and light-headed so was looking forward to tucking into the bread and cheese that her mum had packed for her. It seemed daft that with all the bread, cakes and pies they produced they had to bring their own food, but you could never rely on Mr Epstein's moods. Sometimes he would let them have any imperfect bakes, but at other times he would refuse and if they didn't bring their own lunch they'd be left hungry.

Food preparation was the last thing Dottie could face first thing in the morning, especially after braving the freezing cold of the outside lavvy, and since her morning sickness had begun she was grateful that her mum had taken over making her lunch. She knew Alice was still upset about the pregnancy, but had noticed that she'd begun knitting some little matinée coats and booties. She wondered if, as with her, there was a tinge of excitement setting in. Alice had warned her that, once the pregnancy was out in the open, she should expect a barrage of abuse from the locals, but Dorothy didn't care any more. She was blinded by love for the baby growing inside her and couldn't wait to meet her daughter or son. She was sure her mother was beginning to feel the same way too.

Dorothy eagerly grabbed her wrapped sandwiches from her locker and joined her friend in the small staff room. She was desperate to tell Nelly her secret, but had promised her mother to keep quiet for as long as possible. 'I'm absolutely famished, Nelly. I could eat a horse,' she said, eagerly unwrapping her sandwich before her bottom was properly seated.

'Blimey, Dottie, slow down or you'll give yourself a bellyache,' Nelly said, then looked at Dorothy's stomach, her eyes narrowing.

Dorothy looked down too, and saw she had a bit of a bulge. Half of her wanted Nelly to cotton on, but the other half was reminded of Alice's warnings.

'Dottie, don't take offence, sugar, but I've gotta say . . . you're getting a bit of a tummy on you. You might want to slow up on that bread and cheese. I mean, you don't want to end up looking like me!' Nelly said and laughed a big, bellowing chuckle as she patted her wobbling stomach.

Dorothy didn't laugh along with her friend, but instead gave her a knowing look in the hope that Nelly would guess the truth. Slowly, as the penny dropped, Dorothy could see it dawning on Nelly and the woman's laugh turned into a look of astonishment.

'My God, Dottie . . . have you got a bun in the oven?' Nelly whispered.

Dorothy nodded her head. 'Please don't tell anyone. It's a secret.'

'Oh, blimey! I won't say a word, I promise. I assume it's Robbie's?'

'Of course it is. Who else would it be? But he doesn't know anything about it. I still don't know where he is, and neither does his brother Adrian.'

'Bloody hell, Dottie, what are you going to do? You ain't married so surely you can't keep it.'

Dorothy noted the look of horror on her friend's face and felt disappointed. She'd hoped Nelly would be as excited about the baby as she was. 'If you're suggesting adoption, forget it. I'm keeping my baby, and until Robbie shows his face Adrian is going to help us out. You'll see, Nelly, once Robbie knows I'm pregnant he'll come back to marry me and everything will be all right.'

'Yeah, you live in cloud cuckoo land if it pleases you,' Nelly said sarcastically, 'but I'm telling you straight, that man will *never* marry you. Never in a month of Sundays.'

'I don't care what you say. I know Robbie loves me, and he *will* come back. When he does he'll love his baby too,' Dorothy retorted, but then her tone softened. 'Nelly, please, I don't want to fall out with you about Robbie again. I'm really happy about this baby and I hoped you would be too.'

After a long pause, Nelly finally answered, 'I can't believe you're happy with being up the duff without a husband. I think you've got a long, hard road ahead of you, but if you're determined to have this so-called *love child* then you're going to have to toughen up 'cos you know what people are like around here. You're going to need a friend and I'll be that friend, but I don't want to hear no more nonsense about that Robbie.'

Thanks, probably, to her haywire hormones, and despite what Nelly said about Robbie, Dorothy still felt like crying happy tears. Nelly would stand by her and that felt good. She was fully aware that few others would. The neighbours and locals would be judgemental and no doubt she'd be ostracised by them, and by the other staff in the bakery. Now, though, there was some compensation in knowing that Nelly was there for her.

'Thanks, Nelly. And it's a deal. I won't mention *him* to you again,' Dorothy said.

'Good, I'm glad to hear it.'

Dorothy took another bite out of her sandwich. She might not be able to talk about Robbie, but nothing could stop her from thinking about him, and praying that one day soon he'd come back to her.

Chapter 10

Adrian enjoyed his weekly telephone chats with Myra and would have loved to go up to a snow-covered Scotland for Christmas, but it just wasn't possible. There was far too much to manage with his haulage business, especially at this time of year. It was a shame Myra hadn't heard anything from Robbie; it meant Adrian would have to fulfil his promise to Dorothy to support both her and the child. From what Robbie had told him of their circumstances, once Dorothy could no longer work, he'd have to help out her parents too, and once again he cursed his brother for leaving him to clean up his mess.

As all of his drivers were out on their deliveries and he wasn't expecting any of them back for at least two hours, Adrian decided it was the ideal time to call at Dorothy's house and introduce himself to her mother. He had rifled through the things his brother had left behind and was thankful to find Dorothy's address. Going to see her parents seemed the right thing to do. There was the delicate subject of money to discuss and he thought it best to visit whilst Dorothy was at work.

Since his car was in the garage for a small repair, Adrian hopped on a bus, then made his way through several streets of small terraced houses, noticing that many of them were in a very poor state of repair. It had been a long time since he'd visited this side of Battersea and he hadn't realised the extent of the poverty. The roads had few cars, though there were plenty of scruffy young children with dirty knees and snotty noses playing outside their houses. He'd heard Robbie refer to Dottie as living in the slums, and could see why the area was due for demolition.

Dorothy's parents lived in the middle of their street and as Adrian approached he noticed white curtains twitching in one of the houses. He suddenly felt very out of place. His shiny shoes, smart tailored suit and long wool coat stood out, and he was glad he hadn't brought his car, because if he'd parked it in this area, he doubted it would have its wheels for long.

When Adrian knocked on the street door a thin woman answered it. Frowning, she looked him up and down before saying, 'Yeah, what do you want?'

'Mrs Butler, hello. I'm Adrian . . . Adrian Ferguson, brother of Robbie,' he said as he doffed his trilby hat. 'Please excuse the unannounced intrusion but I believe there are some things we need to discuss.'

The woman looked stunned and opened the door fully as she smoothed her hair. Adrian immediately noticed the sores on her hands, and as she invited him in and he walked behind her, he saw her back was bent.

'Please, take a seat, Mr Ferguson.'

'Thank you, Mrs Butler,' he said, running his eyes over the small kitchen. It was bare and basic but clean, though it could have done with a lick of paint. He twitched his nose at the smell of soap suds and noticed the pile of wet washing on the side, ready, he assumed, to go through the mangle. 'Thank you for inviting me in, and please, call me Adrian.'

'Yeah, well, you can call me Alice, and can I offer you a cup of tea?'

'No, no, thank you, and as I don't want to take up too much of your time I'll get straight to the point.'

Alice nodded, her brow furrowed as she took a chair on the other side of the table, saying nothing as she waited for him to continue.

'I know that my brother has left Dorothy in a rather unfortunate situation, and I have pledged to pay for Robbie's mistake.' He blushed slightly. 'Sorry, I don't like to refer to the child as a mistake, and I apologise for that.'

'It's the truth so there's no need to apologise,' Alice said gruffly.

'To be honest, other than the circumstances, I'm quite chuffed about becoming an uncle again. My sister Myra has three children, but as she lives in Scotland I don't get to see them much. With Dorothy living here, at least I will have the pleasure of seeing this niece or nephew growing up.'

Adrian shifted in his chair, aware that he was rambling on a bit. He cleared his throat before continuing. 'The thing is, as Dorothy is such a young woman with enough to deal with at the moment, I think it best that you and I talk finances.'

'My Dorothy told me you've offered to help,' Alice said, 'and it's ever so kind of you. Let's face it, you're not obliged to do anything.'

'I think I am. Robbie is my brother.'

'I'd like to get my hands on your brother,' Alice said, scowling. 'He's a no good so-and-so, but it seems you're nothing like him.'

Adrian saw Alice's lips purse at the mention of his brother's name. He couldn't blame the woman for holding Robbie in contempt. 'Mrs Butler, you are quite right, I am *nothing* like my brother and I will never condone his actions. Now then, from what Robbie told me, am I right in thinking that your husband isn't well enough to join our discussion?'

Alice nodded sadly. 'He hasn't been himself since he returned from fighting in France during the war.'

'In that case, let's get down to business, you and me. I've given it some thought and I think the fairest way would be for me to give you a fixed sum each week or month, whichever you'd prefer.'

Alice looked down at the table. 'I'm a bit embarrassed about all of this. I don't like charity coming to my doorstep, but I have to be realistic. Thing is, my Bill ain't gonna be in a fit state to work for some time yet, and me, well, I do what I can, but taking in washing won't cover much once Dottie has to give up work. We've gotta put a roof over the baby's head, so what are you offering?'

Adrian was quite taken aback by Alice's words. She had seemed a bit timid at first, but underneath that quiet exterior there was a little firecracker willing to speak out to protect her family. 'As I told Dorothy, I will ensure that the baby wants for nothing. I'm going to suggest nine pounds a week. How does that sit with you?'

'Nine pounds?' Alice squealed. 'But that's more than we have coming in now!'

'Mrs Butler, you will have an extra mouth to feed and the baby will require many things, a pram and a cot for starters.'

'It's . . . it's so generous.'

Adrian smiled. 'Good, that's settled then.'

'Thank you, I'm very grateful, but it doesn't take away the fact that my daughter will be unmarried and her name will be dirt around here. If only that brother of yours would show his face, then he could marry her and make her an honest woman.'

'I doubt any of us will be seeing Robbie for quite some time, but I can at least ease your family's financial burden. I'm sorry there isn't much I can do for Dorothy's reputation.'

Alice scraped back her chair and turned away from Adrian as she looked over the butler sink and out of the window to the small back yard.

'You could marry her,' she said quietly.

'I'm sorry?' Adrian replied, stunned at Alice's suggestion. 'Did you say *I* should marry Dorothy?'

Alice spun around. 'Yes, and it makes perfect sense. From what I've heard you're a single fella and my Dottie is a beautiful girl. Any man can see that, and I'm not being funny but she's the best-looking woman you could hope to have. She would make you a good wife.'

Adrian was at a loss for words. It had never occurred to him to marry Dorothy. Apart from anything else, Adrian didn't consider himself attractive to any woman, let alone one as stunning as Dorothy. He thought his face was nice enough, but his chubby cheeks and double chin detracted from his acceptable features. Dottie would never look twice at him, and anyway, she was still obviously in love with Robbie. No, it was out of the question and he knew that Dorothy would never agree to marry him.

'Yes, she is beautiful,' he said slowly, 'but I can't marry her. It's my brother she loves. Not me.'

'Dorothy is pregnant and needs a husband. What does it matter who she's in love with?' Alice asked.

'I'm afraid it matters to me.'

To Adrian's relief Alice seemed to accept defeat and didn't push the idea of marriage further. She did, however, insist that in future she did all his laundry. Adrian was about to refuse, but then realised that it made accepting the money more agreeable to Alice, and a little less like charity. Adrian smiled inwardly to himself. He did think that nine pounds a week for laundering a few shirts was a little excessive.

They had said their goodbyes and as Adrian arrived back at his office a light flurry of snow began to fall. He was glad to be out of the rough area and in a place where he felt a lot safer. He had to admit that he didn't like the idea of his future niece or nephew growing up in that part of Battersea, but took solace in knowing that from what he'd heard a lot of the houses were to be demolished soon and replaced with modern high-rise flats. The Butlers would be rehoused then, but, from what he could tell, it would take more than a bulldozer to shift Alice Butler from her home.

Fancy her suggesting that he take Dorothy as his wife, he thought. As if a pretty young thing like her would have him. However, Alice had planted a seed in his head, one that he was finding difficult to shift.

As the rest of the day progressed, he still couldn't get Dorothy off his mind, and now, when he thought about her, Adrian saw her in a totally different light.

Chapter 11

Robbie had come to the better part of the town in a bid to find somewhere suitable to rob. He pulled his scarf up over his face against the bitter wind. It hadn't snowed for a few days and what was left on the streets had turned to slush. He was desperate for a smoke and his stomach growled with hunger. With empty pockets he would have to go without until he found somewhere, or someone, to provide the money he so desperately needed.

As he wandered the streets, all filled with Christmas shoppers, Robbie set his mind to planning. The London jeweller's job had been a doddle – he'd almost been spoon-fed the idea – but it wasn't so easy to come up with a plan of his own. It would have to be fail-safe, low risk but high reward. Robbie knew he wasn't the sort of bloke who could handle a prison sentence; he had to ensure he wouldn't be caught.

Robbie glanced in the shop windows at the displays of expensive Christmas goods. Exquisite chocolates, fine jewellery, French perfumes and over-priced woollens. His thoughts suddenly turned to Adrian – these were just the sort of fancy shops that his brother would frequent. More determined than ever, and with jealousy raging within him, Robbie turned into a small side street to evade the howling wind. The shops in this street were mostly the artisan or bohemian type, not the sort that would be worth stealing from. He wasn't quite sure where he was going, but he carried on regardless.

He turned into another street that appeared to be coming to a dead end, and halted. His travels had been fruitless and left him feeling disheartened, hungry, cold and verging on giving up. Robbie was about to turn back when a shiny red MG pulled in to the kerb in front of him and parked up. It looked brand-new, and once again Robbie felt a surge of jealousy. It was just the sort of flashy car he'd love to own. Stepping back into a dark doorway, he watched as a middle-aged man got out of the car. He was dressed in the same style as Adrian liked, wearing a dapper suit and long coat. Robbie guessed the man would be loaded and wondered how much he might have in his wallet.

He waited for the wealthy-looking gent to pass the doorway, then, seizing the opportunity, he jumped out and grabbed the man's neck from behind. The man yelled out and struggled, but Robbie pushed two fingers into his back. 'Don't say a word or I will fucking shoot you,' he warned.

The man stopped trying to fight, his body seemingly frozen in fear as he quickly nodded his head. Robbie was nervous, but his victim's easy submission boosted his confidence. 'Give me your money . . . slowly . . . hand it over and I won't hurt you.'

The man took his wallet from the inside pocket of his suit jacket and, shaking, held it out to his side. Robbie snatched it. 'Now the keys to your car.'

The man reached into his trouser pocket and held the keys out for Robbie to take. He grabbed them, saying menacingly, 'Don't move. Stay where you are and don't turn around. If I see you look at me, I'll kill you.'

Robbie ran to the car, leaped in and sped off down the street without a second thought for his prey. As far as he was concerned the man was easy picking and could afford to lose a car and a few quid. It wasn't as if he'd really hurt anyone, so his conscience was clear.

Robbie knew the police would soon be looking for him, and the car. It wasn't exactly discreet with the bright red paintwork and gleaming chrome finish, but he was reluctant to get rid of it.

There was only one thing he could do: get out of the area. In fact, he thought, it would probably be best to get out of Scotland.

With only a week to go until Christmas, Dorothy was beginning to get excited. She always received a lovely knitted hat and scarf from her mother, but this year she was mostly looking forward to having a couple of days off work.

'Cor, Nel, I really ache this morning,' Dorothy said as she rubbed the small of her back. 'Still, I suppose I should be thankful for small mercies because at least the morning sickness has stopped.'

'Just you wait 'til your ankles blow up like balloons and the little bugger starts kicking your ribs,' Nelly said with a chuckle. 'This ain't nothing yet, not compared to what you've got coming.'

Dorothy smiled. She didn't mind any discomfort that her pregnancy might bring, and she was really looking forward to feeling her baby kick.

'Have you thought about seeing the midwife yet?' asked Nelly.

'No, and I won't until I have to. Can you imagine their faces when they hear I haven't got a husband? Mum knows all about having babies. I mean, she gave birth to me, didn't she? I know she's worried about it, but I've told her I want to have the baby at home. I just don't think I could handle the nasty looks and jibes I'd get in hospital.' Dorothy felt sad at how others would think of her once she started to show, but she couldn't really understand why it was so terrible. She loved the child growing inside her and surely that was all that mattered.

Nelly looked astounded. 'Dottie, you can't do that! This is your first. What if something goes wrong and you need medical attention?'

'I can't see that happening. Women have been having babies since time began. I'm a bit scared, but it's all natural.'

'That may be so, but women have also died in childbirth. I ain't trying to scare you any more than you already are, but Dottie, you need to be realistic.'

'My mind is made up. I'm having a home birth, without an interfering midwife, and that's that.'

'Well, if you're so bloody insistent, will you at least let me help your mum? I'm no nurse, and our Linda had her first baby in hospital, but I was there when she dropped her last two sprogs at home.'

'Really? You would do that for me?'

Nelly gave her friend a hug. 'Of course I will. I told you, I'm your friend and I'll be there for you, come what may.' With a soft smile, she added, 'I just wish you was a bit more blinking sensible at times.'

Chapter 12

Adrian yawned; he was so tired he could barely keep his eyes open. He'd been restless most of the night, thinking about Dorothy. It wasn't any better now during daylight hours. He sat at his desk and tried to keep focused on the job in hand, but as he concentrated on the book-keeping, the numbers in front of him weren't as engaging as thoughts of Dorothy.

The telephone trilled and Adrian reluctantly answered it. He quickly perked up when he heard Myra on the other end of the line.

'He did what?' Adrian screeched, hardly able to believe his ears. Myra had said that Robbie had paid her a fleeting visit and turned up in a brand-new red sports car.

'Did you tell him about Dottie and the baby?' he asked.

Myra said she hadn't seen him as she'd been out shopping at the time. It was one of her lodgers who had told her about the car.

'Where was he heading to next?'

Unfortunately, Myra didn't know, but said he must have come into some money as he'd left the kids a shilling each for Christmas.

'I doubt he earned it,' Adrian said scathingly.

They spoke some more, speculated on how Robbie had found the money for a car, and wished each other a happy Christmas. He and Myra both doubted that in such a short time Robbie could have found a job that paid enough money to buy a sports car, and they discussed the possibility that he'd won the money by gambling. Though he hadn't said anything to his sister, deep down Adrian feared that Robbie had been involved in something illegal again, perhaps another robbery.

He replaced the receiver, lit his pipe and hoped that his brother never showed his face in Battersea again. As far as he was concerned, it would be best for everyone. His forthcoming niece or nephew deserved better than a common thief for a father, and Dorothy should have a worthy husband, one who truly loved her and could look after her.

In the bakery, Nelly glanced at her friend and noticed that she looked pale and clammy. She hoped Dorothy wasn't going to throw up. 'Hey, are you OK, sugar?' she managed to whisper to Dorothy when Mr Epstein wasn't keeping his beady eye on them.

Dorothy just nodded but Nelly wasn't convinced. 'Do you need to go to the toilet?'

'I don't know . . . it's my stomach . . . I've got rotten cramps.'

That didn't sound right to Nelly and she feared it could only mean one thing.

Dorothy gasped as she bent over, clutching her stomach. 'Is this normal, Nel?'

Nelly didn't want to frighten her friend, but she had to get her to the locker room. Her mind raced as she tried to think of an excuse that old Epstein would buy. 'I'm sure it's nothing to worry about, but we need to get you off your feet.'

'How? It's a good hour until our lunch break. Argh, this hurts, but I'll have to grin and bear it.'

'No, you won't. Leave it to me and go along with what I say, OK?'

'Yes, but what are you gonna do?'

'I'm going to have a word with Mr Epstein. Don't worry, love.'

Nelly approached the baker, who was already eyeing the girls suspiciously. He had thin ginger hair swept over the top of his head, and a large pointed nose. His eyes narrowed as he snapped accusingly, 'What is so important that you and Miss Butler find it necessary to talk when you should be working? I saw you both, wasting time. I've a good mind to dock your wages, the pair of you.'

'It's Dorothy, sir, she's not feeling very well. I'm worried she may faint. Can I take her to the back room?'

Before Mr Epstein could answer there was a loud shriek. Nelly spun round just as Dorothy screamed louder and was horrified to see that blood was trickling down her friend's legs and beginning to pool on the floor. Without hesitation, Nelly ran to her, her big chest heaving up and down.

'Shush, it's all right,' she said soothingly, putting her arm round Dorothy's shoulders.

'I'm bleeding! What's happening? Please, Nelly, help me. It's so painful,' Dorothy cried.

'Just come to the locker room with me and try to stay calm,' Nelly urged, hoping that none of their co-workers would work out what was going on.

Her fears were realised when Mr Epstein called, 'What is wrong with that girl? Is she miscarrying?'

Dorothy looked at Nelly, saying fearfully, 'Oh, my God, I'm not, am I?'

'I'm sorry, but yes, you might be, though nobody else needs to know. Come on, lean on me, and let's get you out the back.'

Mr Epstein was shouting again, 'It's a disgrace! How dare she come here in *that* condition! Get that whore out of my sight!'

Nelly felt Dorothy's body flinch and wasn't sure if she was having more pain or if Mr Epstein's words had hurt.

'I'm not having that,' she screeched at Epstein. 'Dorothy ain't a whore, she's just having a bad monthly. You should watch your mouth saying things like that 'cos she could have you up in court for slander.'

Nelly had no idea if that was true, but at least it shut Epstein up as he blustered, 'Yes, well, I can see she's ill so take her home.'

She managed to get her friend through to the locker room and seated on the wooden bench. Dorothy bent over double. 'Oh, God, it hurts. What's happening? Am I going to die?'

'Don't be silly, of course you aren't, but I think you're losing the baby. We must get you to Dr Stubbs.'

'No,' Dorothy shrieked, 'if anyone's in the waiting room they'll see me and guess what's happening.'

Nelly sat down next to her friend. She had seen her sister go through this between her first and second child. 'OK, then, we need to get you cleaned up and home to bed.'

'The pain is getting worse and I don't think I can make

it home.' Dorothy was crying as she clutched her tummy.

'Do you want me to call an ambulance?' Nelly asked worriedly.

'No . . . no!' Dorothy gasped, and, drawing in juddering breaths, she straightened up. 'It's eased off now so I'll try to make it home.'

'All right. I'll help you,' Nelly said, before hurrying into the toilet to get some tissue to wipe her friend's legs. She then took Dorothy's coat from her locker and draped it across the girl's shoulders before putting on her own coat. 'Right, come on, hold on to my arm and we'll take it nice and slow.'

They left the bakery by the side door with Dorothy leaning heavily on Nelly as they made their way to her house. The going was slow as they had to stop every now and then when the pain became too much for Dorothy to walk.

'That's it, girl,' Nelly urged. 'Not far now, we're nearly there.'

Dorothy was becoming weaker so Nelly was relieved when the Butlers' house came into sight. She had the greatest sympathy for her friend's pain, and couldn't imagine what the girl was going through, yet it crossed her mind that maybe, in some ways, this was for the best. She doubted Dorothy would feel the same, but Nelly knew that in the long run it would better for Dorothy if there was no baby.

Alice had just finished changing her bed when she heard a woman's voice shouting from the hallway downstairs. Whoever it was sounded frantic and was calling her name.

'Mrs Butler . . . Mrs Butler!'

Alice sped down the stairs as quickly as her worn-out body would allow and was shocked to see Dorothy, looking as if she was at death's door and being supported by her large friend Nelly. 'What's happened? Alice asked, worried sick at the sight of her poorly daughter.

'She's losing the baby and she needs to lie down,' Nelly answered.

'We can't let her father see her in that state. Somehow we have to get her upstairs,' Alice urged, watching despairingly as with a nod Nelly almost carried Dorothy up the stairs and into her bedroom. It was a good job that Nelly was a big girl with the strength to match, thought Alice, knowing her frail body would have been of little help.

'Mum . . . Mum . . . I'm losing my baby,' Dorothy wept as Nelly laid her down on her bed.

'I know, love,' Alice said sadly.

Dorothy cried out in pain and Alice grew concerned at the amount of blood she was losing. She looked awful, as white as a sheet, and as Alice had known a woman who'd haemorrhaged following a miscarriage she said urgently, 'Nelly, can you run to the phone box and call Dr Stubbs? No, better still, call for an ambulance.'

'No . . . no, I don't want to go to hospital,' Dottie protested.

'You'll do as I say,' Alice snapped, fear making her sound angry.

'Your mum is right,' Nelly said, hurrying off to the phone.

Alice rushed to grab some towels from the bathroom. When she came back, the bedroom seemed to be spinning, so, after placing the towels under her daughter, she was grateful to sit on the edge of her bed. She held her daughter's hand as Dorothy brought her knees up to her stomach and moaned.

'I don't want to lose my baby, Mum.'

'I know you don't, but the ambulance will be here soon,' she said softly, squeezing her daughter's hand. She hated seeing her suffer and regretted the many times she had wished Dorothy would miscarry.

The poor woman who'd haemorrhaged had died, and if her Dottie died too, Alice knew she would never forgive herself.

Chapter 13

Adrian always closed the office early on Christmas Eve but paid his drivers for a full day. It was his way of offering them a little Christmas bonus, plus he included an extra pound in each of their wage packets.

At midday, having locked his office door, he climbed into his car and drove around to the Butlers' house. His back seat was filled with Christmas gifts for them, and a few tasty treats to add to their Christmas dinner.

He rapped quietly on the door and Alice Butler opened it, but Adrian wasn't prepared for what he saw.

'Alice, you look awful. Is everything OK?' As soon as the words had left his mouth Adrian could have kicked himself. What a thing to say, telling a woman that she looks awful, but the truth was that she did. Her hair was unkempt, her eyes were red and she was still in her nightwear.

'You'd better come in,' she said.

'Thank you, but first I need to unload my car. I've got some things for you,' he said, and hurried to fetch them. He hoped Alice wouldn't be offended by his gifts as that was the last thing he wanted, but when he followed her through to the small kitchen and placed his items on the table she showed no interest in them.

'If you've come here to give me the weekly money for the baby, then you needn't bother.'

'I don't understand.'

'Yeah, well, there's no baby now. Dottie had a miscarriage,' Alice said and then sighed heavily before adding, 'I suppose it's for the best.'

Adrian felt like he had been kicked in the stomach. He grabbed a chair and sat down. 'Dorothy . . . is she OK?' he asked, dreading the answer.

'Yes, she's fine. She lost a lot of blood and then got some sort of infection, but they're letting her home today. Funny, that, just in time for Christmas, but I doubt she'll feel much like celebrating.'

'I'm so sorry. Is there anything I can do?'

The woman was quiet for a moment before answering, 'Actually, there is. I can't get up to the hospital to fetch her home, so maybe you could collect her in that nice car of yours. It really would be a weight off my mind. The thing is, it seems they all know about it round here. It happened at Mr Epstein's place and, though Dottie's friend Nelly tried to fob them off, the women in the bakery ain't fools. Word has spread and I think Dottie could do without any snide comments today. I'd feel much better if I knew she was safely tucked away in your car.'

'Of course I'll pick her up. What time is she due to leave?'

'In about an hour. There's something else . . . don't mention it to her yet, but Mr Epstein has given her the elbow. Nelly came round to tell me yesterday.'

Adrian sighed a deep breath. He never had liked Mr Epstein and knew the man treated his employees harshly, though he surmised Dottie losing her job would be the least of her worries. If only he could wrap his arms around her and offer her some comfort. His heart went out to the poor girl, and once again he found himself cursing his brother for the mess he had left behind.

'Don't worry about that now,' he said. 'Let's get Dorothy home and rested, then I'm sure we can sort something out in the New Year.'

'She'll need to find another job.'

'Yes, but one thing at a time for now. I'll be on my way, but before I leave, these are for you.' Adrian indicated the brown parcels on the table. 'I hope you don't mind me bringing you a few gifts. It's Christmas and I thought with Dorothy having the baby, well, we're almost family.'

'Oh, Adrian, that's ever so kind of you. You've put me in an awkward position as I don't have anything for you.'

'I'm glad to hear it. I wasn't expecting anything. I just hope you enjoy what I've brought for you . . . well, the best you can enjoy anything given the circumstances.'

'You'll understand if I don't feel much like opening presents today, but I'm gonna do my best to cheer our Dottie up tomorrow,' Alice said. 'I'm sure she'll love to open them then. What are you doing for Christmas lunch?'

'Me . . . I'm putting my feet up in front of the television. It'll be nice to have a day off work.'

'You mean you'll be alone? On Christmas Day?' Alice sounded astounded.

Adrian shrugged his shoulders. 'Robbie is who knows where, and my sister lives in Scotland, but, as I said, I'll enjoy the peace and quiet.'

Alice shook her head. 'We can't have that. You'll come

here for your lunch and I won't have another word said about it. By yourself on Christmas day? Well, I've never heard the likes of it. I can't promise much in the way of a slap-up meal, but you're welcome to share what we have.'

Adrian was surprised by Alice's invitation. He felt a little embarrassed, but at the same time relished the thought of spending more time with Dorothy. 'Thank you. If you insist, then I would love to accept your invitation. I'll go and fetch your daughter now, and then I'll look forward to spending Christmas Day with you tomorrow.'

Dorothy sat on the edge of her pristine hospital bed. Her small bag was packed and she was dressed and ready to go. She had seen two of the nurses whispering in a corner and passing sidelong glances her way. She knew they were talking about her, which made her feel even more desperate to leave the hospital, but at the same time, home was the last place she wanted to be. She had been pregnant when she'd left her house a few days ago, but now she would be returning with an empty belly and no baby.

She gently rubbed her stomach, consumed by a feeling of barrenness. Her baby was gone, a part of Robbie had died, but Dorothy had cried her tears and was resolute that there would be no more. Apart from anything else, she knew her mother would have no time for weeping and moping. Alice had always been of the 'stiff upper lip and get on with it' mindset.

Dorothy sighed deeply and prepared to make her way home. Her heart thumped in her chest at the thought of facing the world. She was sure word of her losing the baby had spread by now, and knew not to expect any sympathy.

'Dottie, hello. Your mum sent me to pick you up.'

Dorothy looked up, surprised to see Adrian. What a godsend, she thought. He has a car. 'Adrian, you have no idea what a relief it is to see you.'

'I'm so sorry about the . . . the, err . . . you know.'

Dorothy could see the genuine sympathy in Adrian's eyes and almost burst out crying again, but then reminded herself that she had to be resolute. There would be no more tears and she managed to hold them in. 'Thanks Adrian, but I suppose everyone is pleased and thinking this is the best outcome. I won't be an unmarried mother now. It'll be one less thing for my mum to worry about.' Dorothy knew her tone sounded bitter and wished she'd kept her mouth shut. She looked at Adrian, who seemed at a loss for words. 'I'm sorry, Adrian. I shouldn't have said that.'

'Don't apologise to me, there's no need for that. I can't speak for anyone else, but I for one am most definitely not pleased. Now come on, let's get you home. Your mother is waiting and I know she'll be over the moon to see you.'

Dorothy sat in silence during the journey, peering out of the side window as the car trundled through the streets of Battersea. Everything looked so grey and glum to her, echoing her mood. Even the few Christmas decorations she spotted failed to lift her spirits and she sighed heavily.

'I can see how upset you are, and it's understandable,' Adrian said.

His sympathy brought tears to her eyes, but once again

she fought them. 'I know I've got to somehow put this behind me and get on with it. My mum won't stand for any nonsense and, not only that, I don't want to ruin her day tomorrow. We haven't got much, but all the same she makes a real effort every year in the hope of rousing my dad. He used to love Christmas.'

'Your mother has invited me for lunch tomorrow,' Adrian said, 'so I'll help too. I'll even dress up in my old Santa outfit if you like?'

Dorothy smiled; it was the first time she had done so since she'd miscarried. 'You've got a Santa outfit?'

'Yes, and I'll have you know I make a very good Father Christmas.'

Dorothy smiled again as Adrian patted his stout belly.

'Ho, ho, ho,' he boomed. 'See, you'd never guess I'm not the real thing.'

As the sun broke through the dark clouds, Dorothy felt the glimmer of light on her skin. Though she was bereft at losing Robbie's baby, she thought maybe tomorrow wouldn't be so bad after all.

Chapter 14

The pub was full of festive cheer as customers celebrated Christmas Eve. Robbie sat at a table in the corner, supping his pint. He'd been surprised and pleased to find the wallet he'd stolen contained twenty-five pounds, a sizable amount of cash. Jumping that bloke and nicking his car had been easy, but it didn't pay the sort of money he wanted, though he'd enjoyed living the high life for a while. It had paid for fuel to get him to Surrey and afforded him a few nights' stay in some nice hotels. However, it wasn't going to last for much longer and Robbie still hadn't pulled off the big job he was aiming for.

He squeezed his way through the throng of people to the bar and ordered another pint. When the landlord took his money, Robbie noticed the cash register was bulging with notes. This was probably one of the busiest nights of the year and there would be plenty more cash going into the till yet. And there would be no banks open tomorrow. A plan began to form in Robbie's mind.

'And get one for yourself,' Robbie said to the landlord as he was given his change. He didn't like to give away his money to strangers, but, he thought, it would be back in his own pocket later.

‘Thanks very much. Merry Christmas,’ the landlord answered.

Robbie stood and slyly watched as money went over the bar. The landlord was rushed off his feet, but between serving customers he did manage to have the odd word or two with Robbie.

‘You’re not from around here?’

‘No,’ Robbie answered, ‘I’m from London.’

‘Whereabouts? I’ve got family in the Smoke,’ the landlord asked.

‘Knightsbridge way,’ Robbie fibbed.

‘It’s nice around there. My family come from around the East India docks. Tough old game that, being a docker. I got out of it a few years back and set up here. Tom’s my name – you stopping for another?’

‘Nice to meet you, Tom. I’m Graham,’ he lied, ‘and yes, I’ll have another pint. Get yourself another drink too,’ he said, thinking that this was all going according to his hastily put-together plan. Tom seemed like an affable bloke. He was overweight, a bit taller and older than him, but Robbie felt he already had the man on side.

‘Don’t mind if I do,’ Tom said and poured himself a shot of whisky which he drank quickly before having to serve another customer.

By about ten o’clock, the pub was beginning to empty and Tom looked worn out. Robbie would have to be his most charming self if he was going to pull this one off.

‘Err, Tom. Why don’t you grab a drink and come join me for a while? You look like you could do with a bit of a breather.’

‘That’s not a bad idea,’ Tom replied. ‘My daughter was

supposed to come over and give me a hand tonight, but she got stuck indoors with her little 'un. Little bleeder's come down with chicken pox. Never mind, I got through it, but I'm worn out.'

'It's Christmas Day tomorrow so I expect you'll have the day off to spend with your family?' Robbie pried.

'Yeah, but the missus passed away a couple of years ago. Still, I'm off to my daughter's for lunch tomorrow. A few spots won't keep me away from the grandson, not on Christmas Day. What about you, are you driving back to London tonight?'

'I was planning to, but I've had one too many to drive. Are there any decent hotels in the area?'

Tom rubbed his unshaven face. 'You'll be hard pushed to find a room at this time of night.'

'Blast it. Oh well, I might as well have another pint. I can sleep in my car, that's if you don't mind me being parked up outside all night?'

'You can't do that – you'll freeze to death. Tell you what, as it's Christmas, you can have my spare room for tonight, but you'll have to be up and out early in the morning.'

'That's really good of you. Thanks, Tom. I'll pay you for the room and I won't take no for an answer.'

'If you insist,' Tom answered.

'I do,' Robbie said with a laugh. 'Drink up, and let's both have another.'

As closing time approached, Tom staggered over to the bell behind the bar and rang it, signalling last orders. There were only a handful of customers left, who soon finished up their drinks and bade Tom a cheery farewell as they left.

Robbie helped the landlord lock up and then poured him another drink. He reckoned that Tom could only handle a couple more and hoped the man would then pass out.

'So what brings you out to these parts then, Graham? It's a long way from home,' Tom asked as he took a stool at the bar.

'Nothing special. I was on my way home from visiting my sister in Guildford and decided to take the scenic route back.'

'That's a lovely little motor you've got out the front. It must have cost you a packet. What do you do for a living?'

'I've got a haulage business. It's been hard work building it up, but it does me all right. I don't get much time off so this is nice, just sitting here and relaxing with a decent ale and good company. Cheers.' Robbie held out his pint to clink glasses and was pleased when Tom swiftly swallowed his whisky.

'Look at the time,' Tom slurred. 'It's nearly midnight so best we make this the last one and hit the sack.'

'One more for the road, eh? Come on, man, it's Christmas,' said Robbie encouragingly.

'Go on then, jush one more. And mewwy cwissmass . . .' Tom's head was bobbing and his eyes were slowly closing.

Robbie wanted to punch the air with delight but refrained from doing so. This was just what he wanted – an unconscious landlord with a till full of money.

'Let's get you upstairs,' he said gleefully as he heaved the large man up from the barstool.

'I . . . I . . . I've gotta lock the doors and cash up,' Tom moaned, belching loudly.

'You've already done it, remember? Let's just get our heads down and I'll help you clear up the bar in the morning.'

Tom mumbled incoherently as Robbie hauled him up the stairs. 'Where's your room, Tom?'

'Ssthere,' he slurred, staggering towards it.

Robbie helped Tom over to his bed and the man almost fell onto it. He threw some covers over him and then rapidly made his way back down to the bar.

This was a piece of cake, Robbie thought as he helped himself to a quick glass of brandy. His eyes surveyed the bar and he realised there was more than just a cash register full of money on offer. He could help himself to several large bottles of expensive spirits too.

Robbie searched under the bar and found a bag that he stuffed with notes from the till. He quickly calculated that there was about fifty quid, if not more, so it wasn't a bad haul. The landlord had been too drunk to realise that Robbie still had the pub keys, so grabbing a bottle of whisky he made for the doors.

The cold hit him as he dashed outside, where he put the bag of cash and the bottle in the boot of his car before going back inside for more booze. In his haste Robbie let the door slam shut behind him, but he wasn't bothered as he was pretty sure that not even a bomb under the bed would stir Tom.

He filled his arms with bottles of spirits then suddenly spun around when he heard a growling noise coming from the end of the bar. To his horror he saw Tom standing there, looking very dishevelled and twitching with anger. The man was holding a large wooden club in his hand and Robbie was in no doubt that the ex-docker would readily use it on him.

'It's not what you think, Tom. I was just filling up and tidying the bar for you.' Robbie saw Tom's eyes flit to the till and the empty open drawer. He knew his lies were useless.

'You thought I was too drunk to know what you're up to, you lying, thieving bastard!' Tom staggered towards Robbie, brandishing the heavy club, ready to strike.

Astonished that the man had sobered up enough to make it downstairs, Robbie dropped the bottles and fled for the door. He ran outside and jumped into the car.

Tom was surprisingly close behind and haphazardly swung the club, just missing his target. 'You fucking dirty toe-rag! I'll have you . . .' he bawled as he lifted his weapon again, but before he could land a blow the car engine revved into life and Robbie hit the accelerator hard with his foot.

He sped through the dark and winding country lanes, sniggering to himself. It had been a close call but he had got away with it. It saddened him that he'd have to ditch the car now, but it was very noticeable so he had no choice. He'd been mad to keep it this long, but now he'd nick an old banger, one that even if reported stolen the police would be unlikely to pursue.

Robbie smiled to himself. With the money he now had he'd find somewhere nice to stay, well away from this area, and then, after a quiet Christmas, he'd see the New Year in with a bang.

Chapter 15

After driving for half an hour, Robbie had spotted a couple of old cars parked inside a dimly lit industrial area. There wasn't a soul around so he'd driven the MG around the back of the building and managed to break into an old grey Ford. He'd smiled when he found a hidden key, and was relieved when it started the engine. There was petrol in the tank too, so he'd put the booze in the boot and quickly driven away. He'd then travelled for hours, but finally, too tired to drive any further, he'd pulled into a parking area to grab some sleep.

When morning dawned, Robbie rolled his neck from side to side and stretched his arms. It wasn't the most comfortable of places to have slept and he ached all over. He climbed out of the car, stretched his back and blinked in the light, realising that it was Christmas Day.

His stomach growled and he hoped to find a place to eat. He guessed that most establishments would be closed, but he might be able to find a hotel that wasn't fully booked. With that in mind, he got back behind the steering wheel and started the engine. Should he go left or right? Hampshire or Dorset? The heater kicked in and he was grateful to feel the warmth. He took a coin from his pocket and flipped it in the air. Heads for Hampshire, tails for Dorset. The silver shilling landed on heads. Hampshire it is then, he thought, and revved on the accelerator.

The roads were icy and some were covered in snow so Robbie took his time and drove carefully. He wasn't completely sure of the way, but thought as long as he headed south it would eventually lead him to the coast. He liked the seaside and decided it could be a good place to relocate, though it would be cold and quiet at this time of year. A smile crossed his face as he thought about a summer daytrip he had been on with Myra and her children when they had come down on a visit from Scotland. They had visited Southsea and he had ridden the steam-powered gallopers at least four times. He remembered the kids had loved the laughing sailor, a machine that stood outside the fair. It had been worth the penny to see them splitting their sides as the sailor laughed his head off.

He pictured them now, all getting ready to tuck into Myra's Christmas dinner, and felt a pang of longing. He supposed it would have been nice to have enjoyed Christmas with his family, but he shook the thoughts away and shrugged his shoulders. Oh well, he mused, it's only one day. As for Adrian, his boring brother, he would probably be spending Christmas alone too, and after filling his podgy belly full of food he'd sit in his chair, snoring away for the rest of the afternoon.

Robbie's stomach rumbled again at the thought of food, and he hoped he would come across a nice hotel or something soon. He wanted to eat his fill and then get his thinking cap on. As soon as the holidays were over, he planned to find a room in the Southsea area and get his hands on more cash. Once he had plenty of money lining his pockets he'd find himself a pretty young lady or two.

Robbie found he was relishing the more free-spirited life, and enjoying the excitement of not knowing exactly what the future held. There was one thing he was sure of, and that was that he wouldn't work for his cash. Stealing it was much easier.

Alice was up before Dorothy and decided to let the girl sleep in. The walls were thin and she'd heard her crying in the night. She had been tempted to go to her daughter and offer her comfort, but decided against it. Molly-coddling Dottie wouldn't do any good. No, the girl had to be strong and work her own way through her grief.

She crept down the creaky stairs and into the kitchen to set the kettle on the stove to boil, before bracing herself to visit the toilet in the back yard. Alice shivered as cold, wet snow bit at her foot through the hole in the bottom of her slipper.

The kettle was whistling as Alice came back into the kitchen, and to her surprise she found Dorothy was already up, preparing the tea.

'Good morning, Dottie. I thought you were in bed. Merry Christmas,' Alice said with a smile. Her chest felt tight, and though she put it down to the cold air, she hoped her daughter wouldn't notice her discomfort.

'Morning, Mum, and to you.'

Alice saw that Dottie was smiling, but the smile didn't reach her puffy eyes. She was obviously putting on a brave face so Alice went along with it, knowing that any sympathy could shatter the forced cheer. 'Be a love and go light the fire in the front room. We'll get it nice and toasty before we get your father up. And no peeping under the tree in there. We'll wait 'til Adrian is here before we open the presents. After all, most of them are from him. I feel terrible that we ain't got something for him in return.'

'I wouldn't worry, Mum. I shouldn't think he'll be expecting anything.'

'Yeah, he said that.'

'Anyway, it's nice you invited him for lunch.'

'I just hope he likes it,' Alice mused as she drank her tea and then put some toast on for their breakfast.

A short while later, with one meal eaten, Alice busied herself preparing another – the Christmas lunch. Thanks to Adrian there would be extra treats on their plates. She had refused any help from her daughter, because the girl still needed to fully recover from her miscarriage, and now she could hear that Dorothy and Bill were listening to the wireless in the front room. It was something she was looking forward to later, putting her feet up and listening to the Queen's Christmas speech. It would be nice to have a telly, she thought to herself. It might have been a good distraction for her husband but it wasn't a luxury they could afford, especially now that Dottie was out of work. Alice hadn't broken the bad news to her yet. Dorothy appeared to be in quite good spirits, even though they were forced, and Alice didn't want to ruin her Christmas.

With everything cooking nicely, Alice changed, and at one o'clock there was a knock on the front door. She heard Dottie calling out excitedly for her to come and wondered what all the fuss was about. It would only be Adrian as expected, but she walked through to the hall and was stunned to find Father Christmas filling the doorway.

'Merry Christmas, one and all,' Adrian bellowed, with his thumbs tucked into a wide black belt.

'Oh, my goodness,' Alice said, laughing. 'I was expecting Adrian Ferguson, not Santa Claus! You'd better come in and have a mince tart.'

Alice noticed her daughter look over at Adrian and silently mouth, 'Thank you.'

They must have cooked this up between them, the daft buggers, she thought, smiling. She hadn't expected the atmosphere to be so cheery and was glad Dorothy now looked as if she was genuinely enjoying herself.

'It's lovely and warm in here,' said Adrian as he took a seat on the sofa. 'Do you mind if I remove my beard and jacket?'

Alice handed him a mince tart and a glass of stout. 'Of course not, Santa, make yourself at home.'

'I must say, Alice, you look a picture today. I can see where your daughter gets her good looks from.'

Alice felt her cheeks burn. She wasn't used to receiving compliments but was secretly pleased that her best dress and curled hair hadn't gone unnoticed.

'Aw, off with you,' she blustered and hurriedly changed the subject. 'I've got to see to a few things in the kitchen, but then we'll open all those smashing gifts you brought us. I'm sure Dottie is chomping at the bit.'

Alice checked on the turkey that was slowly roasting. They hadn't had a turkey for as long as she could remember. Last year it had been a belly of pork, but this year, thanks to Adrian's generosity, they were having this rare treat.

As she stood up from bending down to the oven, the room began to swim and Alice grabbed hold of the hob to steady herself. She felt light-headed and nausea washed over her. Everything went white in her field of vision and she struggled to focus, fearing she would faint. Then, as quickly as the funny turn had come on, it passed, and Alice took a deep breath. This wasn't the first time she'd experienced this, but she quickly dismissed her fears. It was probably all the anxiety about Dorothy over the past week, nothing to worry about. Anyway, there was Bill to care for and with Dorothy out of work she couldn't afford to be ill.

No, she was fine. She couldn't be poorly, Alice resolved. She wouldn't allow it.

Dorothy looked gorgeous and Adrian found he couldn't take his eyes off her. He doubted that her father would notice as he appeared to be in a semi-comatose state. He hadn't responded to seeing the Santa outfit, or to anything else, and Adrian had seen both Dorothy's and her mother's disappointment.

Adrian watched as Dorothy knelt beneath the small Christmas tree. It was adorned with homemade decorations, adding a lovely personal touch. Adrian wondered if Bill had made any of the ornaments before he'd lost his mind. There were several beautifully carved wooden reindeer and colourfully painted baked-dough elves. Red and silver ribbons were tied in pretty bows to most of the branches and a delicate-looking tissue angel sat on the top.

'Your tree looks very nice, Dottie. I bet it has lots of special family memories.'

'It does. I remember when I was knee-high to a grasshopper, my dad would carve a new reindeer every year. If you count them, there's one for every year of my life – until he went off to war, of course.'

'They're beautiful,' said Adrian, wanting to add that he thought she was too.

'There's so much stuff under here – you really shouldn't have, Adrian.'

'It's selfish of me really. I'll enjoy the pleasure of seeing you and your mum open the gifts. Best of all though, it got me a very welcome invite to lunch, which smells delicious.'

Alice came through carrying a plate of dried prunes and offered them to Adrian, which he politely declined. He couldn't help noticing that she looked sheet white and he wondered if she was overworking herself in the kitchen. He was glad when she announced they could open their presents because he knew there were more appetising delights to savour amongst the gifts under the tree.

Alice sat on the armchair next to her husband and Dorothy loaded her lap with the packages. 'You first, Mum,' she said, flashing Adrian a wide smile.

'No, don't be silly, open yours,' Alice protested.

Dorothy went for the largest box first and eagerly pulled off the wrapping paper. She carefully opened the cardboard box and peered inside. She gave Adrian a puzzled look and then pulled out another wrapped box. Inside that there was another, and another, and another. By now, Alice and Dorothy were chuckling and Adrian was pleased that his 'joke' had the desired effect.

Eventually, Dorothy pulled out the last box, a small one, and gasped when she opened it. 'Oh, Adrian, they're wonderful! It's too much though, I can't accept them. Look, Mum,' she said, and she handed Alice a cream satin-covered box containing a pair of gold and pearl earrings.

'Adrian, whatever were you thinking? I can see they're real pearls and they must have cost you a bomb,' Alice said, clearly shocked.

'The cost is irrelevant. I saw them and thought they'd look nice on Dottie.'

As Alice handed them back to her daughter, Adrian said, 'Try them on, I bet they suit you a treat.'

'But . . .' said Dorothy.

'No buts about it. Go on, clip them on,' he replied.

Dorothy did as instructed and stood to look in the mirror that hung over the mantelpiece. 'They're beautiful,' she said, 'thank you so much.' She dashed over to Adrian and planted a big kiss on his cheek.

At that moment Adrian thought the hefty price he had paid for the earrings had most definitely been worth it. 'You're welcome,' he said, longing to hold her in his arms.

Once all the gifts had been opened, Alice instructed Dorothy to put up the drop-leaf table and set it for dinner. Adrian tried to help but Dottie had everything organised in whippet time. They attempted to persuade Bill to take his place at the head of the table, but their pleas fell on deaf ears and the man refused to budge from his armchair. Instead, Alice pulled a small wooden table in front of his knees and said he could eat his Christmas lunch there.

Alice and Dorothy fetched dishes from the kitchen

until the table was laden with food. Adrian felt his stomach grumble at the sight of steaming turnips, carrots, peas and, best of all, the crispy roast potatoes that were placed around the crowning glory: a succulent-looking turkey. Each setting had a cracker ready for pulling and, though they only had ale glasses to drink from, they all enjoyed a glass of sherry, which Adrian had supplied.

'This looks glorious, Alice,' said Adrian and he raised his glass to toast her. 'Season's greetings, and may your home be blessed with happiness and prosperity.'

Alice clinked glasses with him, took a sip of her drink and then said, 'Would you do the honours, Adrian?' as she handed him the carving knife.

As he sliced through the turkey breast, his mouth salivated. It had been some time since he'd had good, home-cooked fare and he couldn't wait to get stuck in.

'Look, the wishbone,' Dorothy squealed like an excited child.

'Why don't you and Adrian pull it?' said Alice. 'I only have the one wish and we all know what that is.' She looked warmly at her husband who was absently staring at the wall beside his chair.

Adrian offered the delicate bone to Dorothy with his chubby pinkie finger only just managing to grasp it. *You're not the only one with just one wish*, he thought, locking eyes with Dorothy, and hoping, but not really believing, that his one wish would be granted.

Alice saw the way that Adrian was looking at Dorothy, but doubted her daughter would ever feel the same way. It was a shame, because, though he was overweight, if Dottie married Adrian she'd want for nothing.

'Come on now. Let's get this dinner eaten before it turns cold,' she said, but then felt her chest tighten. She rubbed it, regretting eating so many prunes before lunch. They had obviously given her indigestion and she winced as she caught her breath.

'You look a bit peaky, Mum. Are you feeling OK?'

Alice heard her daughter's words but couldn't seem to answer. She felt like she was struggling for breath and the pain in her chest intensified, as though a vice was gripping it tighter and tighter. She grabbed hold of the white cloth covering the table, but her left arm had gone numb. What was happening?

Dorothy was standing up now, looking at her with a shocked expression, and, though she could see her daughter's lips moving, she sounded so far away. The room was swimming and Alice felt herself begin to lean sideways from the chair. Then there was darkness.

Adrian surveyed the scene in front of him. Alice had fallen from her chair to the floor, taking the tablecloth with her. She was lying motionless, covered in vegetables, while Dorothy knelt over her.

'Oh my God, Adrian . . . what should we do? Call an ambulance? Would it be quicker to take her to the hospital in your car? Mum . . . Mum . . . can you hear me?'

Adrian tried to think clearly but felt frozen to the spot.

'Adrian . . . do something . . . ADRIAN, HELP ME!' Dorothy screamed which spurred him to action.

Bill was rocking back and forth in his chair and muttering the word 'No' over and over, so Adrian told her quickly, 'Let me look at your mum. You see to your father.'

Dorothy was beside herself and in obvious distress, though she went to her dad while Adrian got on one knee to place his fingers on Alice's scrawny neck. He couldn't feel anything so took her wrist in his hand, but try as he might he still couldn't detect any sign of a pulse. This can't be happening, he thought, lowering his ear to her face. There was no sound of breathing.

Adrian sat back on his heels. There was nothing that could be done for Alice. She was gone. How on earth could he break it to Dorothy? She was already fragile from the loss of her baby, and now he had to tell her that her mother was dead.

Chapter 16

It was only a week into the New Year, but Robbie was already enjoying 1957. He had secured himself a tidy room in Portsmouth, with his own bathroom, in a decent enough house close to the seafront. Southsea was nearby, just a bit further along the coast, but best of all there was a pub on the corner of the road and Robbie had already made friends with a few of the locals.

The fresh sea air was bracing but Robbie breathed it in deeply, and, as the coldness hit his lungs, he felt alive and vibrant. Life was good. He was on his way to meet a girl he'd bumped into the day before. She'd been coming out of a telephone box when they'd walked into each other and her long legs and blonde hair had caught Robbie's eye. She reminded him a bit of Dorothy, but when the incident gave him the chance to speak to her the similarities stopped, because she spoke with a Welsh accent. He had flirted with her and she'd responded, giving him the opportunity to ask her out.

He now felt excited at the prospect of buying her a few drinks and was sure his luck would be in tonight. After all, she'd been easily persuaded to meet him. It had been a while since he'd enjoyed the pleasures of a woman and his frustration was mounting.

She was there as arranged, waiting outside the pub for him, and as Robbie approached he noticed she was attracting quite a bit of attention from passing men. He wasn't surprised. In her tight skirt and low-cut jumper, he thought she looked very sexy, though she must have been freezing.

'Hello, Gladys. You look cold. Haven't you got a coat?'

'Hi, Robbie. No, I did have a proper fur up until a few weeks ago but I had to sell it. Shame really because now it's cold enough to freeze the balls off a brass monkey.'

Robbie smiled, surprised at Gladys's language but pleased to find it sounded even funnier in her broad accent.

'Best we get you inside and warmed up then,' he answered as he admired her bulging cleavage.

'Hey, cheeky, my eyes are up here, not down there in my bra. Am I going to have to fight against my breasts for your attention all night?'

'Don't you worry your pretty little face about attention from me,' said Robbie with a frisky grin. 'You can have as much of my attention as you like.'

'Is that a promise? *All* your attention,' Gladys purred.

Robbie celebrated quietly inside. She was fast, flirty, and from the way she was playing with him he felt she was definitely a sure thing for tonight. They found a table and Gladys started knocking back gin and tonics at a rate that alarmed Robbie. He would have to get her back to his place sooner rather than later as he didn't want to be spending much more of the cash he had left. At least not until he had done another job.

‘Excuse me a moment, will you? I’m going to powder my nose,’ said Gladys and made her way across the pub to the ladies’ toilet. It didn’t go unnoticed by Robbie that all eyes were on her as she wriggled her hips and clipped her heels on the wooden floor.

‘You’ve pulled a bit of a looker there, mate,’ a burly-looking man called from the bar.

Robbie had shared a few pints with him over the last couple of evenings, learning that his name was Fred and that he was a merchant navy man. He was a rough diamond, but Robbie had enjoyed his company. ‘Yes, I certainly have.’

Fred got off from his bar stool and came to Robbie’s table. He leaned in and whispered, ‘I’ve had a bit of a windfall and come into a few quid. If she’s got any sisters or friends, well, you know what I mean?’

Robbie looked up at Fred. He was a large man with hands as big as shovels, and a bulbous nose that matched his stature. Not only that, his ears were almost as big as his bald head so, all in all, he wasn’t exactly an oil painting. Robbie doubted that Fred had much success when it came to women.

Teasing, Robbie said, ‘So you fancy my new girlfriend, do you?’

‘No, no, Robbie. It ain’t like that. Well, it is actually, she’s a blinder, but she’s your bird and I wouldn’t step on your toes. But like I said, if she’s got any friends I’ve got a pocket full of cash and you know me, I’d be generous.’

Gladys came back to the table and gave Fred a friendly smile as she sat down. ‘This is Fred, a friend of mine,’ Robbie said.

‘Hello,’ Gladys said.

Fred looked awkward and shuffled from foot to foot, but managed to stutter, ‘Pl-pleased to meet you.’

Robbie saw the effect Gladys had on Fred, and as the man had admitted to having a pocket full of cash, an idea suddenly sprang to mind – one that this time didn’t involve robbery.

‘Fred, why don’t you get a round in and join us?’ he asked.

‘Err, yeah, all right. What are you ’aving?’

‘A whisky for me and a gin and tonic for Gladys,’ Robbie said, and, as he watched Fred walk to the bar, his idea expanded into a plan that could be a lucrative long-term venture.

As the evening went on, Robbie turned on the charm and told jokes that made both Gladys and Fred laugh. He noted that Gladys hung on to his every word and had to laugh when she described him as posh. When it was coming up to nine-thirty he saw that Gladys was tipsy and decided it was time to recoup some of the money he’d spent on her. ‘Fred, why don’t you pop along to the off licence to buy a bottle of whisky, and then we can head over to my place.’

Fred looked confused. ‘Your place? What for?’

‘I thought we’d have a bit of a party. What about you, Gladys? Do you fancy coming back to mine?’

She looked a bit disappointed and pouted. ‘I don’t know, Robbie. I thought it was going to be just me and you tonight.’

‘Don’t worry about that, there’ll be other nights and a little party would be nice.’

'Oh, all right.'

'Good girl,' said Robbie and kissed her quickly on the cheek. 'Fred, off you go then, mate. Get the whisky and I'll see you back at mine. You know where it is, number twenty-three, just up this road.'

The cold air spurred Gladys on and Robbie was pleased that she walked quickly. He wanted a few minutes with her before Fred got back. He opened the front door and invited Gladys in before him, slapping her bottom as she passed on the doorstep. Gladys giggled and sashayed up the stairs to Robbie's second-floor room with Robbie following and admiring her backside.

Once inside, Robbie closed the door and pushed Gladys up against it. He furiously kissed her and ran his hands up and down her voluptuous body.

'Hey, easy, tiger,' Gladys breathed. 'What's the rush?'

'Fred will be here soon . . . I want a bit of you before he disturbs us.'

'Robbie, I do really like you but we've only just met. I don't want you to think I'm that sort of girl.'

'Of course you aren't,' he answered as he lifted her jumper over her breasts and reached around her back to unfasten her bra. Gladys's breasts swung loose and Robbie cupped handfuls of them, brushing his lips and tongue against her nipples. 'It isn't important that we haven't known each other for long. You're my girlfriend and it just matters that we would do anything for one another.'

'Oh, Robbie,' Gladys replied, giving into Robbie's advances and caresses, 'I've never met anyone like you before and if I'm your girlfriend now, of course I'd do anything for you.'

Robbie hid a smile of triumph. Perfect! That was just what he wanted to hear.

A knock on the bedroom door brought the canoodling couple to a stop and Gladys adjusted her clothing as Robbie let Fred in.

'This is nice,' said Robbie, pouring them all liberal measures of whisky in white china teacups. 'Cheers!'

Fred and Gladys downed theirs, but then an awkward silence fell between them. 'Come on, lighten up, you two. This is supposed to be a party,' Robbie said.

'Well, a party usually has music,' said Gladys.

'You're Welsh, aren't you? I thought all you girls from the valleys could sing. Come on, give us a song then.'

'Don't be silly,' she replied. 'Haven't you got a record player or a radio?'

'I've only just moved in but as luck would have it, there's an old radio in the cupboard. I don't know if it works but, Fred, pour us all another and I'll see if I can get us some music. Anything to keep my girl happy,' Robbie said and winked at Gladys.

The radio didn't work but Robbie wasn't going to allow that to put a damper on the night. The whisky had gone to his head and was making him feel horny, but he had something else on his mind. Something that was little effort for him and could earn him a bob or two.

Half an hour later, Gladys checked her reflection in the bathroom mirror. She was pleased with what she saw and sauntered back into the room where Fred was sitting, legs splayed on the floor. Robbie was sitting on the bed, casually leaning up against the headboard.

'Come and sit next to me,' Robbie said to her, patting the bed next to him.

The gin mixed with the whisky was making Gladys

feel quite heady and she wobbled a little on her heels as she walked across the room.

'Kick your shoes off,' Robbie urged. 'Relax and make yourself at home.'

Gladys was happy to do just that. Robbie's place was only a room but he had his own bathroom. It was so much nicer than where she lived, a place she shared with her three younger sisters and several other families. She wrinkled her nose at the thought of the stench that was always present in the bathroom they all used. She hated living there and detested the fact that she was forced to make her sisters stay there too, but after their mother died there'd been no choice. Unable to support them, she knew she had to find their father, who was a sailor, and with her sisters in tow they'd travelled down to Portsmouth.

It had been awful to move away from the lush, green small town where they had been born and brought up. Their mother worked as a cook in the big house that came with a tied cottage, but when she died they'd been told they had to move out. It didn't seem right, but she was sure her father would be able to sort it out. She just didn't know when he was due back from sea.

Gladys took off her shoes and snuggled into Robbie. It was comforting to have a boyfriend and she hoped he would help look after her sisters too. She had sold just about everything they owned, including the fur coat her father had bought her mother. She remembered the look on her mother's face when she'd been presented with the coat. 'What a ridiculous waste of money,' she had exclaimed, and sure enough she'd never worn it. Her father had tickled her nose and told the woman to hush up, saying the coat had come to him by good fortune and not a penny had been wasted.

A lovable rogue, that's what her mother always said about her dad. Gladys missed him terribly and hoped she would find him soon, but in the meantime she had Robbie to take care of her now.

Gladys was dozing but was woken from her nap as she felt Robbie's hand move up her leg, as high as her suspenders. It felt nice, and though she had protested her innocence to Robbie, in truth she had lost her virginity to a farmhand about a year ago. They had enjoyed a few tumbles in the hay, and now, as Robbie gently caressed her, she forgot Fred was in the room. She nuzzled Robbie's neck and he turned his head to kiss her on the lips, parting her mouth with his tongue.

Fred cleared his throat.

'Do you like what you see, Fred?' Robbie asked.

'Yes, mate, don't mind me,' Fred replied and licked his lips eagerly.

'Do you want to come over and have a feel?'

'Robbie!' Gladys exclaimed, unable to believe he'd suggest such a thing.

'It's all right, Gladys. Fred's a good friend of mine and I like to see my friends having a good time. Come on, I thought you said you'd do anything for me?'

'Yes, but, Robbie, not *that*!' Gladys replied, annoyed that he would expect that of her.

'Oh, I see, so you talk the talk but don't carry it through. I can't stand girls who do that, so if you want to be my girlfriend you'll have to change your ways. If not, well, we'll call it a day.'

Gladys's mind was fuddled with alcohol but one thing

was for sure: she didn't want to lose Robbie. If it meant letting Fred join in, then so be it. She reluctantly nodded. 'All right then. I'll do it,' she said and laid herself down on the bed, dreading what was coming next.

Robbie beckoned Fred over with his head. 'That'll be a pound,' he said and held his hand out for payment.

Gladys saw the money exchange hands. I'll be having half of that, she thought, and though suddenly aware that she was about to sell her body for sex, she resigned herself to the fact that as she was desperate not to lose Robbie, she'd have done it for free. The money was an added bonus and she needed it to feed her little sisters.

The thought had never before occurred to her to prostitute herself and she wouldn't have had the nerve to do it alone, but with Robbie there to look after her, Gladys could close her eyes and just wait for the big oaf to get it over and done with.

Chapter 17

The church was full of mourners who had come to pay their last respects to Alice. Dorothy was surprised to find there was standing room only, a fine tribute to her mother, especially as she hadn't left the house in years.

Dorothy sat at the front and found a small measure of comfort in having Nelly to one side of her and Adrian on the other. Her eyes were fixed on the coffin – she couldn't believe her dear mother was lying in there. It just didn't seem possible.

The vicar welcomed everyone and led the first hymn but it was all becoming a daze to Dorothy. She looked at the words in her hymnbook, but her brain wouldn't register them. She couldn't shake the thought of how much she was going to miss her mum.

Tears began to well in her eyes and Dorothy felt the urge to run from the church. She suddenly realised that she couldn't go through with this; it was just unbearable. There was still the interment to face but she couldn't deal with the anguish of watching them put her mother into the ground, burying her small, frail body. It was unthinkable. She wanted to escape the all-consuming pain.

'NO . . . NO . . . NO.' Dorothy could hear a woman shouting above the melody of 'The Lord Is My Shepherd'.

She was barely conscious of Adrian's arm around her, or Nelly's voice as she held her hand and said softly, 'Oh, sugar, I know it hurts but it'll be OK, hush yourself.'

Engulfed as she was in a world of grief, everything felt distant, and she wasn't aware that the singing had faded as people listened to the screams in stunned silence. Dorothy felt Nelly's plump hands cup her cheeks, a stern look on her face as she ordered, 'Dorothy Butler, pull yourself together.'

As though dashed with cold water, Dorothy gasped, coming to her senses and realising with horror that *she* had been the hysterical woman. Mortified, she swung around and darted her eyes across the sea of faces staring at her. Some of them looked accusing but others appeared sympathetic.

Her grief turned to an inexplicable anger and she rose to her feet. You can look as much as you like, she thought, but she was *my* mother. She clenched her fists. She wanted to shout at them all, tell them to go away. How could any of them understand the pain she was going through?

'Sit down, Dottie,' Adrian said quietly, 'I know this is difficult for you, but let's get through this together and give your mother the proper send-off she deserves.'

Dorothy peered into Adrian's dark eyes. She hadn't noticed before, but they looked so kind. What on earth was she doing, making a spectacle of herself at her mother's funeral? Suddenly embarrassed, she nodded at Adrian and took her seat. She wasn't sure what had come over her and instantly regretted behaving so badly. It was all so unfair. She had only just lost her baby and now she was contemplating how she was going to live without her mum, the woman she considered her best friend in the world.

The service finally ended and everyone made their way to the graveside, but Dorothy's legs felt weak and she thought they might give way. She leaned heavily on Adrian, thankful he was there to support her. She was dreading this part of the funeral more than the church service, but for her mother's sake she mustered all the inner strength she could find.

With her head held high in the most dignified manner she could manage, Dorothy set her eyes on a tree in front of her. She focused on the branches and began to count each one. It seemed a crazy thing to do but she needed something to distract her from the horror of looking at the coffin being lowered into the muddy ground. One, two, three . . . fifteen . . .

At last it was over and Dorothy felt Adrian gently take her arm to lead her towards his car. A few neighbours stopped her on the way to offer their condolences and she managed to nod politely, yet scarcely absorbed their sympathies. She was vaguely aware of Nelly answering on her behalf.

Three women had collected in the road in front of Adrian's car. Their faces were familiar to Dorothy but she wasn't sure who they were, and in truth she didn't care. She just wanted to get back to the sanctuary of home.

'The vicar's coming this way and we should thank him for conducting the service,' Adrian said.

'I can't, not now, maybe another day. I just want to go home,' she begged, aware of tears forming again.

'All right, get yourself in the car. Nelly and I will talk to him and we'll be as quick as we can,' he said, and they both hurried off.

Dorothy reached out to open the car door, then paused when she heard her name mentioned.

'Yeah, that's her, Dorothy, the wayward daughter,' said one woman to another.

Dorothy recognised her from the bakery, but she kept her head down and didn't let on that she could hear their conversation.

'Poor Alice,' the woman continued. 'No wonder her heart gave in. I mean, fancy having all that worry of her only daughter up the spout without a husband. She's wicked, she is, sending her mother to an early grave like that. And who was the father, eh?'

'Your guess is as good as mine,' said the other woman. 'It could have been either one of them Ferguson brothers, or who's to say it weren't old Epstein's? From what you've told me, he was always a bit generous to her with his cakes and biscuits, especially his ginger nuts!'

Dorothy heard the women laughing as she dived into the car. She sat on the back seat, shocked, and wondered if that was what everyone thought. Was it her fault her mother had died? It was awful enough that she was gone and Dorothy didn't know how she would cope with her death, but it had never crossed her mind that she had caused it.

Had she killed her own beloved mother?

After the funeral they dropped Nelly off, but the rest of the journey home passed in a blur. When Adrian took the key from her shaking hand to open the front door, Dorothy scurried in. She was so grateful to be in the safety of her own home and could understand why her mother had never wanted to leave it.

She went through to the front room to see her father sleeping in his armchair, oblivious that his wife had just been buried. Dorothy managed to thank the woman from across the road for sitting with him, and she saw Adrian slip her a little something before she left. She felt guilty; it should be her paying the woman, not Adrian. Dorothy flopped onto the sofa, unaware that she was wringing her hands with worry. With only her dad's small pension coming in, she would have to find a job, but as he couldn't be left alone, the situation seemed impossible.

'Can I get you a cup of tea?' Adrian interrupted her thoughts.

'Oh, I'm sorry. It should me be offering to make you a drink.'

'No, you've had a tough day. You just sit there and relax while I put the kettle on,' Adrian replied.

Dorothy didn't protest. Adrian was right, it had been a tough day and she was relieved it was over. She didn't think she'd have coped without his help. Her mother had been paying a penny a week to the Prudential for funeral costs but the payout hadn't been sufficient to cover all the expenses. Adrian had insisted on covering the shortfall, and had helped to make all the arrangements.

When he came back from the kitchen, she said, 'Adrian, I don't think I've thanked you for everything you've done for me. Today would have been impossible without your help.'

'No need for thanks. Your mother was a good woman. I just wish I'd known her for longer.'

'Yes, she was. My mum worked so hard to bring me

up, yet look what I did to her,' Dorothy said sadly, the words of the women at the funeral still heavy on her mind. The grief and shame she felt were like a physical pain that tore at her heart, and, unable to control herself any longer, she ran from the room in floods of tears.

Adrian caught up with her in the kitchen where she was standing in front of the sink, her body heaving with emotion. As he placed his arms around her shoulders, she gasped, 'Oh, Adrian . . . it's all my fault.'

'What's your fault, Dottie?'

'My mum . . . I . . . I . . . killed her!'

Adrian turned her to face him and gently lifted her chin. 'Of course you didn't. You had nothing to do with your mother's death. She loved you dearly, and, baby or no baby, she was very proud of you. Wherever did you get such a silly idea?'

'At the funeral. I heard people talking. They said she died because of me; that I caused her so much worry and her heart couldn't take it.'

'That's rubbish. You heard what the doctor said. Your mother had a weak heart, and it wasn't worry that caused the attack.'

Dorothy sobbed and put her arms around Adrian's rotund waist. He pulled her to him and held her as she cried, gently stroking her hair. His strong embrace felt comforting and she cried out her pent-up emotions, the anguish of losing the baby and, even worse, the loss of her mother.

Chapter 18

In Portsmouth, Christmas and the New Year had passed uneventfully, and now spring was in the air. Robbie marched through the docks like a man on a mission. He pulled his collar up and shoved his hands into his trouser pockets against the cold March winds as he stomped along the wet quayside. Anger burned inside him. He was sick and tired of trawling the area looking for Gladys and dragging her back to his place.

Then he spotted her. She was leaning against a wall outside a small hut. She's frigging well at it again, thought Robbie, fuming. He knew the hut was a café which was only frequented by dockers and sailors. There was only one reason any woman would be hanging about outside and no decent woman would be.

'Gladys, what's your game, eh?' Robbie asked. He was attempting to keep his temper under control, especially in front of the men who were in and out of the café. There was no doubt in his mind that some of them would be familiar with Gladys and he didn't want to rile any of them.

'Bugger off, Robbie. I've told you before, I'm not your girlfriend any more so I can go where I like and do what I want.'

Robbie stood close to Gladys and, grabbing her arm, he growled, 'Get your fucking arse back to my place – NOW!'

Gladys looked like she was going to protest so Robbie squeezed tighter on her thin arm. 'Don't defy me, woman,' he said. 'You know what will happen if you do.'

Gladys's body slumped and she relented under Robbie's pressure and allowed him to lead her away. They walked the streets in silence but Robbie's anger didn't subside. Once inside his room he slammed the door and grabbed Gladys's face, digging his thumb into one cheek and his fingers into the other.

'You ungrateful fucking bitch! After everything I've done for you, this is how you treat me,' he spat, shoving her away from him. She landed on his bed and Robbie saw his fingers had left white imprints on her skin. He hoped he hadn't bruised her. It didn't matter if she had marks on her body, but he sold her easier when her face was clean.

'What you've done for me . . . and what exactly is that, Robbie?' Gladys shouted.

'If it wasn't for me, you and your sisters would all be sleeping on the streets now, with hungry bellies and no protection. You've got a short fucking memory, you have.'

'I don't need you, Robbie. I can look after myself and my sisters without you. Why should I get a pittance of the money they pay when it's me who does all the work?'

'All you have to do is open your fucking legs. I get the business in and make sure you don't get roughed up. You've no idea what sort of weirdos are on those streets, or what they could do to you, have you? No, of course not, and do you know why? It's because I look after you,'

Robbie yelled. 'Christ, woman, I'm not going through this again with you. Just stay away from the docks and do what I tell you to do.'

'Or what? Are you going to beat me up again? Punch me in the stomach or kick my legs? Well, go on then, do your worst. I'm not scared of you, Robbie, and I'm not letting you sell me any more.'

Gladys got up and began to walk to the door, but Robbie wasn't going to stand for that. His meal ticket was about to leave, but he wouldn't let her go. He grabbed a handful of her hair and pulled her towards him. 'You're not leaving, do you hear me? I've got three punters lined up for later and you're going to be here to make sure they get exactly what they want.'

'You can't do this to me, Robbie,' Gladys cried. Thick black blobs of make-up were streaking down her face and Robbie thought she looked like a clown gone wrong.

'Shut your mouth and stop your crying or else I'll give you something to cry about. Now, get yourself in that bathroom and get cleaned up.'

'I'll have you for this, I swear I will,' Gladys said scathingly through gritted teeth.

Robbie let go of her hair and pushed her towards the bathroom. 'Yeah, yeah, yeah,' he said but there was something in her defiance that he hadn't seen before and he worried that he might be losing control of her.

When they'd first met he'd been able to manipulate her by using his charms, but that had soon worn off and she'd seen through him. Now he had to resort to violence and intimidation, but, despite what Gladys had said, he'd never really given her a good pasting, just the odd punch or kick here and there to ensure her compliance. Despite that, it seemed Gladys was on the turn, gaining strength from somewhere and daring to confront him. He could probably slap her back into place, but really Robbie wasn't keen on knocking women about, and was reluctant to give her a good hiding. At the same time, he didn't want to let go of the easy money she brought in.

Gladys returned from the bathroom with her face clean and fresh make-up on. He wrapped his arms around her and hoped that a charm offensive might do its old trick again. 'That's better. You look a million dollars and I'm sorry, love. You drive me crazy though. I'm only trying to look out for you but you make it so difficult for me.'

'Look, Robbie,' she said, pulling away from him. 'Me and you, well, I know it hasn't been long, not yet three months, but it's run its course. It's time for me to move on. I appreciate you helping me get straight with money and that, but let's face it . . . we aren't exactly a match made in heaven. To be honest, I can earn a lot more money without you.'

He tried to keep his temper, forcing himself to sound reasonable. 'I know you can make more money if you go it alone, Gladys, but you'll also be in a lot more danger.'

'I'm willing to take my chances on that. I'll see to the fellas you've lined up, but this is the last time. You can't keep me prisoner or make me do things I don't want to do. Yes, you could knock me from here to kingdom come if you like, but at the end of the day I'll still leave, and if I have to I'll get the police on to you.'

Robbie's blood boiled. How dare she threaten him! The audacity of the woman. But she'd hit a nerve as the police were the last people he wanted knocking on his door.

'All right, Gladys, you win. You keep your side of the bargain and sort the customers out tonight and then I'll leave to your own devices. God help you out there all by yourself though, but if that's what you want, then I won't try and stop you.'

'It is, Robbie, and don't worry about me, I'll be fine.'

'Sweetheart, don't flatter yourself,' he said scathingly. 'I'm not worried about you. You're nothing but a filthy whore.'

'Yeah, but one who could still refuse to sort out your customers.'

'Point taken,' Robbie said, still inwardly fuming. Bloody women, some of them had ideas well above their station.

Still, not to worry, he thought, there'd be plenty more like Gladys. He would just have to set himself to finding another one to work for him.

Adrian tidied his desk and sat back in his chair, deep in thought. Robbie had left six months ago and there had been no news of him. He wasn't worried about his brother; after all, as the saying went, no news was good news. Adrian bit his bottom lip, acknowledging the truth if only to himself. He had fallen in love with Dorothy and didn't want Robbie to come home.

He had been to see her many times since her mother's funeral in January, and it was awful to see how she was struggling to stay afloat. Though still beautiful, Dottie now looked worn and weary, her life one of drudgery. He wanted to take her away from it all, to give her the life she deserved, but there was no way Dottie would ever think of him as anything other than a friend.

There was a tap on his office door and one of his

drivers walked in, saying, 'My lorry needs looking at. The brakes are a bit spongy.'

'All right, Joe, leave it with me,' Adrian said, then smiled. 'I hear congratulations are in order. When is the wedding?'

'In two months.'

'No doubt you want to book some time off.'

'Already done, boss.'

Adrian frowned. He must have forgotten, but nowadays, with his mind filled with thoughts of Dorothy, there were a few other things that had slipped past him.

'Night, boss.'

'Yes, goodnight,' Adrian acknowledged as he looked up at the man. Joe couldn't be described as good-looking, and he too was overweight, yet it hadn't stopped him finding someone to love and marry him.

As the office door closed behind the driver Adrian rose to his feet, filled with a new-found determination. If he didn't do it now, he never would, and this was as good a time as any.

Dorothy hardly had time to think about Robbie now. She was exhausted, and ran a hand across her brow. Unable to leave her father, she now took in washing, just as her mother had, and her heart ached at what Alice had endured for so many years. It was hard, back-breaking work that paid little, and, without the money she had once brought in from the bakery, they were now deeply in arrears with the rent and being threatened with eviction.

With the day's washing finally done, she sat down, knowing that the rest would be a short one as her father would be hungry and wanting his dinner. It was vegetable stew again, meat a rare commodity nowadays, but he just ate what was put in front of him and thankfully never complained.

Tiredly she got to her feet, but as she stirred the stew there was a knock on the door. It was a bit early for Nelly, who often popped round for an hour or two in the evenings, and as she rarely saw anyone all day, Dottie felt her friend's cheery conversation saved her sanity.

It wasn't Nelly at the door but Adrian. Though he had been to see her quite a few times, he didn't usually call this late.

'Hello, come on in,' she said.

'Thank you, Dorothy,' he said, removing his trilby hat as he came through the door. 'How are you?'

'I'm fine,' she lied. 'I've got something heating on the stove, so do you mind coming through to the kitchen?'

'Of course not,' he said. He followed her in and his eyes scanned the room before settling on a pile of freshly washed and ironed sheets. He turned to look at her, his expression concerned. 'I know you said you're fine, but you look tired.'

With all the worry about the rent and finding enough money to feed them, Dorothy was close to breaking point and Adrian's sympathy brought tears to her eyes. She blinked rapidly as she flopped onto a kitchen chair and croaked, 'Sit down, Adrian. Yes, I am tired, but I'll be all right after a good night's sleep.'

'I can see how hard you're working to make ends meet. Your mother would be so proud of you,' Adrian said softly.

'Do you really think so?'

'Yes, I do. I know she would be. In fact, did you know she once told me that I should marry you? She said I'd never find a better wife.'

Dorothy gaped in astonishment. Her mother had told Adrian to marry her. It was unbelievable. 'What . . . what did you say?'

'I told her that as you'd never agree, it was out of the question.'

Dorothy gulped, hardly believing she was having this conversation. Adrian wasn't as striking as his brother, though underneath the podginess he was quite handsome, but, more importantly, he was so gentle and kind, a pillar of strength that she could lean on. 'So are you saying that if you thought I'd agree, you'd have asked me?'

Adrian's face turned red and he seemed a bit flummoxed. 'I . . . I would have, yes, but surely that doesn't surprise you.'

Dorothy's mind was in a whirl and she covertly pinched herself to make sure she wasn't dreaming. Adrian was wrong. She was surprised, she really was. She had no idea he felt like that about her and, though she owed him a great deal, she wasn't in love with him. 'I don't quite know what to say,' she said slowly, still trying to digest the madness of it all.

'Say you'll marry me,' Adrian pleaded as he suddenly dropped to one knee and took her hand. 'I can look after you, Dottie, and your father. You can both move into my house and I'll see you want for nothing.'

'But . . . but I don't love you, Adrian, not in that way.'

'That doesn't matter. I can't bear to see you living like this, and though you don't love me now, in time you might feel differently. Give me a chance. Let me try to make you happy. I won't ask for much, just your honesty and loyalty, and, Dottie, you would make me the happiest man alive!'

It was a lot for Dorothy to take in. So much had happened in such a short time. Robbie had run off, breaking her heart and leaving her pregnant. She had lost the baby, and then came the horror of her mother's death and the harrowing funeral. But this man kneeling before her had seen her through it all. Adrian had held her during the worst moments of her life and thrown her a lifeline on more than one occasion. But marry him? Could she really commit the rest of her life to a man she respected but wasn't in love with?

As if Adrian had an insight into her thoughts and could read her mind, he said, 'It's all right, Dottie. As I said, you don't have to love me. I have enough love for both of us.'

Dorothy's mind spun. She hadn't paid the rent for weeks, she struggled to buy food and pay the bills, but if she agreed to marry Adrian all her problems would be solved at once. Yet was that reason enough to marry someone? Eventually, emotionally and mentally exhausted by trying to cope on her own, she said, 'Yes, all right. I'll marry you, Adrian.'

'Oh, Dottie . . . Dottie,' he husked, and standing up he pulled her to her feet and held her closely.

She had thought that all her dreams of becoming Mrs Ferguson had been dashed when Robbie had left her, but here she was, standing in her mother's kitchen and agreeing to become Mrs Ferguson again. It didn't hold quite the same thrill it had when she had said yes to

Robbie, yet Dorothy found that she felt a warmth inside, a safe and fuzzy feeling in Adrian's arms that replaced her fear.

She was going to become Mrs Adrian Ferguson and, though there was no secret about her lack of love for her future husband, she believed that Adrian was a good man, the best in fact.

Dottie inwardly vowed that she would do everything within her power to make her husband a contented man and be a good wife to him. After all, it was the very least he deserved.

Chapter 19

Robbie was getting bored. He'd found himself a replacement for Gladys, but the girl liked a drink and when she was drunk, which she frequently was, he found her quite difficult to handle. He'd left her in his bed to nurse yet another hangover whilst he went for a walk to calm his irritation.

Robbie hadn't ditched the old Ford, sure that the police wouldn't bother to look for such an old car, and mostly left it parked on a piece of ground behind his flat. Today he decided to use it and drove to Southsea, where he pulled up in a side street close to the seafront.

The clouds gave way to June sunshine as he reached the beach. His heels clipped along the wooden decking of South Pier, but wanting a smoke he spied an empty deckchair to sit on. He fished in his jacket pocket for a roll-up and matches, then struggled to light his cigarette in the sea breeze. The grey waters sloshed against the wooden piles beneath him, as early holidaymakers meandered behind him. It wasn't quite the busy summer season but it wouldn't be long before tourists began to swamp the place, and a worrying thought crossed Robbie's mind. He knew the red London buses did trips to the seaside. What if he bumped into someone who knew him? Perhaps it was time for him to move on? He didn't have much cash, but if he could raise more the world would be his oyster. He drew deeply on his roll-up and gazed out to sea. OK, maybe the world wasn't his oyster, but there was nothing keeping him here.

A young couple stopped a few feet along from him, and the man pretended to throw the woman over the side of the pier. 'Argh . . . Leave it out, you silly sod. I'll get me bruvver to knock your bleedin' block off,' the woman said, but laughter took the sting out of her threat.

There was no mistaking her distinct London accent, which made Robbie unexpectedly miss home. He didn't know what it was he missed. He knew it wasn't his dull brother, or the smelly streets, and he certainly didn't miss his job. Maybe it was the hustle and bustle or just the feeling of familiarity. He had always been popular and had a large circle of friends. Everyone knew him wherever he went in Battersea and he'd always felt that people liked him, apart from Stan and Brian, but that was no surprise, considering the money he owed them.

In retrospect, he regretted doing a runner after robbing the jeweller's, and thought back to the panic which had marred his judgement. At the time, he'd thought he was stuck in the jeweller's attic but he'd found an old trunk which he'd upended and together with a box it had given him enough height to climb out of the skylight. He'd made his escape just as the police arrived and didn't think he'd been seen leaving the narrow alley. Yet even if he was, without a criminal record he doubted he'd be recognised.

Panic made him leave Battersea, but by this time, with

no suspects, the police had probably dropped the case. No, it wasn't the law that prevented his return to Battersea. It was the men he owed money to, especially Brian, a nasty piece of work. If he wanted to go back and remain in one piece, there was only one way. He'd need to raise a lot of money to pay off his debtors – with accrued interest, the sum he owed was far larger than the original loan.

As he made his way back to the house where he had a room, Robbie thought long and hard. The drunken old bint indoors would never earn him the sort of cash he needed. So far, he hadn't been successful in planning any big money-making jobs, but then again, he hadn't really tried. Maybe it was about time he did.

Nelly stood outside her mum's house and surveyed the street as she waited for Adrian and Dorothy to pick her up. The clock in the kitchen had said five past one, but you could never tell if it was accurate or not. It was a lovely day and she didn't mind waiting outside. It was nice to get away from the mayhem on the other side of the front door.

Linda, her sister, had been having a bit of a rough time of it with her husband and had left him and turned up here with her three children. Nelly didn't mind as she loved her nieces and nephew, but space was tight in the little two-bedroomed terraced house. She had the two girls top and tailing in bed with her at night and her nephew was on her bedroom floor, whilst Linda slept on the lumpy old sofa. Nelly took after her mother, who was as round as she was tall, and her father was a big man too, which meant there wasn't any room in her parents' bed for the kiddies, but even if there had been she doubted her father would stand for it.

The front door unexpectedly opened and Nelly's nephew ran down the short pathway towards her. Before Nelly had time to react, the three-year-old had wrapped his grubby arms around her leg and left sticky jam hand-prints on her new green dress.

'Oh, no, David . . . what have you done? Look at the state of me now!' Nelly gazed down at the cute boy, who looked back at her with his large blue eyes.

'I is sowwy, Newwy,' he said, his little lips curling down.

His innocent little face melted her heart and she couldn't be angry at the child. 'It's all right, David. Get yourself back indoors, there's a good boy.'

'But I no want to . . . I wants to come wif you,' he cried.

Linda appeared in the doorway. 'There's the little monkey! Come on, you. Inside,' she said but then she noticed the marks on Nelly's dress. 'Bugger it, have you seen what that little toad has done to your nice outfit?'

'Yes, of course I have. Don't tell him off though, he didn't mean to do it,' Nelly replied, ruffling the boy's hair.

'I'll skin the little bleeder alive one of these days! Anyway, come indoors and I'll see if we can't sponge it off. We can't have you going to a wedding looking like something the cat dragged in. And what with you being a witness and all . . .'

Nelly sighed and began to walk up the front path but she spotted Adrian's car coming down the road. 'I ain't got time, Lin, they're here.'

'Don't be daft, it won't take a minute,' Linda said but Nelly was already out of the gate and trudging towards the car.

'Hello, you two,' Nelly said as she climbed into the back seat to sit next to Dorothy's father. 'I'm so bloody excited, I'm like a cat on a hot tin roof!'

Dorothy laughed. 'I must say, I don't think I've ever seen you move so quickly. I love your hat, Nelly, and thanks ever so much for doing this for us.'

Nelly patted her black cloth hat that she'd trimmed with a green band to match her dress, pleased that Dorothy liked it. 'Don't thank me, it's a real pleasure. I've never been a witness at a wedding before. Just think, my signature is going to be on official paperwork for ever. I've been practising a curly bit on the "y" at the end of my name.'

'You are funny, Nel, but I must admit, I've been practising too. It's really weird writing "Ferguson".'

The drive to Wandsworth Register Office didn't take long, and though they all spoke to Dorothy's father, there was no response. Once they were parked up Nelly was first out of the car. Adrian was next and came round to the passenger side to hold open the door for Dorothy. As she climbed out, Nelly thought she looked like a film star in her cream suit, satin-edged jacket and pearl earrings. Her hair was waved and worn up and she wore a cream pillbox hat, with a small veil covering the top half of her face.

'Wow, Dottie,' she said, 'you look amazing!'

'Thanks, Nelly. I just wish my mum could have been here. I think she would have approved of me marrying Adrian.'

'She definitely would. He's a proper gent and you could've done a lot worse.' Nelly didn't need to elaborate and didn't want to mention Robbie's name, especially today. To think her friend could have ruined her life and married the other Ferguson brother. Thank goodness she'd come to her senses and chosen Adrian. Nelly wasn't stupid and knew Dorothy would never love Adrian the way she had Robbie, but at least the girl was giving herself a fighting chance of some happiness.

'Thank you, Nelly,' Adrian said. 'It's nice to hear I'm a gent.'

Nelly looked at Adrian, smart in his dark pin-stripe suit, and thought that, though her friend might not realise it yet, Adrian was the best thing that had ever happened to her.

Adrian had tried many times to talk to Dorothy's father, but he didn't respond. Understandably, Dorothy wanted him at the register office, and Adrian knew she was hoping that it would draw him out, but so far the man seemed to be in a world of his own. They had gently urged him to a seat in the front row, and now Adrian stood before the registrar, turning to gaze at the beautiful woman at his side. He could barely believe his luck. This gorgeous girl would soon be his wife. He patted his jacket to check again that the gold band was still tucked away in his inside pocket. It would sit nicely against the sapphire and diamond engagement ring he had bought her. The ring had cost a lot of money, but when Adrian had seen the blue stones he'd thought they matched Dorothy's eyes, and, as stunning as the ring was, he didn't think it was a patch on the exquisiteness of his fiancée.

Adrian quickly glanced over his shoulder to see that Bill was staring straight ahead, seemingly unaware that his only daughter was just about to be married. Their two witnesses – Nelly and Adrian's driver Joe – both grinned at him. Joe gave Adrian a thumbs-up sign and Nelly was fiddling with her handkerchief. It wasn't a wedding on anything like the scale of Grace Kelly's the year before, and Adrian didn't really have any friends he could call on to be a witness, but nonetheless it was everything he wanted: Dorothy Butler as his wife.

The registrar began to officiate and it was almost time for them to take turns in repeating the marriage vows. Adrian felt his heartbeat quicken and sweat began to run down the side of his face, which owed more to his nerves than to the heating in the large room. He hadn't expected to feel so nervous and he was suddenly worried he might flummox his words. His mouth was dry, and as he began to speak his lips stuck to his teeth. He took a deep breath and cleared his throat, determined to get it right for Dorothy.

Dorothy must have seen how edgy he was feeling and gently squeezed his hand. Her reassuring touch made him instantly relax, and soon he was delighting in placing the wedding ring on her finger. The formal ceremony then came to a close as the registrar announced, 'You may kiss the bride.'

Adrian held Dorothy at arm's length and looked into her eyes. He felt quite awkward. They had been engaged for three months, yet he had only kissed her cheek. Now, feeling embarrassed at kissing his bride in front of Nelly and Joe, he opted to lightly brush her lips with his, so quickly that it could have been missed in the blink of an eye.

Nelly didn't miss it and let out a whoop, which left

Adrian blushing and uncomfortable. It was strange really: in some ways he wished he was more like his brother. But no, Robbie had broken Dorothy's heart and that was something he would never do.

The rest of their wedding day passed pleasantly, and when Adrian walked into the living room that evening he found Dorothy looking quite relaxed with her feet up on the sofa. In the hope that they could have some privacy, he had adapted the cosy dining room at the back of the house into a snug for Dorothy's father, and there was a toilet just outside the back door if he wanted to use it rather than trudge upstairs.

After the wedding Bill had looked tired, so they had driven him home and it had been a relief when he accepted his new surroundings without any sign of agitation. Adrian's neighbour, Mrs Hart, had kindly sat with him while they went for a meal to celebrate their marriage, and now Bill was safely tucked up in bed.

'Penny for them,' he said as he handed Dorothy a mug of warm milk.

'I was just thinking about my mum. I missed her today.'

'I'm sure she was there, Dottie, right by your side and listening to every word,' Adrian said, hoping his words gave his wife some comfort.

'Maybe. It was a really nice day though. That restaurant was smashing, though a bit posh, and I could see that Nelly and Joe were impressed. Thank you so much for paying for that lovely meal.'

'Dottie, you're my wife and you don't have to thank me for picking up the tab for our celebratory wedding lunch.'

Dorothy giggled. 'I suppose I'm not used to being your wife yet. After all, it's only been about nine hours.'

'And they've been the best nine hours of my life. I don't remember if I told you today or not, but you look stunning in that outfit and I'm so proud of you.'

'It is lovely, isn't it? Thank you for giving me the money to buy myself something special to wear, but I think it's time I changed. I don't want to ruin it.'

Adrian decided that this could be his cue to broach the bedroom subject. With her father sleeping in his parents' old room, there were three to choose from, though he thought it wouldn't be appropriate for his wife to sleep in Robbie's old room. That left Myra's old room, or his.

'I've cleared a wardrobe for you in my room and I've had a dressing table put in there. The top three drawers of the chest of drawers are also empty.' Dorothy just looked at him, saying nothing, so he gabbled on. 'I'm . . . err . . . assuming that now we're legally married you'll be moving your things into my room, but I don't want to push you into anything you're not ready for. If you would prefer to stay in another of the rooms, that's fine by me. I've arranged for one of my trucks to go to your house tomorrow and clear it. You can bring back here anything you'd like to keep and, like I said, it's up to you where you want—'

'Adrian,' Dorothy said abruptly but with a smile.

'I'm rambling, aren't I?' he asked.

'Just a bit,' Dorothy agreed. 'I think I'll go upstairs to *our* room and make myself more comfortable. You can join me in ten minutes.'

Adrian felt a jolt but tried not to show it. He was so

relieved to hear he would be sharing a bed with his new wife, but felt terrified at the same time. He couldn't wait to hold her and caress her, but worried that his inexperience would be evident. It was no secret that she wasn't a virgin, but for Adrian it would be his first time, though Dorothy didn't know that. He didn't have the gift of the gab as Robbie did, and being shy with women he'd never fared well with the opposite sex. If he'd been blessed with Robbie's masculine physique it would have given him the confidence, but his stout build and bald head, along with his lack of poise, had always held him back. Instead he'd thrown himself into his business, determined to make his company a success.

Adrian listened as Dorothy went up the stairs and into his bedroom. He nervously gathered the milk mugs, took them through to the kitchen and rinsed them in the sink as though on auto-pilot, all the time silently flustered at the thought of making love to Dorothy. What if she didn't want to? He would feel terrible if she spurned his attentions. Worse still, what if she *did* want to and his lack of skill and knowledge in the bedroom left her unhappy with him?

Adrian suddenly felt very inadequate and frantically tried to think of an excuse to delay going upstairs. However, his mind was a blank and as he approached the bottom step, he held on to the bannister. Pull yourself together, he told himself. You love Dorothy so go and show her just how much she means to you.

Adrian had been very generous with the money he'd given Dorothy to buy her wedding outfit and she had saved some of it to buy a pretty negligée to wear for tonight. She hung her skirt and jacket in the space Adrian had cleared in his wardrobe, and slipped into her silky nightdress, which was adorned with a pattern of exotic peacocks.

She looked around the room. When she had dropped her overnight bag in earlier, she hadn't really taken much notice of anything as the wedding had been on her mind. Now she noted the long velvet curtains and the exquisitely embroidered bed cover. The beige carpet beneath her bare feet had a thick pile, and all the furniture looked to be made from good quality mahogany. She had never been in a room so luxurious.

Dorothy sat down on the stool in front of the dressing table and peered into the mirror, hardly recognising herself in such a sophisticated negligée with her hair professionally styled. It seemed a shame to spoil it, but she began to remove the hairpins, which let her long locks tumble down her back. This room, and in fact the whole house, screamed of everything her mother had never enjoyed and said she never wanted. Dorothy couldn't help but wonder if she'd only said that because she could never have afforded luxuries such as the silver hairbrush on the dressing table or the crystal scent bottle that Adrian had thoughtfully provided. Dorothy picked it up and pulled out the glass stopper to sniff the perfume before dabbing a little behind each ear. She noticed the bottle had a label with words written in French but she couldn't work out what the strange words said.

As she ran the brush through her hair, her thoughts went from her mother to Robbie. His old room was next door but she hadn't seen inside it yet. She wondered if it would look as grown-up as Adrian's room. She knew he had a record player in there and she remembered he had mentioned something about a poster he had on his wall of the British film star Diana Dors.

Dorothy was so confused when she thought about Robbie and felt sick to her stomach when she thought of the possibility of him returning. It would be such a dreadful situation and she feared what would happen. Adrian owned the house. He had paid off the mortgage that his parents originally had, but it was still Robbie's home. She had to be honest with herself: though she was Adrian's wife and would always be true to her husband, deep in her heart she still loved Robbie, and probably always would. It would be better for them all if he never came back to Battersea.

Chapter 20

After a pleasant summer and a mild autumn, late November was wet and cold as Nelly walked along the street holding up her umbrella. It was really nice of Adrian to allow her to have Wednesday afternoons off, and she enjoyed working for him.

Nelly shuddered when she thought of Mr Epstein, her former boss. It had grated on her when he had spoken so unkindly about Dorothy and made jibes at every opportunity, until one day, when he had made nasty remarks about Dottie's marriage to Adrian, she had reached breaking point. She smiled as she recalled the stunned look on Epstein's face when she had retaliated and given the weasel a piece of her mind. It had been a reckless thing to do as she'd been sacked, but thankfully, when Adrian heard about it, he came to her rescue and offered her a job in his office as his secretary.

It worked out well for them both. Once she had grasped the ropes it freed Adrian to spend more time with Dorothy, and it was a step up for Nelly. She found the environment a bit stifling at first but relished learning new administrative skills, along with enjoying some banter with the drivers. Especially Malcolm, a big bloke matching her own stature, who she hoped would soon pluck up the nerve to ask her out.

Nelly folded her umbrella but before she had a chance to knock on the front door Dorothy opened it with a welcoming smile.

'Hello, Nelly. Come in out of that rain, the kettle's already on.'

Nelly was glad to see her friend looking so cheerful. Married life obviously agreed with her. Well, married life with Adrian, that is. She doubted Dorothy would have looked so happy if she had ended up as Robbie's wife.

'Hello, sugar. Do you know what? No matter how many times I walk down this street, it never ceases to impress me. It's a lot bloody nicer than the other side of Battersea, and I don't think I'll ever get used to the idea of you living in this grand house.'

'Yes, I know what you mean. I've been living here for nearly six months now and it still doesn't feel like home. I think my dad feels the same. I thought he'd settled in at first, but nowadays if I don't lock the front door he wanders off. It makes me feel like I'm making him a prisoner, but what else can I do?'

Nelly could hear the sadness in her friend's voice, but Dorothy had her back to her while making the tea, and when she turned round it was with a smile as she proffered a plate of chocolates. 'Here you are, Nelly. Your favourites!'

'Roses! Thanks, Dottie,' she exclaimed, instantly distracted from her friend's mood. She shoved one in her mouth and savoured the creamy milk chocolate, then remembered her concern for her friend. 'I know you said this place doesn't feel like home to you yet, but you're happy enough with Adrian, ain't you? Sorry, I mean *aren't* you? Adrian is helping me to improve my diction, but I still slip up.'

'I'm trying to improve mine too. I don't want to show Adrian up when he introduces me to his business associates and their wives,' Dottie said, and took a sip of her tea.

'You still haven't told me if you're happy with him.'

There was a moment of hesitation before Dottie said, 'Of course I am.'

'I'm not so sure. Come on, Dottie, if something's troubling you, you know you can tell me,' Nelly said as she put another chocolate in her mouth.

'It's nothing really. Take no notice of me, I'm just being silly.'

Nelly knew her friend too well to be fobbed off. 'Is it Adrian? He had better be treating you right or he'll have me to deal with.'

'No, Adrian's good to me, there's no problem there.'

'So what's troubling you then?'

'It's just that . . . I . . . I want a baby but nothing's happened.'

Nelly's brow rose in surprise. She wasn't qualified to talk about bedroom matters, having no experience in such things, and stuttered, 'What . . . what do you mean? Are you saying that you and Adrian . . . well . . . err, you've not consummated the marriage?'

'Don't be silly, Nel, of course we have'— Dorothy rolled her eyes —'but I'm not pregnant. I really want a baby but my period came again yesterday. It's getting me down, Nelly.'

Knowing only what she had gleaned from her sister

and what she'd heard from local gossip, Nelly offered, 'Oh, Dottie, it's early days yet and it'll happen when it's meant to happen. You've got to let nature take its course. Some women take years to fall, not that I'm suggesting it'll take you that long. Look at my sister . . . she's only got to wink at her old man and she ends up with another bun in the oven. Blimey, in June she was living at ours and vowing never to speak to her husband again. Now look at her, back with him and up the duff with her fourth.'

'But that's exactly what I mean, Nelly. How come she's pregnant and I'm not? What if the miscarriage damaged me? What if I can never have children?'

Nelly saw her friend's eyes begin to well up and frantically searched her brain for the right answer. 'Oh, sugar, don't cry. Lots of women have had miscarriages and gone on to have babies. You will too.'

'Oh, I hope you're right. Since I had that miscarriage last year, I've felt so empty and I just long to hold a baby in my arms.'

'Don't worry. You will,' Nelly said assuredly, inwardly praying that she wasn't giving Dorothy false hope.

The clock struck seven in Adrian's office. He'd only stayed late to give his wife and her friend some time together. There wasn't a lot to do and there was no need for him to work such long hours, not since he'd employed Nelly. She'd required a fair amount of training but was making good progress, and her typing was improving from using one finger to several. He'd inwardly cringed at first when she answered the telephone, but she was improving. It still needed a bit of work, but she'd get there, and he'd noticed that Dorothy was making an effort to improve her pronunciation too.

Unexpectedly, he enjoyed having Nelly working in the office. She was like a breath of fresh air and her jolly nature and silly jokes never failed to make him laugh. Now though, eager to get home to see Dorothy, Adrian locked the door and climbed into his car. His wife had appeared a bit miserable that morning, but, after spending the afternoon with Nelly, he hoped to find her cheerful. He felt they had a good marriage and hardly ever spoke a cross word, but worry niggled Adrian as he drove into their street. He didn't like to see Dorothy unhappy, and wondered if it was because she felt trapped, unable to leave her father unless she found someone to sit with him. If that was the case, they would have to find a way to do something about it.

As he pulled up outside their home, he saw Dorothy on the doorstep ready to greet him. He parked against the kerb and took a moment to gaze at his beautiful wife, wondering how he'd became so fortunate. She was a delight to live with and cooked delicious meals, which only added to his flabby belly. Luckily his increasing size didn't seem to bother Dorothy. She always cuddled into him at night, which invariably led to more and they would make love, though despite a healthy sex life they had never seen each other's naked bodies. In his shyness Adrian insisted on turning off the bedside lamp and closing the heavy velvet curtains to block out any light. Dorothy's bare flesh felt so soft and smooth to his touch and he was desperate to see her nude, yet he feared her rejection if she saw his podgy body.

'Good evening, my gorgeous wife,' Adrian said, pushing his thoughts aside as he kissed Dorothy's cheek.

She smiled as she took his hat and coat. 'Hello, husband. I hope you don't mind, but when it stopped raining this afternoon Nelly persuaded me to go out. Mrs Hart kindly sat with my dad, but it means we've only got yesterday's left-over cold pork and some mash for dinner. Is that OK?'

'That sounds fine to me. Did you have a nice time?' Adrian asked as he walked through to the lounge with Dorothy following him.

'We decided to go to the cinema, but there wasn't really anything on we fancied, only one of those Ealing comedies and they're not my cup of tea. Talking of tea, would you like one?'

'Yes, please,' he said, and as he sat down to take off his shoes, Dorothy immediately put his slippers in front of him. 'Thanks, but you don't have to wait on me hand and foot.'

'I know I don't, but I'm your wife and it's the least I can do. You're out working hard all day so it's my job to look after you and the house.'

'There's your father too, and looking after him must be hard on you.'

'I don't mind.'

'Are you sure? I can tell you're unhappy so if it isn't because you're tied to the house, what is it? Is it me? Is it something I've done?'

'No . . . no, of course it isn't.'

'Then what's wrong?'

She bit on her lower lip, and then looked at him, her eyes moist. 'I . . . I want a baby, Adrian, and I hoped by now I'd be pregnant.'

Despite the fact that Dorothy looked close to tears,

relief washed over him. So that was it – she was broody. He stood up and gathered her in his arms. 'It hasn't been long, darling. Give it some time and soon enough we'll have our own little one running around the place. Until it happens we can enjoy trying, and we can have another go tonight if you like?'

He was glad to see Dorothy smile and was quite surprised at his own cheeky suggestion. Nelly's humour must be rubbing off on him, he thought. Maybe he might even be bold enough to leave the light on later.

Dorothy was lying in bed on her back, staring at the ceiling. She could hear Adrian humming to himself in the bathroom but her thoughts were wrapped up in babies.

Her best friend and now her husband too had advised her to be patient and to let nature take its course. Maybe they were right, yet she still feared that the infection she'd had after the miscarriage had caused irreparable damage. After all, she'd fallen pregnant the first time with Robbie.

Adrian came out of the bathroom and stood at the bedside wearing his burgundy woollen dressing gown. She knew he would turn off the bedside light before removing it to climb in bed next to her. She was curious and thought it a bit odd that she was a married woman of five months and still had never seen a man's private parts.

'It's a bit nippy tonight,' Adrian said.

With the light now off, Dorothy felt his side of the bed dip, and then he lay down beside her. 'I don't mind. I've got these lovely thick blankets and my cuddly husband to keep me warm,' she answered and rolled over towards him.

Adrian wrapped her in his arms and began nuzzling her neck. She closed her eyes in the darkness and wished that it wasn't her time of the month. Making love with Adrian wasn't unpleasant, but neither was it very exciting. It was her duty as his wife, but, more importantly, it might lead to pregnancy.

'Adrian, we can't. I'm sorry but it's that time again.'

He immediately pulled away from her. 'I'm sorry, Dottie. I didn't realise.'

'You can still cuddle me though,' she whispered in his ear, and sighed as she relaxed in the safety of her husband's embrace.

It wouldn't be long before they could try again, Dorothy thought. She closed her eyes and as she began to drift off to sleep, she hoped with all her heart that the next time they made love, a seed would be planted and blossom into a beautiful baby.

Chapter 21

Robbie was hunched up against the cold wind on Friday as he walked along the front in Southsea. Money was tight and he hadn't found an opportunity to make more. The woman he'd hooked up with to replace Gladys wasn't as easy to sell to his usual punters. She lacked the charm of Gladys, and, as she was often intoxicated, her personal hygiene left a lot to be desired.

He left the beach and headed for the main road, past Canoe Lake. It had been packed in the summer with kids enjoying a ride on paddle boats shaped like swans. Now, though, the area looked bleak, the sky heavy and grey, and Robbie's expression soured. The seaside was nice during the summer season, but it was dead now and he itched to move on.

A sudden honking made him jump and he halted and turned to see that his mate,Clifford, had pulled up alongside him on his Sunbeam motorcycle. He'd first met Clifford in a pub in Portsmouth, and though he thought the chap was a bit of a goody-goody they had clicked and become firm friends.

'Hello, Rob. I didn't expect to see you here,' Clifford said, his red cheeks matching his peak-capped crash helmet.

‘I felt like a change of scenery and I’m just going for a lunchtime pint. Do you fancy joining me?’

‘Yeah, why not. I fancied a bit of a spin too, but I can only have a couple of pints. I’m supposed to be picking up the laundry for she who must be obeyed. Still, I know just the place for a drink so hop in.’

Robbie took the spare helmet from Clifford’s sidecar before climbing in, pushing his legs down into the bullet-shaped space. ‘Bloody hell, mate, it’s a bit of a tight squeeze.’

‘My wife loves it – stop moaning, you big softie.’

Robbie wasn’t sure he felt the same as Clifford’s wife, and, as they sped along, the cold wind in his face made his eyes water. He pulled the goggles down to cover them, wishing the journey over.

Clifford drove to a pub a little way out of town and pulled up in the carpark. Robbie didn’t recognise it and got out of the sidecar before removing the goggles and helmet. ‘That was a cold ride and a bit bone-rattling,’ he said as he surveyed the area.

‘You loved it really. I saw the smile on your face,’ Clifford replied as they walked into the pub to order their drinks.

‘That wasn’t a smile. It was a grimace. So what are we doing here then, Cliff? It’s a bit off the beaten track.’

‘This is the pub I once told you about, the one near where I work. Anyhow, truth is, my brother-in-law will be in our usual place and I don’t want word getting back to my missus.’

‘She’s not stupid, Cliff, she’ll smell it on your breath, mate.’

‘I’m not worried about that. She won’t mind me having

a quick drink, but she doesn't like me hanging about with you. She reckons you're a bad influence.'

Robbie stared at him. 'Well, I've heard it all now. You really are under her bloody thumb. You're the man of the house; sounds like you need to remind her of that.'

'Maybe, but she knows how you make a living and she's not too impressed by it. The silly cow thinks I might have a skinful and end up as one of your customers.'

'You need to put her straight, Cliff. You and me both know you're not like that.'

'Yeah, I know, but I think since she's had the baby she's put on a few pounds, and she's a bit . . . sensitive.'

'Oh, well, what she don't know won't hurt. Come on, let's get inside, I'm spitting feathers,' said Robbie, unaffected by what Clifford had told him. He couldn't care less what anyone thought about how he earned his money. As far as he was concerned, it was his business and Cliff's wife, the nosy cow, should keep her beak out of it.

From a previous conversation, Robbie knew that Clifford worked in a unit assembling aircraft components. 'How come you aren't at work today?' he asked.

'I've had the day off to pick up the mother-in-law. She's staying with us for a week. Mind you, if it's anything like the last time she stayed I might well be doing time for murder.'

'That bad, eh?' said Robbie.

'Oh, mate, you wouldn't believe it. Take this morning, there's me, minding my own business when . . . Hello, Jack.' Clifford stopped relaying his troubles to Robbie as a short man in a flat cap and braces joined them in the smoky bar. 'Rob, this is Jack. He works down the line from me.'

Robbie eyed the man up and down, always on the lookout for potential customers for his woman indoors. Judging by Jack's age and his miserable-looking face, Robbie thought the old boy would have enough trouble trying to raise a smile, let alone anything else.

'What you having, Jack?' Clifford asked.

'No, you're all right, lad. I'll get my own. They've docked my wages again this week so I don't want to be getting into rounds. Pint, please, landlord, when you're ready.'

Robbie thought it was rather amusing that the short man could barely see over the bar, but something else caught his attention when he pulled a small brown envelope from his trouser pocket and paid for his beer.

'Take a look at this for me, Clifford. I'm not sure why my money's short.' Jack held out his wage packet for him to read the front.

Clifford scanned it then said, 'Look down the bottom there. It says they've taken five shillings out for breakages.'

'Five bloody shillings? The cheeky beggars. My Fanny's going to do her nut when I get this back to her. I just hope we get a decent bonus in our December pay packet. At least it will cheer her up for Christmas.'

'We'd be better off with jobs at that big Giles and West factory up the road. Bloody shame they aren't recruiting.'

Robbie found the conversation drifting over him. He hadn't seen a pay packet for some time and an idea had struck him. A plan was forming, one that could provide him with all the money he needed, and more – enough to go back to Battersea in style.

Malcolm stuck his head around Adrian's office door. He appeared a bit awkward, which Nelly found amusing. He was normally so full of himself so she wondered why he was acting so skittishly.

'Err, sorry to interrupt, but can I have a word with Nelly, please, Mr Ferguson?' the driver asked, his face red and slick with perspiration.

'Yes, Malcolm, but make it quick and don't make a habit of it,' Adrian answered mock-sternly, flashing a teasing smile at Nelly.

'Thanks, I won't be a minute,' she said, her cheeks burning as she stepped outside, where she promptly rounded on Malcolm. 'What on earth are you playing at?' she asked, feigning anger. 'Fancy coming into the office and asking for me. I dread to think what Adrian is going to make of it.'

'Sorry, Nelly. I didn't mean to get you into trouble or nothing,' Malcolm answered with a hurt expression.

'It's all right, I'm only kidding,' Nelly said, feeling the cold and pulling her cardigan closely around her body. 'What did you want to speak to me about?'

Malcolm looked down, shuffling his feet. Nelly found his shyness cute, especially in such a large man. She felt sure he was trying to pluck up the courage to ask her out and secretly had her fingers crossed.

'My sister got engaged yesterday and we're having a bit of a party at home tonight. I wondered if you'd like to come along, you know, as my girlfriend?'

Nelly hid her excitement and said nonchalantly, 'I suppose so. You can pick me up at seven, but now go on, bugger off and let me get back to work.'

Malcolm grinned widely. 'Yeah, all right. See you later.'

Nelly watched as he walked across the yard to his truck, admiring his broad shoulders. She'd never had a boyfriend before and felt like she was floating on air as she returned to her desk.

'So . . . ?' Adrian asked.

'So, what?'

'Did he ask you for a date?'

'As a matter of fact, he did. I'm going to his sister's engagement party tonight. Oh dear, what should I wear? He said I'm to be his girlfriend but what if his family don't like me? Oh, no, look at the state of my hair!'

'Nelly, slow down, woman! I think you need to speak to Dottie. Go on, get yourself off. I can see your mind won't be on your work this afternoon so you'll be no good to me in that state.'

'But, Adrian . . .'

'I said, go!' Adrian rolled his eyes and smiled. 'No doubt Dottie will be pleased to see you.'

Nelly wasted no time in picking up her handbag and dashing out of the door, calling her thanks to Adrian. The sky was grey but nothing could mar Nelly's mood as she hurriedly made her way to see her friend. She couldn't wait to tell Dorothy that Malcolm was her boyfriend.

Distracted in her thoughts and excitement, Nelly stepped out into the road, unaware of the black car hurtling towards her. She heard a loud hoot followed by the sound of brakes screeching on the tarmac, and turned just in time to see the horrified look on the driver's face. Frozen with fear and with no time to react, Nelly braced herself as the car ploughed into her, sending her flying into the air. Excruciating pain ripped through her legs, and for a split second she lost her bearings as the world seemed to tumble and spin around her.

Then she closed her eyes, unconscious, as her heavy body thudded onto the car bonnet before rolling onto the road.

Dorothy was dreading the coming season, but hid her feelings well. It would soon be December, and memories plagued her. She had lost her baby just before Christmas last year, and then her mother on Christmas Day. It made the time of year almost impossible to celebrate, especially as she was still desperately yearning for a child. She would do her best and put up some decorations, but a deep sense of melancholy almost swamped her.

It was difficult to think of much else, but Adrian was due home from work at any minute so she turned the gas up under the saucepan of potatoes. Only moments later she heard the door open and Adrian came through to the kitchen.

'Hello, love,' he greeted her, kissing her on the cheek. 'I bet you're exhausted after an afternoon with Nelly jabbering on about her new boyfriend.'

'What are you talking about? What's all this about Nelly having a boyfriend? Has that Malcolm finally asked her for a date?'

Adrian's eyebrows knotted. 'Hasn't she been round here telling you all about it? I gave her the afternoon off to come and see you.'

'No, I haven't seen hide nor hair of her since last week. Are you sure she was coming round here?'

'Yes, well, I thought so. Oh well, I wouldn't worry. She's going to a party with Malcolm so she probably went home to get herself ready. What's for supper? I'm famished.'

Dorothy drained the potatoes as she spoke. 'Err . . . lamb chops,' she said, but her mind wasn't on the meal. Adrian had said he wasn't worried about Nelly, but she was. It didn't take all afternoon to get ready to go to a party and she wondered what could have happened to her best friend.

Chapter 22

A week passed and in Southsea Robbie was lining up his next big job. He needed to do a bit of fact-finding before he put his plan into action and intended to stake out the unit where Clifford and Jack worked, but he didn't want to be seen.

At nearly six o'clock, knocking-off time for the workers, Robbie lit a roll-up and smoked it until he heard the sound of activity. He popped his head around the corner and looked towards the unit, seeing men and women leaving, some riding bicycles, with faces showing their pleasure at finishing work for the day. The poor buggers, he thought, having to slog it out from eight until six. You wouldn't catch him going back to the daily grind.

This was the first stage of his fact-finding mission and Robbie tried to gauge how many workers there were as he calculated their wages. He counted about twenty, and some would earn more than others, but best of all, a Christmas bonus had been mentioned which would swell their wage packets.

Satisfied with what he had observed, Robbie went back to collect his car. He would have to come back again to check out how the staff wages were collected. He hoped they weren't delivered as that would scupper his idea and he would have to come up with an alternative plan.

It had been a week since Nelly's sister Linda had sent her husband to Dorothy's house to inform them of Nelly's accident. Now, with Nelly in hospital, Adrian had to work longer hours so was home later than usual. Dorothy was pleased when she heard his car pull up outside. It had been a testing day for her and she longed for a comforting cuddle from her husband.

'I'm so glad to see you,' she said, throwing her arms around Adrian as soon as he walked through the front door.

'What's wrong? Is it Nelly?'

'She's doing as well as can be expected. It's just so upsetting to see her like that. She's normally larger than life but she's still not responding to very much,' Dorothy answered as she left her husband's embrace to walk through to the lounge.

Adrian sat in his armchair and picked up his pipe from the side table. 'Try not to worry, love. Nelly took a nasty blow to her head, but the doctor said he expects her to make a full recovery.'

'Yes, I know, but I'm worried about my dad too. I think his cough is wearing him down and he's been tetchy today. I didn't stay long at the hospital as I didn't want to leave him with Mrs Hart for too long. It's very neighbourly of her to offer to sit with him, but it didn't feel right when he's so unwell.'

'She's a good woman and I doubt she minds.'

Dorothy's thoughts drifted back to the first time she had met Mrs Hart. She had appeared on her doorstep when Dorothy had been hammering on Adrian's front door in search of Robbie. So much had happened since then that it felt like a lifetime away.

Quickly dismissing thoughts of Robbie, she said, 'Nelly's sister was there today. I thanked her for sending her husband round to let me know what had happened to Nelly and tried to give her his cab fare. She wouldn't take it though. The poor woman looks run ragged, what with being pregnant and going back and forwards to the hospital. She seemed to think that Nelly looks a lot better. I don't know, maybe she is, but I can't see past her swollen face and plastered leg.'

'The accident only happened a week ago, and if Linda thinks Nelly is on the mend already you can stop worrying your pretty little head. You know Nelly, it'll take more than a car to stop her.'

Dorothy thought that Adrian was probably right. Nelly would be OK and her dad's bad chest would hopefully improve soon too. In truth, what really hurt her was seeing the swell of Linda's belly. Linda already had three children and was now pregnant again, whilst despite trying, Dorothy's dreams of having a baby remained unfulfilled.

When Friday came around again, Robbie woke early. It was payday at the industrial unit and he was keen to put the next stage of his plan into action.

He followed the same route, and left his car in the wooded area before inconspicuously tucking himself around the corner from the unit. He was thankful to find the area was very quiet; the fewer people who spotted him the better. In a bid to disguise himself, he hadn't greased his hair back but instead let it flop across his face. He was also wearing glasses, and hoped that would be enough to make it difficult for any witnesses to identify him.

As Robbie waited, a woman with a small child came around the corner. He instantly dropped to his knee and kept his head low as he pretended to tie up his shoelace. The woman passed and Robbie was confident that she hadn't got a look at his face.

It was ten o'clock and Robbie was shivering with the cold as he began to wonder if he'd missed the wages run. Perhaps whoever collected the money from the bank had been the day before, or maybe it had already been dropped off. His doubts diminished somewhat when he saw a middle-aged woman and a young man leave the unit. Were they going to the bank to collect the wages? He intended to follow them to find out, and if they were he'd look for a spot where he'd be able to make the snatch.

As he watched them walk towards a small car, Robbie cursed his lack of forethought. The industrial unit wasn't in the town centre and the nearest bank was quite a walk. Of course whoever picked up the wages would need transport. He hadn't thought of that.

As they drove off, Robbie was thinking fast. His car was parked too far away to follow them so that left only one thing to do. He would have to wait for them to return, and if he spotted they were carrying a money bag he'd know they were the target. If they were, the theft would have to happen a lot closer to the factory than he'd anticipated. He'd bide his time and come back again, but there was no way he was going to back out of his plan.

Chapter 23

Though she tried to be cheerful for Adrian's sake, as Christmas drew ever closer, it was a hard time for Dorothy. She had done her best and put up some decorations, along with a Christmas tree, but sometimes a deep sense of sadness almost overwhelmed her.

Nelly had recovered enough to leave hospital. Her leg was still in plaster and she was on crutches but apart from that she had mended well. Since she had nowhere to sleep downstairs in her own home, Dorothy had insisted that she come and stay with them, saying that, as she was there all day to look after her father, she might as well nurse her friend too. She genuinely wanted to help her, but there was some self-interest as well: Nelly was always so cheerful and maybe having her there would make Christmas more bearable.

'Are you ready?' Adrian asked, breaking into Dorothy's thoughts.

'Yes, I'll just have a quick word with Mrs Hart and then I'll get my coat. It's kind of her to sit with Dad again.'

'It is, but are you sure Nelly's parents are happy for us to have her here? After all, it'll soon be Christmas.'

'They're pleased about it as they're spending Christmas with Nelly's sister and her children,' Dorothy assured him, inwardly thinking that it would be lovely at Linda's house with the children so excited about Santa Claus coming. Oh, if only she was pregnant, it would have given her so much to look forward to, and might even have eased the painful memories of last year and of losing her mother.

Nelly was waiting to be collected. Adrian had agreed to her moving in with them, which was no surprise to Nelly. The man was obviously head over heels in love with Dorothy and, as long as it kept her happy, Adrian went along with anything she wanted. He was a bit like Malcolm in that way. Granted, she didn't know Malcolm well, but he'd been to the hospital every day to see her, and never turned up without some sweets or something equally thoughtful. They still hadn't had their date, but they'd shared a discreet kiss when no nurses were buzzing around. At first, Nelly had been mortified when she realised Malcolm was sitting at her bedside. Fancy the man seeing her in that state! She soon relaxed as she came to realise that he must be pretty keen on her. For him to see her at her worst and still come back for more spoke volumes.

It wasn't long before Dorothy and Adrian arrived and, after saying her thanks and goodbyes to the nurses who had cared for her, Nelly gingerly hopped along the corridor on crutches to the lifts.

'I can't wait to get you home, Nelly,' Dorothy said. 'I've got a big black pen and I'm going to write something on your plaster.'

'Trust you,' said Nelly. 'What are you going to write?'

Something along the lines of, "Look at me, I'm plastered."'

Nelly laughed along with Dorothy and began to think that maybe it wasn't so bad to have a broken leg. She was looking forward to enjoying Christmas with her best friend.

The following morning, Adrian woke up to the sound of the alarm clock. Dorothy was up before him and he could smell the unmistakable aroma of fried bacon wafting up from the kitchen. His stomach growled in anticipation of a breakfast feast. Dorothy would normally prepare porridge or something she deemed healthy, but he guessed she was pushing the boat out on account of Nelly being there.

They'd made up a makeshift bed on the sofa for Nelly, but it wasn't ideal. With her large frame he thought she might find it uncomfortable, but there was no way Nelly could have made it upstairs to one of the bedrooms, even with them helping her. However, the sofa would only be temporary as he intended to make arrangements for a proper bed to be delivered as soon as possible. It would've made life easier if they could have put it in Bill's sitting room, but moving him out of there might be too much of a disruption for the old chap. When the bed arrived it would be a surprise for Nelly, and it would mean he would have to say goodbye to his living room for a while, but anything to keep Dorothy happy.

Adrian was already out of bed and half-dressed when his wife called that his breakfast was ready. The lounge door was open when he went downstairs and he could see Nelly sat with her broken leg up on the sofa, a tray on her lap.

Dorothy appeared in the hallway. 'Good morning. Go and sit yourself down. We can't have Nelly eating alone so we're eating off trays today.'

Adrian didn't mind and walked into the living room. Before Dorothy had moved in, most of his meals were taken in his armchair but that had all changed when she insisted they ate at the table.

'Morning, Nelly. I don't suppose you got much sleep last night?' he asked, watching as she cut into a juicy sausage.

'I managed to doze on and off, but I tell you what, if that wife of yours keeps this up, I won't want to go home,' Nelly replied, indicating the food on her plate.

Dorothy came into the room carrying Adrian's tray. 'Don't get too used to it,' she said to Nelly. 'I'm only spoiling you today because you've had to put up with that horrible hospital food.'

'Thanks, Dottie, you're a real good mate. I've got something else to ask you, but I don't want to put you out.'

'Ask away.'

'Would it be OK for Malcolm to come here to see me?'

'That's fine with me. Adrian, you won't mind, will you?' Dorothy asked.

'No, of course not.'

'That's settled then,' Dorothy told Nelly. 'He can call in any time he likes, and I expect your family will want to visit you too.'

'Yes, if that's all right. Malcolm said that if I cleared it with you he'd call in on Sunday and I'm really looking forward to seeing him. Will you do something nice with my hair?'

‘I can do better than that,’ Dorothy answered with a smile. ‘My hairdresser mentioned she does home visits so we’ll get her to come here and pamper us both, my treat.’

‘Blimey, Dottie, I’ve never seen a hairdresser in my life! You know my mum always cuts and sets it for me. Cor, I really am being spoilt.’

‘I think we should invite Malcom to join us for Christmas dinner too. What do you think, Adrian?’

‘Yes, good idea,’ he said as he dipped his toast into his runny fried egg. It was good to see Dorothy so animated and having the confidence to spend money without asking for his permission. Perhaps at last she was really beginning to feel like his wife rather than a housekeeper.

Chapter 24

It was funny how things worked out, Robbie thought. It was Christmas Eve and this time last year he'd stolen cash and booze from a pub. Now he was about to commit a riskier crime and his nerves were jangling. The last time he'd watched the unit, he had seen the middle-aged woman and the young man returning from the bank. When they'd pulled up outside, the woman had taken a cloth bag from the car that looked like it was bulging with money.

Now Robbie was back again, and this time he was set on getting that cloth bag out of the woman's hands. He'd parked a little distance away, watching, and as expected they climbed into the car and drove off. He waited until they were out of sight then quickly drove his car closer. He then did a three-point turn so that he was facing the right way for a quick getaway, parking the Ford where their car had been. On their return he would spring into action, but for now he would have to wait. His nerves were still jumping and he held his hands out in front of him. They were shaking. Pull yourself together, he told himself as he slouched low in the seat. They wouldn't be long, forty minutes at the most, but the time passed slowly for Robbie.

Eventually he heard the murmur of an engine, and sat up to see the target car coming into focus. As it drew closer Robbie's heart thumped hard in his chest, and he took several deep breaths as he slouched low in his seat again. It crossed his mind that it might not be as easy as he'd first thought, but steely determination and the greed for easy money spurred him on.

As the car pulled up behind Robbie he started the Ford's engine whilst looking in his rear-view mirror to see the young man get out and walk round to open the door for the middle-aged woman.

This was it: time to react. Robbie leaped from his car, leaving the door open, and ran towards the other car just as the woman climbed out with the cash bag. The young man saw Robbie, and for the briefest moment the two locked eyes, but before the chap could react Robbie had his hands on the cloth bag and was tugging it hard to pull it from the woman's grasp. She struggled and tried to keep hold of it but she didn't have the strength, and her shrill screams didn't deter Robbie. It took very little to yank it from her hands, but as he turned to run the young man was blocking his path.

'Oi, you, give it back,' he shouted as he made a grab for the bag.

Robbie had expected a confrontation and was ready for it. He pushed hard on the man's chest, shoving him so violently that it sent him flying onto the pavement, leaving Robbie unrestricted to flee to his car and speed off.

Robbie raced through the streets, heading out of Southsea, relieved not to hear the sound of police sirens.

His heart was still pounding, but he glanced at the bag of money beside him on the passenger seat and laughed heartily.

It had been so easy, much easier than he had estimated. He had a small flick knife in his jacket pocket, and with one hand on the steering wheel he fished around for it with the other, then threw it out of the window. He hadn't wanted to use the knife and risk being done for armed robbery, but had brought it with him just in case. If the young man had been able to restrain him, he'd have been forced to use the knife against him, yet he had resolved to make sure he only stabbed the man in his arm or leg – just enough to escape.

Pleased he hadn't needed to use that sort of violence, Robbie began to relax and to believe he had literally got away with daylight robbery. He kept driving, heading for London, aiming to put as much distance between him and the local police as possible. He wanted to pull over to count his haul of stolen money, but didn't dare risk stopping yet.

However, sure that with Christmas bonuses there was a lot of cash in the bag, Robbie knew he'd be able to pay off his debts. He thought about Adrian. His brother's face would be a picture when he handed him the money he owed him.

Robbie had hated the way Adrian looked at him every time he'd asked to borrow a few quid, and now the risk he'd just taken was worth it if only to knock that patronising expression off his brother's face.

Dorothy washed up, dried her hands and smoothed down the front of her skirt. It would be Christmas Day tomorrow and she was dreading it. She would have to prepare Christmas dinner knowing it was the last meal her mother had cooked.

With a determined effort, she took a deep breath and walked through to the living room, where Nelly was lying on the single bed that Adrian had bought for her. He was such a generous, considerate man and though she didn't regret marrying him, there was still something missing. She hadn't fallen in love with him, and wondered if she ever would.

'I'm looking forward to tomorrow,' Nelly said as she eyed the pile of gifts under the Christmas tree.'

'Yes, me too,' Dorothy lied.

'You can't fool me,' Nelly said kindly. 'I know this must be hard for you, and Adrian does too, but try to remember that your mum wouldn't want to see you unhappy.'

'Yes, I know,' Dorothy said softly.

'I bet Adrian will give you some lovely presents.'

The only thing Dorothy really wanted was a baby, but she still wasn't pregnant and it added to her unhappiness.

'Thanks for getting my present for Malcolm. They're lovely gloves and I hope he likes them.'

Dorothy hoped so too, but, wanting to turn the talk away from Christmas, she said, 'Time's getting on so I'd best pop along to the butcher's to pick up the turkey I put on order, and then go to the greengrocer's for the vegetables.'

'All right, love, but don't get too many sprouts. I can't stand the bloomin' things.'

Dorothy put her coat on and after tying a scarf around her head she hurried out. Her energy dissipated when she reached the high street; the shop windows were dressed with garish Christmas decorations and her heart sank. It was impossible to ignore the time of year. She whispered to herself, 'Oh, Mum. I miss you so much.'

Chapter 25

Whilst Dottie was out, Nelly's ears pricked, sure she had heard Bill call out. She grabbed her crutches, cursing how uncomfortable they were to use as she manoeuvred her way along the hall. Dorothy's father rarely made any sort of noise, and would just sit all day gazing out onto the back garden. Dottie often put the radio on in his room, hoping a programme would stimulate him, but so far there had been no reaction. Maybe that was what she'd heard, Nelly thought. Perhaps it was the radio. However, as she limped into Bill's room she was astonished when he turned to look at her and a smile spread across his face.

'You all right there, Mr Butler?' she asked.

Bill didn't answer and turned his head again to the window.

'Can I get you anything? A cup of tea? I'm sure I can manage to make one.'

'Bad leg,' he answered slowly.

Nelly thought, if she hadn't been on crutches, she would have fallen over with shock. The man had spoken his first real words in years! What a dreadful shame Dorothy wasn't home to witness it.

'Yes, Mr Butler. I got hit by a car and my leg is broken. What about you? How are you feeling?' She held her breath, hoping for a response.

Nelly waited but was disappointed when he remained silent. She hadn't imagined it though; he had spoken and acknowledged her plastered leg. She was reeling with excitement at hearing Bill's voice, and she couldn't wait to tell Dorothy, who would no doubt be over the moon.

As Nelly headed back to the living room, there was a knock on the front door. She tutted, but at least she was already on her feet. She struggled along the hallway, but when she opened the door it was her second shock of the day – though this one filled her with doom.

'Well, well . . . Nelly the News. Don't tell me you're shacked up with my brother? Bloody hell, he must be either blind or desperate.'

Nelly couldn't believe her eyes and blinked hard, but it was true – Robbie bloody Ferguson was back and that could only mean trouble. She refused to be baited and ignored his nasty remarks, asking instead, 'What do you want?'

'That's really none of your business, Nelly. More importantly, what are you doing in my house?' Robbie answered, his tone unfriendly.

Nelly panicked. Dorothy would be home any minute, and, worried that her friend still harboured feelings for Robbie, she gabbled, 'You can't be here. The police are probably still after you for that jeweller's robbery, and this isn't your house, it's your brother's, so clear off!'

'The police have got nothing on me, and who the hell do you think you are, telling me to clear off? I've got more right to be here than you have, unless of course you really *are* shacking up with Adrian.'

'Don't be bloody ridiculous!' Nelly snapped, her newly learned diction forgotten. 'How could I be? Just piss off, Robbie, you ain't welcome. Your brother and Dottie are happy and they don't need you turning up to ruin things for them.'

'What are you talking about? I intend to spend Christmas with my brother so move over and let me in,' said Robbie as he tried to push past Nelly.

'No, Robbie. They're married and Dottie lives here now,' Nelly said through gritted teeth while she tried to hold one of her crutches across the threshold.

'Married? My brother and Dottie? No way! You're kidding, right?' Robbie stepped backwards. It was obvious he didn't believe her.

'No, I ain't kidding. They got married about six months ago and they're very happy together.'

Robbie took another step backwards and for a moment he just stood there, his eyes narrowed in thought, but then he sneered and said, 'Funny, I never took Dottie for a gold-digger, but the only reason she'd marry my brother is for his money. Huh, and with you living here too the pair of you have really landed on your feet. Well, you can tell Adrian from me that I'll be seeing him . . . and soon.'

Robbie spun on his heel to march towards an old grey car and when he drove off Nelly closed the door, her stomach in a knot. From what he'd said, she knew it wouldn't be the last they would see of Robbie Ferguson.

Dorothy was pleased to arrive home. Her shopping bags were heavy and made her arms ache. She trudged down the hallway to the kitchen, but just as she put the bags down, Nelly called her.

'What's wrong? Are you in pain?' Dorothy asked as she walked into the living room to see Nelly looking agitated.

'No, I'm fine, but I've got something to tell you.'

Dorothy could tell from her friend's expression that it was something serious. 'What is it?'

'Sit down, Dottie.'

'Nelly, just spit it out.'

'Do you want the good news first or the bad?'

'The bad . . . give me the bad.'

'I hate to tell you this, but . . . but Robbie is back.'

Dorothy's mind reeled as she stood, transfixed. Robbie back. No! Oh, no!

'Are you all right?' Nelly asked urgently. 'You've gone as white as a sheet.'

With a supreme effort she found her voice, and managed to sound nonchalant. 'I'm fine, Nelly. I knew this would happen one day, but I'm well over Robbie. I'm married to Adrian now and I'm happy.'

'You don't look fine.'

Dorothy gripped the back of Adrian's armchair to steady herself. 'How do you know he's back?'

'He knocked on the door, as bold as brass, but I sent him off with a flea in his ear. He didn't look too happy when I told him about you and Adrian.'

'He was upset to hear we're married?' Dorothy asked, unable to help feeling a surge of pleasure, but then common sense took over. 'Actually, it doesn't matter if he was. Forget I asked. What's the good news?'

'You won't believe this, but it's your dad. He noticed

that I've got a bad leg and spoke to me. I could hardly believe it myself, but honestly, he smiled and said a couple of words.'

This was the news Dorothy had waited years to hear, but the return of Robbie had marred it. She tried to smile and pretended to be delighted, even though her mind was still reeling. 'I'll pop in to see him. This could be the first step in the right direction, but what a shame my mum missed it.'

'I know, but one step at a time. Don't expect too much.'

Dottie found her father sitting in his usual chair, facing the window. She placed a hand on his shoulder and spoke softly. 'Hello, Dad. Nelly tells me you spoke to her today.'

There was no response, but hoping to pique his interest she continued, 'There aren't any flowers in the garden at this time of year, but if you'd like to plant some spring bulbs, I'm sure Adrian wouldn't mind.'

Bill began to rock back and forth in his seat, but didn't answer, his eyes fixed ahead.

'I don't know when bulbs need to be planted, and I can't tell a daisy from a daffodil. I expect you miss your job in the park. I can just remember the flowers you used to bring home for Mum. She loved them.'

Bill shook his head from side to side and began to flay his arms wildly. 'Alice . . . Alice . . .' he grumbled.

Dorothy tried to hold his arms down while pacifying him. 'It's all right, Dad,' she said, repeatedly, but instead of calming he became more agitated. He managed to break loose from her grip and swung an arm back, his elbow thumping into her face, just below her eye.

Momentarily dazed, Dorothy stepped back, and when she lifted her fingers to her cheek she found blood on them. 'Nelly, help, it's Dad,' she called, watching as he thrashed around in his seat, still shouting for his wife.

It felt like ages before Nelly appeared, struggling on her crutches. 'Your face, Dottie! You're bleeding!'

'Don't worry about me. Look at my dad – he's going berserk and I don't know what to do. Oh, no, he's foaming at the mouth now!'

'You can move quicker than me. Call the doctor,' Nelly ordered, 'and Adrian.'

Dorothy ran to the telephone in the hall. She rang the surgery asking for an urgent visit and then replaced the receiver to ring Adrian. That done, for just a moment she paused, her thoughts again on Robbie's return. She felt sick with guilt. How could she think of Robbie at a time like this? She felt awful, but the image of his face remained in her mind even as she tried hard to dismiss it.

Robbie was back and Dorothy feared the impact it was going to have on her life.

Chapter 26

Robbie had driven to the other side of Battersea and pulled over outside a pub that seemed to attract most of the local villains. He owed Stan and Brian nearly a hundred quid between them, and though the two men ran separate gangs, they worked together when it came to debt collection.

He had received threats from them before he'd done a runner, and feared their heavies seeking him out, so on his return he decided that for his own safety he'd better repay the debts first.

Robbie killed the engine but sat holding the steering wheel, his mind still on what Nelly had said. Dorothy was probably the best-looking girl in Battersea so, apart from his bank balance, what on earth did she see in Adrian? He scowled and then shrugged. He wasn't bothered. His brother was welcome to his cast-offs, though it would be amusing to see Dorothy's face when she discovered that Adrian wasn't the only one with money now.

He reached under the passenger seat for the stolen cash bag, which he'd found contained just over four hundred pounds. There was more than enough to pay off his debts and leave plenty to enjoy the high life. He counted out one hundred and fifty pounds for Stan and Brian, calculating that the extra fifty-pound payment on top of his original loan would be enough to pacify them.

Robbie got out from his car and nervously sauntered towards the pub. This wasn't a meeting he was relishing and his normally confident demeanour was in tatters. He pushed open the door and paused a second while his eyes adjusted to the gloom, caused by the shuttered windows that were designed to stop prying eyes from seeing what went on inside. The bar fell silent as the punters stopped talking to check who had come in. Strangers weren't welcome.

'You've got some nerve, showing your face in here.'

Robbie didn't see who had spoken, but recognised Brian's hoarse, raspy growl. All eyes were on Robbie as he spotted Brian and walked over to his table. 'I've come with the money I owe you,' he said, in the hope it would pacify the man enough to save him from a beating.

'It's about time.'

Robbie saw that Stan was there too, and on a nearby table were three of their heavies. 'I've got your money too.'

'Pull up a chair,' Brian said with a snarl as ash fell from the cigarette hanging from the side of his mouth. 'We need to have a little chat.'

Robbie uneasily did as he was told, and noticed that Stan was looking at him as if he was a bad smell under his nose. It was Brian, though, who spoke. 'You've taken the piss out of us, Rob, and we're none too pleased.'

Stan swigged from a pint glass and Robbie wished he had a drink too. His throat felt dry and he coughed before answering. 'I'm sorry. I got into a bit of trouble and had to leave a bit sharpish. I'm back now and I've got all the money I owe you, plus a bit more.'

'Let's see it then,' Stan growled.

Rob pulled the wad of notes from his denim jacket pocket and placed it on the table. 'That's one hundred and fifty quid. All I owe you plus interest,' he said, watching tensely as Stan and Brian exchanged looks.

'I don't think so, Robbie. There's nearly fifteen months of accrued interest, so your debt has doubled, and it's Christmas Eve so we would've expected a good drink too, considering you ain't had a slap,' Brian said.

Both men were a good twenty years older than Robbie but their age didn't slow them down in a fight. Not that either of them did much fighting these days. It was left to their heavies to do their dirty work. Robbie knew he didn't stand a chance against them, and said, 'All right, I'll pay you double.'

Stan stood up from his chair and placed his hands on the table as he leaned forward and said through gritted teeth, 'Huh, we've listened to your fucking bullshit before and you ain't gonna get away with it again. We want our money now. If we don't get it, tomorrow you'll owe us double again, and then treble, along with our boys re-arranging your face.'

'I'll get it for you,' Robbie said as he hastily scraped his chair back. 'Just give me a minute.'

'Not so fast,' Brian said and gave the nod to two of his heavies, who surged up to grab Robbie's arms. 'Where do you think you're going?'

'I was just going to get your money from my car.'

'Big John will go with you,' Brian growled.

Robbie instantly regretted his words, but nodded, his mind in overdrive as he walked out of the pub with John on his heels. He desperately tried to think of a way to get the money from the cash bag without the man seeing it, knowing that if Stan and Brian found out how much cash he had sitting in his car, he could kiss it all goodbye.

When they reached the vehicle, John was standing so close behind that Robbie could almost feel him breathing down his neck. He opened the car door and leaned inside to fish under the seat, hoping to pull out enough money whilst blocking John's view of the cash bag. With a wad of notes in his fingers he quickly counted them and straightened up, saying, 'Got it.'

The man just snorted and stood back, indicating that Robbie lead the way back into the pub.

'That should cover it,' he said, placing the money on the table, 'but it's cleaned me out.'

Big John leaned over to whisper something to Brian, but Robbie couldn't hear what was said. He felt sure the man hadn't seen the cash bag, so wasn't worried about that as Brian counted the money before looking up at him to say, 'Yeah, that covers it, Robbie. We're straight now and no hard feelings. Why don't you sit down to join us for a drink and a few rounds of poker?'

Robbie watched as Brian shuffled a deck of cards. 'I'd love to, but I haven't got any money left,' Robbie lied.

'We'll stake you another loan, and it'll give you a chance to win some of this back.'

'No, but thanks for the offer. Maybe another time,' Robbie said, anxious to get away from the men and the charged atmosphere.

'I never thought I'd see the day that Robbie Ferguson

turned down a card game,' said Brian with a sickening chuckle. 'What's the world coming to, eh?'

Robbie faked a smile and said goodbye, glad to leave the pub. He hurried to his car, and though he hadn't heard or seen them coming, he found himself boxed in by the three heavies.

'I'll have them,' one of the men said as he snatched Robbie's car keys and moved to open the door.

'You'll find it under the passenger seat,' Big John told him.

Robbie felt a surge of anger and his fists clenched, but he knew he didn't stand a chance against even one of these huge men, let alone three.

The man emerged from the car with the cash bag in hand and as he looked inside, a huge, broken-toothed grin spread across his face.

Robbie didn't feel like smiling, but then all thoughts turned to self-preservation when he saw Big John's fist coming towards him. He didn't have time to dodge the punch and as the huge knuckles connected with his chin, pain shot upwards through his head. The blow knocked him off his feet and he soared backwards and landed with a thud on the pavement.

The man who'd found the cash bag threw the car keys at him. 'We won't be wanting that pile of shit,' he said, nodding towards the car.

'Don't show your face here again,' Big John growled, ''cos if you do, we've been told to finish you off.'

Robbie was dazed. His ears were ringing, but he'd heard what the men said. When they disappeared inside the pub, he somehow managed to scramble to his feet and made it to the car. He couldn't believe it; all the money he'd stolen had in turn been stolen from him and he was once again left with nothing.

He was furious with himself for letting this happen. How could he have been so stupid? And what the hell was he going to do now?

Robbie's head thumped as he started the car, but his thoughts turned to someone he knew would take him in. He might be broke, but he still had his charms and she always fell for them.

Chapter 27

In his frantic state, Bill had thrown himself around so much that he had fallen out of his chair. He'd been thrashing on the floor when the doctor arrived. It had upset Dorothy to see blood on her father's chin from where he'd bitten his tongue, and she was grateful when the doctor gave him an injection to calm him.

'He needs to be in a hospital, Mrs Ferguson,' the doctor said. 'I'm sure you do a splendid job of caring for him but he requires specialist attention.'

As Adrian dashed into the room, Dorothy cried, 'Oh, Adrian, I'm so glad you're here. Dad's had some sort of funny turn and the doctor said he should be in hospital.'

'I think he's right, love.'

'But my mum would turn in her grave.'

'If she saw this happen, she'd be the first one to call for an ambulance.'

No, she wouldn't, thought Dorothy, and though at one time she'd wanted her dad to have specialised care, she now wanted to keep to her mother's wishes. She couldn't stand the thought of letting her down.

'The doctor's calling for an ambulance now,' Nelly said, 'and I'm sorry, but I have to agree with him and Adrian.

Your dad needs to go to hospital, and look at you, you're injured too.'

Dorothy wiped her cheek with the back of her hand as she pondered their words. Her cheek felt sore, but the blood had dried. 'All right, I'll accept that my dad needs help, but I want him home as soon as possible. Mum always said if she let him go to the nuthouse, he would never come out.'

'They're not taking him there,' said Adrian. 'He's going to the local hospital to have his injuries looked at and then he'll soon be home again.'

Dorothy felt reassured and shortly afterwards the ambulance arrived. Adrian went to open the door, and Dorothy helplessly watched as her sedated father was stretchered into the back of the vehicle. 'Can I go with him?' she asked the driver.

'It's all right,' said Adrian, 'we'll follow in my car.'

'But I want to be with my dad,' Dorothy pleaded.

'He'll be fine with us, and, looking at him, he won't know what's happening,' the ambulance driver said.

Dorothy reluctantly agreed and as they closed the ambulance doors she called a hasty goodbye to Nelly before rushing to the car. As Adrian drove off she was silently praying that her father would be all right. If anything happened to him she wouldn't be able to bear it. Last Christmas she'd lost her mum, and now, almost a year later, she feared losing her dad too.

Aware of her anguish, Adrian said, 'Try not to worry, love. Your dad has had some sort of fit, but physically he's fine.'

Despite his words of reassurance, Dorothy couldn't help but fret, and she still felt guilty that Robbie's return had the power to plague her mind. There was a time when she'd prayed for him to come back, but then, as time had passed, she'd begun to feel resentful. She'd been carrying his child, and her mother wouldn't have been racked with worry if he'd been there to marry her. Adrian had said that worry hadn't caused her heart attack, but she wasn't so sure. Yet, despite that, news of Robbie's return made her heart thump at the thought of seeing him again.

Dorothy turned her head to glance at Adrian. He had no idea yet and, if she didn't want him to know how Robbie's return had affected her, she would have to feign indifference. 'By the way, we had a surprise visitor today. Thankfully I was out shopping and missed him.'

'You were thankful? Why was that?' Adrian asked, but then his eyes flicked to her before they returned to the road. 'Don't tell me it was Robbie.'

'Yes, I'm afraid it was.'

Adrian was quiet for a while, but then he said, 'I hope he doesn't think he can move back into our house, because I won't allow it.'

Dorothy was relieved. She had wondered if Adrian would let his brother have his old room back and didn't think she could stand it. It would mean having to see Robbie every day, and at night she would have to sleep in a room knowing that he was just next door.

As they drew up outside the hospital, Dorothy pushed all thoughts of Robbie to one side. She had bigger things to worry about now, primarily her father, and she was praying as hard as she could that he would be all right.

Chapter 28

Robbie woke early the next morning and wondered for a moment where he was. He turned over to see Cynthia asleep next to him. She looked even older in the morning with her make-up worn off, but he appreciated her putting him up for the night, especially as he'd admitted to her that he was broke.

He felt the cold biting as he threw his legs over the side of the bed, yawned and stretched his arms. When he felt fingers running down his bare back he knew that Cynthia was awake. 'Morning, love,' he said. 'Any chance of a cup of tea?'

'Yeah, you know where the kettle is, but I'm out of sugar. Stick the gas on under the pan but top it up a bit. I could do with some hot water to wash my face.'

Robbie noticed the black smudges of mascara under her eyes, and looked away with distaste to scan the room. Other than the bed there was a small sink, a gas stove, a small, rickety table, and a couple of chairs strewn with tatty-looking clothes. It was a far cry from the luxury of Adrian's house, but even he had to admit it would've been weird living there now that Dorothy was married to his brother. This dump would have to do, at least for the time being.

'How long are you planning on staying?' Cynthia asked a little later as she sipped her cup of tea.

'I don't know yet. I need to get some cash together. If it wasn't for Brian and Stan I'd be laughing now.'

'You were daft to go there with a bag of loot.'

'Don't you think I know that?' he scowled.

'Yeah, well, I can hardly chuck you out on Christmas Day, and like I said last night, you can stay here but I can barely afford to make ends meet so you'll have to pay your way.'

Robbie's mind turned. He didn't want to go back to it, but for the time being it would at least provide him with some much-needed money.

'When I was in Portsmouth, I had a girl working for me,' he said. 'It didn't make me a lot of money, but it was more than enough to live on.'

Cynthia's eyes widened. 'Are you telling me you were pimping?'

'Yes, but it was only small-time.'

'I'm surprised. I never saw you as a pimp, but I suppose you could do the same here.'

'I could, but I'd have to find a girl and that isn't easy.'

Cynthia frowned. 'I hope you ain't got me in mind.'

'No, of course not,' Robbie protested, knowing that he needed someone a darn sight younger. Years ago Cynthia had told him she'd been on the game, and though she considered herself retired, he knew she wasn't averse to charging for her services when the situation presented itself.

Cynthia's eyes narrowed in thought and Robbie remained quiet, wondering if she'd come up with something. A lot of people in Battersea didn't have much time for her and considered her a tart, but Cynthia was actually one of the few women Robbie trusted. When they had first met he'd used her for one thing, but over the years they'd become friends, and now Robbie found she was probably the only real friend he had.

'I might be able to help you out, Rob,' she said with a cunning smile, 'but I'll want compensating, if you know what I mean?'

'I'll take any help on offer and you know me, Cynth, I'd see you all right.'

'Right then. Recently a girl has moved in upstairs and she's a pretty young thing. Her name is Yvonne, and to be honest, from the few chats we've had I don't think she's the sharpest tool in the box. The thing is, I reckon she's all alone up there and from what I can tell she's hard up for a bob or two. She might be just what you need, so how about I introduce you?'

Robbie grinned. 'It sounds like she could be just the ticket.'

'You're a good-looking bloke, Robbie, and I'm sure you'll be able to use your charms on this girl.'

'Right then, get yourself dressed, woman,' Robbie urged. 'Time is money.'

On the other side of Battersea, Nelly called, 'You're up early, did you wet the bed or something?'

Dorothy walked through to the living room. 'Sorry, did I wake you? I couldn't sleep.'

'I can see that. You look knackered, sugar.'

'I've been up half the night,' Dorothy admitted. 'I've got a pot of tea made and I expect you want a cup.' She left the room and came back carrying two cups of tea and a plate of digestive biscuits.

'I'm guessing you're worried about your dad?' Nelly asked, as she dunked a biscuit in her tea.

'Yes, I am.'

As perceptive as always, Nelly asked, 'Have you been worrying about Robbie being back on the scene too?'

Dorothy had, but didn't want to admit it. She was married to Adrian now and, though she hadn't come to love him, he had her loyalty. She couldn't let on that the thought of Robbie being back in Battersea had stirred up old emotions. 'No, he doesn't bother me. I've wasted too many tears over that man in the past and I won't let him get under my skin again.'

Nelly flashed her a look that told Dorothy her best friend didn't believe her. She said defensively, 'What are you looking at me like that for? It's true.'

'Whatever you say, sugar,' Nelly answered sarcastically. 'Bugger! I always do that. You'd think I'd be an expert at dunking biscuits by now. I've had years of regular practice, yet still I manage to leave it in too long and the biscuit goes soggy and drops off in my tea.' She held out her cup to Dorothy. 'Is there another one in the pot?'

Dorothy took the cups back through to the kitchen and poured two more. Adrian would probably be up soon so she filled the kettle to make a fresh pot.

'I know it was a shock when I told you that Robbie's back,' Nelly said when she handed her the tea, 'but think about how he treated you. It was the best thing you've ever done when you married Adrian, and I can tell you're happy with him.'

'How can you tell?'

'I can hear them bed springs up there going!' Nelly said and giggled.

Dorothy felt her cheeks flush. She and Adrian tried to make love quietly, but with him being so large, the bed springs always protested. Nelly was going to be with them for another couple of weeks, and Dorothy didn't want to abstain for that long, not when she so desperately wished to fall pregnant. 'Oh dear, that's embarrassing. I'm sorry, Nelly.'

'Don't be daft. You know how thin the walls are in my mum's house. I've heard my parents at it for years. Anyhow, you're a married woman and it's only natural.'

'What's only natural?' Adrian asked as he came into the room and caught the last bit of Nelly's sentence.

Dorothy and Nelly looked at each other and burst out laughing.

Smiling, he said, 'Happy Christmas. I'm glad to see you're in a good mood this morning.'

'Take no notice of us, we're being silly. Cuppa?' Dorothy asked and kissed her husband on the cheek.

'Yes, please, love.'

Dorothy went back to the kitchen, determined that, after she'd poured yet another cup of tea, she'd ring the hospital to see how her dad was and try to set her mind at rest a little. 'Here you are, love,' she said, handing it to him and then heading for the telephone.

It took a little time to get through to her father's ward, but at last a nurse answered, and soon afterwards she replaced the receiver, a little reassured. 'I've just spoken to the hospital and a nurse said he had a comfortable night,' she told Adrian and Nelly.

'I'll take you to see him after breakfast,' Adrian offered.

'We can't go until visiting time, which is just as well as it'll give me time to start preparing our Christmas dinner,' Dorothy told him, fighting not to let memories of last year engulf her.

'If it's too much for you, we can scrap a roast. I'll be happy with egg and chips.'

'No, Adrian, I've got a turkey and I'm going to cook it,' she said with determination. 'Don't forget we've got a guest joining us and I don't think Malcolm would appreciate egg and chips for his Christmas dinner.'

'Just make sure you don't give me any sprouts. They give me terrible wind,' Nelly said, obviously trying to lighten the atmosphere. 'I mean, imagine how embarrassing it would be if I let out a big blow-off in front of Malcolm.' Her hand went to her mouth, her eyes wide, 'Whoops, sorry, Adrian.'

Dorothy giggled, then the giggle turned to a laugh, which grew louder and had her doubling over as she gasped, 'Oh, Nelly.'

'You don't have to apologise to me, Nelly.' Adrian said. 'I won't say that was very ladylike, but you've made Dottie laugh and that sound is music to my ears.'

Dorothy managed to pull herself together, feeling guilty that she could laugh on the anniversary of her mum's death, then was reminded of something Nelly had said. Her mother wouldn't have wanted to see her unhappy. Maybe that was true, but with her father in hospital and Robbie back on the scene, she wasn't sure how long she could keep up her façade.

Chapter 29

'Hello, love, this is Robbie, a good friend of mine. Do you mind if we come in?' Cynthia asked the young woman, who looked unsure of the two visitors at her door.

Robbie eyed her up and down. Cynthia was right, the girl was pretty, but she looked very young too.

'I suppose,' she answered timidly and opened the door wider.

'I bet you're wondering what we're doing here, especially so early on Christmas Day,' Cynthia said as she sat on a sofa that had seen better days.

'Well . . . yes,' Yvonne said.

Robbie sat next to Cynthia, noting that the only window was covered in muck, making the room dim and dingy. It was the same size as Cynthia's, yet it appeared much larger as, apart from the sofa, the only other items were a small double bed and a few clothes stacked neatly in the corner. There wasn't even a stove next to the tiny sink.

'Well, love, I know it's none of my business, but how do you get by? I mean, I don't see you going out to work so how do you pay the rent?' Cynthia asked as she lit a cigarette and puffed on it, leaving bright pink lipstick on the filter.

Yvonne rummaged in a cupboard under the sink and pulled out a small china bowl which she handed to Cynthia for her ash. 'I've got a job. I pack pencils in boxes at Stanford's. You ain't seen me going out 'cos I've been laid off, but it's only for a bit, just until Mr Stanford gets a big order in, then he'll have me back. He says I'm one of his best girls and he don't want to lose me to no other factory.'

'Oh, I see. So how long have you been waiting for him to get this big order?'

'I think it's been about seven weeks now. That's why I took this room, 'cos it's cheaper than my last place.'

'Seven weeks? Are you mad or something?' Robbie asked.

Cynthia shot him a warning look as she stubbed out her cigarette, and then said, 'What he means is, Mr Stanford is having a laugh if he expects you to wait around for all that time with no wages. What does he think you're living on, fresh air?'

'I . . . I . . . don't know. I ain't got no savings left. My mum and sister moved to Clacton, and Mum said I had to stay here 'cos she says I'm a lia-lia-liability, but honest, I don't ever tell lies. She said when it's Christmas I could go to see her, and it's Christmas now, but I ain't got my train fare.' Yvonne's bottom lip pouted and her eyes filled.

Neither Robbie nor Cynthia were ones for sympathy, but they were both good manipulators and Yvonne was playing right into their hands. She's not that bright, thought Robbie, but he didn't need a girl with brains. Look where that had got him with Gladys. She'd been capable of earning her own money without him and had left him high and dry. He doubted he'd have the same problem with Yvonne. From what he could see the girl had trouble looking after herself, and that was perfect for Robbie's requirements.

'Don't upset yourself, Yvonne. I can help you,' Robbie said softly. 'You can work for me and before you know it you'll have all the money you need to get to Clacton. You'll even be able to buy something nice for your mum and I bet she'd love that.'

Yvonne's face lit up. 'Really? What sort of work? I can do packing. I'm good at that.'

'I'm sure you are, but I've something else in mind. There's no need to worry your pretty little head about it for now, just leave it all to me. One question, how old are you?'

'I'm seventeen,' Yvonne answered, 'and do you really think I'm pretty?'

'You certainly are,' Robbie told her and looked at Cynthia.

'I told you,' she mouthed.

Robbie smiled. Yes, Yvonne was perfect, and soon he'd put her to work.

Later that morning, sick of looking at Cynthia, Robbie went for a walk. Some Christmas this was turning out to be, he thought, but at least he now had the chance to make a bit of money. As he turned a corner, Robbie almost walked straight into Mrs Hart and his eyes widened.

'Hello, Mrs Hart. I'm surprised to see you in this part of Battersea.'

'Hello, young man. I'm on my way to spend the day with an elderly relative,' she told him, while adjusting the knot under her chin that secured her scarf. 'I haven't seen you for a while, Robbie. Are you back home now?'

'I'm in Battersea, but I'm not living at home.'

'Oh, I see. I suppose that's because your brother is married now, and I must say I'm surprised you missed his wedding.'

'It was unavoidable, but they seem happy together, don't you think?' Robbie asked, knowing that like most women she probably enjoyed a good gossip.

'Oh, they are, but such a shame about Dorothy's poor father.'

'Mr Butler – what about him?' Robbie asked, pretending to be concerned.

'Haven't you heard? He was taken into hospital. There was an ambulance outside yesterday. Dorothy looked beside herself with worry.'

'No, I hadn't heard.'

'I do hope he's going to be all right,' Mrs Hart said.

'Yes, me too, but I'm in a bit of a hurry so I must go,' Robbie lied. 'Bye, Mrs Hart, and merry Christmas.'

'Goodbye, and merry Christmas to you too.'

Robbie threw her a smile and walked quickly away, his pace increasing to stay warm. If Dottie's dad was kept in hospital, once Christmas was over and Adrian was back at work, he'd have the opportunity to make sure he bumped into her when she went to visit her dad. He'd have to make doubly sure that Adrian wouldn't be around, and he knew just how to do that.

Chapter 30

Adrian had seen how close to tears Dottie had been on Christmas morning, but she'd managed to cook them a lovely meal. Then, after going to see her father in the afternoon and finding he was no worse, her spirits had lifted.

They had waited until teatime to open their presents, and Dorothy had loved the Brownie camera, along with the gold locket and chain he'd chosen for her. Having Nelly and Malcolm there had helped, but now the festivities were over and he was back in the office.

It was the twenty-seventh of December, and in a few days they would be seeing in the New Year. He'd hoped it would be a good one, but now with Bill in hospital and his brother back on the scene, worry clouded his mind.

Adrian looked at the watch that Dottie had given him, noting it was nearing lunchtime, then the office door opened, and, seeing who had come in, he looked up, unsmiling.

'I guessed you'd show your face here eventually.'

'That's a fine welcome for your little brother,' Robbie said. 'I thought you'd be pleased to see me.'

Adrian snorted. 'You thought wrong, Rob. After you left, gossip spread about the robbery, and your debts too. No wonder you disappeared, and no doubt you've come back from wherever you've been because you've messed up and run out of money. If you think I'm going to lend you another penny, or that you can move back into my house, you can forget it.'

'There's no proof I did a robbery, but you always think the worst of me, don't you? As it happens, I don't want your money, or a roof over my head. I'm sorted and I wouldn't want to intrude on your perfect little life, with your perfect little wife. I just came to say hello, but if that's how you feel, I'm off.'

As Robbie turned to walk out, Adrian hung his head. From the moment he'd heard that his brother was back, he had feared how Dottie would react. He didn't want to lose her, but as she'd barely shown any interest in Robbie's return, maybe he was overreacting. After all, when all was said and done, Robbie was his brother. He took a deep breath.

'Rob, stop. I'm sorry.'

Robbie swung around again. 'What are you sorry for? Nicking my girl?'

Adrian instantly regretted his apology. 'Your girl? The woman you left high and dry, you mean! You didn't deserve her, Rob. She was always too good for you.'

'Too good for me! How do you work that one out? She's from the slums, as common as muck, and without a penny to her name. That's why she married you, for your money, and surely you know that.'

Adrian seethed, but he wasn't going to let Robbie see how his words had affected him. Instead he asked, 'What's the matter, Rob, are you jealous?'

'No, I'm not. If you can't see that she's using you, you're welcome to her,' Robbie answered and sauntered out of the office, leaving Adrian with a bad taste in his mouth.

Adrian took a deep breath to calm down. He'd had his apology thrown in his face, and the things Robbie had gone on to say about Dorothy had overstepped the mark. He was glad to see the back of his brother, but with no idea where Robbie was living, and with a lingering fear of losing Dorothy still on his mind, he hoped he'd stay out of their lives. And for good.

The bus pulled up outside the hospital and Dorothy got off with a heavy heart. She hoped to find more of an improvement in her dad's health but the doctors had warned her that progress would be slow.

It was a busy building with a throng of visitors coming and going, but as she approached the main entrance Dorothy stopped in her tracks. Despite the cold wind a familiar figure was leaning casually against the wall and her pulse quickened. Her legs felt weak and shaky, but she forced herself to put one foot in front of the other. She'd been dreading this, yet at the same time part of her had been hoping for it. Robbie looked self-assured and as handsome as ever. Her heart hammered in her chest.

'Robbie, what are you doing here?' she asked, trying to sound irritated, though inside she was melting.

'Hello to you too, Dottie,' he answered, and threw his roll-up to one side as he stood up straight.

'You haven't answered my question.'

'I heard about your dad and wanted to make sure you're OK. How's he doing?

Dorothy struggled to keep her composure, but when she looked into Robbie's eyes, she was captured by his gaze. Like a moth to a flame she was drawn to him, but she didn't want to get burned again and she hoped Robbie couldn't read how she was feeling.

'How did you hear about my dad?'

'I bumped into Mrs Hart. So how is he?'

'You've no right to be here, Robbie, and since when have you given a toss about me or my dad?' Dorothy snapped, and not waiting for his response she stomped into the hospital.

Robbie caught up with her and marched alongside. 'Don't be like that, Dottie,' he said, and pulled a sad face. 'I know I went off without a word, but I had to leave. I didn't have a choice, but not a day passed that I didn't think about you.'

Dorothy didn't want to hear it. It was difficult enough to wrestle with her confused emotions without Robbie trying to pull her heartstrings. 'In that case, you could have at least written to me,' she spat.

'Dottie, please. I'm sorry, give me a chance to explain . . .'

Dorothy spun around, and with her arms stiff at her side she glared at Robbie. 'Tell it to someone who cares. Just leave me alone.' The love she had felt for him was bubbling close to the surface but still mixed with anger. A part of her wanted to melt into his arms and feel his tantalising touch, yet another part wanted to slap his face and run to the security her husband offered. 'I'm not interested in anything you have to say. I'm married to Adrian now, so don't waste your breath.'

'I know that, Dottie, but can't we still be friends?' Robbie asked and then with a cheeky grin he added,

'Come on, after all, you're my sister-in-law so that makes us family, and I'm sure Adrian wouldn't want us to be at each other's throats.'

The comment cut through Dorothy. He had run off, leaving her pregnant, but she didn't want him to find out. Now that he was her brother-in-law it was too weird. It made her feel sick inside, but she said, 'All right, for Adrian's sake I'll make an effort, but please, keep your distance.'

'I'll try, Dottie, but it won't be easy. I mean, look at you. You're a beautiful woman.'

'Robbie, stop!' Dorothy warned.

'All right, I get it, you don't want to be disloyal to Adrian, but it was just a compliment, that's all. I wouldn't want to upset Adrian either, but there's no reason why we can't go for a coffee and a chat about things, clear the air.'

'I can't. I've got to see my dad.'

'I'll wait. You go and check on him then we can go for that coffee. It'll make Adrian happy to see that we've put the past behind us and become friends.'

Dorothy had always found it difficult to resist Robbie's pleading eyes and though all her instincts were screaming at her to run for the hills, there was something about him she couldn't resist. 'OK, I'll see you in a bit,' she found herself saying, but instantly felt a pang of guilt.

I'm meeting him for the right reasons, she told herself, and as she made her way to her dad's ward, Dottie repeated the words over and over in her head, hoping to make herself believe them.

Robbie was pleased with himself. He'd seen that a romantic route wasn't going to wash with Dorothy so he'd played the family card and, bingo, the woman had caved. Not everything he'd said had been a lie, though: she did look bloody gorgeous, but he didn't plan on bedding her. He reckoned she'd be a softer touch than his brother and, since she had access to Adrian's cash, he hoped to wangle some of it from her.

He'd left Cynthia busy with Yvonne, showing the girl how to apply make-up and stuff, so Robbie hung around just inside the entrance to the hospital until he saw Dorothy walking towards him. Time for the second part of his charm offensive, he wickedly thought to himself. 'You look a lot happier. I take it your dad's on the mend?' he said, smiling warmly.

'Yes, he's a lot better. Well, he's calmer at least. I'm pretty sure he knew who I was too.'

Robbie felt Dorothy flinch as he took her arm, but he ignored it and said, 'That's good. Come on, there's a nice coffee shop round the corner and we can talk in there.'

'All right, but I can't stay for long.'

Robbie led Dorothy to an empty table and sat opposite her. When a waitress appeared he ordered their drinks, and then focused on Dottie again, asking, 'How did you end up marrying my brother?'

'It's a long story. A lot happened when you left, and I had my reasons, but it's water under the bridge now and I don't want to dwell on the past.'

Robbie felt that Dottie was fobbing him off. The only reason she'd married Adrian was for his money, but she didn't want to admit it. Fair enough, he thought as the waitress placed two cups of frothy coffee on the table. He might have done the same if a rich woman had been in his sights. 'You sound different, Dottie, less common.'

'Common? Is that what you thought of me?'

'No, of course not. I found the way you spoke endearing,' Robbie lied. 'You dress well too. That outfit you're wearing looks lovely, and I bet that fur cost a pretty penny.'

'Adrian's business is doing well and he likes me to look nice.'

'I'm sure he does and who could blame him? I popped in to see him this morning, but I think he got the wrong idea about some of the things I said.'

'Why? What did you say?'

'He thinks I'm jealous that you're married to him, and I suppose I am a bit,' he said. 'But I'm happy for you too.'

Just before Dorothy took a sip of coffee their eyes locked and Robbie hid a feeling of triumph. He was sure he'd seen something in hers, and if he was right she still loved him. That would make her easy to manipulate. 'When Nelly told me you'd married Adrian, it came as a bit of a shock,' he continued, 'and to be honest, it's left me a bit up the creek without a paddle.'

'What do you mean?'

'When I came back I planned on moving into my old room until I found a job and sorted myself out. Of course, I can't do that now so I'm in a bit of a predicament. I've got to find somewhere else to live, but until I find work I can't afford to pay any rent.'

'Oh dear, what are you going to do?'

'I don't know, Dottie. Jobs seem scarce and nobody seems to be taking on mechanics. I had enough money to stay in a cheap hotel for a few nights, but I'm broke now so I'll just have to sleep in my car until something turns up.'

'No, Robbie, you can't do that. You . . . . you'll have to move in with us,' Dorothy said, though she didn't look pleased at the idea.

'Adrian has already vetoed that, so it's the car until I can find some money to rent a flat.'

Dorothy was quiet for a moment, her head lowered as though in thought, but then she took a purse from her handbag and said, 'I know you're a proud man, Robbie, but please, let me help.'

'No, Dottie, before you offer, I can't take money from you.'

'Don't be silly,' she argued, holding out two pound notes. 'Adrian is more than generous with housekeeping money, but I've been shopping so this isn't much. I've got more at home. Anyhow, if it wasn't for me, you wouldn't be in this predicament. It's all my fault.'

'Dottie, I couldn't . . .' Robbie falsely protested.

'Don't be silly. As you said, we're family now, and it's only until you're back on your feet.'

Robbie took the money and stuffed the notes into the pocket of his denim jacket. Two quid wasn't much, but it was a start and better than nothing.

'Thanks, Dottie. I don't know what to say. It's a bit awkward though. Because of the way things were left with me and Adrian earlier, I don't think he'd be happy about you giving me money.'

'I wouldn't want to upset him so he doesn't need to know. I've got a bit of money saved, enough for you to rent somewhere, but we'll have to meet here again tomorrow. With Nelly staying with us, it's best you don't come to the house.'

'With Nelly the News around, that's understandable,'

Robbie said, and smiled. 'I really do appreciate this, Dottie, and I'll pay you back as soon as I can.'

'There's no need. I'll see you here tomorrow at midday, if that's OK?'

'That's fine,' Robbie replied.

They said their goodbyes and Robbie headed for the nearest pub for a celebratory drink. He'd thought Dottie would be easy to manipulate, but that had proved even easier that he'd expected. She'd near enough thrown her cash at him, begging him to take it, and was happy to give him more.

Robbie smiled to himself; perhaps Dorothy marrying his brother was the best thing that could have happened. He had two potential sources of income lined up now and his future was suddenly looking much brighter.

Chapter 31

Early the following morning, Yvonne yelped and grabbed some cotton wool. It was the third time in a row she'd prodded her eye with the mascara brush. When Cynthia had done it she made it look easy and Robbie had been pleased with the results when he'd seen her, but now Yvonne was struggling to apply the make-up herself.

She thought it was ever so nice of Cynthia to leave her a couple of bits. She liked the shiny blue eyeshadow and the red lipstick, though she wasn't so keen on the block of mascara.

At last she managed to apply the final touch but, as she gazed at her reflection the mirror, Yvonne could have sworn she was looking at someone else. She hardly recognised her painted face, and wasn't sure if she liked it or not. Still, as long as Robbie approved, that was all that mattered. The mascara stung her eyes and her lips felt greasy, but she would have to put up with it now while she was waiting for Robbie to arrive. He was ever so good-looking, just the sort of bloke her sister would've fancied. She couldn't wait to start working for him and get enough money together to go to see her mum and sister. They would never believe she was working for such a dishy fella, or that she was all glammed up now.

Robbie had told her she was pretty. In fact, he'd said she was the prettiest girl in Battersea. No one had ever said that to her before. She'd only known him a little while, but Robbie made her feel special. It was an unusual feeling for Yvonne, but one she was relishing. She wondered what sort of work she'd be doing for Robbie, especially as Cynthia had been adamant about wearing the make-up. She looked at her reflection again and it suddenly came to her: modelling. Robbie must be a photographer. Of course, it all made sense now – he thought she was pretty and wanted to take photos of her. As much as Yvonne had enjoyed working at Stanford's, she was excited and looking forward to putting her pencil-packing days behind her and starting her new job.

Who knows, she thought, she could soon have her picture on the front cover of *Vogue*!

Robbie had said he would call in that morning, so at nine o'clock when there was a gentle tap on the door she hurried to answer it.

'Hiya,' she said happily as she let him in. 'What do you think of my make-up?'

'Yeah, lovely,' Robbie replied, though he didn't seem very interested, his eyes scanning the room instead of looking at her properly. 'I suppose this place will do for us for now,' he said, 'but we'll move out of here as soon as I can raise the money for something better, maybe a nice flat down by the river.'

'What do you mean, Robbie?'

He turned to look at her and his eyes sparkled as he said, 'If we're going to be working together, it makes sense that we live together. You must admit this place is a bit of a dive, and I can't have my girl living in a dump. You just leave it to me and I'll soon be able to find us a nice little pad.'

Yvonne's head began to swim. Robbie had said she was his girl and they would live together, but surely that wouldn't be right? She knew a bit about what went on between a man and a woman, but not very much, only that when you married a man you would have a baby. She liked the idea of that, but Robbie hadn't said they were getting married. 'Li-live together?'

'Yes, it makes sense,' Robbie said.

'Bu-but . . .'

'Don't worry your pretty little head about it. Just leave it all to me. I'm meeting someone later who can provide me with the money I need to buy a few nice new bits of furniture for this place. You'd like that, wouldn't you?'

Yvonne's head was in a whirl. This was all happening so fast but she didn't want to let Robbie down. She was out of her depth but believed she could trust him; after all, he was very sophisticated and, apart from her old boss Mr Stanford, Robbie was the only man who had ever shown any interest in her. 'Yes, I'd like that, Robbie.'

'That's my girl,' he said, grinning. 'Now I've got to go, but I'll get my stuff together and see you again later.'

Yvonne was still struggling to take in all that Robbie had said as he left. He was going to buy some furniture, and if he was going to move in with her, that must mean another bed.

Nelly awoke late to the sound of Dorothy humming in the kitchen. She wondered what had put her friend in such a good mood, especially considering her dad was still in hospital. She struggled to her feet, sorted out her crutches and headed for the toilet.

'Good morning, Nelly,' Dorothy called as she passed the kitchen, 'or should I say afternoon?'

'You cheeky moo. It's only nine-thirty.'

'Do you need any help?'

'No thanks, I can manage, but my mouth feels like the bottom of a budgie's cage so—'

'You could do with a cuppa,' Dottie finished for her.

'Yeah, thanks, sugar,' Nelly said, smiling as she continued on her way, but she was shivering with the cold by the time she made it back to her bed.

'Here you go,' Dottie said, soon coming in with a tray.

'Thanks, love. I can't help noticing that you're full of the joys of spring this morning. Is there something you want to share with me?' Nelly asked suspiciously.

'No,' Dorothy answered, 'should there be?'

'I don't know, you tell me. I haven't seen you this jolly for a while and I'm wondering what's happened to make you so happy. You aren't pregnant, are you?' Nelly asked, but when she saw the smile vanish from Dorothy's face, she instantly regretted her question.

'I wish I was,' Dorothy replied, 'but no, still nothing.'

'So what is it then?' Nelly asked, though if Dorothy wasn't pregnant she guessed there was only one other thing that would have this effect on her friend. 'Don't tell me you've seen Robbie?'

'No, of course I haven't,' Dorothy said, avoiding eye contact as she turned to walk back to the kitchen.

Nelly eyed her retreating back worriedly. It was obvious to her that Dorothy wasn't telling the truth, and with

Robbie back on the scene, Nelly feared it was all going to end in tears.

Later that day, Dorothy began fidgeting as the bus drew nearer to the hospital. She drummed her fingers on her handbag and briskly tapped her foot as her leg jigged up and down. She felt terrible about lying to Nelly and keeping secrets from Adrian, but if she was honest and told them about Robbie it would create a barrage of questions. They weren't questions she felt able to face at the moment, so she'd decided that until she could look them both in the eye, with no trace of guilt, she would keep quiet. As her mother used to say, 'Least said, soonest mended.'

The bus stopped and Dorothy got off, but it crossed her mind to jump back on again. Her deceit could cost her dearly as she risked losing her husband and her best friend, but her reservations were forgotten the instant she saw Robbie walking towards her.

'Hello, Dottie. You're looking as gorgeous as ever.'

'Thanks, but I don't think you should say things like that to me,' Dorothy replied, though secretly cherishing his compliment.

'Yes, you're right, sorry. I take it you haven't told Adrian about our arrangement then?'

'No, of course not. Like you said, he wouldn't approve. For the moment, what he doesn't know can't hurt him.'

'Thanks, Dottie. I really appreciate you doing this for me.'

They walked to the café and sat at the same table they had the day before. Dorothy took a small bundle of notes from her bag and handed them to Robbie. As he reached for the money, his fingers brushed her hand, causing Dorothy to catch her breath.

'There's seventeen pounds,' she managed to say as she quickly pulled her hand back.

'That's amazing, Dottie. I wasn't expecting that much.'

'It's just sat in a tin at home doing nothing. I'm sure you'll find it helpful.'

'I will. I'll be able to pay enough rent up front to keep me going until I find work. Thanks again,' said Robbie, and tucked the money away in his pocket.

'So did you sleep in your car?' Dottie asked.

'I thought I'd have to, but thankfully an old friend, Cynthia, came to my rescue. She lives in Grant Street and her place is a bit of a fleapit, but she told me the room above hers on the top floor is empty. It isn't much, but better than my car, and now, thanks to you, I'll be able to rent it.'

Cynthia, there's that bloody name again, thought Dorothy as jealousy consumed her. She remembered Nelly telling her that Robbie had stayed with the woman the night he'd disappeared. She'd never spoken to Cynthia, but had heard the woman talked about. There weren't many people in Battersea who didn't know of Cynthia and her questionable reputation. Surely Robbie wasn't involved with someone like that? The woman was old enough to be his mother.

'I can see by your face what you're thinking, Dottie, but there's nothing going on between us. Cynthia's all right, and she's been a good friend to me. That's all she is though. A friend.'

'It's up to you what you do, Robbie, and it's none of my business,' Dorothy answered, feigning indifference.

She felt consoled to hear Robbie say Cynthia was just a friend, and then reprimanded herself for allowing her feelings to get the better of her. 'I've got to go before visiting time ends. If you don't find work and need more money to tide you over, I can get you some next week.'

'That would be great, Dottie, but it isn't just the money. Do I really have to wait a whole week until I see you again? Couldn't we meet up sooner?' Robbie urged earnestly.

Dorothy lowered her eyes and stared at her lap. She had to resist him, but it was so hard. 'Please don't, Robbie,' she begged quietly. 'I can't do this . . . I just can't.'

Robbie didn't say anything, but she stopped herself raising her head. If their eyes locked, she could be lost. A minute passed and at last she looked up, but the seat opposite was vacant. Robbie had silently slipped away.

A tear fell from the corner of Dorothy's eye and she fumbled in her bag for a handkerchief. The delicate white hanky with lace edging had been a gift from Adrian and was embroidered with her initials, DF . . . Dorothy Ferguson. She stared hard at the hanky and the pink cotton embroidery as her mind raged. Dorothy knew that despite everything she still loved Robbie and wished with all her heart that she had been more patient.

A sob escaped her lips. He had come back at last, but it was too late. She had made her bed and would have to lie in it, yet in her heart Dorothy knew she had married the wrong brother.

Chapter 32

After meeting Dottie, Robbie went back to Cynthia's, sorted out his stuff and then went upstairs. When Yvonne let him in he dumped his suitcase on the floor and pulled the bundle of notes from his pocket. Yvonne's eyes bulged as though on stalks. She probably hadn't seen so much money before and watched in awe as he peeled off five one-pound notes.

'There you go, Yvonne. Treat yourself to something to wear that's a bit more grown-up and sexy.'

'What! Spend all this on clothes?'

'Yes, of course. You just stick with me. There'll be plenty more where that came from,' Robbie said, winking at her.

'Thank . . . thank you, Robbie,' she gushed.

It irked Robbie to give Yvonne his money but she'd be earning her keep soon enough, and in the meantime he had to gain her confidence. She looked delighted with the cash and Robbie grinned to himself, pleased with what he saw. The bit of make-up she was wearing made her look a little older, and the dark mascara enhanced her green eyes, which were now rather striking. She's quite a looker, he thought, albeit a bit on the dim side. Robbie walked across the room and sat on the edge of the bed. 'Come and sit next to me,' he coaxed.

The girl looked nervous, but did as he asked and as she sat down he said, 'Don't worry, sweetheart, I don't bite.'

'Dogs bite. You're not a dog.'

'No, you're right,' Robbie said softly as he gently brushed her brown hair from her cheek. 'So do you want to be my girl?'

Yvonne kept her eyes lowered but nodded her head.

'Good. You just do as I tell you, and everything will be fine. I'll treat you like a princess and you'll have more money than you've ever dreamed of. You trust me, don't you?'

Yvonne nodded her head again.

'Have you ever been with a man before?' Robbie asked.

Yvonne quickly shook her head this time.

'Well, don't worry. It only hurts a bit the first time, then you'll like it after that.'

'But my mum said to wait 'til I get married,' Yvonne said anxiously.

Robbie contrived laughter. 'That's a bit old-fashioned and you'd better stop being so naïve if you want to be my girl. Everyone's doing it these days,' he lied. 'The trick is not to get caught out, you know, up the duff.'

'The duff? What's the duff?'

Robbie heaved a sigh. The girl didn't seem to have a clue. 'Yvonne, do you know how women get pregnant?'

'Yeah, a man puts his thingy in the woman. My sister told me about it but said only a husband can do it to his wife. I . . . I don't know what a thingy is though,' Yvonne said, her cheeks flushed.

Robbie found her innocence suddenly quite sweet. 'Your sister was right about some of it, but not all of it. The thing is, if you want to be my girl and earn lots of money, you're going to have to get used to doing it with men. But you won't have to worry about a thing because I'll be looking after you, do you understand?'

'No . . . I don't,' Yvonne said, looking confused.

'You said you trust me, so trust me. I promise you, Yvonne, it'll be a piece of cake.'

'My sister said that women who let men do it to them before they're married are tarts, and I don't want to be no tart.'

'Oh, Yvonne, honestly, love, your sister, though I'm sure she's a lovely girl, hasn't got it right. Not only that, it seems that she's left you here to fend for yourself, and though I know you've tried, you haven't coped very well, have you?'

'N-no.'

'Right then, forget everything she told you and listen to me. You're my girl and I'll look after you from now on,' Robbie assured her and, gently touching her cheek again, he softly pulled her face around. 'Close your eyes, I'm going to kiss you.'

Robbie gently brushed his lips over hers, and then pushed his tongue into her mouth. Yvonne didn't respond, so he began running his hands over her body, then squeezing her breasts. Still nothing, and his own excitement was beginning to wane. He pulled away from her. 'Yvonne, you've got to join in. There's nothing to be scared of,' he said and moved his hand under her skirt and up her bare thigh.

'But I . . . I am scared. Nobody has done that, touched my . . . my . . . and I . . . I don't know what to do.'

For a moment, Robbie thought she was going to cry, and that would put him right off. 'Hey, relax. It's perfectly normal and I'll show you what to do. I've told you, I'll look after you, so come on, take off your top, bra and knickers, and then lie back.'

Yvonne was nervous but did as Robbie said. He lay by her side and looked her over. She had rounded, pert breasts and soft, milky skin. With her long brown hair fanned out around her head, she really was a picture. 'You're gorgeous,' Robbie said huskily, and slowly traced his fingers across her flat stomach, up her body and over her nipple then back down again. He was pleased when he saw her nipples become erect so he repeated the movement.

'That feels nice. You like that, don't you?' he whispered.

Yvonne nodded.

'I knew you would. Now close your eyes and open your legs. If you like what I just did to you, then you're going to love this,' Robbie said and used his tongue to work his way down from her stomach to between her legs.

Yvonne gasped as Robbie pleasured her with his mouth and soon she was writhing on the bed and moaning in delight. He felt pleased with his efforts and could feel himself bulging in his trousers. The thought of taking her virginity and breaking her in added to his excitement.

She winced a bit at first, but Robbie was gentle with her, and after some further reassurance from him, she relaxed and dug her fingers into his back until Robbie was ready to finish. He made sure that he quickly pulled out in time. Satisfied, he flopped to one side, panting. 'See, I told you it would be all right. You liked that, didn't you?' he asked, and stood to pull his trousers up from around his ankles.

Yvonne was coyly pulling her clothes over her naked body. 'Yes, Robbie. It wasn't like I thought it was going to be, but why do you want me to do it with other men?'

Robbie took a roll-up from his pocket and lit it before answering. 'Stop asking daft questions. I told you I'd look after you and that's all you need to know for now. Get yourself dressed and I'll be back later with a friend. You just have to do exactly the same thing with him.'

Yvonne pulled her knickers on. 'I thought I was going to be a model,' she said, looking close to tears. 'I thought you was going to take photos of me.'

Robbie almost laughed, but then realised that it wasn't such a bad idea. If he had a good enough camera, he could take some risqué shots of her and sell them for a few bob.

'I don't know how you got that idea into your head, but I'll give it some thought. For now, be a good girl. Have a nice wash and tidy yourself up.'

'I . . . I don't think I want to do that with another man, Robbie.'

'In that case, I'll have to find myself a girl who does, and you'll just have to manage on your own again.'

'No! No, Robbie.'

'If you want me to stay, you'll have to do as I say. Are you willing to do that?'

Tears falling in earnest now, Yvonne whispered, 'Yes, Robbie.'

'Right. I'll be back later and don't worry, it'll be fine,' Robbie said, wanting away from her miserable face. He fancied a pint and the pub was always a good place to find some willing punters. It would probably be best to only get the one customer tonight though, ease Yvonne in gently to the job.

As he left the semi-derelict house he glanced back at Yvonne's window on the top floor. Once she was in full swing and the money was coming in, the first thing he planned on doing was finding a decent place to live.

Chapter 33

With Nelly on crutches and Dottie unwilling to go out, they had seen the New Year in at home without fuss. Adrian's paperwork was beginning to pile up so he'd gone back to work the next day, and had come home that evening to tuck into a strange-looking meal. It was a new recipe Dorothy had dished up from her Constance Spry cookbook.

'Do you like it?' Dorothy asked.

'It's scrummy,' Nelly answered with her mouth full.

'Different,' said Adrian. He found it was edible but not his favourite of Dorothy's culinary experiments.

'It was invented for the coronation of Queen Liz, hence the name, Coronation Chicken,' Dorothy said.

She spoke with such animation that Adrian didn't want to say anything negative and curb her enthusiasm. 'How was your dad today?' he asked instead.

'Much the same. I'm not sure if he knew I was there or not. It was funny though because he seemed to recognise one of the nurses who's been caring for him.'

With Bill in hospital, Adrian had expected his wife to be a bit down in the dumps but she was remarkably upbeat, which made him wonder if she was putting on a brave face.

'You know, your father could be in hospital for quite some time yet, and I'm not happy with you trudging back and forward on the bus,' he said. 'It'll wear you out. So how about I take you tomorrow to give you a break? I can leave the office for a while, it's no bother.'

'No, it's fine, honest. You've enough to do, especially with Nelly being off work. Thanks, darling, but I'll manage.'

'Well, at least get a taxi.'

Dorothy smiled. 'I'll think about it.'

Adrian doubted she would, but just in case, he'd increase her weekly housekeeping allowance to cover the cost. Alice had brought her daughter up well, he thought, teaching Dorothy to be frugal. She never took advantage of him and was far from extravagant with her spending. It further proved to him that Robbie had been very wrong about Dorothy marrying him for his money. If anything, he had a problem getting her to spend it.

'I've been thinking,' Nelly said. 'It's about time I moved back home. Don't get me wrong, I've loved being here, but I don't want to be an added burden for you.'

'You're not a burden to me. It's really nice having your company,' Dottie insisted, then turned to Adrian, her eyes pleading. 'Nelly doesn't have to leave, does she, Adrian? Tell her.'

Adrian cleared his throat. He didn't mind Nelly staying with them but he was looking forward to having his lounge back and his wife to himself. 'Dottie's right. Of course you don't have to leave. You're always welcome here.'

'See, Nelly,' Dottie said.

'But if Nelly wants to go home,' Adrian continued,

'then you should let her. You aren't here all day to look after her now, and if she had a fall on those crutches, she'd have a job to get up without help.'

'Oh, I'm sorry, Nel. I didn't think and I didn't mean to neglect you.'

'You haven't, Dottie, quite the opposite. I've never been so spoiled, but circumstances have changed, that's all. Tell you what, though, I'll really miss this bed, it's very comfy.'

'I'll arrange for it to go home with you,' Adrian said, glad to make the gesture – it would make him feel better about being pleased that Nelly was moving out.

'No, Adrian, I couldn't, that's far too generous.'

'It's no good to me,' Adrian answered. 'All the rooms upstairs have perfectly good beds so I really don't need it. It's yours, Nelly, so no more arguments.'

Adrian climbed into bed that night and snuggled up close behind Dorothy. His wife was happy, Bill was none the worse and Nelly was moving back home. There was only one blot on the landscape, but hopefully they had all seen the last of him.

'I've been thinking about getting decorators in to do up Robbie's old room. We could turn it into a nursery,' Adrian said in Dorothy's ear. He felt her body stiffen but assumed it was because she still wasn't pregnant, though not through lack of trying. 'You might like to think about colours?'

'I'm not sure that's such a good idea, Adrian. What if we jinx it or something? Isn't it unlucky?'

'You make your own luck in this life. Look at me, married to the most beautiful woman in the world and

I don't believe in all that mumbo-jumbo stuff. Still, we don't have to decorate if you don't feel comfortable with the idea. I'm sure you'll fall pregnant soon and we can do it then.'

'I hope you're right. I really do.'

Adrian hoped he was right too. He'd given Dottie everything he possibly could to make her happy, apart from the one thing she really wanted. A baby. He silently cursed Robbie. If Dorothy was damaged and couldn't conceive, it would be his brother's fault and he would never forgive him.

There was nothing he wanted more than to see his beautiful wife contented and smiling, but he feared she wouldn't ever be truly satisfied until she had a child in her arms.

Chapter 34

A week had passed since Dorothy had seen Robbie, and the house was very quiet, almost too quiet now. Nelly had moved back home, Adrian was at the office and her dad was still in hospital. She flicked the duster over the lounge furniture, thinking how large the room looked without Nelly's bed in it, and how she missed her friend's chattering, which had been a welcome distraction.

The quietness gave her too much space to think and her thoughts were filled with Robbie: his voice, his face and his irresistible touch. She tried to block him out because fantasising about Robbie left her feeling guilty towards Adrian, but it was useless to even bother to try, especially as she was due to meet him later.

Dorothy turned on the radio to alleviate the silence and her mood lightened when Elvis belted out across the airwaves. She flitted around the room with her duster, wriggling her hips to 'All Shook Up'. That was her, all shook up over Robbie bloody Ferguson, she thought. It wasn't right to feel like this over another man besides her husband, but she couldn't help herself.

Her lips tightened resolutely. She would never act on her feelings, never in a month of Sundays.

Later that morning, the bus pulled up near the hospital and Dorothy made her way to the café. She'd been keen to get there and took a seat at their usual table. Her heart was pounding hard again and it felt like there were a hundred little drummer men in her stomach, playing out a frenzied beat.

She looked at the cash she had managed to squirrel away from her housekeeping, a sizable four pounds. Not a bad amount to have saved in a week, she thought, imagining Robbie's elated face when she gave it to him. Ten minutes passed, then twenty, which soon turned to nearly an hour. Another cup of coffee later, her heart sinking, Dorothy had to accept that Robbie wouldn't be coming. She'd been a fool, expecting him to meet her when they hadn't made any firm arrangements last week. Robbie had just left without a word, but nevertheless she'd felt sure he would turn up today. It was her fault, of course, she'd rebuffed him, but she was married to Adrian so what choice did she have?

Robbie had told her he was going to rent a room above Cynthia's, and if she shortened her visiting time with her dad, she'd be able to make it over to the other side of Battersea and back again before Adrian got home from the office.

It was daring, but Robbie might be in need of the money and it was the only way she could think of to get it to him.

Yvonne was shivering with the cold as she came out of the bathroom and almost walked straight into Cynthia. She thought her new friend from downstairs looked a bit messy with her mascara smudged and her hair still in rollers.

Cynthia squinted at Yvonne as if trying to work out who she was. 'Blimey, I hardly recognised you. Look at you, all done up like a dog's dinner in all that fancy clobber.'

Yvonne turned her face from the foul stench of alcohol on Cynthia's breath, but wished she hadn't when with a scowl Cynthia said, 'I see, like that, is it? Turning your nose up at the likes of me now you've got your fancy man taking care of you. Just you remember, girl, it was me who introduced you to him.'

'No, I . . . I wouldn't turn up me nose, honest I wouldn't.'

Cynthia softened. The girl sounded as dim as ever. 'Take no notice of me, love, I've got a stinking hangover. I didn't mean to snap at you, but tell that fella of yours not to be a stranger. He ain't bothered to come to see me since he moved in with you. Not that I blame him for not wanting to gawp at an old wrinkly like me when he's got you to look at.'

Yvonne smiled, but as she did her lip split again and she tasted blood. She licked it away, but not before Cynthia had seen it.

'Oh, dear Lord, look at your lip. What happened to you?' Cynthia asked.

Yvonne's brain floundered for an answer, 'I . . . I walked into a door.'

Cynthia leaned in closer. 'Are you fibbing? Has Robbie given you a slap?'

'No, he wouldn't hit me, he loves me.'

'Yeah, right, if you say so. But take note from this old

girl who's been around the block a few times. If you let Robbie get away with it, he'll do it again and it'll only get worse. I've put up with a lot of crap in my life but I'd never let a bloke hit me, and neither should you. Now that's all I'm going to say on the subject, so come on, move out of my way. I'm busting for the loo.'

Yvonne walked back upstairs to her room. It looked a lot nicer than it had a week ago. Robbie had furnished it with some bits of good second-hand furniture and some pictures. She sat on the blue sofa and pulled out a compact mirror from her handbag. Her lip had nearly stopped bleeding, but it looked quite swollen. She frowned. Robbie had said she'd been a naughty girl and it was her own fault he'd had to slap her, but Cynthia had just said that she shouldn't let Robbie get away with it. The things they'd said tumbled round and round in her head and she found it too hard to make sense of them.

In the end, Yvonne clung to the one thing she could remember clearly. Robbie had promised her that as long as she did as she was told, he wouldn't hit her again. Her bottom lip trembled and she fought tears. She had upset Robbie, but from now on she'd be a good girl and then he wouldn't be angry with her. Would he?

Dorothy hadn't ventured to this side of Battersea since she'd left her family home to move in with Adrian as his wife. She walked through the streets, close to where she used to live, and fought to control the mixed emotions that bubbled so close to the surface.

The streets felt narrow and gloomy, the January sky looking heavy with possible snow. These slums were all she had known growing up, but Dorothy suddenly felt very out of place in her smart attire. She picked up her step and pondered how she'd ever found any happiness amongst all this poverty and hardship. 'What's the matter with you?' she muttered to herself. 'You've become a right snob.' She reminded herself that Nelly lived just around the corner.

As Dorothy turned into Grant Street, the narrow, three-storey house where Cynthia lived loomed up in front of her, and she unexpectedly felt very uneasy. Maybe this wasn't such a good idea, and she questioned her motives for being there. Well, she was here now, so with a deep breath she braced herself to walk up the mildew-covered concrete steps to the front door.

As Dorothy went to knock, she was surprised to find the door already open, and pushed it wide before walking into a hallway that reeked of damp. As her eyes adjusted to the dim light, it dawned on her that she didn't know which room Robbie was renting, but as he'd said it was on the top floor, she'd go upstairs.

Dorothy held on to the loose wooden bannister, and took the stairs slowly. The whole house felt a bit rickety and she feared the stairway would collapse. She passed the first floor, pleased to get away from the revolting smell emitting from an open door that revealed a bathroom, then stopped in front of a room on the top floor, wondering if this was Robbie's. Dorothy held her breath and tried to listen. She could detect movement but no voices, so she couldn't tell if Robbie was behind the closed door. Oh, well, she thought, what's the worst that could happen? Bravely throwing caution to the wind, Dorothy rapped hard on the door. It took a while, but eventually a pretty young woman answered.

'Hello,' she said.

'Sorry, I think I've come to the wrong door. I'm looking for Robbie, Robbie Ferguson. Do you know which room is his?'

'He lives here but he ain't in. Who are you?'

'Oh, I'm Dottie, his . . . his sister-in-law,' Dorothy replied, not sure what to make of the slip of a girl who was staring nervously at her.

'He's never mentioned you, but you can come in to wait for him if you like.'

'Thanks,' Dorothy answered and walked into the room where she immediately set eyes on the double bed against the wall.

'I dunno how long he'll be. Do you want a cup of tea or somefing?'

'That would be nice, and though I've introduced myself, I don't know who you are.'

'My name's Yvonne and I'm Robbie's girl.'

Robbie's girl! The words hit Dorothy like a punch to the stomach. She couldn't believe this little thing, who looked like she wasn't long out of her gymslip, could possibly be Robbie's girlfriend. 'How long have you been with Robbie?'

Yvonne smiled, but then frowned. 'Err . . . for nearly two weeks, I think, but we loves each other and he buys me lots of nice things.'

Dorothy felt sick. What on earth was Robbie playing at? Despite her painted face this girl looked so young and her eyes flicked to the double bed again. No . . . no, surely not! Her stomach rolled at the thought that they had been sleeping together. Surely the money she'd given Robbie hadn't been spent on this young girl, who didn't seem very bright. 'Where did Robbie get the money from to buy you things? Has he got a job now?'

Yvonne's frown deepened. 'I'm not allowed to talk about that sort of stuff. Robbie doesn't want me to.'

'Why not? It's only a simple question.'

'I . . . I dunno,' Yvonne said.

The thought of facing Robbie now was too much for Dorothy and she turned to leave. 'Look, I won't wait, and I think it's best you don't tell Robbie I was here.'

'Why not?'

Dorothy fought to find a reason, stuttering, 'It . . . it's complicated. I'm . . . I'm married to Robbie's brother and they don't really see eye to eye. It was probably a mistake to come here uninvited and I don't want to cause any trouble. Please, don't tell him.'

'Trouble! No, I-I don't want that neither. All right, I won't tell him.'

'Thanks. It's for the best.'

Yvonne still looked puzzled, but Dorothy hastily left, glad to be out of the house and away from its musty smell. She headed towards the bus stop, her mind a muddle of confused thoughts as she tried to fathom what Robbie was doing with a girl like Yvonne. She would've liked to pop round to Nelly's house to have a chat with her about it, but it was out of the question. Nelly had no idea that she'd been seeing Robbie, or that she had given him money, and there was no way her friend would approve.

It would have to remain a secret, but the young girl and the situation played on Dorothy's mind. It was all a bit peculiar, and once again she felt there was something very wrong with the set-up – very wrong indeed.

Chapter 35

Two weeks passed, and Dorothy bustled around her father's bedroom, preparing it for his homecoming later that day. As she made his bed with freshly laundered sheets, the subtle aroma of washing powder brought back memories of her old kitchen and her mother scrubbing laundry over the sink.

She still missed her mum so much – missed her more in moments when she found herself doing something and wishing she was there to share it. Today was one of those days. Nelly had said that time heals, but though the death of her mother had changed everything, time hadn't healed her grief. The pain still felt as raw as it did on the day she died. Dorothy ran her fingers through her hair and drew in a long breath. She had to think positively. Her mum wouldn't have allowed her to wallow in grief, and today was a good day. Her dad was coming home.

Dorothy paused when she heard a knock on the front door. She ran downstairs to open it, but then froze in her tracks when she heard Robbie's voice.

'Yes, it's just a flying visit, Mrs Hart.'

Robbie was obviously talking to their next-door neighbour, and Dorothy considered pretending she wasn't home. She was about to make a dash for the kitchen when the letterbox opened and Robbie called through.

'I know you're in there, Dottie. I can see you.'

Her mouth went dry and a racing heart made her feel quite giddy. What was he doing here? Bracing herself, Dorothy went to answer the door. 'What do you want, Robbie?' she asked harshly.

'So it's all right for you to come to my house, but I'm not welcome here?' he said. 'By the way, you look lovely as always,' he added, his smile disarming her.

Dorothy flicked her head from side to side, worried who might see him standing on the doorstep. She hoped Mrs Hart wasn't being nosy and listening in to what Robbie had said.

'Get in, quick,' she said, and ushered him into the hallway.

'What do you think you're playing at?' she asked once the front door was shut.

Robbie slowly ambled up the hallway and into the lounge, where he sat on the sofa. 'Now, now, Dottie, don't be like that. I hear you came looking for me the other day so I thought I should find out why.'

Dorothy couldn't believe how brazen Robbie could be. What if Adrian had been home and heard his brother, or if Nelly had still been staying with them? 'You shouldn't be here, Robbie. You could have put me in a very awkward position.'

'Why? We're alone, aren't we?'

'Yes, but you couldn't have known that.'

Once again Robbie's smile was unsettling. 'Well, I'm here now,' he said slowly, 'and it's good that we can talk freely.'

'No, Robbie, you can't stay. Adrian will be home any minute,' Dorothy said in panic as she glanced at the mantelpiece clock to see that it was midday.

'Dottie, we both know Adrian is at work and he won't be home for some time yet.'

'You're wrong. My dad is being discharged today and Adrian is taking me to the hospital this lunchtime to pick him up. Please, Robbie, just go.'

Their eyes locked and he said, 'Not until you tell me why you came to see me.'

She managed to pull away from his gaze. 'I thought you might have been in need of money, and when you didn't show up at the café I was worried.'

'It's nice to know you still care about me.'

Dorothy had the distinct impression he was teasing her and chose to ignore his comment.

'Seriously, though, I mean it – thanks, Dottie,' Robbie said, actually sounding sincere. 'As it happens, I really do need some money. You've seen the state of my room and it's hardly Buckingham Palace.'

'Yes, and I've also seen the young woman you're living with.'

'There's nothing going on between us. Yvonne's father threw her out and she had nowhere to go. I found her wandering the streets and I could hardly leave her out there to fend for herself.'

'She said you're in love with each other,' Dorothy snapped.

'That's all in her head. Come on, Dottie, you must have noticed that she's just a kid and isn't very bright. I think she's got a bit of a crush on me, but you're the only woman for me, you know that.'

As their eyes met, Dorothy's stomach knotted again. Why, oh why, did Robbie always have this effect on her? 'So the two of you aren't sleeping in that double bed?'

'Of course not, I sleep on the sofa. I can't believe you think I'd take advantage of Yvonne. What sort of man do you think I am?' he asked indignantly. 'I'm doing the girl a good turn, that's all.'

'I'm sorry, Robbie, it's just . . . well . . .' Dorothy found herself at a loss for words. She'd had a bad feeling about the set-up, but maybe it was just jealousy, and jealousy was something she had no right to feel.

'Don't worry about it. And another thing, I didn't turn up at the café because taking your money made me feel like a shit. Sorry, excuse my language. Don't get me wrong, I really need it, especially with an extra mouth to feed, but it isn't right, Dottie. I should be standing on my own two feet. It's hard though; I've worn out the soles of my shoes looking for work, and still I haven't had any luck.'

'If I hadn't married Adrian, you could have come back here to live, so don't feel bad, Robbie. I've got a comfy roof over my head whilst you've been left homeless. Just wait there a minute,' Dorothy said, and hurried into the kitchen. She returned to hold out ten pounds. 'Here, I want you to have it, no arguments. Adrian won't miss it, and I don't need it.'

'I don't know, Dottie, it feels wrong,' Robbie said as he shook his head.

'Come on, that girl looked like she could do with a good meal inside her and how else are you going to manage? Please, Robbie, just take it and go before Adrian comes home.'

Robbie grabbed the notes and jumped up from the

sofa, then quickly planted a kiss on Dorothy's cheek. 'Thanks, Dottie, you're a lifesaver,' he said before walking up the hallway to the front door. 'My brother is a very lucky man.'

Dorothy stood in the hallway, but as the door closed her legs felt wobbly. She sat on the stairs, third one up, cupping her face with her hands. From what Robbie had said, she was sure he still loved her. A sob escaped her lips. She loved him too, but they could never be together. She had married Adrian and there was no way she would ever leave him. Once again Dorothy knew that she had made her bed and would have to lie in it, but it was with the wrong man.

She rose to her feet, fighting tears, her heart aching for what might have been.

It was gone two-thirty that afternoon when Adrian pulled in to the kerb.

'It's all right, Bill, we're home now,' he said to pacify the man who was mumbling incoherently in the back seat of the car.

'Come on, Dad,' Dottie urged. 'I'll help you out of the car.'

'Hold on a minute, love,' Adrian cautioned. 'I'll go and open the front door first and then give your dad a hand.'

'Hello, Adrian. It's good to see Mr Butler coming home,' Mrs Hart said, appearing from next door as he put his key in the lock. 'It must be such a weight off Dottie's mind. I took the liberty of baking a sponge cake. Here you are . . .'

'Err, would you mind holding on to it for a minute,

Mrs Hart? Just until we get Bill in. He's a bit testy in the car.'

'Of course not. Go on, don't let me keep you.'

With the door now open, Adrian went back to the car and held Bill on one side, while Dorothy took the other. They slowly walked the old man into the house, with Mrs Hart following behind with the cake.

Adrian left Dorothy to settle Bill in his sitting room and walked into the kitchen to find Mrs Hart putting the cake in the larder. 'That's very kind of you. Thanks, Mrs Hart. I'll enjoy a slice with a cup of tea later and I'm sure Dottie and Bill will too.'

'You're welcome, it's my pleasure. I don't find the need to bake much these days, not since my Cyril passed on. I know you and your brother have always been fond of my sponge cakes, and it's nice for me to have an excuse to do some baking. Talking of your brother, I saw him when he was round here earlier. Such a polite young man.'

'I'm sorry, did you say Robbie was here earlier?' Adrian asked, confused.

'Yes, that's right, but he said it was just a flying visit.'

For a moment, Adrian felt like he had been smacked between the eyes. 'I'm sorry, Mrs Hart. If you'll excuse me I have to help Dottie,' he said as he ushered the woman up the hallway and out of the front door.

Thankfully she didn't seem offended, and when he had closed the door behind her, Adrian leaned against it, still trying to digest what she'd said. Why hadn't Dorothy told him? What was she hiding? Was she secretly seeing Robbie behind his back? His mind raced with so many questions, but if he asked Dorothy would he believe any answers that she gave him?

For the first time since he'd married her, Adrian wondered if he could trust his wife.

Once Dorothy was satisfied her dad had settled in his sitting room, she walked into the kitchen to see Adrian sat at the kitchen table. He was unsmiling and looked serious as he said, 'Sit down, Dottie. We need to talk.'

'What is it? What's wrong?' Dorothy asked worriedly.

'Why didn't you tell me that Robbie was here this morning? It's only thanks to Mrs Hart that I found out.'

'I . . . I . . . I forgot to mention it, what with my dad and everything,' she answered and hoped her feeble excuse would be believed.

'What did he want?' Adrian flatly asked.

'Nothing – well, nothing much.' She fumbled for an answer. 'Some things from his room.'

'What things?'

'I don't know, he didn't say.'

'What did he take?'

'He didn't take anything. I told him to come back when you're home,' she said, trying to maintain eye contact to make her lies more convincing, although she felt sure that Adrian could see straight through them. It made her feel awful and she wished she'd just told him the truth. It was too late now and she was on a downward slide of deception.

'How long was he here?'

'Only for about ten minutes.'

'Yes, that ties in with what Mrs Hart said.'

'Sorry, I should have told you, but it just slipped my mind.'

'So he hasn't been round here before today?' Adrian asked.

'No, well, not since Christmas Eve and, as you know, I wasn't in then. He spoke to Nelly,' she said, relieved that she could at least answer that question truthfully. Trying to change the subject, she asked, 'Did I see Mrs Hart with a cake?'

'Yes, it's in the larder, but Dottie, if there's anything you want to tell me, now would be a good time.'

Dottie wanted to tell him, she really did, but it would mean telling him everything. If not in reality, she'd been unfaithful to Adrian in her mind, and that was almost as bad. How could she admit that she was still in love with his brother? It would break his heart and Adrian didn't deserve that. 'No, there's nothing,' she said, and stood up to leave the table.

'No, Dottie, sit down. Maybe I'm just being paranoid, but I need peace of mind. Have you been seeing Robbie behind my back?'

She looked into Adrian's eyes and could see his pain – this man who had always shown her nothing but love and kindness. She couldn't stand it any longer and blurted out the truth. She told Adrian about the money she'd given Robbie, and her reasons for helping him, but that was as far as she went. She couldn't hurt Adrian, couldn't confess her feelings for Robbie, and now sat nervously waiting for his reaction.

Without so much as a glance at her, Adrian stood up and walked into the lounge. His silence felt worse than if he had screamed and shouted at her. But of course, he wouldn't do that – angry outbursts weren't in Adrian's nature.

Dottie followed and, seeing that he had sat down, she knelt on the floor in front of him. 'Adrian, I'm sorry I didn't tell you. Please, say something, anything. Tell me how much you hate me, throw me out, but please don't give me the silent treatment.'

Adrian looked into Dorothy's eyes, his own watery. 'Dottie, I could never hate you. You're my wife, I love you, and I'd never throw you out. This is your home, our home. I can understand why you helped Robbie. You're kind, caring, and I know how persuasive my brother can be, but he had no right to come to you for money. I want you to promise me that in future, if Rob asks you for more money, you just send him to see me.'

'All right,' Dorothy agreed. She felt so much better for telling Adrian the truth, and was quite overwhelmed at how understanding he was. She placed her head in his lap, and as Adrian stroked her hair she wished she could give him the love he deserved, but her heart still belonged to Robbie and she feared it always would.

Chapter 36

The following week, Malcolm sat in the bar, looking at the glass of dark ale in front of him. He'd managed to finish early and had been to a jewellery shop, and though he hadn't been in a pub since he'd met Nelly, he was now taking the time to celebrate his purchase.

His eyes savoured the smooth-looking liquid with the creamy, frothy head. He was going to enjoy this pint and make the most of it. The overtime he'd been doing had paid off, and he was pleased that he'd managed to find the perfect engagement ring for Nelly. It was going to be a surprise for her birthday. She'd be having the plaster removed soon, and then he was going to take her to a nice restaurant where he planned to go down on bended knee to propose. The thought of it made him nervous. He was pretty sure that Nelly liked him, but would she agree to marriage? Well, he thought, if he didn't ask, he'd never know.

He picked up his glass and supped the ale. Nelly was worth giving up a drink for and he got a warm feeling inside when he thought about her. Malcolm grinned. His little pudding on legs, as he liked to call her.

The door opened and Malcolm saw Robbie Ferguson

walking in. Nelly had mentioned that Robbie was back in town but it was the first time he'd seen him, and as Robbie owed him a fiver, now was his chance to get it back.

'Oi, Rob, over here,' Malcolm called.

'Hello, Malcolm. How are you?' Robbie asked.

His breezy manner peeved Malcolm but he faked a pleasant smile before answering, 'I'm all right and if you're on the way to the bar, mine's a pint.'

Robbie nodded and sauntered off, returning a few minutes later with two beers. 'So how's tricks? Are you still working for my brother?'

'Yes, I am, and as it happens I've been doing a few extra hours lately to earn a bit more money. Talking of which, you still owe me a fiver.'

Robbie shifted in his seat. 'You've got a good memory.'

'I suppose you thought that after all this time I'd have forgotten about it, but I ain't and I want it back.'

'I intend to give it to you, but I need a bit of time to sort myself out. I've been back in London for about a month but I haven't managed to find a job yet. I will, though, and as soon as I do, I'll square up with you.'

'Don't take me for a mug,' Malcolm growled. He wasn't a violent man, but Robbie didn't know that. Nelly called him her big teddy bear, but his size and stature gave a different impression. 'You buggered off owing me that money, but now you're back with enough in your pockets to come in here for a drink. I want the fiver you owe me and now. Or else!'

Robbie paled but blustered, 'Honest, Malcolm, I haven't got much money, just enough for a couple of pints and I was hoping you'd buy the next round.'

Malcolm didn't believe him and his temper rose. 'Don't take the piss, Robbie. I don't want to hurt you, you're my guv's brother, but if you don't give me what I'm owed I'll rip your head off and shove it up your backside.'

Though still pale, Robbie obviously wasn't intimidated. 'OK, OK, I get it. You're a big fella, Malcolm, and I wouldn't want to be on the receiving end of your fists, but it doesn't change anything. I haven't got your money, but I'll tell you what I can do for you . . .' Robbie said, winking at him.

Malcolm breathed heavily to calm himself, intrigued despite himself to hear what the cheeky so-and-so was going to offer. 'Go on then, surprise me.'

'I've got this smashing young, gorgeous girl. She's a firecracker between the sheets, if you get my drift . . .' Robbie said and nudged Malcolm with his elbow.

'What's this got to do with the fiver you owe me?'

'If you saw her, you'd pay good money for her. If you like, I can take you to her now, and pay off my debt that way. You can have her more than once too, so how does that sound?'

Malcolm was sickened by Robbie's offer. 'A young girl? You dirty fucking toe-rag,' he shouted. 'Get out of my sight before I do something I'll regret.'

Robbie scarpered, leaving Malcolm with a bad taste in his mouth. So that's how he had money in his pocket to buy a drink, the dirty bastard, thought Malcolm. Robbie Ferguson was now a pimp, a dirty rotten pimp, and he wondered if his boss knew what his brother was up to.

What Robbie was doing played on Malcolm's mind. He liked his boss, finding Adrian Ferguson a fair man to work for, but he had no time for his brother. He wasn't sure what to do with what he'd found out about Robbie, but he knew someone who would point him in the right direction.

Malcom finished his pint, went home, ate his dinner and then got spruced up a bit to go to see Nelly. No sooner had he been invited in than he said, 'Nelly, you ain't going to believe what that Robbie Ferguson is up to now.'

'Nothing would surprise me when it comes to that man, but go on, tell me.'

'He's got a bird working for him and he's selling her for sex, you know, prostituting her.'

'You've got to be kidding,' Nelly said, her eyes wide with surprise. 'How did you find out about it?'

'I bumped into Robbie in the pub. The cheeky git owes me a fiver but offered me the woman for a bit of how's your father instead of the money.'

Nelly knew Robbie was a lowlife, but this was too much. 'I hope you told him where to stick his offer?'

'Of course I did,' Malcolm replied. 'But do you think I should have a word with Adrian?'

Nelly took out a packet of fruit Spangles and sucked a sweet in thought. 'Robbie is dragging the Ferguson name through the mud, and Adrian is going to be fuming when he finds out. He won't thank you for telling him, so I think you should keep out of it.'

'Yeah, maybe you're right.'

'Do me a favour, darlin', pass me that knitting needle. My leg is itching like mad but I can't get to it.'

Malcolm passed Nelly the knitting needle and took a seat next to her as she pushed the length of it down the side of her plaster, sighing with pleasure when it reached the itch.

'Are you sure I shouldn't have a word with the governor? I'd hate him to find out that I knew but said nothing.'

'Yes, I'm sure. Adrian's your boss, and though you were invited for Christmas dinner, that doesn't make him your friend. Keep out of it, and as it will kill two birds with one stone, I'll have a word with Dottie. I've been worried that she's still got feelings for Robbie, but this should leave them dead in the water, and then it'll be up to her if she wants to tell Adrian what his scumbag brother is up to.'

'Do you think she will?'

'I don't know, but you'll have to go round to her place as soon as you get the chance and tell her I want to see her. The sooner she finds out about Robbie the better.'

Chapter 37

Adrian had left for work when Dorothy opened the door to Malcolm, surprised to see him there. He told her that Nelly wanted to see her, but was vague about why, only saying it was important. Dorothy smiled. She could guess what Nelly wanted to tell her and no doubt her friend was itching to pass on the good news.

It meant she had to ask Mrs Hart to sit with her father, but thankfully the woman didn't seem to mind. At ten-thirty, after saying she'd be back as soon as she could, Dorothy didn't walk or wait for a bus to get to Nelly's house. For once she hailed a taxi.

When she arrived, Nelly's mum opened the front door and led her through to the front room. Dorothy smiled at the sight of her best friend sat with her plastered leg resting on a pile of old newspapers and perming lotion dripping down the side of her face.

'Wotcha, Dottie. Mum's doing me one of them poodle perms. She's used tiny little rollers and the bloody things are pulling on my scalp. That setting lotion stuff stinks too. Still, I want to look my best for Malcolm,' Nelly said and patted the sofa next to her for Dorothy to sit down.

'Sorry I haven't been round this week,' Dorothy said, 'but having to keep an eye on my dad makes it difficult for me to get out. Malcolm said you wanted to see me, so I asked Mrs Hart to sit with him.'

'Don't worry, sugar. I understand. How's your dad doing?'

'I don't know if it's the pills he's on, but, other than having a chesty cough again, he seems better. He's calm now and he gave me a lovely smile this morning.'

'That's good,' Nelly said, then, raising her voice, she shouted, 'Did you hear that, Mum? Bill's on the mend.'

Nelly's mum came through to the living room with two cups of tea. 'That's nice, love. I'll leave these cups here and let you two have a natter in peace.'

No sooner had she left than Nelly said, 'Dottie, I've got something important to tell you.'

'Let me guess. Malcolm has proposed.'

'No, it isn't that, but watch this space,' Nelly said, smiling briefly before her face straightened. 'Look, Dottie, I'll get right to the point. It's Robbie. That man is the lowest of the low, bloody pond life.'

Dorothy knew that Nelly had no time for Robbie and said, 'Look, I know you don't like him, but what's brought this on?'

'It seems he's found himself a new line of business – as a pimp.'

It sounded so ridiculous that Dorothy almost laughed. 'What? Selling women for sex? You must be joking.'

'It's no joke, Dottie.'

'I know you like a bit of gossip, Nelly, and I don't know where you heard this, but I'm sure it's rubbish.'

'I heard it from Malcolm so I know it's true. Robbie

offered him a woman in exchange for the money he owes him.'

Dorothy sat in stunned silence. It couldn't be true, not Robbie, the man she loved. 'Are you sure, Nel? Malcom could have been mistaken.'

'There's no mistake. Robbie told Malcolm that he's got this young and gorgeous girl, and said he could have her to pay off the debt.'

Dorothy felt her stomach lurch. She felt sick, and blurted, 'Oh, Nelly, I think I've met her. Her name is Yvonne and she's young, very young. I can't believe Robbie would put her on the game.'

'Well, he has, but how did you meet her?'

Dorothy suddenly realised she had dropped herself in it and would have some explaining to do to her friend. 'I thought Robbie was desperate for money, so I went to his place to give him a few pounds.'

'When it comes to you and that man, once a mug always a mug,' Nelly said, sighing. 'I should have bloody guessed you'd been seeing him, even though you denied it.'

'I'm sorry, Nelly. I should have told you. Can you forgive me?'

'Of course, you twit, but I knew you was up to something. So tell me, are you still in love with him?' Nelly asked. 'And don't give me a cock-and-bull story this time.'

Dorothy thought hard before replying. There had been enough lies over the past few weeks and it was time to come clean, with Nelly at least. 'Yes, I love him and I think I always will. I can't help myself, and I think Robbie must be in dire trouble, desperate for money, to do what he's doing.'

Nelly shook her head in disgust. 'You've always been blind when it comes to Robbie Ferguson and I should have known you'd make excuses for him. I just hope you're not going to do anything silly, like running off with him.'

'No, I won't be doing that. Adrian has been so good to me; he loves me and I can't hurt him. I just can't love him in return.'

'You could if you'd see Robbie for the nasty piece of work he is. The man's a bloody pimp!'

Dorothy pictured Yvonne's young face and remembered her swollen lip. She wondered if one of Robbie's clients had been a bit rough and hurt Yvonne. It was bad enough that the girl was being used for sex, without being physically abused too.

'Robbie told me he was just letting the girl stay with him because her father had chucked her out and she had nowhere else to go,' she said.

'For goodness' sake, open your eyes! Robbie is sick, Dottie. I reckon he's got that pathological lying disease thing that I read about last week.' Nelly paused, her look intent. 'Are you all right? You look terrible.'

'Yes, but now that I know the truth, I'm really worried about Yvonne. I can't just ignore this. I have to do something.'

'Like what? If you're thinking about going round there to rescue the girl, forget it. You're out of your depth here, and, after finding out that Robbie's a pimp, you don't know what else he's capable of.'

Dorothy could see that Nelly was worried about her, but felt she had no choice. 'I'll be fine. Robbie may be a lot of things but he isn't violent. I know he would never hurt me.'

'You can't be sure of that. Robbie isn't the man you think he is. You should tell Adrian what's going on and leave him to sort his brother out.'

Dorothy shook her head. 'No, I've brought enough trouble to his doorstep already. And anyhow, I know Adrian. He'll want to protect me and tell me to keep out of it. I'll have to deal with this myself. I just want to talk to the girl. She's so young, and as she isn't very bright she may not understand what's happening. As for Robbie, I'm finished with him,' she said, but deep down Dottie knew that she still had feelings for him.

After leaving Nelly, Dorothy set off on a determined march to Grant Street. She had told Mrs Hart she wouldn't be long, but this was something she just couldn't put off, and after talking to Yvonne she'd save time by getting a taxi home again. She hoped that Robbie would be out, but if he wasn't, then she'd deal with him too. She'd tell him that what he was doing was disgusting, sick and depraved, and maybe hearing it from her would shame him into seeing sense.

Soon Dorothy was climbing the rickety staircase to the top floor again, where she knocked on Robbie's door. There was no answer, so she knocked again, this time harder.

'All right, all right, don't get your knickers in a twist,' she heard Yvonne shout. The door opened and Yvonne stood there, biting her bottom lip worriedly when she saw who it was. 'Robbie ain't in.'

'Good. It's you I've come to see.'

'Me?'

'Yes, so can I come in?'

'I don't know. Robbie might not like it.'

'I just want to talk to you and it won't take long. Please, love, it's important.'

'All right then,' Yvonne said, though she looked nervous as she stood to one side.

'Do you mind if I sit down?' Dorothy asked.

'If you want, but you mustn't stay long.'

'I won't, but I've come to see you because I'm worried about you.'

'Why? I'm all right.'

'I don't think you are. Tell me, is Robbie making you do things you don't want to do?'

Yvonne frowned as though in thought and then said, 'He does sometimes, but I don't think I really mind.'

'Does he make you have sex with other men?'

Yvonne's face paled and she shook her head vigorously. 'I'm not allowed to talk about it. Robbie told me not to.'

'I just want to help you,' Dorothy told her. 'I wish I could make you see that Robbie is just using you.'

'No, he's not. He loves me and we're happy together.'

'If he loved you, he wouldn't offer you to other men for money.'

'But . . . but he said it makes him happy.'

'Yes, of course it does. Every time you have sex with another man, he gets paid for it, but you don't have to agree to it.'

'I do.'

'No, you don't,' Dottie insisted. 'I wish I could make you understand that Robbie has turned you into a prostitute, and it can be dangerous.'

'But Robbie looks after me.'

'Does he? Last time I was here I noticed you had a

split lip. Did one of the men he made you sleep with do that to you?'

Yvonne lowered her head, and just mumbled, 'No.'

'So who hit you then?'

'It was my fault. I asked for it. If I'd done what Robbie told me to do, he wouldn't have slapped me.'

Dorothy felt her face stretch in shock. She couldn't believe that Robbie had hit this young girl and it sickened her.

'Yvonne, men that hit women are the lowest of the low, and if Robbie has hit you once, then you should leave him before he hurts you again.'

'No . . . he . . . he told me he won't hit me again. He loves me, he takes care of me and . . . and I think you should go now!'

Dorothy knew she hadn't got through to Yvonne and could see that the girl was getting upset. She pulled a piece of paper out of her handbag and scribbled on it before standing up. 'All right, I'll go, but take this, it's my telephone number. If you ever change your mind about leaving Robbie and need help, please, call me.'

Yvonne took the note and quickly tucked it away in her bra. Dorothy had the feeling that one day Yvonne would need her help, and hoped the girl would keep the number somewhere safe.

Sadly Dorothy made her way home, close to tears and still unable to believe that Robbie had sunk so low.

Chapter 38

On the first Sunday in February, Nelly was flexing her leg, doing the exercises she'd been given to strengthen the muscles. She'd been glad to discard the crutches, but still had to use a walking stick. She was hoping to return to work soon and was also itching to tell Dorothy her news. For her birthday the previous evening, Malcolm had taken her out for a lovely meal, and just before their last course he had actually gone down on one knee in front of the whole restaurant to propose. She'd been gobsmacked. Malcom never struck her as being extrovert or romantic, and everyone in the restaurant had applauded when she had said yes. The manager had even sent over a bottle of champagne, and the bubbles had tickled her nose.

'Here, Mum, you'll never believe it, but I didn't really like the taste of champagne,' she said now. 'I might sound a bit posher nowadays, but you can't take the girl out of Battersea. I prefer Babycham.'

Her mum laughed. 'If you ask me, you can't beat a nice glass of stout.'

'Malcom will be here soon so I'd best get ready. We've been invited to Dottie's for dinner.'

'That girl has done well for herself. To think she was once engaged to Robbie Ferguson, and what a toe-rag he's turned out to be. I bet his brother is ashamed of him, and Dottie certainly made the right choice with Adrian.'

'Yes, she did,' Nelly agreed. As far as she knew, Dottie still hadn't told Adrian what his brother was up to, but at least she was keeping well away from Robbie for now, so that was something. Nelly felt it was only a matter of time before the gossip reached Adrian, and wondered what would happen when it did.

'Have you set a date for the wedding?'

'Give us a chance, Mum. We've only just got engaged.'

'Yes, well, don't leave it too long. Long engagements lead to temptation and I don't want you walking down the aisle with a bun in the oven.'

'I won't be doing that,' Nelly told her, but as she was already sorely tempted when she was in Malcolm's arms, she wanted to set the date sooner rather than later.

Adrian's stomach grumbled as the smell of roast beef wafted through the house. He always looked forward to his Sunday lunch and the apple pie he knew would follow. He walked through to the kitchen to find his wife busy draining potatoes. 'Do you want a hand with anything, love?' he asked, knowing she would decline his offer and probably usher him out of the kitchen.

'You can lay the table, if you like,' she answered to his surprise.

Dottie had seemed a bit distant for the last few weeks, probably worried because her father had a bad chest again, though Adrian couldn't help but wonder if she'd seen Robbie again. He wouldn't ask her as he wanted to trust his wife, but he didn't – and never would – trust Robbie.

The telephone trilled in the hallway and Dorothy quickly threw the sieve and saucepan in the sink, looking almost panicked as she said, 'I'll get it.'

Again, niggling doubts began to bite, and Adrian wondered what his wife was so obviously trying to hide. He stood in the kitchen doorway and eavesdropped on the one-sided conversation.

'Where are you? OK, stay right there and I'll be there as soon as possible,' she said, then turned to look at him, her face ashen.

'Who was that?' He asked.

'Adrian, it's a long story but I have to go and fetch a friend who needs my help,' she answered.

'What friend? What sort of help? Tell me what's going on.'

'It's a long story. I met this young lady called Yvonne. She's really sweet, but she got mixed up in a bad crowd and now she needs to get away. I said to call me if she ever needed me, and well, now it appears she does. I'm sorry, I know I should have told you about it, but it just sort of happened.'

Typical of Dorothy, thought Adrian, always caring about other people. He was a bit peeved that she hadn't discussed it with him, but how could he be angry at his wife for trying to help a young woman who was in trouble?

'OK,' he said, 'but what do you want to do? I heard you say you were going to fetch her, so I suppose you're bringing her back here?'

'I don't think she's got anywhere else to go, so yes, if you don't mind.'

'Of course I don't, but this bad crowd, are they likely to come here looking for her?' Adrian asked. He wasn't bothered about a bunch of yobs, but he was concerned for his wife's safety.

'No, I shouldn't think so. They won't know where she is.'

'Where is she then? I'll drive us.'

There was a knock on the door and Dottie ran to answer it. 'Nelly, thank goodness you're here. We've got to go out for a little while, so can you keep an eye on my dad? I'm sorry about dinner, but I'll finish it off when we get back.'

'Yeah, all right, but where are you off to?'

'I haven't got time to explain now,' Dottie said, looking even more anxious. 'Come on, Adrian, we must go.'

They left a flummoxed-looking Nelly and Malcolm watching them from the hallway as they hurriedly left and climbed into the car. He started the engine and then said, 'Right, where to?'

'She's waiting at the telephone box on the corner of Falcon Road. Adrian, thank you so much for doing this. You are such a good man.'

He would have liked Dottie to add, 'and I love you' to the end of her sentence. He was so desperate to hear those words from his wife, and still hoped he would one day. After all, he did everything within his power to make her happy – even, it seemed, taking in street urchins now.

'Adrian, there's more I need to tell you,' Dorothy said in a serious voice. 'It's about Robbie.'

His heart sank. Was that why Dottie had been so

distant? Was she going to confess that she'd been seeing Robbie? However, when she spoke again it shocked him to the core.

'This girl, Yvonne, has been working for Robbie as a prostitute. He's used her and he's been hitting her too. She's so young, Adrian, barely a woman, and she doesn't have anyone. I just couldn't stand by and do nothing so I went to see her a couple of weeks ago. I tried to talk some sense into her, but she refused to listen. She said she loves Robbie and wouldn't leave him, but something must have happened to change her mind. She sounded terrified on the telephone.'

Adrian's grip tightened on the steering wheel. He was sickened by what he'd heard, but also annoyed.

'Did you hear what I said, Adrian? Your brother is a pimp.'

'Yes, I heard you, but you said you went to see this girl two weeks ago. If that's the case, why am I only just hearing about it? Are you trying to protect Robbie?'

'No, of course not! What he's doing disgusts me, but as Yvonne refused to leave him, there was nothing more I could do. I was going to tell you, but it's just been one thing after another lately. I'm really sorry.'

Adrian accepted her explanation, and though he was disgusted that his brother was now a pimp, he now knew that if that was the case Dottie would never have anything to do with him. Shortly afterwards he turned into Falcon Road, and, seeing the telephone box, he drew in to the kerb.

'There she is, Adrian,' Dottie exclaimed. 'Stay in the car. If she sees you it might frighten her off.'

'Yes, all right,' he agreed and watched as Dottie walked

up to a young girl who was hunched up in a corner next to the telephone box. Her face was streaked with tears and she looked so young and vulnerable. He couldn't hear what was being said, but then Dottie was leading Yvonne over to the car and opening the back door.

'Come on, love, get in. This is my husband Adrian, and there's no need to be afraid. We're going to take you home to our place and you'll be safe there.'

Adrian looked at Yvonne through the rear mirror, and, seeing the state she was in, he silently cursed his brother. Robbie had put the Ferguson name to shame when he had robbed a jeweller, and now he had dragged it further down into the mire. He cursed the day his brother had returned to Battersea.

Robbie returned from the pub after a Sunday lunchtime drink to find that Yvonne was gone. He'd told her to be ready by two-thirty, yet here he was, bang on time and she was nowhere to be seen.

He ran down the stairs and knocked on Cynthia's door. 'Have you seen Yvonne?' he asked when Cynthia opened the door. 'Is she here with you?'

'No, Robbie, I haven't seen her for a few days. Why, has she gone missing or something?'

'Don't worry about it,' Robbie said dismissively and ran back up the stairs to his room.

He looked around for some sort of clue, anything that could indicate where Yvonne was. It didn't look as if anything was missing, so she couldn't have gone far. It was Sunday, the shops were closed, and she had no friends or family to visit. Anger coursed through his veins. He had a punter due at any minute and the bitch had let him down.

Robbie paced the room, swearing under his breath, even more so when the punter arrived and he had to turn him away. He was losing money, and Robbie was determined to make Yvonne pay for that when she returned. His fists clenched. He'd make sure she never disobeyed him again.

Gradually Robbie's anger subsided, and he began to worry that Yvonne might not be coming back. If she had gone for good, then so had his income, and he cursed as he took a roll-up from his tin. His matchbox was empty, but he knew Yvonne kept a box in the kitchen drawer by the new gas cooker. As he rummaged through it he saw a small clip-top purse and wondered where it had come from. Hoping it might contain a few bob he opened it, but only found a piece of tightly folded paper. Curious, he unfolded it and when he saw a telephone number, his blood ran cold. It was the number for his brother's house, but there was only one person who could have given it to Yvonne. Furious, he snatched a saucepan from the top of the stove and threw it against the wall, yet it wasn't enough to vent his anger. He knew where Yvonne was now. She was with Dorothy, his fucking goody-two-shoes so-called sister-in-law.

He stomped out of the room and took the stairs two at a time. He wouldn't go around there today; Adrian would be home. No, he'd wait, have a few pints for now, but tomorrow he would get Yvonne back and ensure Dottie never stuck her uppity nose in his business again.

While Malcolm sat with Bill, Nelly took over in the kitchen. She propped her walking stick up, and, though her leg was weak and it wasn't easy, she managed to finish off the dinner just as Dorothy and Adrian returned. She was surprised to see they had a young girl with them, but Dorothy hurriedly told her that explanations would have to wait for now and she would tell her everything once they were alone. The girl clung to Dorothy as Nelly dished up the food and then they all sat down to eat.

With a silent, nervous virtual stranger sitting with them, the atmosphere was a bit strained, and, though Nelly was eager to tell Dottie her news, she was hesitant.

'Yvonne, would you like some cabbage?' Dottie asked, holding a serving spoon and her hand hovering over the vegetable dish.

Nelly's jaw dropped. She had heard that name before. Yvonne was the girl Dottie had once spoken about, the one that Robbie had put on the game. Why was she here? Nelly wanted to ask questions, but knew she would have to wait.

'Here, Dottie, I think I may know why your dad's chest is playing him up,' Malcolm said. 'I noticed that the fire in his sitting room smokes a bit so maybe the chimney needs sweeping.'

'Thanks, Malcom, I'll get onto it straight away,' said Adrian.

'My granddad used to suffer with bronchitis, but it improved when we stopped lighting a coal fire and got an electric one.'

'That might be a good idea. What do you think, Dottie?' Adrian asked.

Nelly saw that Dottie wasn't really listening. Her eyes had spotted her engagement ring and she was grinning widely.

'Nelly, you're engaged!' she squealed. 'When did this happen and why didn't you tell me?'

Nelly blushed. 'Malcolm proposed last night.'

'This calls for a celebration,' said Adrian. 'I'm afraid I haven't got any champagne, but I think I've got a bottle of white wine.'

'That's all right. I'm not keen on champagne,' Nelly told him.

'How do you know you don't like champagne?'

'I had some last night, when Malcolm proposed.'

'If you can afford champagne, Malcolm, I must be paying you too much,' Adrian quipped.

'It was from the manager,' Nelly said quickly.

'I'm only joking, my dear.'

When she tasted the wine, Nelly tried not to pull a face. It wasn't nice and sweet like Babycham, but it was lovely to be toasted on their engagement.

'Have you set a date for the wedding?' Dottie asked.

'Blimey, you're as bad as my mother, and, as I told her, no, we haven't. We've only just got engaged.'

Malcolm smiled fondly at her and Nelly's heart soared. She knew she wasn't an oil painting, and her figure left a lot to be desired, but she could see the love in his eyes. He looked at her in the same way she would often look at chocolate cake.

Yvonne was so quiet that it was hardly noticeable that she was there, Nelly thought. When the meal was over she helped Dottie to clear the table, and at last managed to talk to her alone.

'What's that girl doing here, Dottie?' she whispered.

'Yvonne has run away from Robbie and we've taken her in.'

Nelly was shocked. 'Are you mad? What if Robbie finds out she's here?'

'What if he does? There's nothing he can do. He can't force Yvonne to go back.'

Nelly wasn't so sure about that. She had a sinking feeling that there was trouble ahead and hoped that Dottie and Adrian wouldn't live to regret taking the girl into their home.

Chapter 39

The following morning, Dorothy lightly tapped on the door of the bedroom which had once been Myra's. 'It's only me. Would you like a cup of tea?'

'Yes . . . yes, please,' Yvonne called.

Dorothy went in and placed the cup and saucer on the bedside table. She could see from Yvonne's puffy eyes that she had been crying. 'Are you all right?' she asked gently.

Yvonne nodded, but her eyes pooled with tears and Dottie's heart went out to her. 'Yvonne, I didn't pry yesterday, but is there anything you want to talk about? Do you want to tell me what happened to make you change your mind about leaving Robbie?'

Yvonne pulled her thin legs to her chest and started chewing on her thumbnail. 'It . . . it's good of you to take me in, and . . . and thanks for lending me this nightie.'

It was obvious that Yvonne didn't want to answer her questions, so Dottie left it for now. 'You're welcome, and as you didn't bring any clothes with you, we'll pop up to the Junction today and get you a few things.'

'No . . . no . . . I don't want Robbie to see me!' Yvonne said as she violently shook her head.

'It's all right, we don't have to go out if you don't want to,' Dorothy said soothingly. 'I'll sort out some of my clothes for you to wear for now, though they will probably be a bit big for you.'

'Th-thank you.'

'Robbie doesn't own you and you can't hide away for ever. You'll have to face the big wide world again one day,' Dorothy said firmly, thinking that she sounded like her mother with her no-nonsense attitude. 'I'll put some bread under the grill. Are you going to come downstairs for some breakfast?'

When Yvonne nodded, Dorothy stood up and said more kindly, 'All right, love, I'll see you downstairs in a bit.'

'He . . . he . . . he made me do bad things,' Yvonne cried out.

Dorothy sat down again and pulled Yvonne into her arms. 'It's all right, love, don't cry.'

'He said if I didn't do what he told me, he'd send some bad men to Clacton to beat up my mum and my sister,' Yvonne cried. 'And . . . and . . . he . . .'

Dorothy could feel the girl trembling in her arms and said soothingly, 'It's all right. You don't have to talk about it if you don't want to.'

'I'll tell you,' Yvonne choked out. 'When Robbie made me have sex with men, I didn't like it, but it made him happy and . . . and he's nice to me when he's happy. But . . . but on Saturday night he . . . he . . . brought two men back with him. Robbie told me I had to do what they wanted and then he went to wait outside. I didn't want to do it . . . it was nasty and I was scared. I said no, but . . . but they held me down . . .' Yvonne's body was wracked with sobs as she told Dorothy the sordid details. 'It hurt . . . it hurt so much and I screamed for Robbie, but he didn't come.'

Dorothy felt bile rise in her throat, but she had to hold herself together for Yvonne's sake. The bastard, she thought: rape, beatings, prostitution – Robbie's behaviour was so depraved that she wondered if she had ever really known him at all.

'I'm so sorry this happened to you, Yvonne,' she said. 'Those men were sick, they raped you and shouldn't be allowed to get away with it, nor should Robbie. I think you should report it to the police.'

'No, please don't make me,' Yvonne cried in panic, and began to tug at her hair.

'It's all right. I won't make you do anything you don't want to do, but what happened to you wasn't your fault,' Dorothy told her. She didn't blame Yvonne for not wanting to report the rape. From what she'd heard, the police and the courts would make the poor girl feel more like the criminal than the victim.

'Please, don't tell Adrian, or . . . or anyone,' Yvonne begged.

'I won't. I promise. Now, I know it won't be easy, but it's time to put this all behind you, and you won't be able to do that while you're lying in bed thinking about it. Come on, no more moping about, get yourself up for breakfast,' Dorothy said firmly, once again thinking that she sounded just like her mother.

After breakfast Dorothy put the television on and Yvonne watched it, fascinated. Dorothy said the programme was called *Mainly for Women*, and though she didn't really understand it, the pictures on the screen amazed her. The telephone rang in the hallway and the shrill sound made Yvonne jump.

'It's all right, it'll only be Adrian,' Dorothy said as she went to answer it.

Yvonne slumped with relief. She was still so scared – so frightened that Robbie would find her.

'Yes, she's fine,' she heard Dorothy say. 'OK, love, I'll see you later.'

Dorothy walked back into the lounge. 'Told you. Adrian always calls about this time, just to see if I'm OK.'

Yvonne found it nice. Nobody had ever cared for her that much, not even her own mum. Robbie said he did, but he had lied and he had let those men hurt her.

'I need to pop out to the shops for a few bits,' Dorothy said. 'It's all right, don't look so worried. I won't be long, but I'll call in next door first to ask Mrs Hart if she can sit with my dad.'

'I used to help my granny to look after my granddad. My mum couldn't, she was too busy working at the flour mill,' Yvonne answered, and beamed at the fuzzy feeling she got at the memory of her grandparents.

'In that case, maybe you can keep an eye on my dad. Do you think you could manage to do that?'

'Yes, it'll be nice to sit with him,' Yvonne said.

'Right then, I won't be long, but if anything happens, anything at all, call Adrian. I'll write his number next to the telephone.'

'You don't have to. I've remembered it,' Yvonne said proudly. 'I saw a number on the pad by the telephone and it said Adrian's office. I ain't that good with reading and writing, but I always knows my numbers. Mum used to say I'm as useless as a chocolate teapot, but with a head like an abacus. That's how I called you yesterday. I forgot the bit of paper, but I remembered the number.'

Yvonne wondered why Dorothy looked worried.

'So you don't have that bit of paper with you, the one I wrote my telephone number on?' Dorothy asked.

'No, I told you, I didn't need it 'cos I remembered it,' Yvonne said.

'Did you throw it away then?' Dorothy asked.

'No, it's in my purse in the kitchen. I thought it'd be safe there.'

'I'm sure it is,' Dorothy answered but Yvonne could tell there was something bothering the woman. She hoped she hadn't done anything wrong as the last thing she wanted was to upset the lovely people who had come to her aid.

'My dad should be fine, he's had his breakfast, and he's got his radio on, and, as I said, I won't be long.'

Dorothy left and, after peeking in Bill's room to see him dozing in his chair, Yvonne settled down to watch the telly again. Only about five minutes later, she heard someone hammering on the front door. Fearing it was Robbie, Yvonne huddled in the chair, but Dorothy had said she was safe here so maybe it wasn't him. She tiptoed towards the window to sneak a look through the net curtains, but was stopped in her tracks when she heard Robbie's voice shouting through the letterbox.

'Open the door! I know you're in there, Yvonne.'

Yvonne's heart felt as if it was going to thump right out of her chest. Frozen to the spot, her mind raced. Maybe she could call Adrian, but the phone was in the hallway and Robbie would see her. If she kept as quiet as a mouse and as still as a statue, maybe he'd go away. She closed her eyes, hardly daring to breathe, but then heard his voice again, louder this time and full of venom.

'If you don't open this fucking door, I'll break it down.'

Yvonne heard a thump from Dorothy's father's room and then a faint groan. Had the man fallen over? Her granddad had never done that and she didn't know what to do. Yvonne remained standing in the same spot while minutes passed. Dorothy said that Mrs Hart had looked after her dad, so if Robbie had gone, maybe she could run to her house and fetch her. Bill groaned again and knowing that she had to do something, Yvonne crept into the hall and nervously opened the front door, just enough to peep her head through.

In that moment, Robbie pushed hard on the door and before she knew it, he was standing in the hallway in front of her, his eyes blazing with anger. 'You thought you could do a runner, you stupid bitch, but you can't get away from me that easy!'

Yvonne wanted to tell him to go away, to leave her alone, but fear gripped her as she backed herself up against the wall. 'Go . . . go . . .' she gasped.

'No, and don't bother calling for Dottie. I know she's out, I saw her leave. It's no good calling for the old man in the back room either. He doesn't know his arse from his elbow so he won't be able to help you.'

'Pl-please, Robbie . . .'

'Please Robbie what?' he sneered. 'Spit it out.'

'I . . . I . . . don't want to be your girl no more,' Yvonne stuttered.

'Well, that's tough shit. The thing is, you owe me, Yvonne. All that new furniture, the fancy clothes, the rent money . . . it amounts to a fair few bob, so you'll have to work for me until you've paid back every last penny. I'm not a charity, and if you don't pay what's owed, you'll find I'm not a very nice man.'

Yvonne tried to make sense of what Robbie was saying. When he'd given her clothes and things, she didn't know she had to pay for them. He hadn't told her that. But now he wanted his money back, and she didn't have any money. Robbie reached out and grasped her arm and, too scared to fight him, her body slumped in submission.

'Good girl. Now let's get you back home with no fuss,' he said, leading her out to his car.

Yvonne looked up and down the street, but there was no sign of Dorothy. She felt so lost, so alone, as Robbie shoved her into the passenger seat. Dorothy had said she was safe here, but she wasn't, and now Robbie had come to take her away.

Chapter 40

Dorothy put her key in the front door and called out to Yvonne, 'It's only me,' knowing how jumpy the girl was and hoping to reassure her. She walked straight through to the kitchen and unloaded her shopping before putting the kettle on the stove.

'Would you like a drink, Yvonne?' she called. 'I've got us some nice fresh teacakes to go with it.'

That's funny, she thought. She could hear the television, but Yvonne hadn't answered. She walked through to the lounge and frowned at the sight of the empty room, so went to see if she was in with her father.

She found him sitting in his armchair, the newspaper he was looking at upside down, and, though it was still plugged in, the radio was lying on the floor. 'Hello, Dad. What happened, did you knock the radio off the table?'

'Man bang door.'

Dorothy was shocked to hear her dad's voice, but his words chilled her. She called out to Yvonne again, but there was no reply and with a sinking heart she realised the man banging on the door must have been Robbie. He had come for Yvonne and, after seeing the terror on the girl's face at the thought of bumping into him,

Dorothy knew there was no way she'd have gone voluntarily. Robbie must have forced her, with violence or the threat of it.

Dorothy worried that her dad might have witnessed it and been scared or upset, though he appeared perfectly settled now. 'Yes, Dad, a man banged on the door. Did you see him?'

Her dad had gone back into his own world and her question fell on deaf ears. It chilled her to think that he'd been left on his own, but he seemed fine. She worried about Yvonne though. She'd promised the girl a safe haven, and she couldn't bear to think about what would happen to her now that she was back with Robbie.

She dashed to the telephone to call Adrian, picked up the receiver and put it to her ear, but then quickly hung up. If Adrian went after Robbie there might be a fight. He was no match for Robbie and she didn't want him hurt. Robbie would never lay a hand on her, though, so she wasn't worried about herself. She'd ask Mrs Hart to sit with her dad, and then she'd grab a taxi to Robbie's place to confront him. He was no more than a sick, despicable pimp and she'd tell him that to his face.

Then she'd bring Yvonne back here again and there would be nothing that Robbie Ferguson could do to stop her.

Robbie paced the floor of their room, ranting at Yvonne, who was white-faced and shaking, but that didn't bother him. 'If you ever try to run off again, I'll skin you alive, you little slag.'

'I . . . I'm sorry, Robbie. I won't do it again.'

He rolled himself a cigarette and lit it before he

continued. 'You made a big mistake, Yvonne, but let that be the last. And if that bitch Dottie comes round here again you tell her to fuck off.'

'All right, Robbie.'

'Stop snivelling. You've got work to do later and I want you looking your best. Now wash your face and get yourself dolled up.'

Yvonne meekly did as he asked, and soon she was sorting through a bag of make-up, about to apply some, when there was a thump on the door. Robbie opened the door and scowled. 'I might have guessed, Florence flaming Nightingale. Come on a rescue mission, have you?'

'As it happens, yes, I have. I'm here for Yvonne,' Dorothy said resolutely.

'Bugger off, Dottie, and mind your own business,' Robbie snapped.

'Let me in. I want to talk to Yvonne.'

'You're not coming in and Yvonne's not coming out, so just go away.'

'I'm not going anywhere until I've seen her.'

Robbie opened the door wider and indicated the sofa, 'There, you've seen her. Now get out of my sight, you interfering, money-grabbing bitch!'

'Call me what you like, Robbie, but I'd never sink as low as you,' she spat, and then called, 'Yvonne, are you all right?'

'Ye-yes.'

'See, she's fine, but if you insist on talking to her, O righteous one, come on in. You've got two minutes.'

Dorothy stepped over the threshold and gave Robbie a dirty look before saying, 'Hey, Yvonne, are you sure you're all right?'

Yvonne looked at Robbie, and he narrowed his eyes at her. He was pleased when she said, 'Yes, s'pose so.'

'Don't worry about Robbie. He's just a low-life and he can't force you to stay here. Come with me, I'm taking you home,' Dorothy said gently, and held her hand out to Yvonne.

That really got Robbie's back up – the audacity of the woman! He quickly stepped between Dorothy and Yvonne, a snarl on his face.

'I don't know who you think you are, coming here and acting like you're better than me. Just remember, Dottie, I know you and you're nothing but a common little tart from the slums who married my brother for his money. You've as good as prostituted yourself to Adrian since the day you married him. Now take your airs and fucking graces and get out,' Robbie shouted as he pointed to the door.

'I'm not leaving without Yvonne,' Dorothy replied as she pushed her shoulders back in defiance.

Robbie stepped closer to her until there was just breathing space between them. He glared down at her face and warned, 'You *are* leaving without her, or do you want me to physically throw you out? Is that it? You like it rough? Does it turn you on?'

Dorothy stepped back. 'You disgust me, Robbie. Yvonne, come on, we're leaving.'

Dorothy reached out to pull Yvonne up, but Robbie acted quickly. He grabbed her arm tightly and said menacingly, 'I told you, she's not going anywhere.'

'Get off me, Robbie, you're hurting me,' Dottie said as she tried to yank her arm free.

'I could hurt you a whole lot more,' Robbie growled

before releasing her arm, 'but it's not going to come to that now, is it, Dottie?'

'You can't threaten me, Robbie. I'm not as gullible as Yvonne and I'm not scared of you. One way or another, I'm taking her with me.'

'Don't push me, Dottie, my patience is wearing thin. She doesn't want to go with you. Go on, tell her,' Robbie demanded, looking at Yvonne.

'I . . . I stay here.'

'See, you heard her,' Robbie said. 'Now bugger off, Dottie.'

'She only said that because she's too afraid to defy you. If you don't let her leave, I'll call the police. I'm sure they'd like to hear about your little prostitution racket, not to mention the robbery at the jeweller's that I heard about. It may have been some time ago, but I'm sure they'd still be interested.'

Robbie glared at Dottie, his temper at breaking point. It was all right for her, in his brother's nice house with all of Adrian's money, but what about him? He'd been left with nothing and had to make some cash one way or another. He was furious and as a black mist began to descend over his eyes, he lifted his hand and slapped Dorothy. 'I told you,' he screamed. 'Get out!'

She staggered sideways, her hand holding her cheek, as she stared at him dumbfounded.

For a moment he regretted hitting her, but the moment passed and he yelled, 'See, look what you made me do. Now piss off before I give you more of the same, and you'd be wasting your time calling the police. There's no proof that I robbed a jeweller's, and when I tell them I'm not a pimp, Yvonne will back me up.'

Dorothy just continued to stare at him as though transfixed, but then she lowered her head, stepped over to the door and walked out without a backward glance.

Dorothy's unsteady legs only just got her down the stairs. Once she was at the bottom, she grabbed hold of the newel post and paused to catch her breath. She felt her throbbing cheek with her hand, hardly believing Robbie had hit her.

Her mouth was dry and she felt sick to her stomach. She was close to tears and as she was near to where Nelly lived, she almost ran there.

Nelly's mother opened the door, and looked surprised to see her, but then her expression changed to concern. 'Gawd, love, what's wrong?'

Dorothy found herself unable to speak and almost staggered inside, where she collapsed in a heap on the sofa next to Nelly.

'Nelly, look after Dottie. I'm gonna make her a cup of hot sweet tea. She looks like she needs one.'

'Dottie, what's wrong?' Nelly asked worriedly. 'Has something happened to your dad . . . or Adrian?'

At last Dottie found her voice. 'Robbie came round while I was out and he took Yvonne. I . . . I went round to his place to get her back and . . . and he hit me.'

'He what?'

'I couldn't believe it. It's like he's a different person. Something's changed him. He's not the Robbie I used to know.'

'Dottie, he hasn't changed. He's always been a bad 'un. The difference is that now you're seeing him for what he really is.'

'I didn't think he was capable of violence, not Robbie.'

'Yeah, well, he isn't getting away with hitting you. Just you wait until I tell my Malcolm.'

'No, please, if Malcolm goes round there it'll only make things worse and any more violence might rebound on Yvonne. I'll have to find a way to go back there when Robbie's out and hopefully she'll agree to leave him again.'

'Leave it out, Dottie. He could come back while you're there and you can't risk that. If he's hit you once, he'll hit you again. You've got to tell Adrian, and I'll tell Malcolm. We'll leave it to the men to sort out.'

'No, no, Nelly, please don't say anything to Adrian. He's never been involved in fights and I don't want him going up against Robbie.'

'Look in the mirror, Dottie. You've got a big bruise coming up on your face and Adrian is going to see it. How are you going to explain it away?

'I'll think of something, but, more importantly, I've got to think of a way to get Yvonne away from Robbie,' Dorothy answered as her mind whizzed with ideas.

'No, Dottie, enough is enough. I won't let you put yourself in danger again. Sorry, sugar, but like it or not, if you won't tell Adrian, I will.'

With a feeling of defeat, Dorothy sat back on the sofa. Her head was pounding, her cheek burning, and her heart was broken. Even when she had confronted Robbie and seen how nasty he'd become, she had still believed she could reach him, that he still loved her as much as she did him.

She had stubbornly refused to believe the man she'd loved could really be such a monster and hoped in her heart, that, like her father, he would find his way back from the dark place.

Chapter 41

As usual, Adrian's desk was covered in a mountain of paperwork and he had to admit he missed Nelly. Thankfully, though she was still using a cane, her leg muscles were stronger and she was coming back to work next week.

When there was a knock on the office door he looked up to see Malcolm walking in. The man looked a bit uncomfortable, as if he wasn't looking forward to what he had to say.

'I thought you'd knocked off for the day,' Adrian said. 'Is there a problem, Malcolm?'

'Nelly wants to see you, and she said it's urgent.'

'Do you know why?'

'No, guv, she didn't say. I went round to have dinner at her place when I finished work but she sent me straight back here again.'

'All right, Malcolm. I'll lock up and go to see her. Do you need a lift?'

'No, thanks. I came on my motorbike.'

'I'll see you there then,' Adrian said, wondering what could be so urgent, and twenty minutes later he pulled up outside Nelly's house. The street was alive with young children playing hopscotch or kicking a ball around. Many had snotty noses, and most had dirty faces. He was instantly reminded that Dorothy had grown up like this, in dire poverty, yet she'd emerged through her struggles with such grace.

As he climbed out of his car he beckoned to a group of four boys who were playing marbles against the kerb. He reached into his trouser pocket, pulled out a coin, a shining sixpence, and said, 'If you look after my car and make sure that no one touches it, there'll be one of these for each of you.'

'Yes, mister,' said one of the lads. 'We can do that for you.' The rest of the boys nodded enthusiastically.

Nelly's mother showed Adrian into the small front room where Malcolm was sitting next to Nelly on a sofa. 'Am I glad to see you,' she said. 'Thanks for coming so quickly.'

'Malcom said it was urgent, so I came as soon as I could.'

'Sit down, Adrian. I've been up half the night thinking about this, and though Dottie doesn't want you to know, for her sake I just can't keep it to myself. What did she tell you about Yvonne leaving your place?'

'She said the girl had gone back to Robbie. I must admit I was surprised. I know she's young, but she's an adult so there isn't much we can do about it.'

'Yvonne didn't leave voluntarily,' Nelly said, going on to report what had really happened, along with Dottie's attempt to get her back.

When Adrian heard about Robbie hitting Dottie, his temper immediately flared. That explains her face, he thought, his teeth grinding. Dottie had said she'd walked into a door, but in truth his brother had dared to strike her. He wanted nothing more than to march round to Robbie's and batter his brother to a pulp, but he remained outwardly calm.

'So you can see why I had to tell you, because that stubborn wife of yours refuses to.'

'I don't know why.'

'She doesn't want you going up against Robbie and getting hurt, but I don't think you're the sort of man to let him get away with hitting Dottie.'

'No, I'm not,' Adrian said as visions flashed through his mind of kicking Robbie's head in. He could imagine his hands round his brother's throat as he squeezed tighter and tighter. He was usually a mild man and this was out of character, but his chest heaved with fury. 'I need to get some fresh air, Nelly. I'm so angry I'm seeing red and I can't think clearly.'

'No, wait,' Nelly said. 'I know what you're thinking of doing, and I'd like to wring Robbie's neck too, but—'

'Sorry, Nelly, I intend to get there first,' Adrian interrupted.

'No, Adrian. If you go round there the chances are you'd come off worse and that's the last thing Dottie needs. We both want Robbie to get his comeuppance, but you can't do it alone. You need a bit of muscle with you.'

'I fit that bill and I'll come with you,' Malcolm offered.

'Thanks, but this isn't your problem and I can't ask you to become involved.'

'You ain't asking. I'm offering.'

'Think about Dottie,' urged Nelly. 'I told you, Dottie doesn't want you hurt, but she wants to get Yvonne away from Robbie. You'll have more chance of doing that if Malcolm is with you.'

Adrian knew that Nelly was right and, though he wanted revenge for what his brother had done to Dottie, he doubted he'd be able to get Yvonne away from him without help. There had been a time when he had looked after Robbie, felt protective towards him, but now he questioned the way he and Myra had brought Robbie up after their parents died. Had they done something wrong? Had they indulged and spoiled him? Yet even if they had, surely that wouldn't have made him turn bad? He remembered Robbie's uncontrollable temper tantrums and the way he would kick the cat, or steal toys from other children. They had always made excuses for Robbie's bad behaviour, but, looking back, Adrian concluded Robbie must have been born that way: nasty, reckless and with an evil streak.

'All right, Malcolm. I'll accept your offer and thanks,' he said, then, realising that he couldn't have gone to sort Robbie out without his address, he added, 'Nelly, do you know where Robbie lives?'

'Yes,' Nelly answered, and told him where to go.

'Right, if it's all right with you, Malcolm, we'll go round there now.'

'Yes, that's fine, boss. Let's go.'

Robbie thought Yvonne looked sexy and felt a stir in his groin but was immediately put off by the thought of all the men she'd been with. No, he wouldn't go there again, even though he'd made sure she was always clean and protected. Even so, just the thought of all the punters turned his stomach. Yvonne was a good worker, he'd give her that, credit where credit's due, he thought, but he wasn't prepared to mix business with pleasure any more.

A knock on the door brought Robbie out of his thoughts. He wasn't expecting anyone, and his lips tightened. It had better not be Dorothy again. But when he opened the door, a man mountain filled it. 'Hello, Malcolm. Have you come to take me up on my offer?'

The man took a menacing step towards him, but then Adrian pushed him to one side. 'It's all right, Malcolm. I'll deal with this and I think you know why *I'm* here, Robbie.'

Robbie shrugged. 'If it's about that little incident with Dottie yesterday, well, I'm sorry, it was an accident, but you need to keep that wife of yours on a leash. She's out of order coming round here and laying down the law.'

'I ought to knock your bloody head off for what you did to her. How dare you hit my wife and try to fob it off as an accident!'

Robbie had never seen Adrian so wound up. Even when annoyed he usually came over as placid, but now his eyes were blazing with anger. 'All right, calm down. I said I'm sorry, so what more do you want?'

Adrian turned to Yvonne. 'Get your things together. You're coming with me.'

'No, she isn't,' Robbie argued.

'Yes, she is, and if you try to stop her from leaving I'll let Malcolm loose on you,' Adrian warned. 'And another thing, if you dare to come round to my house again, you'll live to regret it.'

Robbie looked on angrily as the flustered Yvonne shoved clothes into a bag. She couldn't leave, he needed her, but he wasn't stupid enough to think he could get past Malcolm. The man was built like a brick shithouse.

Within minutes, Yvonne scurried out of the door, and then Malcolm marched up to Robbie, and said, 'This is for Dottie.'

Before Robbie had time to react, a huge fist landed, the force of the punch almost knocking him off his feet, and he staggered backwards, recoiling in pain. He held his hands over his bleeding nose and hazily saw Adrian leaving. He shook his head, trying to clear it, and then raced after him.

'Adrian,' he shouted from the top of the stairs as his brother reached the landing on the floor below, 'you can't do this!'

Adrian stopped and looked back, his eyes flickering to the room behind his brother. Robbie quickly turned and the movement made him dizzy. He saw Malcolm reach out for him, stepped back to avoid his grasp but lost his footing. Arms flailing and unable to save himself, Robbie tumbled backwards down the stairs. He could feel every bump and thud as each step bashed into his bones and threw his body around into unnatural shapes, until he landed with a sickening crash that knocked the air out of his body. Almost unconscious, he lay in a twisted and broken heap at the bottom of the stairs. He opened his eyes to see Adrian leaning over him with a concerned expression, and he groaned in pain.

'Don't move, Robbie, I'm going to call an ambulance,' Adrian instructed before disappearing from view.

Robbie wanted to turn his head to see where his brother had gone, but it wouldn't move. From where he was lying he could see his leg, but, to his horror, his foot was facing the wrong way. It was strange; everything hurt yet felt numb at the same time. Confused, he closed his eyes again and the last thing he remembered was hearing Yvonne's shrill scream before he fell into unconsciousness.

Chapter 42

Dinner was ready and, as Adrian was much later than usual, Dorothy was keeping it warm. At last, hearing a car pull up outside, she went to the window to see Adrian get out, followed by Yvonne and Malcolm. How had that happened? Had Yvonne run away from Robbie again? Had Adrian seen her and stopped to pick her up? And Malcolm – what was he doing here?

She ran to open the door, but when she looked at Adrian he was troubled and pale. 'What's going on?' she asked, 'How have—'

Adrian interrupted her. 'Come and sit down, Dottie, we've just got back from the hospital and I've got something to tell you.'

'What's wrong? Do you feel ill?' she asked worriedly.

'No, I'm fine, but there's been a terrible accident,' he said. He turned to Yvonne. 'I know you're upset, but would you go through to the kitchen to make a pot of tea?'

Yvonne looked hesitant, but then nodded before she scuttled off. Then Adrian turned to Malcolm.

'Nelly must be worried. Take my car, tell her what happened and then bring her back here. Speak to no one except Nelly, do you understand?' Adrian said with authority.

'Yes, guv,' Malcolm answered with his head lowered, and he took Adrian's keys and left.

'Please, Adrian, you're scaring me. Tell me what's happened,' Dorothy asked urgently.

'Don't be angry with Nelly, but she told me what Robbie did to you. You should have told me, Dottie, and you shouldn't have gone to his place alone.'

Dorothy could tell from his tone that he wasn't angry with her, and said, 'I know and I'm sorry, but please, tell me what's going on.'

'I took Malcolm with me and we went to see Robbie. We went for two reasons. One, to have it out with him for hitting you, and two, to get Yvonne back. I must admit I was furious with Robbie, and I was happy to see Malcolm give him a punch, but the retaliation stopped at that.'

Adrian's voice was shaky and Dorothy feared there was more. He paused for a moment, and her fears were realised when he reached out to take her hand before he spoke again.

'Dottie, Robbie's been hurt. It was all so quick, I'm not quite sure what happened, but Robbie fell down the stairs.'

'Oh, no! Is he OK?' Dorothy blurted out.

'No, Dottie, he's not. He's alive, but he'll never walk again.'

Dorothy instantly yanked her hand away and walked to the window to hide her face from her husband, afraid he would see how upset she was. She was fighting back tears and felt as though her breath was caught in her throat, rendering her unable to speak.

'Dottie, it was an unfortunate accident, but the police will want to talk to me. I've spoken to Malcolm and

Yvonne, and we've all agreed not to mention the prostitution, or that Robbie hit you. We'll simply say he tripped, and in all honesty, from what I saw, that's the truth.'

'But what about Robbie?' Dorothy managed to say, 'Will he say the same?'

'I don't see why not. He's hardly going to tell the police that he's a pimp and that Malcolm punched him in retaliation for hitting you. And anyway, that had nothing to do with him falling down the stairs.'

'You said Robbie's never going to walk again. Does that mean he's totally paralysed?'

'Not from the neck, but he's paralysed from the waist down. He'll be in hospital for quite some time, and when he comes out he'll be in a wheelchair.'

Dorothy felt dizzy and the room began to sway. She edged sideways and grabbed hold of the curtain to steady herself, but then felt Adrian's arms supporting her.

'Here, sit down. I know it's been a bit of a shock for you, for all of us, but when Robbie leaves hospital, he'll need our help. He won't be able to go back to that top-floor room in Grant Street, and Myra won't be able to look after him. He'll have to come here.'

Dorothy looked up into Adrian's eyes. She'd always found them so kind and gentle, but now she thought there was something in them that she hadn't seen before. She couldn't put her finger on it, but, as he quickly looked away, she wondered if it was guilt. A terrifying thought crossed her mind. Had Adrian deliberately disabled his brother? Or, even worse, had he tried to kill him?

Nelly put her flabby arms around Malcolm and held him to her generous bosom as he broke down and sobbed like a baby. My big teddy bear, she thought, loving what a softie he was and desperately wanting to take away his pain. 'It's all right, darling. From what you've told me, it wasn't your fault,' she said tenderly.

'But you should have seen him, Nel. I've never seen anything like it . . . just lying there, all twisted the wrong way . . . it was . . . weird. I swear, Nel, I didn't push him. I was trying to grab him, but he stepped away from me and . . . and just fell.'

'I know, I know, shush now,' she said and rubbed her hand up and down his back. It broke her heart to see Malcolm so upset. Though some might think her hard, she didn't care about Robbie. As far as she was concerned, the man got what he deserved.

'He's in a bad way, Nelly. Robbie can't move his legs and when the doctor spoke to Adrian he said that Robbie's spine is so badly damaged that there's little chance of recovery.'

'So he's going to be in a wheelchair now?'

'Oh, Nel, if Robbie never walks again I'll never forgive myself.' Malcolm began crying again.

Nelly pushed him away from her and looked him straight in the eyes before saying firmly, 'Malcolm, you've got to stop blaming yourself. You didn't push Robbie. He fell, so come on now, pull yourself together and take me round to Dottie's.'

Malcolm nodded but still sounded very sorry for himself when he said, 'Yeah, Nel, you're right, as usual. I'm acting like a stupid baby. Sorry, love, I don't like you seeing me like this.'

'It shows you've got a heart, you big oaf,' she told him, which was more than anyone could say about Robbie

Ferguson. He'd put a young girl on the game to line his own pockets, and to Nelly that was unforgivable. If a woman wanted to sell herself for money, that was her decision, but to be forced into it was a different matter.

Yvonne had made a pot of tea, and while Adrian and Dottie were talking she retreated upstairs to the bedroom she'd stayed in for just one night. She sat on the bed, pulled her knees to her chest and rocked back and forth, unable to forget the sight of Robbie's broken body lying at the foot of the stairs. She hadn't wanted that to happen to him, but at least he wouldn't be able to make her do things with men any more. She stretched out on the bed, tired from all that had happened that day, but she hadn't had anything to eat and was too hungry to sleep. She didn't want to go back to that room in Grant Road; she wanted to stay here. She curled into a ball, fearing that soon they would tell her to leave. Yvonne had no idea how long she'd been lying there before there was a tap on the door.

'Can I come in, Yvonne?' called Dorothy.

'Yes,' she called back.

When the woman walked in Yvonne could see that she'd been crying, but when she spoke, her words made her feel very happy.

'I'm glad that Adrian brought you back here and you're welcome to stay. If you're hungry, come downstairs. I'm afraid dinner is a bit dried up, but it's still edible. Nelly and Malcolm will be back soon to talk about the . . . the accident so I'd like us to eat before they arrive.'

'Fanks, I'm a bit starving,' Yvonne said as she scrambled off the bed. 'I want to stay here, I really do, but does Adrian think it's all my fault?'

'No, love, of course he doesn't. Robbie brought this on himself. It wasn't anybody's fault except his own. So I don't want you hiding away in this room for ever. I'll do a deal with you – you help me look after my dad and I'll help you get your life back on track,' Dorothy said and held out her hand.

'Deal,' Yvonne replied.

'Good,' Dottie said. 'It'll make my life so much easier if I don't have to ask Mrs Hart to sit with him every time I go out.'

Yvonne clapped her hands with excitement. 'I'd like to do that,' she said, and for the first time in a while she smiled happily.

Chapter 43

It had been six weeks since Robbie's accident but Dorothy still hadn't managed to bring herself to visit him in hospital. When she'd first heard about the accident, she had planned to go, but when it came to it, she couldn't face seeing Robbie so badly injured.

Adrian kept trying to encourage her, saying it would be good to clear the air with Robbie before he came home, but she fobbed him off with feeble excuses. It was strange: each time Adrian referred to Robbie, a black look would veil his eyes, one that she couldn't fathom. She'd thought at first it was hatred for his brother, but now she chastised herself and regretted thinking so badly of him. It was probably guilt, she decided, though, from what she'd been told, Adrian had nothing to feel guilty about.

She heard a key in the front door and checked the time on the mantelpiece clock. It was already twelve-thirty, and she wondered where the morning had gone. 'Hello, love, have you had a good day?' Dorothy asked Yvonne.

Yvonne threw herself back on the sofa next to Dorothy and kicked off her shoes, saying, 'Yes, but my feet ache.'

'Put your feet up and I'll make us a cuppa,' Dorothy said and walked through to the kitchen. Yvonne had found herself a part-time cleaning job that wasn't far away, in a big, fancy house near Battersea Park. She appeared to really enjoy the work and was coming out of her shell.

As the kettle began to whistle, Dottie thought it might be a good time to have the conversation with Yvonne, the one she had been dreading. When the drinks were made she drew in a steadying breath and carried them through to the lounge. 'Here you are,' she said, handing her a cup. 'While you're drinking that, there's something I want to talk to you about. Now, the thing is, according to Adrian, the doctors have said that Robbie can leave hospital soon, probably in a week or two. His sister lives in Scotland, but, with three children and a house full of lodgers, she can't take him in. There's nobody else, so it means that Robbie is going to have to move in here.'

'In here? With us?'

'It's that or an institution, and as I think Adrian feels partly responsible for what happened to Robbie, he's offered him a home. I know it won't be easy for you, but if you think you can cope with it, you're more than welcome to stay.'

'I . . . I don't know, Dottie. I really like living here, and I love looking after Bill now and then. He's such a funny old sod . . . but living with Robbie again? I don't think I could . . .'

Dorothy didn't want Yvonne to leave. She wasn't bright, but she had a nice nature and Dorothy enjoyed her company. More importantly, the girl had managed to bring her father on in leaps and bounds. He responded well to Yvonne, more so than he did to anyone else, and Dorothy worried he would slip backwards if she left. 'I know it's a big ask, but I'd love you to stay and I know my father would too. Give it some thought. After all, Robbie isn't the man he used to be. He can't hurt you now or make you do anything you don't want to.'

'All right, I-I'll think about it,' Yvonne replied.

That was good enough for Dorothy for now, though it did make her think. She'd told Yvonne that Robbie wasn't like he used to be, but she didn't know that for sure. Just because he'd lost the use of his legs, it didn't mean he wasn't still capable of nastiness. Maybe it was time to bite the bullet and go to see him in hospital – if only to put her mind at rest.

Robbie had come to accept that he would never walk again, yet he persisted in trying and wasn't prepared to give up yet. As he lay in his hospital bed, he lifted his head and looked at his feet, willing them to move. 'Shit,' he muttered, exasperated, as yet again his feet refused his command.

He rested his head back on the pillow and closed his eyes. At least he still had use of his manhood – an unexpected display of morning glory had proved that. It had been a concern for him, but he hadn't been able to bring himself to ask the doctors. Thankfully, this morning's event had answered his question. He wasn't sure how he'd manage to perform without the use of his legs, but surely there'd be a tart out there who'd take on the leading role. In the meantime he could still use his hands and that would have to do.

It wouldn't be long until he was discharged from

hospital and went to live with Adrian and Dottie, but then what? He could at least use the toilet unaided, and mostly dress himself, but what about getting out and about? He didn't want to become a prisoner, unable to pop down to the pub, like Dottie's father, who was stuck in a room day in and day out. It wasn't so bad for the old man, he was as nutty as a fruitcake and didn't seem aware of anything around him, but Robbie knew it would be different for him. He was young, with his whole life in front of him, but his future had been ruined. He'd have been better off if the fall had killed him, he thought bitterly, feeling sorry for himself.

'Hello, Robbie,' someone said, interrupting his thoughts.

Robbie instantly recognised Dorothy's voice, but kept his eyes closed. If she thought he was asleep, she'd go away.

'It's no good pretending. I know you're awake.'

He snapped his eyes open. 'Yes, well, I'm pretending for a reason. Doesn't that tell you something?'

'Can't we just talk civilly for a while? Adrian tells me you'll be coming home soon and I wanted to see you to clear the air.'

Robbie glared at Dorothy. He had to admit she looked knockout, but 'clear the air' – who was she kidding?

'What you mean is, you want to know if I blame you for what has happened to me. Well, then, I'll tell you. Yes, I do. If you'd kept your nose out of my business, none of this would have happened.'

'But I couldn't stand by and let you get away with what you were doing to Yvonne. It wasn't right, Robbie, and now that you've had time to think about it, surely you can see that?'

Robbie's temper was rising and he ground out, 'For fuck's sake, who are you to lecture me?'

'There's no need to use foul language.'

'I'll swear if I want to, especially in front of the likes of you,' he sneered. 'You can come down off that high horse because I know you for what you are. As I've said before, you're a slum girl who's gone up in the world because you married a man with money, but one day my brother will wise up to you and then you'll be out on your ear. Let's see how you cope when you're left with nothing . . . just as I was. You'll be back where you started and I can't wait to see that happen.'

'You can accuse me of it as many times as you like, Robbie, but I didn't marry your brother for his money, and another thing, he'll never throw me out, because he loves me.'

'Yes, but do *you* love him?' Robbie snapped, and when Dottie just looked down at the floor he smiled triumphantly. 'No, I thought not. You might have pulled the wool over Adrian's eyes, but you can't kid a kidder. Now do me a favour and piss off!'

'I can't bear it when you talk to me like this, Robbie, and I don't think I'll be able to stand living in the same house if we don't get on.'

Robbie realised that he'd gone too far and fought to rein in his anger. If Dottie told Adrian that she didn't want him to move in, then his brother would withdraw his offer. He couldn't risk it, not if he wanted to stay out of a care home. 'Look, I'm sorry,' he forced out, 'but I'm in a lot of pain and it makes me short-tempered. I shouldn't be taking it out on you.'

'Oh, Robbie, it's all right. I understand.'

He was pleased to see that her eyes were full of unshed tears, and almost smiled at what a daft, soft cow she was. Not only that, when he'd asked if she loved Adrian he had hit a raw nerve and found her vulnerability. When he went to live with her, it was sure to be useful, but for now he'd keep it under his belt. He'd fooled her for now, but he didn't want to keep up this façade. To get rid of her he said, 'I'm sorry, I'm tired, so would you mind leaving now?'

'No, of course not. Bye, Robbie,' she said softly.

'See you,' he said and as she walked away Robbie watched her shapely hips swing from side to side. He had to admit that Dottie was a lovely-looking woman, but she had ruined his life and he would do all he could to make hers an absolute bloody misery.

'Good afternoon, Ferguson Haulage. How may I help you?' Nelly said as she answered the telephone. 'Yes, sir, if you could hold the line for just one moment, I'll have that information for you.'

Nelly held her hand over the Bakelite mouthpiece and beckoned to Adrian. 'When is Joe due to drop at Smythe's and Co? I've got a right miserable git on the phone chasing him up . . .'

Adrian fumbled through some paperwork and answered, 'That's Joe's last delivery, he should be there within the hour.'

Nelly removed her hand, and passed on the information, ending the call with, 'If there's anything else I can help you with please don't hesitate to call again. Good day, sir.'

As she replaced the receiver, Adrian said, 'Well, I never.

Nelly, that was spot on. You almost had me believing you're the Queen's cousin! I've got to hand it to you, you've come on leaps and bounds and I'm chuffed to hear you answering the telephone so eloquently.'

Nelly chuckled. 'What the bleedin' 'ell does "eloquently" mean? Oops, sorry for swearing and dropping my aitches. I still slip up at times.'

'Never mind,' said Adrian, and shook his head. It was good to have Nelly back at work. There had been so much misery lately, and he was worried about the future, but he could always depend on Nelly to put a smile on his face.

Adrian could see Nelly's thick legs jigging under her desk, and she was tapping her fingers on the edge of her typewriter, which was beginning to grate on him.

'Nelly, what's on your mind?' Adrian asked. 'You haven't stopped fidgeting since lunchtime.'

'I'm so excited, I think I might burst,' Nelly answered.

'I can see that, but please don't, it would make a hell of a mess,' Adrian said jokingly.

'Adrian, do you mind if I pop round to see Dottie after work? I've got something to tell her.'

'You could ring her. I won't charge you for the call,' Adrian jested.

'I want to see her face when I tell her my news.'

Adrian's brows rose. 'Well, come on then, spit it out.'

'We've set a date for the wedding,' Nelly said, smiling happily.

'When's it to be?'

'We didn't want a long engagement, so we're getting married in May.'

Adrian only had to think about it for a moment before

he said, 'Well then, you might as well go to see Dottie now.'

'But it's only four o'clock.'

'I know, but if you leave now, by the time I arrive home all the talk of dresses and flowers and venues will be done and dusted so I can eat my dinner in peace.'

Nelly rose to her feet, put her coat on and picked up her handbag. As she hurried out she called, 'Adrian, you might have an ulterior motive for letting me leave early, but you're a diamond and I love you.'

Adrian knew Nelly didn't mean it in the same way, but he wished Dottie would say those words to him. He rubbed his hands across his face, fearing it would never happen. He worried that he was mad bringing Robbie to live with them, but what choice did he have? He couldn't see his brother going into an institution, but he was concerned that Dottie still harboured feelings for him.

Chapter 44

The first thing Robbie noticed was that the front step had been adapted. Adrian had obviously gone out of his way to make the house wheelchair friendly, but Robbie didn't feel any gratitude towards his brother. When Adrian pushed his wheelchair into the living room where Dorothy and Yvonne were standing, he said mockingly, 'Ah, the welcoming committee. You needn't have bothered to make such an effort for the cripple.'

Dorothy paled, but said, 'We've put a bed in what was my father's sitting room for you, and Adrian managed to find builders to do a rush job so there's a small bathroom too with everything you need.'

'I see, so there's a new set of legs in there for me?' he asked.

'That's enough, Robbie,' said Adrian. 'Dottie has been working hard to get everything prepared for you and you could at least thank her.'

'Oh, I'm so sorry, where are my manners? Thank you, Dottie, thank you for instigating my so-called *accident,* and thank you for reminding me that I'll have to sleep downstairs as I can't walk up the fucking stairs.'

'I said, enough!' Adrian barked, and proceeded to push Robbie through to Bill's old room.

'You don't need to push me. I may be stuck in a wheelchair, but I'm working on strengthening my arms and shoulders,' Robbie barked. The thought of being dependent on Adrian and, worse, Dottie was abhorrent to him. He was growing stronger by the day and he was determined to gain as much independence as possible.

'Until you do, it's no problem,' Adrian said.

'I said I can manage,' he growled, taking control of the chair, and as he manoeuvred it past Dottie he glared at her with all the venom he felt inside. This was all her doing and he'd make sure she never forgot it. The bitch, he thought, he'd see her downfall soon enough. He'd make sure she hated seeing him in his wheelchair as much as he loathed being in it.

As Robbie disappeared, Dottie sat down, reeling from the way he had spoken to her.

'I'm sorry, Dottie. I can't believe Robbie behaved like that.'

'It wasn't your fault. He'll come round eventually. He can't be that angry for ever,' Dottie said, but she had seen the look in Robbie's eyes, a look so hateful that it physically hurt her.

'I hope you're right,' said Adrian as he sat down to light his pipe. Smoke billowing round him, he continued, 'Or he's going to make life difficult for us. Are you sure you can cope with him? I feel like I'm asking too much of you.'

'I'll manage,' Dorothy said, 'and anyway, what choice do we have? We can hardly pack him off to your sister in Scotland, and it wouldn't be right to put him in a home. At the end of the day, he's still family.'

'Dottie, I've said it before and I'll say it again, you're an amazing woman. To take this on after everything my brother has done, along with caring for your father, well, you astound me.'

'My dad doesn't need a lot of care. He mostly just needs watching to make sure he doesn't wander off. I've got Yvonne to help me with that now, haven't I, love?' she said, turning to the young woman.

'Yes, I like helping. I'll pop up and see if Bill's all right,' Yvonne answered and left the room.

'Thanks, love. Try to encourage him to come downstairs. It might do him good,' Dorothy suggested, just as the sound of Elvis Presley singing 'Hound Dog' blasted out. She'd put Robbie's old record player in his room, but hadn't expected him to play his discs at full blast.

'That's a bit much,' Adrian commented.

The music was so loud that Dottie struggled to hear what Adrian said, but if she asked Robbie to turn it down, he would probably snap at her again. It was in that moment she realised that life was going to be very different from now, and probably far from perfect.

Yvonne was glad to be upstairs with Bill. It was a sanctuary from Robbie downstairs, and it gave Adrian and Dorothy some private time to talk.

She'd been nervous about seeing Robbie again. The thought had kept her awake for many nights, and when she had slept it had been fretful, full of nightmares about him and what he'd made her do. Yet now that she'd seen Robbie, and knew it was really true, Yvonne felt she'd sleep soundly. Robbie couldn't get upstairs to her room. He couldn't walk. It made her feel something she hadn't felt before, and though Yvonne couldn't put her finger on it, she felt empowered and smiled.

'Hiya, Bill. How are we today?' she asked.

'See garden.'

'Robbie's in the back room now, but it's a nice day so if you get dressed you can sit outside.'

Bill slowly climbed out of bed and put his slippers on. He shuffled over to the window and looked down, a wide smile appearing on his face. 'Lots tulips.'

'Yes, and them yellow things.'

'Daffodils.'

Yvonne knew that Bill was going to miss his sitting room. She'd grown fond of him and didn't want to see him upset, especially if it was because of Robbie. 'You go and have a wash. I'll make your bed,' she offered.

'Where's my suit?'

'What do you want your suit for?' Yvonne asked, puzzled. Bill couldn't go anywhere alone and rarely wanted to leave the house.

'Special day.'

'What's special about today?'

'Baby,' Bill said, his face beaming.

'Baby?' Yvonne asked, more confused than ever. 'Who's having a baby?'

'You are, silly. You're having baby,' Bill said, looking delighted.

Yvonne stood in stunned silence. When her monthlies stopped she didn't know why, but now Bill was saying she was having a baby. How did he know? Her mind was all over the place and she flopped down on the side of

Bill's bed. She knew that women's bellies swelled when they were having a baby and now ran her hand over her own and felt a small lump. No, no, she thought frantically. If Dottie and Adrian found out they might throw her out and she had nowhere to go. She'd have to hide it from them.

'Baby,' Bill said again, pointing at her stomach.

'Shush, it's a secret. You mustn't tell anyone,' Yvonne pleaded.

'Secret,' he repeated.

'Yes, that's right,' Yvonne said, hoping that it was a secret she could keep for a long, long time.

Chapter 45

Dorothy sat dabbing her watery eyes and turned to smile at Adrian. She'd found the lovely May wedding ceremony quite moving, even amidst the chaos of Nelly's nieces and nephews running around and causing havoc.

Adrian returned her smile and gently stroked the back of her hand.

'Doesn't Nelly look gorgeous,' Dorothy whispered.

'Yes, and it's nice to see her so happy.'

With the officiating completed, Nelly and Malcolm stood on the steps of Wandsworth Register Office. Nelly had her arm linked through Malcolm's and was holding a small bouquet of pink roses with white gypsophila. The colour of the roses perfectly matched her pale pink dress, secured with a wide white belt, and she wore a white crocheted bolero jacket over her shoulders.

Dorothy pulled her Brownie camera from her handbag. 'I knew this present you bought me would come in handy,' she said to Adrian, then called to the newly-weds, 'Say cheese.'

'Dottie, I'd like a photo with you and Adrian,' Nelly said, beckoning her friend over.

Dottie turned to Yvonne. They hadn't wanted to leave

her out, so they had asked Mrs Hart to sit with her father and the woman had kindly agreed. 'Yvonne, if I show you how to work the camera, do you think you could take a photo?'

'I'll give it a go,' she agreed.

The camera wasn't hard to use and, when Yvonne seemed to have grasped it, Dottie went to stand alongside Nelly, and Adrian stood next to Malcolm.

'Cheese,' Yvonne called, and they all beamed, but suddenly the girl placed the camera on the floor and fled to the other side of the building.

Puzzled, Dottie ran after her to find her around a corner. She was bent over and holding onto a wall as she vomited. 'You all right, love?' Dottie asked, concerned, as she walked up to her.

Yvonne jumped, obviously startled, and when she looked up Dottie could see that her face was drained of colour. 'I . . . I'm fine. It . . . it must be something I had to eat.'

'Here,' said Dorothy, offering the girl her handkerchief. 'You had the same as me this morning, just a bit of toast and marmalade, so I don't think it's your breakfast that's upset your stomach.'

'It's all right now.'

Dorothy couldn't help noticing that Yvonne looked nervous and she was avoiding eye contact as though she had something to hide. In fact, when she thought about it, Yvonne had been acting strangely for a while now. It had started when Robbie had come to live with them, so she'd put it down to that, but that had been about a month ago. She looked at the baggy blouse Yvonne was wearing and it was then that the penny dropped. 'Yvonne, are you having a baby?'

For a moment Yvonne said nothing, her head low, but then she nodded.

'How far gone are you?'

'It's not gone. It's here,' Yvonne answered as she pointed at her stomach.

Dottie heaved a sigh. 'How many times have you missed your period?'

'Lots of times.'

Dorothy knew she would have to take Yvonne to see a doctor and her heart went out to her. She had been in this situation herself and knew how she'd be treated as an unmarried mother. Though it was a cruel thing to cross her mind, she felt that Yvonne would be better off if she lost this baby too. Yvonne had slept with any number of men and, though it seemed a bit pointless to ask, she still posed the question. 'Yvonne, I don't suppose you have any idea who the father is?'

'Of course I do!' Yvonne replied indignantly, 'Robbie's the dad.'

Dorothy gasped but tried to hide her shock. 'Considering how many men you slept with, how can you be sure?'

'Robbie was the first one who did it to me, and . . . and he didn't use anything, but when he made me sleep with other men, he told them they had to use a . . . a thing he called a Johnnie. He said it would stop me from having a baby, but I am, so it must be his,' Yvonne wailed as tears flooded her eyes. 'Are you going to chuck me out now?'

'No, of course not. This isn't your fault, it's his, and for goodness' sake stop crying,' Dottie said, rather more sternly than she meant. Robbie had left her pregnant too, but this time he wouldn't get away with it. He'd be there to face the music. 'Now come on, pull yourself together. We don't want to spoil Nelly's big day so we'll keep it quiet for now. I'll talk to Adrian tonight and we'll work out what's the best thing to do.'

As they walked back to join the others, Dottie's emotions were all over the place. Robbie had been a complete pig to live with this last month, constantly insulting her whenever he could and going out of his way to be inconsiderate. Her patience was beginning to wear thin and she'd been wondering how much more she could take. Yet, on hearing that Yvonne was having his baby, jealousy burned and her buried emotions resurfaced once again. Though Dottie hated to admit it, and raged against her feelings, she wished it was her who was carrying Robbie's child.

Adrian was pleased to put his feet up and relax in his armchair. It had been a nice day but a long one, and with the cost of the cake, the celebratory meal and Dorothy and Yvonne's new outfits, it had been an expensive day too. Not that he minded; he'd enjoyed seeing Nelly and Malcolm so happy together, and it reminded him of the day he'd married Dottie.

As Dorothy came into the lounge, he noticed the frown on her face and wondered why she looked so worried. Robbie couldn't have upset her as he wasn't in, probably in some seedy pub spending his 'pocket money' on a game of cards. So what had happened to put that look of consternation on his wife's pretty face?

'We need to talk,' Dorothy said as she sat on the sofa. 'It's Yvonne and you're not going to believe this, Adrian. She's pregnant.'

Adrian nearly choked on his pipe. 'What?' he spluttered. 'You have got to be kidding me. Who's the father?'

'Please, keep your voice down. I know Yvonne's upstairs but she still might hear you. As for the father, she said it's Robbie's baby.'

Adrian cleared his throat, thinking hard. Yvonne wasn't really their problem, but if Robbie was the father of her unborn child, then that put things in a whole different light, though he doubted Robbie would agree to marry the girl.

'Bloody hell, Dottie . . . sorry for swearing, but, well, I'm at a loss for words. Robbie will have to be told, and I hope he does the decent thing, but I think we both know that won't happen.'

'No, I can't see him agreeing to marry her.'

'With Yvonne living here, it's going to make things very awkward.'

'I know, but this isn't her fault and we can't throw her out.'

'Of course not. She'll stay, have the baby and then we'll help her to support the child.'

'The more I think about it,' Dottie said, 'the more I realise how hard it's going to be for Yvonne. You know what people are like when it comes to unmarried mothers. She'll not only lose her little cleaning job, she'll be shunned. At least talk to Robbie and try to make him see that he's got to marry her.'

Adrian rubbed his chin. Dorothy was right in what she said, but he doubted that his brother would listen to him. 'All right, I'll talk to him, but I can't force him to marry her. I suppose I could threaten to kick him out, but you know how obstinate he can be.' Adrian paused to relight his pipe. 'Still, you never know, Robbie might be over the moon to find out he's going to be a father.'

Dorothy looked doubtful, but nevertheless he'd talk to Robbie when he came home. He had to try, and not just for Yvonne's sake.

'It's getting late so why don't you go on up to bed?' he said gently. 'I think it's best I talk to Robbie alone so I'll wait up for him.'

'All right,' Dottie agreed, leaning down to kiss him. 'Night, love.'

Adrian said goodnight and then poured himself a large whisky. It had been a long day, and now it looked like it would turn into an equally long night.

Robbie slammed the front door behind him, hoping it would disturb the rest of the house. He'd worked hard on improving his physique and was pleased with the width of his shoulders and the way his biceps bulged. However it had been impossible to find a cab and despite his new bulk his arms ached from wheeling himself home from the pub. At least the roads had been clear so he'd used them rather than the pavements and it had saved him from trying to tackle the challenging kerbs.

He wheeled himself into the sitting room and was surprised to see Adrian asleep in an armchair.

'Ha, she's chucked you out of the bed then?' Robbie said with a sneer into his brother's ear.

Adrian woke up, shaking his head to clear it. 'Robbie, you're home, good.'

'Yes, I'm home, but there's nothing good about it,' Robbie said, 'I'm going to bed, so sweet fucking dreams to you.'

'Wait,' Adrian called, 'we need to have a little chat.'

This could be interesting, thought Robbie. It must be important for Adrian to have waited up. He wheeled his chair over to the sideboard and poured himself the last of the whisky. 'Come on then, out with it,' he said, then knocked back his drink, expecting to get another earful about his bad language and being nicer to Dorothy.

'Robbie, I know life hasn't turned out how you were expecting it to, but that wheelchair isn't the end, you know.'

'What are you going on about? It's a bit late for any pep talks about my legs, and anyhow, it's you that put me in this thing so you're the last person I want any advice from,' Robbie said and swung his chair to leave the room.

'Robbie, you have a child on the way,' Adrian blurted out.

Shocked, Robbie stopped in his tracks and, unable to take it in, he said, 'I think you'd better elaborate on that.'

'It's Yvonne, she's pregnant with your baby. I'm hoping that for once in your life you'll do the right thing and marry the girl.'

Adrian sounded as pompous as usual and Robbie started laughing.

'What's wrong with you? I've just told you that you're going to be a father and you find it funny?'

'It's not being a father I find funny. It's the bit where you think I would marry that tart. Yvonne's a fucking whore and, baby or not, I'd never marry her.' Robbie paused, his eyes narrowing. 'And anyhow, who's to say it's mine? I'm telling you, the amount of blokes she's had, her knickers have been up and down more times than the big dipper ride in Battersea Park funfair.'

'Robbie, you disgust me. Yvonne only slept with men because you forced her into it. For goodness' sake, she's carrying your child and this is a chance for you to turn things around. You could have a family of your own, and being in a wheelchair won't stop you from being a good father.'

'Don't lecture me, Adrian. Do you think this wheelchair stops me from finding women? Well, newsflash, it doesn't, and the tackle is all in good working order. There's plenty out there who'd take pity on a poor cripple, so don't think for one minute that I couldn't have kids if I want them, but I don't. So I'm telling you, I'm not being lumbered with one on the word of that tart. As far as I'm concerned, that bastard Yvonne's carrying has nothing to do with me.'

Before Adrian could protest any further, Robbie wheeled himself to his room and slammed the door shut. He sat in his chair in the darkness and clenched his fists. Fuck them all, he thought to himself. Adrian had plenty of money, he could look after Yvonne and her child. In fact, it was the least his brother could do, seeing as it was Adrian and his bitch of a wife who'd caused his accident in the first place.

He didn't want the responsibility of a child, especially as nowadays he was having so much fun. It had taken him a while to adjust to life in his chair, but Adrian was generous with his weekly allowance and it afforded him a good lifestyle, one in which he didn't have to work for a living and could drink and gamble to his heart's content.

There was no way he was about to give all that up for that whore.

Robbie smirked. No, the dirty slag could go take a running jump, and preferably down the stairs.

Chapter 46

Dorothy yawned and stretched as she waited for the kettle to boil. It was a Friday morning at the end of May and she was making Adrian a cup of tea to have in bed before he came down for his breakfast. It wasn't quite seven o'clock so she'd just make tea for the two of them, leaving her father and Yvonne to sleep in for a while. They were planning a rare day out to Battersea Park and Dorothy hoped the memories of where her father used to work would help with his rehabilitation.

It had been two weeks since Adrian had spoken to Robbie about the baby and nothing had changed. Robbie still refused to accept that the child was his, even when the doctor said that she was already over four months pregnant. It had come as a shock to Dorothy who thought that morning sickness only lasted for the first three months, but Yvonne was proving to be the exception to the rule.

Deep in her thoughts, Dorothy nearly jumped out of her skin when Robbie's door flew open. She hadn't expected him to be awake yet – he didn't usually emerge from his room until about midday.

She was aghast when she saw a dishevelled young

woman stood in the bedroom doorway wearing Robbie's robe. The woman looked about the same age as her, but her brown hair had the appearance of a bird's nest on her head, and dark mascara was smudged under her eyes. Her skin was deathly pale, and Dorothy thought the woman could have walked straight out of a ghost film.

'Good, I thought I heard the kettle going on. I'm bleedin' gasping,' the woman said, and walked into the kitchen, dragged a chair out from under the table and flopped onto it. 'I'll have a spoonful of sugar in mine.'

Dorothy was astounded. 'Who are you and how did you get in here?'

'I stayed the night with Robbie. I'm his girl, Violet, and you must be Dottie. Ain't he told you about me? He's told me all about you.'

'No, he's never mentioned you.'

'Oh, well, nice to meet you. Any toast going with that cuppa?'

What a cheek, thought Dorothy, her nerves grating at Violet's squeaky and shrill voice. 'No, I'm only making tea.'

Violet pulled a roll-up from the pocket of Robbie's robe and went to the gas stove to light it from under the kettle. As she passed, Dorothy wrinkled her nose at the pungent smell of body odour and alcohol emitting from her body.

'You ain't got a pair of stockings I could pinch off you, have you? Only mine got caught last night and laddered all the way up,' Violet asked as smoke wafted over Dorothy's face.

'I'll see what I can find,' Dorothy reluctantly answered,

and after pouring three cups of tea she put one in front of Violet before heading upstairs. Adrian was still asleep when she placed a cup next to him, but she gave him a gentle shake. 'Adrian, wake up.'

His eyes slowly opened and he smiled at her. 'Good morning, darling.'

Dorothy didn't greet her husband with any morning niceties. Instead she said angrily, 'Honestly, I'm gobsmacked at the audacity of your brother!'

'What's he done now?' Adrian asked tiredly.

'He brought a woman home with him to stay the night and she's sitting in my kitchen as bold as brass.'

'Well, darling, we've never laid any ground rules. It's Robbie's home too, so he has every right to invite someone to stay, within reason of course.'

Dorothy huffed. 'It would have been nice to have been consulted,' she said sulkily, 'and what about Yvonne? She's carrying his child so how is she going to feel about him bringing a woman home?'

'I don't know, love. It's a funny situation. Yvonne keeps out of Robbie's way as much as she can, and if he sees her, he acts as if she doesn't exist.'

'Well, I'm not happy about him bringing strange women back to my house,' Dorothy snapped. But then when Adrian looked at her intently, she quickly looked away. She was genuinely thinking about Yvonne's feelings, but she also recognised her own jealousy. She just hoped Adrian hadn't picked up on it, and prudently decided to say no more on the subject.

An hour later, Robbie was trying to ignore Violet's annoying voice, but she wouldn't shut up. 'For Christ's sake, woman, I'm trying to sleep,' he eventually said through gritted teeth.

'But, Robbie, they've all gone out now. I heard them leaving,' Violet said and shook Robbie's shoulder.

'So what,' Robbie snapped, giving up on getting any more sleep.

'Now they're gone we can have a root around upstairs.'

'What for?' Robbie asked, not quite with it yet.

'Well, it ain't 'cos I'm nosy, silly, I want to see if there's anything worth nicking.'

'Hold on. I don't know about that. It wouldn't be difficult for them to work out who's pinched their stuff.'

'Don't worry, I'm not stupid. I'll just take a couple of bits, you know, stuff they could have mislaid. I ain't talking about wiping them out!' Violet said and pouted. 'Oh, come on, Robbie, it'll be a laugh.'

Robbie rolled his eyes, 'You seem to have forgotten that I'm in a wheelchair.'

'Oh, blimey, yeah, sorry. Well, never mind, I can do upstairs on my own, and you can keep a lookout in case they come back.'

Robbie heaved a sigh and pulled on some clothes. He then hauled himself onto his chair and wheeled it into the living room, where he positioned himself at the bay window. He could see up and down the street and if he spotted them coming home he'd be able to give Violet plenty of warning.

While Violet poked around upstairs, Robbie drummed his fingers on the arm of his wheelchair, and realised he was excited at the possibility of getting caught. It had been a while since he'd felt adrenalin in his veins, and he found he was enjoying this daring antic. It made him feel alive.

Before long Violet rushed into the living room and Robbie eyed her up and down, taking in her slim figure, ruined by her scruffy appearance and matted hair. Her crooked smile revealed several missing teeth, but when he'd met her he'd been fuelled with beer. It was true that alcohol turned you blind, he thought wryly, but she was good in bed and had been happy to be on top doing all the work. Now, though, seeing what a mess Violet looked, he regretted his drunken decision to bring her home. Dorothy had met her and he could imagine her reaction. She probably thought that Violet was dirty and common – but hold on, why did he give a toss about what Dorothy thought?

'Look, Robbie, I found this watch in a drawer. It looks like it's worth a bob or two. And this ring, I reckon it's gold, a bit old-fashioned, but I'm sure I could flog it down the hock shop.'

Robbie instantly recognised Adrian's Rolex watch with its gold rim and brown leather strap. He saw that the strap was broken, which explained why Adrian wasn't wearing it, but surely he would notice it was missing. The gold ring wasn't familiar to him, but it probably belonged to Dottie, and for a moment he had second thoughts about stealing the items. Still, Violet kept yapping on about how much the Rolex could be worth and Robbie gave in.

'All right, pipe down, will you? Get yourself tidied up and I'll come with you down to the pawnbrokers.'

'You cheeky sod. I don't need tidying up, I'm ready to go!'

Robbie regretted saying he would accompany Violet; the woman looked like a vagabond. He didn't want to be seen with her, let alone have her push his chair, but if he wanted a share of their spoils, he'd have to put up with it. He wouldn't trust her to split the profits without him keeping a watchful eye.

Chapter 47

At the end of the day Adrian closed the office and drove home, looking forward to a nice dinner and a peaceful evening in front of the television. However, he'd barely walked through the door when he heard Dorothy calling from upstairs.

'Adrian . . . Adrian, is that you?'

Adrian thought she sounded irritated and called back, 'Yes, sweetheart.'

'Can you come here, please?'

He trudged upstairs and entered their bedroom. Seeing Dottie's pale face he asked anxiously, 'What is it, darling?'

Dorothy was surrounded by scattered items that she was frantically pulling from her bedside drawers. 'My mum's ring, I can't find it. It . . . it's missing.'

'It must be there somewhere,' Adrian said soothingly. 'Where did you last see it?'

'In my top drawer. It's always been in my top drawer, but when I opened it to get my make-up out, I noticed that my things aren't how I left them. It worried me so I checked to see if my mum's ring is still in the box, but it isn't. It's gone!'

'Are you sure that's where you left it?'

'Yes, of course I'm sure! I've never worn it so why would I take it out of the box? I'm telling you, Adrian, it's not here. I bet that bloody woman has been up here. I knew there was something dubious about her.'

'Calm down, Dottie, you can't go jumping to conclusions.'

Dorothy put her hands on her hips defiantly. 'Check your things then. See if there's anything missing,' she said.

Adrian began rifling through his drawers and it wasn't long before he noticed his watch was missing too. He turned to Dorothy. 'Looks like you're right,' he said regretfully. 'I can't find my Rolex.'

'I told you! I'll bloody kill her when I get my hands on her. My mother's ring – oh, Adrian, I know it wasn't very valuable, but you know how much it means to me,' Dorothy said and then slumped onto the bed as her tears began to fall.

Seeing the state that Dottie was in, Adrian's anger flared. 'Don't cry, I'll sort this out,' he said, and marched downstairs, cursing Robbie all the way. He hammered on his brother's door but there was no answer.

It wasn't long before Dorothy appeared, dashing tears from her face. 'I could have told you he wasn't in. They'd both gone out by the time we arrived home from the park. I don't suppose Robbie will turn up again until he's drunk, or maybe he'll be too guilty to show his face here again and that suits me just fine.'

'Robbie feeling guilty? Huh . . . never in a million years,' Adrian answered, trying to contain his anger. Losing his temper would achieve nothing, but that didn't stop him feeling bitter. Though Robbie hadn't deserved it, he'd given him a roof over his head, money in his pocket – and this is how he'd repaid him.

Adrian breathed deeply to steady himself. He wasn't going to stand for it. This was the final straw, and Robbie would find that out when he came home.

Robbie had been glad to see the back of Violet, thankful that she hadn't hung around for long once they had sold the goods. He thought the pawnbroker had ripped them off, offering them a fraction of the worth of the items, especially the Rolex, but, with no proof of purchase or ownership, they'd reluctantly accepted his offer.

Robbie's cheeks puffed. It was after eleven and, despite the work he'd put in, the muscles in his arms were burning as he wheeled himself home. Bugger this, he thought, and decided he would try to persuade Adrian to buy him one of those new electric chairs.

At last he arrived home and as he reached up to turn the key to the front door, Robbie regretted his extravagant bets over the card table. He'd blown the money he got from the pawnbroker, but, sure that he could recoup his losses, he'd got into more debt with Brian. He wasn't too worried about it as he'd be getting his allowance from Adrian on Monday, and that would enable him to pay back some of the money he owed, at least enough to keep Brian quiet for a while.

He pushed open the living-room door, deciding to help himself to a whisky from Adrian's decanter, but then paused on the threshold. 'Well, well, what are you two doing up?'

His mind was a bit fuddled with drink, but he could see that Dottie looked angry, while Adrian was looking at him with an expression of disgust. It was Adrian who spoke.

'My watch and a ring are missing. Show some dignity by not trying to deny your involvement, Robbie.'

'I don't know what you're talking about.'

'You know full well. Granted you couldn't have got up the stairs, but that girlfriend of yours certainly could. I can't prove you were in it together, or if she took it upon herself to steal from us, but either way, I want our things back, especially the ring. It belonged to Dottie's mother and means a lot to her.'

Robbie hid a smirk. As Adrian had pointed out, he couldn't get upstairs so they had nothing on him. 'Firstly, Violet isn't my girlfriend, and secondly, it's got nothing to do with me if she's pinched things that don't belong to her.'

'I expected you to deny any involvement, but it doesn't wash with me, Robbie. My watch is very valuable, you know that, but Alice's ring is priceless to Dottie and I don't how you could stoop so low as to steal from your own family.'

'I told you, I didn't have anything to do with it. It's Violet you should be talking to, but I haven't a clue where she is, so good luck finding her.'

'Robbie, my mum's ring is all I had left of her,' Dorothy interjected tearfully.

'What a shame,' he sneered, and for a brief moment Robbie thought Dottie was going to jump from the sofa and launch herself at him in a blind fury. Instead she lowered her head and he knew she was crying. Unexpectedly he felt a surge of compassion towards her and wished now he hadn't sold the ring.

Adrian put a consoling arm around Dottie as he said, 'I don't believe you weren't involved, Robbie, and until our things are returned I'm cutting your allowance in half.'

Robbie suddenly went from confident to a state of panic. Adrian couldn't cut his money; he had debts to pay. 'You can't do that! Why should I be punished for a crime I didn't commit?' he asked furiously.

'I didn't get off the last banana boat. I know full well you and that woman were in cahoots. Either return the goods or live with the consequences. If you're desperate for money you could always find employment with Remploy. Just because your legs don't work, there's no reason why you can't work with your hands.'

The pompous bastard, thought Robbie, talking to me as if he's my father. He wanted to punch his brother's lights out, just the same as Brian would do to him if he couldn't pay the man back.

'And another thing . . . as you're obviously such a poor judge of character, I don't want you bringing any more women back to my house.'

Robbie couldn't give a toss about the women. His main concern was the beating he could expect from Brian. He knew his brother and could see that he wasn't going to change his mind, and after stealing Alice's ring he doubted Dorothy would be a soft touch. Perhaps Brian would settle for some minimal payment each week? If the man agreed it would mean cutting out the booze and cards for a while, but it would be worth it to keep him off his back. He might as well ask – after all, his face was pretty much all he had going for him, so he didn't want Brian's heavies messing it up.

'If you've finished with your accusations, I'm going to bed,' he snapped, wondering what on earth he was going to do if Brian didn't agree to his offer.

Chapter 48

It had been a month since her mother's ring had gone missing, and Dorothy had given up any hope of seeing it again. It upset her, but now she had other things on her mind to worry about too.

She'd noticed Yvonne had been moping around the house for a couple of weeks now. At first, Dorothy had thought it was the girl's hormones playing havoc with her emotions, but now she wondered if there was something more to it. She glanced at the clock. Yvonne would be home soon, and she decided to try to get to the bottom of what was troubling her friend. Yes, she thought, she considered Yvonne a friend now, albeit a very young one.

Just as the kettle began to whistle, Yvonne walked through the door. Right on cue, thought Dorothy with a smile. Yvonne's reliability was one of the qualities Dorothy liked about her. 'Hello, love. You look hot. Sit yourself down and I'll get you a cold drink.'

'Ta, Dottie,' Yvonne said as she sat at the kitchen table, her head low.

'What's the matter, love?' Dottie asked as she gave her a glass of orange squash. 'You look so sad and have done for a while now,' she added gently.

'The . . . the mistress saw my tummy and . . . and I've been sacked.'

'I'm surprised she hasn't noticed it before this, but it doesn't matter as I was going to tell you to leave anyway. You're six months gone now and I think doing cleaning is too much for you.'

Yvonne bit her lower lip, looking like she was about to cry, so Dottie said, 'I know it isn't just losing your job that's upsetting you. My mum used to say that a problem shared is a problem halved, so come on, tell me what the problem is and maybe I can help.'

Yvonne said nothing at first, but then she burst out, 'I-I'm having a baby, but I ain't married. What would your mum have said if it had happened to you?'

The question caught Dorothy off guard, but she thought quickly and answered truthfully, 'It did happen to me, Yvonne, and at first my mum wasn't too happy about it. She came round though and started to knit things for the baby, but . . . but then I lost it.'

'Sorry, Dottie,' Yvonne said sadly as her eyes welled up and tears rolled down her cheeks. 'I-I miss my mummy, and . . . and I got one of the other girls at work to help me to write her a letter . . . but . . . but I ain't had nothing back. I'm scared, Dottie. They said it hurts when you have a baby and . . . and I want my mum!' She sobbed, and wiped her snotty nose down the arm of her blouse.

Dorothy's heart went out to the poor girl. She knew how it felt to want to speak to your mum. There wasn't a day went by when she didn't miss Alice, and there were numerous times when she'd have loved to turn to her for advice. This was the first time Yvonne had ever mentioned missing hers. When she'd moved in with them, it hadn't occurred to Dorothy to ask Yvonne if she had any family that could take her in, assuming that, if she had, she'd have gone to them for help. 'Yvonne, where is your mother?'

'She . . . she lives in Clacton.'

Puzzled, Dottie asked, 'When was the last time you saw her?'

'I dunno . . . last year, I fink. She moved to Clacton with me sister, but she said I had to stay in London.'

'Really? Why?'

'It's like I told Robbie. She . . . she said I'm a lia-lia-bility.'

'Robbie told me that your father threw you out. Is that why you didn't go to him?'

Yvonne frowned. 'No, that's not right. My dad didn't throw me out. He left my mum a long time ago.'

That was bad enough, but Dorothy wondered what sort of mother could leave her daughter behind, especially one as vulnerable as Yvonne. The girl needed looking after and surely her mother had known her daughter's limitations. Poor Yvonne – despite being abandoned, she was still desperate to see her mother. 'I'll have a word with Adrian and I'm sure he'll be happy to take you to see her. If you'd like that, we could drive down to Clacton on Sunday.'

'Oh, yes, yes, I'd like that, but . . . but what do you think she'll say about the baby?'

'Once she gets over the shock, I'm sure she'll be happy. Now come on, no more tears, and we'll take my dad with us. I'm sure he'd love a day at the seaside.'

'Oh, Dottie, thank you,' Yvonne said excitedly.

It was lovely to see Yvonne looking happier now, but

Dottie was beginning to wonder if she'd done the right thing. It worried her that Yvonne's mother had left her behind to fend for herself.

What sort of mother would do that? And what sort of reception was Yvonne going to receive?

Chapter 49

On Sunday, Adrian enjoyed getting out of London. He had been driving for an hour, and the air was now fresher and the surroundings greener. It was nice to get away from the heavy atmosphere that lingered at home whenever Robbie was around.

'How about a sing-song then?' he suggested, hoping to lift Yvonne's spirits. She looked ever so worried, sat on the back seat chewing her nails. 'I'll start us off – "There once was an ugly duckling, with feathers . . ."'

Dottie burst out laughing, 'Adrian, we aren't eight-year-olds. Let's try this one – "Que sera sera, whatever will be, will be . . ."'

Yvonne joined in, and though Adrian didn't know the words he hummed along, and was pleased to hear Bill whistling. They sang a few more popular songs, but then Adrian glanced in the mirror to see that Yvonne was beginning to fidget. 'Everything all right back there?' he asked.

'Err, yeah . . . but . . . I . . . err . . . need the lavvy,' Yvonne said and visibly squirmed.

There wasn't much further to go, but there was only countryside around them. Adrian pulled over. 'Sorry, Yvonne, that bush over there is the best I can offer.'

Yvonne wasted no time in jumping out of the car and making a dash for cover, calling out a thank-you to Adrian over her shoulder.

Adrian turned to look at his wife, who was busy applying some fresh lipstick. 'You don't need more make-up. You already look stunning,' he said.

'Thank you. I wish I could say the same for Yvonne. The poor girl looks pale and drained.'

'Maybe she doesn't travel well.'

'I don't think it's that. It's probably because she's nervous about telling her mother that she's pregnant.'

'I thought you said she's already written to her.'

'Yes, but as she hasn't had a reply, Yvonne thinks her mother didn't get it. I haven't said anything to Yvonne, but my worry is that she didn't write back because she wants nothing to do with her.'

Before Adrian had a chance to reply, the back door opened and Yvonne climbed into the car. He drove off, frowning at the thought of what sort of reception they might receive in Clacton.

Unaware of the conversation that went on in the car while she was out of it, Yvonne settled down in the back seat and saw that Bill had dozed off. She smiled. It wasn't long before they came to the brow of a hill and she could see the sea in the distance. She'd only been to the seaside once, and recalled a sweet memory of building sand castles with her sister. They had taken their shoes and socks off to paddle in the sea, jumping the small waves that rolled to shore. It'd been smashing, until she had lost one of her shoes, which had annoyed her mother. She'd got a good hiding for it, and no dinner that night.

'Here we are,' Adrian said after he'd driven for another fifteen minutes, and he pulled the car over to stop outside a small bungalow.

Yvonne's jaw dropped at the sight of the pretty pansies in troughs on the window ledge and the roses blooming in the well-kept garden. It was a far cry from the two rooms she'd shared with her mother and sister in a flat in Battersea.

'It looks really nice,' Dorothy commented.

'Yeah . . . lovely. Blimey, fancy my mum living somewhere posh like this!' Yvonne said, and scrambled out of the car.

'Wait for me,' Dorothy called, but Yvonne was already down the neat path and was about to knock on the smart front door.

She turned to Dorothy who had caught her up on the doorstep. 'What if me mum goes mad when I tell her?'

'Don't worry, love, I'll help explain everything to her.'

'But you won't tell her what I did . . . you know . . . what Robbie made me do?' Yvonne said, suddenly panicking.

'Of course not!' Dorothy answered.

'Your dad's still asleep so I've left him in the car,' Adrian said as he joined them and leaned forward to rap the door knocker. 'So, what were you waiting for?'

'Yvonne is just a bit nervous,' Dorothy told him.

The door began to open and as it did, Yvonne felt a surge of excitement. She was going to see her mum . . . but instead she saw a short, tubby, older woman and bewildered she blurted out, 'Who are you?'

'I could ask you the same, young lady,' the woman replied.

'I'm Adrian Ferguson, this is my wife Dorothy, and this is Yvonne,' Adrian said, stepping forward. 'We're here to see Yvonne's mother, Mrs Woodman. I believe she lives here with Yvonne's sister?'

The old woman shook her head. 'No, she doesn't and she never has. I've lived in this house all my life, and I've never heard of a Mrs Woodman round here.' She paused. 'But come to think of it, I have seen that name on a letter that was mistakenly delivered here.'

'That was me. I wrote that letter. But if my mum isn't here, where is she?' Yvonne asked.

'Sorry, dear, I don't think I can help you,' the old woman said.

'Well, thank you for your time and I'm sorry we disturbed you,' Adrian said.

'Come on, Yvonne, let's get back in the car,' Dorothy urged quietly as she wrapped an arm around her shoulders.

Yvonne allowed herself to be led back up the garden path, confused as she climbed back into the car. Adrian turned to her from the front seat and said, 'Let me have a look at that address again.'

Yvonne handed him the piece of paper that her mother had left for her. Adrian looked at it, hoping that he'd come to the wrong place, but then said, 'There's no mistake. This is the same address.'

'I don't understand . . . where's my mum?' Yvonne asked.

'I wish I could tell you. Have you got any other family – cousins, aunts, your mum's friends, anything?' Dorothy asked.

'I don't think so. After me dad left, my mum moved

us around a lot. My sister said it was ’cos she couldn’t pay the rent and that’s why we always did a midnight bunk. I had lots of new uncles, but they didn’t stay long and I don’t know where any of them are now.’

‘In that case, I’m sorry, love,’ Dorothy said gently, ‘I’m not sure what we can do to find her.’

Yvonne didn’t want to cry again, but she couldn’t help it. Her mum had given her the wrong address. She’d done another midnight bunk, only this time she’d left her behind too, and that must mean she didn’t want to be found. ‘She . . . she doesn’t want me,’ she choked, unable to stop the tears from flowing.

‘I know you’re upset, and it might not be much consolation,’ Dottie said kindly, ‘but you’ve still got us.’

Yvonne hadn’t realised until a hand reached out to grasp hers that Bill was awake. She clung on to it, and that, along with Dottie’s words, made her feel less alone.

Chapter 50

Malcolm rolled over in the bed he shared with his wife in their new home. It was a few doors down from Nelly's parents' house, and just about affordable. He reached underneath and pulled out a small package wrapped in red Santa Claus paper. It was a Saturday morning in mid-August, a long way from Christmas, but the paper had been going cheap. Adrian was generous with the wages he paid, but his and Nelly's earnings had to cover their own rent and bills as well as his mum's.

He rolled over onto his side and raised himself up on his elbow to gaze at his sleeping wife. He studied her face, admiring her upturned nose and full lips. Even her snoring like a steam train endeared him.

As if aware of his scrutiny, Nelly opened her eyes, yawned and asked, 'What are you looking at, you silly bugger?'

'The loveliest girl in the world,' Malcolm replied and placed the small package on Nelly's heaving chest.

'What's this?' she asked, pushing herself up.

'Open it and see.'

'What have I done to deserve a present? It isn't my birthday or anything.'

'You've been my wife for three months today, so it's a

sort of an anniversary,' Malcolm said, and kissed Nelly's rosy cheek. 'Happy three-month anniversary, darling.'

'You're a proper softie,' she said, smiling at him affectionately before unwrapping the present.

Malcolm delighted in seeing his wife's face light up as she looked at the home-made wooden plaque he had carefully made. 'See, it says,

We hope you find our home to be,
a wellcum plase for a cup of tea.
Its full of love and happynis to,
so heres a bit from us to you

and then I've signed it, '*Malcolm & Nelly x*'. What do you think? I thought it would go nice in the hallway near the front door.'

Nelly's eyes welled up which made Malcolm think she must really like it. After all, his wife wasn't one for soppy sentiment. She refused to give Malcolm any sympathy about Robbie, even though he was still plagued by nightmares and guilt over the accident. It had got to the point where she wouldn't listen to his feelings on the subject, so he'd found it easier to just shut up about it.

'I love it, thank you, but we're going to have to give you some spelling lessons,' Nelly said with a chuckle.

'Oh, no,' Malcolm said, feigning hurt, 'have I cocked it up?'

'No, it's perfect as it is,' Nelly answered. 'Actually, I've got something for you too.'

'Really? What is it?' Malcolm asked like an excited child at Christmas. He hadn't been expecting Nelly to realise the significance of the date, let alone get him a present.

Nelly took his hand to place it on her flabby stomach, a soft smile on her face as she said, 'Say hello.'

It took a moment, but then the penny dropped. 'Nel, you're pregnant?'

'Yes, and it didn't take you long. I'm two months gone and somewhere under all that fat there's a little baby growing.'

'Oh, Nel, that's bloody marvellous! I'm chuffed to bits, I really am,' Malcolm said, feeling overcome.

'I am too, but I'm worried about telling Dottie. You know how much she wants a baby and what with Yvonne being pregnant too . . .' Nelly said.

'Don't be daft. She's your friend and she'll be happy for you.'

'I know, but I'll keep it to myself for now and that means you'll have to keep your gob shut too.'

'But I'd love to tell my mum.'

'Just leave it for a few weeks, love. It can be our little secret until then, something that only we know about to cherish.'

'All right,' Malcolm agreed but he felt he was bursting at the seams to announce the news.

'I don't know how we're going to cope financially. I'll work as long as I can, but when this baby makes an appearance we'll only have your wage coming in. I know Adrian will find you some overtime, but I don't want you working all the hours under the sun.'

Malcolm hadn't had time to think that far ahead, but he could tell his wife was very concerned. 'Don't worry, love, we'll manage. If Adrian will let you do less hours, and one of our mums or your sister will watch the baby, you could still go to work.'

'Possibly,' she answered. 'I hadn't thought of that. I know my sister would appreciate a bit of extra cash so I could bung her a few bob.'

'There you go,' he said, glad he'd offered a solution.

'Right, that's sorted, now you get a hammer and I'll put the kettle on,' Nelly said.

'What do you want a hammer for?'

'It isn't for me, you daft sod. I want you to put that plaque up.'

'Give us a kiss first,' Malcolm said as he pulled his wife into him.

'Get off, you big lump. I haven't got time for hanky-panky this morning. I'm going up the Junction with Dottie. We're going on a shopping spree for Yvonne's nipper-to-be.'

'Cor, I drove past her last week and she looks like she's ready to drop. Big as a bleedin' bus, she is! I feel sorry for the poor kid though – there's some right horrible things being talked about her,' Malcolm said as he pulled his trousers on and his braces over his shoulders.

'I know, but what can you expect? She's got no husband and Robbie won't have nothing to do with her. Still, she's lucky to have Dottie and Adrian looking out for her. Gawd knows what would have happened to the little blighter without them on her side.'

Malcolm felt his stomach knot at the mention of Robbie's name. Every time he heard it, he saw the image of the man lying at the bottom of the stairs and wondered if it would ever go away.

'Yvonne . . . surprise,' Yvonne heard Dorothy shout. She rushed out into the hall to see Dorothy pushing a new navy-blue pram over the threshold, with things piled on top of it. Nelly was laden with shopping bags too.

'It's a Silver Cross pram and one of the best,' Dorothy said.

Yvonne was overwhelmed. Speechless but grateful, she ran to Dorothy and threw her arms around her neck.

'All right, calm down,' Dorothy said, laughing, 'it's only a pram. I'll leave it there and we'll go into the living room. I can't wait for you to see the things we've got for the baby.'

Like an excited child, Yvonne clapped her hands together, and finally squealed, 'Oh, Dottie, thank you.'

'I really enjoyed our shopping spree,' Nelly said as she opened one of the bags to pull out a white bedding set for the pram. 'Look at this. Isn't it gorgeous?'

Yvonne reached out to feel the lovely soft material. 'I love it,' she said and soon more baby things were being pulled out of bags.

'Do us a favour, love, put the kettle on, I'm parched,' Nelly said as she flopped back on the sofa.

Yvonne nodded and waddled through to the kitchen. She was excited to see what other goodies the bags held, and tapped her foot impatiently as she waited for the kettle to boil. As she walked back through to the lounge, she tensed when she heard Robbie's voice.

'What the fuck is this doing here?' he shouted.

'The pram must be blocking his wheelchair,' Dottie said, and when she walked out to the hall her voice carried when she spoke to Robbie. 'I'll move it, but there's no need for that kind of language.'

'It's my fucking house and I'll say what I like. Get this shit out of my way!' Robbie yelled. 'Don't you think it's hard enough for me to get around without finding this bloody thing blocking my path?'

Yvonne didn't hear Dorothy answer but she must have moved the pram because the wheelchair appeared in the living-room doorway. She tensed when Robbie looked at her, and quickly turned away, but she couldn't avoid the sound of his voice.

'I'm warning you, Yvonne, when you give birth to that bastard I don't want to see its shit all over this house, and you'd better keep the fucking thing quiet!'

'You're a nasty piece of work,' Nelly yelled after him as he wheeled himself away.

Yvonne let out the breath she'd been holding, but tears pricked her eyes. Robbie was so cold and cruel, and still said the baby wasn't his.

'Take no notice of him,' Dorothy said as she walked back into the room. 'He's still bitter and twisted about his disability, but I'm sure that once he sees the baby he'll soften.'

'I don't think he will, but I won't let him hurt me no more. I don't need him and neither does my baby,' Yvonne said. She wished she believed her own words, but in truth she dreamed of Robbie being the perfect father, better than her own bullying dad had ever been.

'That's the spirit,' Nelly said. 'I wonder if you've got a boy or a girl in there.'

'I think it's a girl,' Dottie said.

Yvonne knew that they were trying to cheer her up and managed a smile as she said, 'You must be hungry after all that shopping. If you like I'll make you some sandwiches.'

'No, love, your ankles are swollen and you need to take the weight off your feet. I'll make the lunch.'

'While you're at it, get me a bit of cotton. You can guess what I want it for,' Nelly said.

'As long as Yvonne doesn't mind,' Dottie said.

'Mind what?'

'Nelly reckons if she puts her wedding ring on a bit of cotton and holds it over your belly, she can tell what you're having.'

'But how?' Yvonne asked.

Nelly smiled. 'If you have the gift, it's easy. I inherited it from my gran. She could see the future and she said I could too. I have to admit I do get strange feelings about stuff, but not visions like my late gran. Mind you, I'm always right when it comes to babies. I used to use a threaded needle, but I reckon my ring is more powerful. I was right about all four of my sister's babies. Isn't that right, Dottie?'

'Yes, Yvonne, it irks me to say it but she was right, though of course there's a fifty-fifty chance either way,' Dorothy said jokingly.

'Oh, please, do it to me, Nelly,' Yvonne urged.

Dorothy went to the kitchen to prepare the food and then came back with a piled-high plate and a reel of cotton from her sewing box. 'Here you are,' she said, handing the cotton to Nelly.

Yvonne watched as Nelly threaded her ring onto it and then as instructed she lay perfectly still while it was suspended over her tummy.

'Ooo, look at that, your tummy moved. It must be the baby kicking,' Nelly observed.

Yvonne smiled, used to feeling her baby kick, but then the ring started to move, slowly going round and round, gathering momentum.

'It's a girl!' Nelly pronounced.

'Told you,' Dorothy chirped, 'though I think you might be making the ring move.'

'No, I'm not,' Nelly protested.

Yvonne sat up and said, 'I believe you, Nelly. I think I'm having a girl and I'm going to call her Rosie . . . my beautiful little Rosie.' Yvonne rubbed her stomach tenderly.

'Oh, that's a lovely name,' Dottie said, 'and I can't wait to meet my niece.'

Yvonne smiled. Robbie might never love this baby, but Dottie would, and she'd be a lovely auntie. Adrian would be a lovely uncle too, and Rosie would have a family, which made her feel a surge of happiness. She'd try to be a good mum, and unlike her own mother, she'd never abandon her baby. Never!

Chapter 51

August passed and it was a Friday evening in mid-September when Adrian came home from work to hear Dorothy humming in the living room. It had been a long time since he'd found his wife in such good spirts. He knew it was hard for her to watch Yvonne's stomach swell, and had held her at night when she'd cry, yearning for a baby herself.

He couldn't understand why she hadn't yet fallen pregnant and was beginning to think that Dottie was right, that the miscarriage had damaged her beyond repair. She'd been to see the doctor, who had found nothing wrong, so he'd offered to pay for a specialist, but Dorothy refused, saying she couldn't stand to be poked and prodded about any more.

'Well, what's all this?' he asked, walking into the room to see another pile of baby paraphernalia.

'It's a Moses basket. I thought we should get one as there isn't long to go, and I don't believe that silly superstition about not buying stuff before the baby's born. It's amazing how much stuff a baby needs, but I think we've covered all the essentials now, with a few irresistible extras. I've had such a lovely time buying baby things. I just wish it was for our own.'

Adrian sat next to Dottie and pulled her into his arms. 'I'm sure you'll be buying things for our own baby one day,' he said to console her.

'I hope so, but in the meantime I'll enjoy lavishing my niece with beautiful things,' Dorothy said.

'Niece? How do you know she's having a girl?'

'Just a hunch.'

'Oh, right.' Adrian smiled, then looked more serious. 'I don't want this to sound like I'm a miser, but I want you to work out how much you've spent so far on just the essential items.'

'OK,' Dorothy answered, 'but can I ask why?'

'Because I'm going to deduct the cost from Robbie's allowance. Despite him denying it, Yvonne insists the baby is his and one way or another I'm going to see that he pays towards the child's keep.'

Dorothy raised her eyebrows. 'I see your point and I agree with you, but Robbie's not going to be too happy about it, especially as you're still giving him only half his allowance.'

'I don't care. It's about time he accepted his responsibilities towards the child,' Adrian said. He wasn't looking forward to telling Robbie and decided to wait until the next day. No doubt he'd get a torrent of abuse then and it wouldn't be a good start to the weekend, but Adrian was determined to stick to his guns.

'Yvonne's gone to bed. I'm worried about her,' Dottie said. 'She was fine earlier, but now she's got a terrible headache. I noticed that she's all swollen and puffy too.'

'Keep an eye on her. I'm sure she'll be fine, but if she's no better tomorrow, call the doctor. And what about Robbie, is he home?' Adrian asked.

'He's in his room, no doubt sprucing himself up for the pub again tonight. He was really horrid to Yvonne earlier. I wish there was something we could do about his behaviour.'

'Is it getting worse?'

'No, he's just the same, along with his bad language. Yvonne avoids him as much as she can, and I let his wicked remarks wash over me. It's such a shame though. I remember the old Robbie – surely he's in there somewhere.'

Adrian saw the sadness in Dottie's eyes and the old niggling doubt he always carried reared its ugly head. He tried to quash it and not give it credence, but he'd never been completely convinced that Dorothy didn't still harbour feelings for Robbie.

'Let's be honest, he wasn't the nicest of people before the accident, Dottie.'

'You didn't see him the way I did.'

There it was again, Adrian thought sadly, Dottie defending Robbie. He wanted to ask her outright if she was still in love with his brother, but fear of the truth always stopped him. He couldn't face losing her. If only he could make her really happy by giving her the child she so desperately craved. He gave her everything else, but a baby was the one thing money couldn't buy.

On Saturday morning, Robbie heard a knock on his door. He'd chosen to eat all his meals in his room so it was probably Dottie with his breakfast, but it was a bit flaming early. He liked giving her extra work to do, but he wasn't going to put up with being disturbed before nine in the morning. He'd give her a piece of his mind and he'd enjoy doing it. In fact, he liked making her life as miserable as he could. As long as he was stuck in this chair, he had no intention of letting any of them off the hook and he would do whatever he could to make them feel uncomfortable in their own home.

'It's me, can I come in?' he heard Adrian ask.

'If you must,' Robbie answered unenthusiastically.

He braced himself for another confrontation as Adrian walked into the room.

'You've probably noticed the array of baby items amassing in the house,' Adrian said.

'I could hardly miss that fucking great pram.'

'From what I've seen all the baby clothes and equipment are proving to be expensive. It'll be an ongoing expense too.'

'And your point is?' Robbie asked.

'I think you should be paying towards the costs. I'll deduct a weekly amount from your allowance and—'

'You can't do that!' Robbie feverishly interrupted. 'You can't even prove that the bastard is mine.'

'I expected this from you, Robbie, but I was hoping you would listen to reason.'

'Reason? There isn't any reason why I should be left short because of what that slut is carrying in her belly. For fuck's sake, Adrian, I'm a grown man but you're treating me like a naughty child having my pocket money deducted. You're already stopping half my allowance and I can't afford to lose any more. I won't have it, do you hear me? I'll never buy that . . . that *thing* anything. Not even a nappy pin!'

'I'm sorry you feel that way, but it's the right thing to do. If you choose to neglect your responsibilities, as usual, then you leave me with no other option than to take charge. I hate to say it, Robbie, but you know what you can do if you don't like it.'

Robbie's anger was boiling and he cursed his legs for not working. He wanted to run at his brother and batter the living daylights out of him. 'I HATE you. Don't you think it's bad enough that you ruined my life, and now this! GET OUT, go on, fuck off!'

Adrian didn't say another word and quietly left the bedroom, closing the door behind him. Robbie sat staring at it, thumping the arm of his wheelchair in frustration.

How dare Adrian inflict this on him! Apart from anything else, he was counting on the money to keep up with his payments to Brian, though his debt was rapidly increasing because of the ridiculous interest the shark kept lumping on. 'Fuck . . . fuck . . . fuck,' he cursed under his breath, knowing that Brian would soon have his heavies on him again, and this time he doubted he would avoid a beating – especially as he couldn't run away.

'That went well then?' Dorothy said with a note of sarcasm in her voice as Adrian walked into the kitchen.

'I take it you heard our little exchange?' Adrian said.

'Yes, most of it.'

'We both knew he'd scream and shout about it, but, like it or not, he's going to have his allowance cut. I hope he doesn't take it out on you, but if he does he'll have me to deal with. Anyway, where's Yvonne? I said I would run her up to Walter's shop this morning to collect the high chair and cot you ordered.'

'I haven't seen her. She must be still in bed or too worried to come down after hearing that. I was just about to take Dad some breakfast so I'll give her a shout, though I think she really ought to spend the day in bed. She looked awful yesterday.'

Dorothy found her father sitting up in his bed and she thought he looked a little agitated. 'Morning, Dad. Here's your breakfast, but after you've eaten it, why don't you have a nice wash and come downstairs?'

'Vonnie . . . Vonnie,' he said, his name for Yvonne.

'She's still sleeping, Dad, but she'll be in to see you soon.'

'Vonnie . . . Vonnie . . . bad . . . Vonnie bad . . .' he said, his arms flapping as he pushed her to one side to get out of bed.

The tray went flying, and, frightened that her dad was going to have another fit, she tried to push him back onto his pillows while yelling, 'Adrian! Adrian!'

Shortly afterwards he came into the room, panting from running up the stairs.

'Quick,' Dorothy said urgently, 'take over here while I fetch Yvonne. She always calms him.'

'Yes, all right, but if he gets any worse we should call the doctor.'

Dottie ran to Yvonne's room and without knocking threw open the door. 'Yvonne, sorry to get you up, but it's my dad and . . .' The words died on Dottie's lips. Yvonne's face was so bloated that she was barely recognisable, and sweat matted her hair. When she groaned, Dottie stood frozen for a moment before dashing from the room and back to her father's.

'It's all right, he's calmed down now,' Adrian said.

'It's Yvonne,' Dottie blurted, panic in her voice. 'Something's wrong with her. We need help.'

'Has she gone into labour?'

'No, well, I don't think so, but she's badly bloated. I'm going to call the doctor.'

'I'll do that. You'd best get back to her.'

While Adrian went downstairs to make the phone call, Dottie ran back to Yvonne's room to find her groaning and clutching her stomach.

'The baby . . .' she cried.

'It's all right, love, Adrian's gone to call the doctor,' said Dorothy soothingly, but her voice shook.

'I . . . I think the baby's coming. Oh . . . oh . . . it hurts.'

'It's normal to feel pain,' Dottie said, fighting to stay calm. She remembered her miscarriage, but she'd never seen childbirth. Yvonne's pain was obviously so much worse, but when she screamed in agony before passing out, Dottie knew something was wrong – badly wrong. She felt helpless, at a loss to know what to do, and lightly slapped Yvonne's cheeks, trying to revive her, 'Come on, Yvonne, wake up, love,' she pleaded.

Yvonne half opened her puffy eyes and groaned, 'My head hurts so bad.' Then there was another loud scream. 'ARGH, no . . . make it stop.'

Dorothy was floundering and felt completely ineffectual as Yvonne continued to cry out in pain. She wished Nelly was with her now, she'd know what to do. It looked like she was slipping in and out of consciousness and seemed to be getting weaker by the second.

Adrian stuck his head around the door, and his face went grey at what he saw. 'I rang the doctor but when I told him about the bloating he advised me to call an ambulance. What do you want me to do now?'

'I don't know,' Dorothy cried, 'I haven't got a clue what I'm supposed to do, let alone you.'

Yvonne suddenly sat up and gasped, 'I feel funny. I . . . I think the baby's coming.' She then leaned forward, making a long grunting noise from deep in the throat.

'I think that's what they call pushing,' Dorothy said, and glancing over her shoulder she saw that Adrian looked about to faint. 'Get out of here,' she snapped.

Dorothy wanted to run from the room too, but she knew she couldn't as she silently panicked. 'Hurry up,' she whispered under her breath, praying for the ambulance to arrive.

Yvonne grunted, pushing again; she knew there was no way to stop this baby coming before the ambulance.

Adrian came back into the room with a bowl of water and fresh towels.

'What do I do with these?' Dorothy asked, looking at what he was carrying.

'I have no idea but it's what I hear the midwife always asks for,' Adrian replied.

His ignorance didn't help to calm Dorothy's fears, especially when Yvonne began to make a noise in her throat.

'Adrian, what do we do? I don't know what's wrong, but I do know this isn't normal,' she asked fretfully.

'Cool her down, mop her brow. If nothing else, it'll make her more comfortable,' Adrian said.

Dorothy dipped one of the towels in the bowl of water, wrung it out and began gently dabbing Yvonne's brow.

Yvonne sank back on the pillows, exhausted, her voice weak and husky as she croaked, 'Dottie, my head feels like it's going to burst. Promise me . . . promise me you'll look after Rosie.'

Dorothy flashed Adrian a look. He was stood with his mouth agape. This wasn't a man's territory, so Dorothy knew she'd have to deal with this alone.

'Don't talk daft, Yvonne. You'll be looking after Rosie yourself,' Dorothy said in Yvonne's ear.

'Please . . . Dottie . . . promise me . . . you have to . . .' Yvonne begged.

Yvonne must think she was going to die, Dorothy thought, and the enormity of the situation overwhelmed her. 'Yes, of course I will, but it won't come to that. The ambulance will be here shortly.'

'Thank you,' Yvonne said, but then she sat forward and with an enormous howl she pushed hard until she cried out, 'My head . . . it feels like it's exploding, but I think Rosie is coming out.'

Dottie pushed up Yvonne's nightie, in awe of what she saw. 'Yes, I can see the baby's head,' she said eagerly as she heard the siren of the ambulance as it pulled up outside. 'Come on, love, keep going . . . she's nearly here.'

She turned to look at Adrian who was making a hasty retreat from the room, muttering something about going to check on Bill.

She was amazed when Yvonne managed to find strength from somewhere and with another push the baby was delivered.

'You did it, Yvonne! Look, it's Rosie!' Dorothy said through tears as she picked up the baby and held her up for Yvonne to see.

There was no response, no expected cry of joy. Instead Yvonne had slumped back, her head turned to one side and her mouth open. Dorothy felt a shiver of fear as she noticed her eyes were strangely fixed too and she wasn't blinking. 'Yvonne . . . Yvonne, love.'

A midwife suddenly appeared in the bedroom alongside two ambulancemen. The midwife cut the baby's cord, but Dottie hardly noticed, unable to tear her eyes away from the vacant expression on Yvonne's face. Rosie was wailing, but Dottie was barely aware of the baby being taken from her arms. Then she was ushered away from the bed to the back of the room, and, feeling as if she was looking at the scene from a distance, she took in the blood-drenched sheets and saw that Yvonne still hadn't moved. She watched as if in slow motion as the midwife gave the baby to one of the ambulancemen to hold while she leaned over the bed to check on Yvonne. She then looked at the man and shook her head. What did that mean? Why was the midwife shaking her head?

The ambulanceman who held Rosie in his arms turned to look at Dorothy and said, 'I'm so sorry.'

Sorry? What was he sorry for? What was going on?

She became aware that Adrian was by her side, lightly pushing her towards the door. 'She's gone, darling. Come on, there's nothing you can do.'

'I don't understand . . . she . . . she just had Rosie,' Dorothy muttered and as though coming out of a fog and realising what had been said, her voice strengthened. 'No, Yvonne isn't dead. She can't be. She must have passed out again.'

Dorothy pulled away from Adrian and flew over to the bed. Shaking Yvonne, she cried, 'Wake up! Yvonne . . . please . . . come on . . . love . . . WAKE UP,' but when she saw the unchanged vacant look on Yvonne's face and her fixated eyes, it finally sank in. Her legs gave way and she crumpled to a heap on the floor next to the bed. 'I'm so sorry. I'm sorry I let you die. I didn't know what to do . . .'

'It wasn't your fault, Mrs Ferguson,' the midwife said. 'There was nothing anyone could have done. It appears she died of toxaemia. It can come on very quickly and looked quite advanced. You did very well to deliver the baby.'

The baby, Dorothy thought, climbing to her feet. She walked over to the ambulanceman who was holding Rosie and said, 'I'll take her.'

When Rosie was placed gently into her arms, Dottie turned to look lovingly at her deceased friend. 'I made you a promise, Yvonne, and I intend to keep it. I'll look after Rosie and make sure she knows all about you and what a wonderful mother she had.'

She turned with Rosie in her arms and, crying hard, she looked at Adrian, who had tears streaming down his face too. 'We will love this child as our own, give her the world and always keep Yvonne's memory alive.'

Adrian nodded and Dorothy could tell he was unable to speak. 'We should get Rosie out of here. I don't want the image of her mother's lifeless body to be imprinted on her brain for ever,' Dorothy whispered protectively.

Adrian put his arm around her, and together they left the bedroom. 'Hey, my pretty little girl, let's go and meet your grandpa,' Dorothy cooed through her snivels.

Adrian held his hand out to Rosie, and Dorothy watched astonished as she gripped hard on his pinkie finger. Robbie may be Rosie's biological father, she thought, but Adrian is going to be her daddy.

Robbie was abruptly woken by the sound of heavy footsteps going up and down the stairs above his bedroom.

He'd been hoping for a morning lie-in, but checking the clock on his bedside he saw it was only nine-thirty. The night before, he'd drunk enough ale to sink a battleship, and now he was paying for it.

He rubbed the sleep out of his eyes and tried to focus as he sat himself up. The room was spinning and his mouth felt dry and furry. Then he heard a distinct noise which he recognised as a crying baby. I don't believe it, he thought, the fucking tart has only gone and dropped the sprog a few weeks early.

He didn't feel the delivery of his so-called child warranted getting out of bed early, but the need for a cup of tea to rehydrate his hungover body forced him to make the effort. As he pulled on his robe, the baby's persistent screaming grated on his nerves, and he wanted to shout to Yvonne to shut the thing up.

Thankfully, he found some warm tea already brewed in the teapot, and poured himself a welcome cup before venturing into the lounge.

Dorothy was standing with her back towards him, swaying from side to side as she rocked the baby in her arms. He was grateful that the nipper had finally quietened down.

'So, the bastard is born,' Robbie said.

Dorothy spun around and he immediately noticed she'd been crying. Then, through the lounge door, he saw two ambulancemen carrying a stretcher down the stairs. There looked to be a person on the stretcher but the face was covered over – like they do to dead people, he thought – and he quickly looked away, believing it was unlucky to see the deceased.

'Don't start, Robbie,' Dorothy said. 'I'm in no mood for your antics today'.

He thought she sounded exhausted, and he saw the sadness in her eyes, but still hadn't worked out if Bill or Yvonne had been on the stretcher. Either way, he thought Dorothy must be pretty cut up, and for a moment he felt sorry for her.

'So who are they carting off in that ambulance?' he asked as, looking through the net curtains, he saw it drive away.

'Yvonne,' Dorothy answered. She kept her back to him as she said, 'She died in childbirth.'

Robbie could hear Dorothy was crying, and though he felt nothing over the loss of Yvonne, his heart did go out to his sister-in-law, and for a change he decided to keep his ugly comments to himself.

Adrian walked into the room looking just as glum as his wife. 'I assume Dorothy has informed you of Yvonne's death?'

'Yes, she has, but if you think I'm taking on that kid, you've got another think coming. Send it to her mother or take it down the orphanage, whatever you want to do, but I'm having nothing to do with it.'

Much to Robbie's surprise, Adrian said, 'Good.'

'What do you mean, "good"?' Robbie asked. He'd been expecting yet another onslaught from his brother about the virtues of responsibility.

'I'll see my solicitor and get the relevant paperwork drawn up. Dottie and I will adopt Rosie. We'll bring her up as our own.'

His brother's voice was steely, and, glad to be let of the hook, Robbie had no intention of arguing.

'Yes, well, that suits me fine,' he said, and then spun the chair around. He could hear the baby crying again and with his head thumping he wheeled himself back into his room.

He'd had a drink with Brian and managed to get a two-week extension on his debt, but a fortnight wasn't long to come up with eighty-odd quid, especially as Adrian was docking his money to pay for baby things. Then a thought occurred to him. If Adrian and Dorothy were planning on adopting the child, then surely it would be their responsibility and he would get his full allowance back.

He smiled, thinking that, thanks to Yvonne popping her clogs, his pocket was going to be a bit fuller.

Chapter 52

Nelly had decided that she could no longer hide her condition from Dorothy. Malcolm was itching to tell his mother, and she wanted to tell her parents and sisters too. Last week they'd been invited to Dottie's for Sunday dinner, and now that the day was here it was as good a time as any to break the news.

'Stop worrying,' Malcolm said as they knocked on Dottie's door. Adrian opened it.

'Hello, Adrian,' Nelly said, nerves making her voice higher than usual.

'Shush,' he said gently, smiling. 'She's only just gone to sleep.'

'Who you talking about?' Nelly asked in a puzzled whisper.

'Rosie,' Adrian answered. 'Go through to the lounge and Dorothy will explain everything.'

Nelly walked in and her eyes popped when she saw her best friend sitting on the sofa with a sleeping baby in her arms. 'Oh, Dottie, how wonderful! Yvonne's had the baby.'

'She was born yesterday, and, as Yvonne wanted, her name is Rosie.'

‘I was right about it being a girl then. How’s Yvonne doing? I expect she’s still in bed. I’ll pop up to see her if that’s OK?’

‘I’m afraid you can’t,’ Dottie said, and then burst into tears.

‘What is it? What’s wrong?’ Nelly asked, but then an awful feeling swamped her. ‘She . . . she’s not dead, is she?’

‘Yes,’ Dottie said, still crying as she went on to tell them what had happened.

Nelly flopped down on the sofa next to her friend and instinctively rubbed her stomach protectively. ‘Oh, poor Yvonne.’

‘I know, it’s heartbreaking, but we’ve decided to adopt Rosie.’

‘What about him in there?’ Nelly asked, nodding her head towards Robbie’s room. She held the man in such contempt that she could hardly bring herself to mention his name.

‘He’s agreed to it, and for a refreshing change he’s being civil,’ Dorothy answered. ‘By the way, dinner might be a bit later than expected. I’ve had my hands full with this one and haven’t even peeled the spuds yet.’

‘I’ll see to dinner. You look worn out and in need of a rest, and before you start, no arguments,’ Nelly said as she rolled up her sleeves and made her way through to the kitchen. ‘But I’m not cooking a morsel for him,’ she muttered under her breath, referring to Robbie.

As she stood at the sink peeling the potatoes, Nelly’s thoughts were on Yvonne and a deep sadness washed over her. The girl had been so young and hadn’t had much of a life. What a waste, she thought, and silently cursed God for taking such a sweet girl who didn't have a bad bone in her body.

'Are you all right, love?' Malcolm asked as he came into the kitchen.

'I'm sad and upset, but I'll be all right. One life has passed, but another has come into the world and I hope Rosie's life will be better than her mother's. With Dottie and Adrian as parents there'd be little doubt of that, but I just hope that Robbie stays out of the child's life.'

'Are you still going to tell Dottie that you're pregnant?'

'With what has just happened, I don't think it's the right time.'

'No, I suppose not,' Malcolm said. 'Adrian wants me to take a look at his car. He had a problem starting it but thinks it could just be that the battery is flat. If you need me, I'll be outside.'

'Yeah, all right,' Nelly said, going on to finish peeling the potatoes. Her thoughts went back to Yvonne, but a few minutes later Robbie wheeled himself into the kitchen. She glared at him and clenched the knife in her hand, thinking how she would love to sink it into his flesh. If it hadn't been for him, Malcolm would sleep soundly at night. Instead, she heard him torturing himself in his sleep night after night, blaming himself for Robbie's accident.

'Nelly the News,' he drawled. 'Well, you've heard the latest now so no doubt all of Battersea will know about Yvonne by tomorrow.'

Adrian came in before Nelly had a chance to retaliate and said, 'I'll thank you not to talk to my guests like that.'

'Fine. Actually, Adrian, it's you I want to talk to. In private.'

'I hope this won't take long. Malcolm is outside taking a look at my car and I want to join him.'

'I only want a quick word with you,' Robbie said, wheeling himself away.

Adrian followed Robbie into his room and Nelly was glad when the door closed. She liked spending time with Dottie in her lovely home, but if Robbie was in, seeing him was always unpleasant. She tried to rise above it and let his ugly comments wash over her, but it wasn't always easy. She wondered how Dottie put up with it and thanked her lucky stars she didn't have to see him very often.

Adrian stood in Robbie's room, worn out after being up half the night, with Dottie either crying or having to get up to attend to the baby. 'What do you want to talk to me about?' he asked.

'I've been thinking about you and Dottie taking on the baby. What's its name, by the way?' Robbie asked.

'*Her* name is Rosie,' Adrian replied, his suspicions aroused. He knew his brother of old and guessed he was after something. He waited to hear what was coming next.

'Rosie, that's nice, but the thing is, Adrian, Rosie is my baby, not yours,' Robbie said with a smug smile on his face.

'So, you've finally owned up to it, but why now? You've made it abundantly clear that you don't want her.'

'I know, but that doesn't change the fact that I'm her father, and as such what happens to Rosie and where she goes is ultimately my decision.'

'I can guess what you're after, Robbie, but let me make

this clear. Rosie is not a commodity to be bought, sold or made profit on. She's a dear, sweet baby who deserves love, security and decent parents, so forget any stupid ideas you might have about me paying you to adopt her.'

'I think you may want to rethink your position, Adrian. After all, it's me who has the upper hand on this one. I mean, I'm her father and it's my responsibility to ensure she goes to people who really want her. You've been banging on at me about responsibility for years now, so I'm stepping up and doing what you've told me to. If you want her that much, you'll have to prove it to me by putting your money where your mouth is.'

Adrian shook his head at his brother's audacity and ran a hand tiredly across his face. 'So now you're resorting to blackmail. It was bad enough that you used Yvonne to make you money, but now you're trying to use an innocent child too. You sicken me, but I don't think you've thought this through. You see, Robbie, you previously tried to duck your responsibilities by insisting there was no proof that you're the baby's father. Now, equally, there's no proof that you are.'

'I can still make things difficult for you – make a claim, hold things up.'

'Be careful, Robbie, because I'm almost at the end of my tether with you. Once again you haven't thought things through. You see, if you carry out your threats I will simply cut off your allowance and throw you out of my house.'

'You . . . you . . .' Robbie ground out.

Adrian could see Robbie was fuming and thought steam might come out of his ears. It felt good to hold the upper hand and he secretly smiled to himself. 'Have you got anything else to say?' he calmly asked and when there was no reply he added, 'No, I thought not.'

With that, Adrian walked out of the room. He passed the kitchen to see Nelly was busy preparing dinner and without stopping he went on to the living room to find that Rosie was sound asleep in her pram and his wife had taken a well-deserved nap on the sofa.

He'd go to give Malcolm a hand now, but first he looked at the baby's little rosebud lips. She really was a cutie, he thought, her features reminding him of his sister Myra's first child. He just hoped that Rosie hadn't inherited any of Robbie's personality and that she had a sweet nature like her mother.

Chapter 53

Mrs Hart had been kind enough to look after Rosie and keep an eye on Dorothy's father on the morning of Yvonne's funeral. When they returned, close to midday, Dottie, puffy-eyed from crying, thanked the woman and saw her out.

'I've got a lot of work on, so if you're sure you can cope, I'm going to the office,' Adrian said.

'Nelly's here and I'll be fine,' Dottie told him.

'I know you've given me the day off, but are you sure you don't need me to come into the office too?' Nelly asked.

'No, I can manage without you.'

Dorothy kissed him on the cheek before he left, appreciating his thoughtfulness. She hadn't wanted to be alone for the rest of the day and it was good to have Nelly there. When her friend volunteered to make a fresh pot of tea, Dorothy sat on the sofa, holding Rosie close to her chest. 'We said goodbye to your mummy today,' she said softly. 'But don't worry, my little one, I'll try my best to look after you in her place.'

Nelly came through with two cups of tea. 'It was sad to see so few people at the funeral,' she said, shaking her head. 'I can't believe Yvonne's mother and sister weren't there.'

'I know,' Dorothy responded, 'but with no idea where they are, we couldn't inform them about her death. I don't have much time for that Cynthia but at least she made the effort and turned up with some flowers.'

'It's such a bloody shame. Poor Yvonne didn't have much of a life.'

'I don't even have a picture of her to show Rosie when she gets older,' Dorothy said sadly.

Robbie appeared in the doorway and Dorothy felt her body tense. She had noticed that since Rosie had been born he appeared to have mellowed and she wondered if it was a sign that the old Robbie was emerging, the man she had fallen in love with. However, as he began to speak, his quiet demeanour didn't stop her being on her guard, and she braced herself, waiting for a spiteful comment.

'You can take that look off your face,' he said. 'I won't bite.'

Dorothy relaxed a little before she said, 'I thought you'd have come to the funeral.'

'Well, you thought wrong, and now I'm off out.'

As the front door closed behind him, Nelly said, 'I don't know how you do it. You deserve a medal for putting up with him under your roof.'

'It's not like I have a choice – he's Adrian's brother.'

'Well, if it was me, I don't think I'd be quite so charitable, family or not. Now come on, let me cuddle that little 'un, and you drink your tea.'

Dorothy smiled and reluctantly handed over the baby. She loved the feeling of having Rosie snuggled into her and would happily have held her all day long. Not only had Rosie fulfilled her yearning to be a mother, she also felt she had a little bit of the 'good' Robbie close to her.

'She really is beautiful,' Nelly said. 'You all right, sugar? You look a bit peaky.'

Dorothy stood up, but feeling dizzy, she immediately sat back down again. 'Yes, I'm fine, thanks, Nel, just a little light-headed. I didn't have any breakfast.'

'Right then, take this gorgeous little bundle back, and I'll fix us a bite to eat.'

Dorothy was happy to accept Nelly's offer. She'd been feeling extremely tired lately, but it was little wonder considering she was up three times a night tending to Rosie. Adrian must be feeling it too, she thought, but he never complained. She looked down into Rosie's blue eyes. 'But you're worth it,' she whispered, and brushed her lips over the baby's soft forehead. She couldn't understand how Robbie could ignore Rosie, his own flesh and blood, but he'd made no attempt to hold her. It seemed so wrong that Rosie had a father who rejected her, but for a silly moment she imagined what it would have been like if she hadn't miscarried. Would Robbie have been the same, or would he have come back wanting to hold their child in his arms?

After his brother had called his bluff, Robbie had been forced to think of another way to acquire some quick cash. Eventually, what Adrian had said about Rosie not being a commodity had given him an idea. The baby would be worth money to someone who wanted one desperately enough – he just had to find that person.

'Do me a favour, mate,' Robbie said to a middle-aged

man who was coming down the front stairs from the building where Cynthia lived. 'I can't manage the stairs, so I'd be much obliged if you would knock on someone's door for me and tell them that Robbie's outside.'

'Yeah, all right, but whose door?'

'Cynthia's. Do you know her?'

'Yeah, of course I do, everyone knows Cynthia. I won't be a tick,' the man said and disappeared back into the tenement, to return quickly with Cynthia behind him.

'Hello, Robbie,' she greeted him warmly. 'I was expecting to see you today at Yvonne's funeral.'

'I didn't think I'd be welcome,' Robbie lied. He'd had no intention of going to the funeral. Why would he? That tart meant nothing to him, nor did her offspring.

'Cynth, I need a chat, but not here on the street. Fancy a gin and tonic?'

'You know me, I never say no to a drink,' Cynthia answered, smoothing her bouffant hair.

Once sat in the pub, Robbie supped on his pint. He was bored of the small talk between them, and Cynthia's prattling, most of it going over his head as he tried to think of a way to tell her what was on his mind without totally alienating her. When there was a pause in her chatter, he said cautiously, 'I know nothing much shocks you, but what I'm about to say might.'

'Go on, Robbie. I'm intrigued.'

Robbie leaned in closer to Cynthia and glanced around, ensuring there wasn't anyone within earshot. 'I've got myself in a bit of bother with Brian again, and I need to pay off the debt or, well, you know what he'll do to me.'

'I would help if I could, Robbie, but you know I don't have two pennies to rub together.'

'I don't want your money. I just need a bit of advice. The thing is, with me stuck in this bloody chair, my options are limited. My brother won't help, so the only thing I can think of to raise the money is to . . . err . . . find a willing buyer for Yvonne's baby.'

Robbie looked at Cynthia for her reaction, but she remained pan-faced as she stirred the ice in her drink with her finger. He half expected she might throw it at him, but instead she said quietly, 'I know a bloke who could help.'

'I knew I could rely on you,' Robbie said excitedly. 'How soon can you introduce me?'

'Ain't you going to ask what he might want the baby for?'

'I don't give a shit,' Robbie said, not caring if he sounded callous. 'She's a bastard, and the sooner she's out from under my nose, the better.'

'OK, if you're sure, but you've got to promise that my name will never be mentioned in any of this,' Cynthia insisted.

'You know me. Mum's the word,' Robbie said as he tapped the side of his nose.

'Right then, finish your pint and I'll take you to Jack's Yard. You know the place I mean? The scrappy up near the candle factory. I'll leave you with him and he'll point you in the right direction. I think, from what Jack once told me, his cousin is the bloke you'll need to talk to.'

Robbie gulped his pint, eager to set the wheels in motion. He'd run out of time with Brian, and if he didn't pay off the loan, he feared the next thing to be broken would be his arms.

Chapter 54

The following morning, a Saturday, Dorothy placed Rosie in her pram and pushed it back and forth. This always had the desired effect of getting her off to sleep and would give Dorothy the opportunity to fix her father some breakfast. Pleased when she saw Rosie close her eyes, she hurried upstairs.

'How are you today, Dad?'

'Vonnie . . .' he said quietly.

'I know, I miss her too, but why don't you come downstairs for your breakfast?'

'Vonnie . . .' was his same response.

'Come on, Dad,' Dottie urged. 'You don't want to stay up here all day. Come downstairs and when Rosie wakes up you can hold her. You'd like that, wouldn't you?'

Though she hoped to get some reaction, there was still none. Since Yvonne's death her father had hardly said two words, and she wished she could work the same magic on him as Yvonne had.

He got out of bed to shuffle to the bathroom, and Dorothy was thankful that he still carried out this part of his morning routine. Though she knew that her father was physically in good health, she stood outside the bathroom as he ran a flannel over his face. He turned and looked at her with an angry expression.

'Go . . . do it myself . . .' he said, grumpily.

Dorothy rolled her eyes but appeased him by walking away. She knew he was more than capable of washing himself, but as he was a bit unstable on his legs, she liked to make sure he didn't fall over. She stood outside Yvonne's room; since that fateful morning she hadn't been able to face going in there. Slowly, she pushed the door open to see the bed freshly made up, with no evidence of the tragedy that had taken place. Adrian must have done it and once again she was touched by his thoughtfulness. There were no ghosts, just painful memories as Dottie walked into the room, but as her eyes went to the bed she felt a sudden wave of nausea. Unwanted memories of seeing blood and Yvonne's lifeless body filled her mind and with a hand over her mouth she fled the room as another wave of nausea struck. Thankful to see her father heading back to his room, she dashed to the toilet and was violently sick. With perspiration beading her forehead, Dorothy splashed cold water on her face, vowing that it would be a long time before she'd risk going into Yvonne's room again.

As Robbie left Jack's Yard, he grinned to himself, satisfied with the sizable sum Jack's cousin Pete had offered in exchange for the child. Of course, Pete had assured Robbie of his utmost discretion, so now all Robbie had to do was get his hands on the baby.

He'd heard through Cynthia that Sid, his old partner in crime, had recently been released from prison, and, realising he'd need help to execute his plan, he'd popped a note through Sid's door.

Later that evening, Robbie went into the pub, eager to put his idea into action. He hoped Sid would turn up, as he couldn't think of anyone else he would trust to keep their mouth shut.

As he waited at the bar for his drink, the door opened again and Robbie was pleased to see Sid walk in and make a beeline for him. Robbie eyed the scruffy-looking man as he approached. A three-year stretch hadn't changed Sid: he still looked just as wormy as he did back then. They greeted each other with little enthusiasm, picked up their pints and made their way to a quiet booth.

'Let's get down to business,' Robbie said.

'Is this going to be a nice little earner?' asked Sid.

'It could be, Sidney, but it's a bit delicate, and, well, I'm not sure I can trust you.'

'You know me and of course you can. I helped you with that whisky heist off your brother, and you know I kept shtum about it. Come on, mate, you know I've only just got out so I really need the cash, Robbie. Let me do it, whatever it is.'

'OK, but you'd better not let me down.'

'I won't. You can count on me.'

'All right, I'll give you the chance, Sid, but not a word to anyone.'

'Yeah, don't worry, I've never said a word to anyone before, have I?' Sidney replied.

Robbie agreed, Sid had never grassed him up on his part in the robbery. It had been four years ago. Robbie had known the details of a large haul of premium whisky Adrian was transporting, and he and Sid had pinched the lot and made good money. Sid wasn't as bright as

Robbie and eventually got caught trying to sell off some of his share of the whisky to one of Adrian's best customers. For some reason unknown to Robbie, Sid confessed to the whole crime, leaving Robbie out of it. The man's misplaced loyalty was the reason Robbie felt he could trust him now. He knew at the time that Adrian had suspicions of his involvement, but, with Sid keeping quiet, nothing could be proved, so Robbie had got away with it while Sid had served his time.

Robbie began to explain to Sidney the details of what he wanted the man to do, and was pleased to see Sid didn't seem at all daunted by the idea.

'So let me get this straight, Robbie. You're gonna be out on Monday, but before you go you'll unlock the back door. You want me to sneak in, grab the baby and keep her overnight. What then?'

'I'll meet up with you the following morning.'

'But what if that sister-in-law of yours finds me in the house?'

'She won't. I told you, I've been watching her movements and she's like clockwork. At nine o'clock every morning, she always puts the baby in its pram and then goes upstairs to sort her father out. What you're going to do will only take a couple of minutes and you'll be in and out before she comes back downstairs.'

'Yeah, OK, but how the bloody hell do you think I'm going to be able to look after a baby all day and overnight?'

'You won't have to do much. Just leave her in a drawer or something. She'll be fine. She might cry a bit, but no one will hear her at your place.'

'I bleedin' will.'

'Well, give her a bit of gin or something, that'll knock her out.'

'I don't get this, Robbie . . . why have I got to kidnap the baby for you? If you want her, surely you can just take her. After all, you said she's yours.'

'I don't want the bastard . . . but I know a man who does. That kid is worth a packet to me, and if you don't fuck this up you'll get your share.'

Sid clapped his hands together, before spitting into one palm and offering it to Robbie to shake. 'Deal,' he said.

Robbie declined the handshake but picked up his pint and repeated, 'Deal.'

Chapter 55

As Dorothy prepared her dad's breakfast on Monday morning, she was surprised to see Robbie's bedroom door open and him nowhere to be seen. It wasn't like Robbie to be up and out so early, and she breathed a sigh of relief, instantly relaxing. Her nerves always jangled less when Robbie wasn't in the house.

She poured warm milk over Bill's porridge oats and tapped her foot as she waited for the kettle to boil. Rosie had been running a slight fever and had kept Dottie up for most of the night, but thankfully the baby now seemed more settled. Adrian must have realised she'd had a restless night, so she guessed he had sneaked out to work quietly and allowed her to sleep in. The only problem with having a bit of a lie-in was Bill's mood. She was running late and knew her dad would soon become tetchy if his usual routine was disturbed.

Finally, the kettle whistled and Dottie poured boiling water into the teapot. As she turned to place the kettle back on the stove, something in the back garden caught her eye. She leaned towards the window and peered out, sure she had seen movement.

Then she gasped and stepped back with her hands

over her mouth as she saw a short, thin man slowly mincing up the garden path. He looked very suspicious as he weaved his way in and out behind the shrubs and trees, obviously trying not to be seen.

In a blind panic, Dorothy ran from the kitchen and up the stairs. She had to protect Rosie. She gathered the sleeping child from her cot and raced back to the top of the stairs, holding the baby protectively to her. From here, she had a vantage point, though now she wished she had picked up the phone and called Adrian.

She stood silent, holding her breath and willing Rosie to stay asleep. The house was so quiet, she could hear her heart hammering in her chest. Her mind raced. She hadn't checked the back door. Was it locked? What if the man got into the house?

Hardly daring to move, Dorothy craned her neck in a futile bid to look along the downstairs hallway. It was no good, she couldn't see further than the telephone table. Daringly, with her back against the wall, she took one step down. If she could get to the telephone, she'd call the police.

Then, to her horror, Dorothy heard the distinct sound of the hinge on the back door squeaking. Before now, Adrian had mentioned oiling it but she was glad he hadn't, as now she knew for sure that there was an intruder in the house.

She froze in fear, but could feel her body trembling.

From her viewpoint at the top of the stairs, she saw the top of the man's head as he crept along the hallway. She couldn't believe he was in her house, but she didn't want to scream and scare Rosie or her father.

Thinking quickly, Dorothy took a deep breath and tried to make her voice sound deep and booming as she called, 'Get out of my house!' She hoped she didn't sound as scared as she felt.

The man was near the bottom of the stairs and turned to look at Dorothy. She thought he looked as surprised to see her as she did him. For a fleeting moment, their eyes met, and Dorothy thought he might run up the stairs to attack her, but instead he turned and fled, leaving her relieved but still shaking in fear.

Slowly and cautiously, she made her way down the stairs. She couldn't be sure he had left the house; he could pounce on her at any moment. She sidled up to the telephone table in the hallway and dialled Adrian's number in the office.

'Dottie, good morning, sweetheart,' she heard Adrian say. The sound of his voice felt so soothing and reassuring, Dorothy found herself in tears and unable to speak.

'Dottie . . . what's wrong?' Adrian asked.

She drew in a long, juddering breath, 'There was a man in the house,' she managed to cry.

'Take Rosie into Bill's room, shut the door and stay there. I'll be straight home.'

Dottie heard the line go dead as Adrian hung up. She held the telephone in her hand as she gathered her thoughts, then quickly followed Adrian's instructions.

Bill was sitting up in bed, oblivious to the fright Dorothy had just had.

'Tea time,' he said, smiling.

'In a minute, Dad. I thought you might like a cuddle with Rosie first,' Dorothy said, as she placed the sleeping baby in Bill's arms.

Dorothy stood against the bedroom door, inconspicuously leaning hard against it. She flashed her father a fake smile, relieved to see him in a good mood and unaware of the uninvited house guest.

'Rosie sleeping, bad night,' Bill said.

'Yes, Dad, she was a bit poorly but she's much better this morning. She loves her cuddles with Grandad. Let's be really quiet so we don't wake her.'

'Grandad . . .' Bill said, and smiled down sweetly at the child.

Dottie strained her ears, listening for any movement in the house, and wished she could hear Adrian's car pulling up. It felt like she'd been stood there for ages when she eventually heard the rumble of a car engine.

She could hear footsteps pounding up the stairs, and pushed harder against the door. What if it wasn't Adrian?

'Dottie, it's me.' Her body slumped with relief at the sound of his voice. She opened the door and fell into her husband's arms.

'It's all right, love,' he said, as he held her shaking body.

'Oh, Adrian, I was so scared. I saw him coming up the garden, and panicked. I didn't even think to check if the back door was locked, I just made a dash up the stairs to get Rosie. The next thing I know, he was stood at the bottom in the hallway as bold as brass!'

'You stay here, I'll check he's definitely gone,' Adrian said.

Dottie nodded, and watched with trepidation as Adrian went downstairs.

He soon returned. 'All clear. Come on, you look like you need a cup of sweet tea.'

Dottie looked at Bill, who appeared to be very content with Rosie, and followed her husband downstairs.

'Had you unlocked the back door this morning?' Adrian asked as he came into the lounge with two cups of tea.

'No, to be honest, I haven't been up long.'

'Robbie must have then. I always check it at night, so I know it was locked. But why would Robbie do that? He never goes out there. Where is he?'

'I don't know, he was gone when I got up,' Dottie answered.

'Did you get a look at the man?'

'I did, but I didn't recognise him. He was short and thin, with dark, dirty hair and very tatty clothes. What do you think he was after?'

'Probably just a vagrant chancing his luck. I'll call in to the police station on my way back to the office and let them know what's happened. They'll keep an eye out. If he didn't get anything from here, he might have tried some other houses in the area.'

'Oh, Adrian, he might still be in the street! You need to call the police now, and check on Mrs Hart.'

'It's all right, Dottie, calm down. He won't be anywhere around here, not now he knows he's been seen. He would have scarpered as far away from here as possible.'

Dottie could feel her heart pounding again. 'Are you sure?'

'Yes, I'm more than sure, so don't worry. I'll pop next door and have a word with Mrs Hart now. Are you OK?'

'Yes, I'm fine. It was a bit of a shock, but you're probably right, he'll be well away by now.'

Adrian went next door whilst Dottie drained the last of her tea. Well, that was an eventful morning, she thought, and wondered what her mother would have made of it.

The streets she'd grown up in might not have been as fancy as these ones, but you could usually leave your back door open and still feel safe. She could understand why Alice had never wanted to leave the slums. They didn't have much, but they did offer a sense of community, and though Dottie enjoyed the luxuries of her grand home, it was at times like this that she missed her old place.

After ensuring Dottie felt secure enough to be left alone, Adrian drove back to his office. He hadn't let on to his wife, but he was sure there was more to the break-in than met the eye. It was all a bit coincidental – the back door being unlocked and Robbie being out of the house that early.

He couldn't gauge what was going on, but had a niggling feeling his brother was behind it. It wouldn't be the first time Robbie had stolen from them, if that was the man's intention. Alice's ring and his Rolex were never recovered, and, though Robbie denied it, Adrian knew his brother was responsible for the theft. Then there was the whisky heist. Robbie would have been the only person who knew about the cargo, but yet again, though Adrian had known Robbie was involved, his brother had got away with his crimes.

Robbie had shown he had no scruples, yet Adrian found it hard to accept that his own flesh and blood would send a strange man into the house, knowingly putting his daughter, Dottie and an ill old man at risk.

He knew it wouldn't be easy to concentrate at work, all the time worrying about his wife, so decided he'd finish as early as possible. He thought Dottie would appreciate him coming home, and if Robbie came back too, he'd be able to catch and question him before he disappeared out down the pub.

Robbie breezed through the front door, putting on a carefree façade. He was surprised to see Adrian's car wasn't parked outside the house, and even more surprised to see Dottie sitting on the sofa giving Rosie her bottle.

He fumed as he realised Sid hadn't done the job, and assumed the scallywag must have bottled out. So much for him needing the money, Robbie thought, vowing never to trust the man again. He just had to hope Sid had at least kept his mouth shut.

As he wheeled himself into his bedroom, his mind was already scheming how he could steal the baby, when he heard Dottie call out to him.

Irritated at the interruption to his thoughts, he went into the lounge. 'What?' he snapped.

'You should know, a man broke into the house this morning. He ran off when he saw me, but just keep your eyes open,' Dottie said.

Robbie's mind raced. Sid hadn't bottled it, he'd been caught.

'Did you speak to him?' Robbie asked, then regretted his question.

'No, of course not, only to tell him to get out.'

'Did you know him?'

'No, never seen him before. By the way, did you unlock the back door this morning?' Dottie asked, as she lifted her eyes from the baby to look at him.

'No, why? Is that where he came in?' Robbie asked, knowing he could tell Dottie anything and she'd believe him.

'Yes, but Adrian was sure the door was locked. Oh, well, maybe I left it unlocked when I put the washing out yesterday. You were out early this morning. That's unusual for you,' Dottie added.

Robbie felt fairly certain that it was an innocent remark, but he had to be careful. He didn't want to rouse her suspicions. 'I thought I had an appointment at the hospital for a check-up. Seems I got my dates mixed up and it's next month, not that it's anything to do with you.'

He had been to the hospital; it was the perfect alibi, though normally he would have badgered Adrian to fork out for a taxi. Dottie seemed satisfied with his answer and returned her attention to the baby.

Robbie went back to his room and hauled himself from his chair and onto his bed, cursing as he did so. Damn it, he thought, angry that his plan had been foiled and Sid had been seen. He wondered if the man would still want to go through with it, if he'd be bold enough to try again. If Sid refused, Robbie had one up on him. Dottie would be able to identify Sid, so if it came to it, he was more than willing to resort to a bit of blackmail to get Sid to carry out the kidnapping.

Chapter 56

On Wednesday evening, Malcolm went into the pub. It was something he rarely did these days, but Nelly had gone to her sister's to babysit whilst Linda and her husband attended some sort of works do. When Nelly had told him her plans for the evening, Malcolm hadn't really been listening to the details, but as he sat in the corner of the pub with his whisky chaser, he had to admit he was glad of some time to himself. He was annoyed with Nelly. He wanted to break the news to his mother that his wife was pregnant, but she still wouldn't have it. He knew that Dottie was her best friend, but surely family came first.

To lower his mood even further, Malcolm saw Robbie wheeling himself into the pub. Every time he saw the man he felt a surge of guilt at the part he'd played in his dreadful accident. Remembering the sight of his twisted body at the foot of the stairs, Malcolm felt his eyes well with tears and fought to pull himself together. He couldn't be seen in a pub blubbering like a baby – he'd never live it down. He knew he was a big softie and so did his wife, but because of his mammoth size, he was known to have a bit of a reputation as a hard man and didn't want to lose it.

Malcolm hunched down in his booth, glad that Robbie hadn't spotted him as he wheeled himself to the bar. Before Robbie had a chance to order, a snidey-looking, weedy bloke joined him. They ordered drinks and Malcolm quickly picked up the evening paper that had been left on the table and held it in front of his face as he pretended to read. He hoped that once the two men were settled he'd be able to sneak out of the pub, but as he peeped around the newspaper he saw that they were heading his way. He ducked sideways as though picking something up from under his table, and thankfully they didn't see him as they sat in the neighbouring booth. There was only a dark wood partition, topped with misted glass, between him and Robbie, and though Robbie spoke quietly, Malcolm heard every word.

'So what went wrong then, Sid?' Robbie asked.

'I dunno, Robbie. You said she'd be upstairs and the baby in the pram, but she weren't. I got in all right, but the pram was empty and your sister-in-law spotted me,' Sid replied.

Malcolm wasn't normally the nosy sort; he thought all that gossip and stuff was best left to his wife. However, Nelly had mentioned something about an intruder in Dottie's house and from what he was hearing, it sounded like something shifty was going on, so his ears pricked.

'You're going to have to go back and try again,' Robbie said.

'I don't know about that, Robbie. I mean, it's a bit risky now, ain't it? They'll be extra vigilant now.'

'It'll be fine. I've been watching her the last couple of mornings and she's back to her old routine as if nothing happened. Anyway, you didn't get properly caught so you've got nothing to worry about.'

'I ain't happy about risking it. You know I've only just got out from being banged up, and I can't face going back to prison.'

'Stop being so soft in the head, Sid. This is going to be a good earner for you, easy money too.'

'You say that, Robbie, but it seems it's me taking all the risk here. All you've gotta do is sell the kid, I'm the one nicking it!' Sid said.

'Oh, and you think there's no risk in selling a baby? Come off it, Sid, it's hardly legal to trade in children. Where else are you going to get your hands on this sort of cash, eh? The bloke who said he'll have Rosie is willing to pay more money than you'd make in a year of hard graft.'

'I suppose, but I still ain't convinced. Who are you selling the kid to?'

'You know Jack, he's got the scrapyard up near the candle factory, well, his cousin said he'd have her.'

'What, Pervy Pete? He's a . . . you know . . . he likes—'

Robbie sounded like he was growing impatient with Sid's chatter and quickly interrupted him. 'Let me put it another way, Sid,' Robbie said, 'If you don't do it, I might be tempted to have a little word in Dottie's ear. She saw you, and I bet she'd have no problem pointing you out in a line-up.'

'You wouldn't grass me up, would you? I'd tell them it was your idea and tell 'em about the whisky job too,' Sid said.

'Who do you think they would believe, Sid? You're an ex-con fresh out of jail. Look, I don't want this to get nasty, I just want that baby. I'll level with you, Sid . . . I need the money.'

Sid agreed and as Robbie began to go over the details of what he wanted the man to do again, Malcolm's hackles rose.

'Right, not tomorrow, Friday morning it is. Cheers.'

Malcolm was seething, sickened by what he'd heard. He wanted to leap over to the other booth and knock the shit out of both of them, but as it was only hearsay and his word against theirs, he'd probably end up behind bars. Anyway, giving them both a hiding wasn't enough. He wanted everyone to know what an evil bastard Robbie was, and he'd start by telling Nelly.

However, things didn't go according to Malcolm's plans. He'd been shaken by what Robbie had said and felt he needed a strong drink to calm his nerves. Thankfully, Robbie didn't hang around and left the pub sharpish, closely followed by Sid. As soon as Malcolm saw them leave, he went to the bar, ordered a large whisky and quickly swallowed it. He was still reeling and that whisky was followed by another. By the time the landlord called last orders, Malcolm was unsteady on his legs and after staggering home he went to bed and passed out in a drunken stupor.

When he awoke in the morning, bleary-eyed, he remembered what he'd heard the previous evening. He drank greedily from the glass of water on his bedside table and then said, 'Nelly, I've got something to tell you.'

'You don't need to. I can smell it on your breath. You went out for a drink last night. You should know better, you've got work today.'

'Yeah, but it's not that,' he said, and went on to tell her what he'd heard.

'He said what?' Nelly turned her face from Malcolm's stale, beery breath and threw back the covers to get out of bed. 'We've got to get round to Dottie's. We've got to warn them.'

'Can't we have a cup of tea first?'

'Yes, I suppose so,' Nelly agreed as she dressed, 'but then get a move on. I'm not risking that filthy low-life git getting his hands on Rosie.'

'From what I heard, it won't be happening until tomorrow.'

'I don't trust him. Something could happen to make him bring things forward, and that Sid has already been in their house once.'

By a quarter past seven, Nelly was pounding on Dorothy's front door, not caring if she woke the neighbours.

Adrian opened it, looking sleepy. 'Nelly, what on earth's the matter?'

'Your bloody brother, that's what,' Nelly answered as she pushed past Adrian. 'Get Dottie. This is important.'

Adrian went upstairs while Nelly and Malcolm waited in the living room. Nelly paced up and down, fuming, wanting to go screaming into Robbie's room.

Dorothy walked in with Adrian and looked bewildered as she asked, 'What's wrong?'

'This is going to knock you both for six, so you'd best sit down and I'll explain,' Nelly said. 'As for Robbie, I take it he's still in his room?'

'He might be, though I'm not sure if he came home last night,' Adrian answered.

'And Rosie, is she upstairs in her cot?' Nelly asked.

'Yes, sleeping soundly after keeping us up half the night,' Dorothy said wryly.

'OK, Malcolm, tell them,' Nelly ordered.

'Well, Nelly was out last night; she was babysitting while her sister and her hubby went to a do. Anyway, I don't normally drink, but I fancied a pint so I went to a local pub and found a seat in a booth—'

'Oh, for goodness' sake, Malcolm, I'll tell them,' Nelly interrupted irritably. 'Robbie's planning on stealing Rosie, but he's going to make it look like he had nothing to do with it. That's what that bloke was here for on Monday. He's working with Robbie to take Rosie.'

Nelly saw Adrian and Dorothy look at each other with open mouths and went on to tell them all that Malcolm had overheard, then adding, 'I was shocked to the core when Malcolm told me. Robbie said he was going to sell her to Pervy Pete, and we've all heard about him and them schoolgirls—'

'Sell her?' Adrian interrupted. 'You're telling us that Robbie plans to kidnap Rosie and then sell her?'

'Yes! I know, it sounds ridiculous, but, well, I wouldn't put anything past him,' Nelly answered.

'I can't believe this,' Dottie said, her face wan as she flopped back on the sofa.

Adrian got up and pulled the curtains open, letting bright sunlight stream into the room. 'This man that Robbie met. What did you say his name is?' asked Adrian.

'Sid,' Malcolm told him.

'What did he look like?'

'He was short and skinny, with dark hair, and about the same age as Robbie.'

'Sidney Cole . . . I should have guessed.'

'You know him then, Adrian?' Nelly asked.

'Oh, yes, I know him all right. He was an old

schoolfriend of Robbie's, a right little so-and-so. I had him arrested a few years ago for pinching one of my trucks which just happened to be loaded with quality whisky from Scotland. Robbie swore blind he had nothing to do with it, but I always had my suspicions. It seemed a bit too convenient that Sidney knew the exact time and place to execute the robbery. He was never that bright so someone had to have given him inside information.'

Nelly sat next to Dottie, worried that her friend looked as white as a sheet. 'Are you OK, sugar?'

'That sounds exactly like the man who broke in here. I just can't believe that Robbie would do this,' Dorothy answered sadly.

'I always said he was low-life, but even I didn't think he'd sink this far,' Nelly said.

'Malcolm, thank you, and you too, Nelly,' Adrian said. 'I'm not sure how I'm going to handle this yet, but trust me, I'll deal with my brother.'

Nelly was inwardly seething. Any trouble, upset or worries always involved Robbie bloody Ferguson and whether it was wicked to think it or not, she wished he'd died when he'd fallen down those stairs. She didn't know how Adrian was going to deal with him, but if she had her way she'd get someone to knock the wicked bastard off. Or, better still, she'd throttle the bloody life out of him herself.

Chapter 57

Robbie was sitting in a strange kitchen, his mind on the previous evening. He already regretted intimidating Sid. He only wanted the man to kidnap the baby, but had been daft enough to lay it on thick and force Sid into doing as he wanted by blackmailing him. Not only that, but he'd told Sid who he'd lined up to buy the child. What if Sidney took umbrage at Robbie's threat and opened his mouth? Robbie slumped in his chair as it dawned on him that he might have completely buggered up his only chance of getting his hands on some much-needed cash.

He looked at the girl sitting opposite him, thinking that she must be a bit naïve, as he tucked into the sausage sandwich she'd made him. Fancy believing he was a war veteran and had sustained his injuries during a battle in Holland. He didn't think he looked old enough to have served in the war, but he didn't care, as long as it got him his leg over. Fat from the sausages dripped down his chin as he remembered snippets from the night before. When he'd parted from Sidney, he'd gone on to another pub and had found some mugs to buy him drinks. He had a vague memory of chatting to the girl outside, but couldn't remember her name or coming back to her place. Actually, he wasn't sure where he was, and hoped he wasn't too far from home.

The girl stood up and Robbie stared at the shortest nightdress he'd ever seen. He was impressed with her large, bulging bosom too as she sashayed towards him. He smiled with appreciation.

She leaned over the table, almost pushing her breasts into his face as she asked, 'Do you fancy going back to bed?'

Robbie's head felt thick. He didn't think he was up to it, and, with tomorrow looming, he had more important things on his mind. 'Maybe later, love. I've got to get off now, but I could come back this evening if you like,' he said, fobbing her off.

'Yeah, all right,' she agreed and when she stood up to leave she walked in front of him, wriggling her bottom all the way to the front door.

Once outside, Robbie surveyed the street. It didn't look familiar to him, but he spotted Battersea Power Station in the near distance. He knew if he headed in that direction, he'd soon find his way home and hoped he had the strength in his arms to wheel himself that far. He hoped to see a taxi on the way, but on a Sunday morning the chances of that were slim. Still, with the thought of the money he'd soon have in his pocket, he set out, planning to pay back the money he owed Brian, and then have a good time with the rest.

A tense silence fell across the room when they heard the front door open. Dorothy had never seen Adrian so incensed, and steeled herself for the coming confrontation.

She didn't know what he was going to do – he hadn't said – but he'd told them all to leave Robbie to him.

Dorothy's stomach knotted in fear, but she didn't doubt Adrian. He'd never let her down before, and had always looked after her and protected her. Now she felt sure he would do the same for Rosie, and she was glad the baby was asleep safely upstairs. Nelly grabbed her hand as if sensing her distress.

'Robbie, in here,' Adrian called, sounding deceptively calm.

When he wheeled himself into the room, he quickly scanned them all before asking, 'Yeah, what do you want?'

This was going to be ugly, thought Dorothy.

'I'll put this simply, Robbie . . . go to your room, pack your things and get out,' Adrian snapped. 'I never want to see your face again. You're dead to me.'

Robbie looked shocked. 'But why? Why are you throwing me out?'

'I think you know. Now get out. This is my house and I don't want you in it. Oh, and don't bother calling Myra – your sister doesn't want to be lumbered with you. In fact, like me, she no longer wants anything to do with you. Dottie and Rosie are my family now, and you're no longer a part of it. I've given you chance after chance, but what you're planning is the final straw.'

'What's the final straw? What am I supposed to have done?'

'You know full well. I don't understand how a man could even consider selling any baby into God knows what, let alone his own flesh and blood!'

'Hold on, Adrian, where did you get that idea from? As if I would sell Rosie,' Robbie said.

Dorothy could tell he was lying; there was no sincerity in his voice.

'Don't try and worm your way out of it. I know all about your chat with Sidney last night. You got him to break in here on Monday. He frightened the life out of Dottie. Thank God Dottie and Rosie are OK, but no thanks to you.'

'What chat with Sidney? It was him who broke in? I didn't even know he was out of prison. You've seen him, have you? Is that what he's told you? I bet he asked you for money for info. And you believe that fucking idiot over your own brother? You know he's a thief and a bloody liar!'

'It's you who's the liar, Robbie. You see, someone was in the pub last night and saw you with Sid. He also heard every word that you said to him.'

Robbie's eyes flicked to Malcolm and as they narrowed suspiciously he said, 'So that's why you're here. Well, whatever you've told Adrian, it's all lies.'

'You little shit,' Nelly spat, breaking her silence. 'My Malcolm has told the truth and if you don't apologise to him I'll knock your bloody block off.'

'Not if I get to him first,' Malcolm growled.

'Robbie, enough of this!' Adrian said, his voice rising. 'You can't bluff your way out of this, so just get out. I've told you, I no longer have a brother, so just go, or I'll be forced to call the police. I'm sure they'd be interested to hear about the jeweller's in Knightsbridge.'

Robbie gritted his teeth and quickly moved forward, surprising them all with his strength as he rammed himself into Adrian's legs. 'No!' Dorothy screamed.

Malcolm flew across the room, and before Dorothy

could fathom what was going on, she saw that Adrian was all right as between them he and Malcolm picked up Robbie's chair, with him in it, and marched him down the hallway.

'You can't do this,' Robbie was ranting. 'You can't do this . . . you fucking dicks, put me down.'

With that the front door slammed closed, but Dorothy could still hear him screaming outside. 'Let me back in or I'll smash this door down! I'm warning you, Adrian, I'll have you fucking killed, I will, and that fucking bitch of a wife!'

'Ignore him,' Adrian said. 'Nelly, can you throw Robbie's stuff in a case, or anything else you can find?'

'Yes, of course,' Nelly answered.

'Blast, I should have taken his key,' Adrian said as they heard a key in the lock.

'I'll make sure he doesn't come in,' Malcolm said as he rushed from the room.

Dorothy heard Malcolm scuffling with Robbie on the doorstep. Then the door slammed again, and she heard the letterbox open.

'You're dead, do you hear me? You and Dottie . . . I'll make sure you die slow and painfully, then what'll happen to your precious bastard baby, eh? I'll do what I fucking like with her, that's what! Who gives a shit about a whore's child? She's nothing, just like her mother, and soon she'll be used just like her too.'

Dorothy felt like a knife had stabbed her in the heart at the thought of anything bad happening to Rosie. Robbie's words repelled her and, as though a veil had suddenly lifted from her eyes, she realised that he repelled her too. He was an animal, despicable and revolting. A shiver ran through her as she finally saw Robbie's true colours. She hated him – but she hated herself even more for ever loving the man in the first place.

Robbie finally calmed down and gave up. He realised Adrian wasn't going to let him back in, and then anxiety struck him.

He wheeled himself onto the pavement and scanned the street. Some neighbours were on their doorsteps, others were twitching curtains. Considering the scene he'd created, it was little wonder the nosy parkers were out in force with wagging tongues. He managed to hold back, but almost told them all to bugger off and mind their own.

He checked his pockets, but was sorely disappointed when he found he had no money. Feeling helpless, he headed towards Cynthia's. She'd help him, she always did, but then he realised there wasn't much she could do. The woman never had any money and she wouldn't even be able to offer him a bed for the night, not with all the stairs in her building that he'd have to contend with.

He could go back to the girl he had left earlier, he thought, trying to recall her name. Maybe he could spin her another yarn and she'd put him up for a few days or longer. He needed some time to collect his thoughts and work out what to do. One thing he knew for sure was that, no matter what, he would not be going into any hospital or asylum.

'What do you want me to do with his stuff?' Nelly asked.

'Just leave it where it is, thanks, Nelly,' Adrian replied.

'I think Robbie has gone for now, but he'll no doubt be back, with his tail between his legs.' Not that Adrian was prepared to forgive his brother.

'I think we should call the police, Adrian,' Dorothy said.

'No, it's all hearsay. I despise the man, and there's nothing I'd like more than to see him behind bars, but at the end of the day I think fate will deal him a fair blow.'

'What do you mean?' Dorothy asked.

'Well, there's not much left for him. I can't see anyone else putting him up, so he'll either be living on the streets or he'll have to go into the infirmary. Let's face it, it's not a nice choice. In fact, I think I would rather be homeless than live in one of those places. It's only his body that's broken, his mind is all there, but he'll be locked up with all sorts of disturbed people,' Adrian replied.

'I don't like to think of anyone in one of those sort of places, but Robbie doesn't deserve any better,' Dorothy said. 'I'm just so glad Rosie slept through all the shouting,' she added. 'But now I could really do with a cuddle.'

Adrian walked over to his wife, and though he wasn't usually demonstrative in front of people, he pulled Dorothy from the sofa and held her to him. 'You can have a cuddle any time you like, Mrs Ferguson,' he said.

Dorothy smiled and whispered, 'A cuddle from Rosie, I meant, but I like this one too.'

'Oi, you two,' Nelly interrupted, 'time and place.'

'Don't be such a prude,' Dorothy teased her friend over her shoulder, 'I'm allowed to cuddle my lovely husband.' She faced Adrian again and said, 'Unhand me, kind sir, I need to check on my dad.'

Adrian felt proud to hear Dorothy speak about him like that, and it was nice she was smiling again too. She'd looked horrified when Robbie had been shouting his threats and abuse. Hopefully she'd put it behind her, and they could resume a happy family life, just the three of them and Bill.

Chapter 58

Robbie's uncertainties had disturbed his sleep, and he woke up feeling exhausted. Not only was he worried about where he was going to live and what he was going to live on, worse was the thought of the money he owed Brian.

After sticking a note through Sid's door to tell him the job was off, he'd managed to find his way back to where he had stayed the previous night. He'd eventually remembered her name, Eileen, and he could hear her in the kitchen clattering around. She'd seemed pleased to see him when he had turned up, but he hadn't yet broached the subject of staying for longer. Her flat was tidy and comfortable, and, once she'd moved a few bits of furniture around, access with his wheelchair was relatively easy, though she had to help him over the front step.

Eileen walked into the bedroom carrying two cups of tea.

'Here you go, love,' she said, and handed Robbie one.

'Cheers, Eileen,' Robbie said, and wondered if now would be a good time to mention staying for a while.

'I've got to go to work soon so you'll have to leave.'

'I was hoping you'd let me hang around here and wait for you to come home,' he said, and rubbed his hand up her bare thigh.

'Oh, I see. Thing is, Robbie, it's . . . awkward, if you get my drift.'

'What's awkward about it? You fancy me, don't you?'

'Yeah, of course I do, but . . . I'm married,' Eileen said quietly.

Robbie hadn't seen any sign of a man living in the flat and he thought maybe Eileen was telling fibs. He frowned. 'So where's your old man?'

'He's banged up in Wandsworth nick doing a three-year stretch. Silly bugger got caught turning over some posh gaff in Chelsea,' Eileen answered.

'When's he due for release?'

'In a couple of months.'

'In that case, we've still got plenty of time,' Robbie said and winked at Eileen.

'No, sorry, I don't want a proper relationship. I don't mind the odd one-night stand here and there – I mean, a girl's got her needs – but I have to draw the line at that.'

Robbie could tell Eileen wasn't going to budge, so decided to come clean. 'I'll be honest with you. I don't have anywhere else to go. I was staying at my brother's house, but we had a bit of a falling out and he asked me to leave. Can I just stay here for a few days until I get myself straight?'

Eileen didn't look too pleased. 'You're an old soldier with war wounds and there's places for people like you.'

'Well, that's not strictly true,' Robbie told her, deciding

to come clean. 'I was never a soldier. I was too young to fight in the war.'

'But you told me . . .'

'Yes, I know and I'm sorry. I was trying to impress you, but the truth is I broke my back by falling down some stairs.'

Eileen's brow knotted into a frown, but then her face softened. 'We're as bad as each other. I didn't tell you I was married so I suppose that makes us even.'

'Can I stay then?'

'Yeah, for a few nights, but that's all.'

'Thanks. One more thing . . . could you lend me a few bob? I'll pay you back . . .'

'You're taking the bleedin' micky now. I'm scrubbing floors five days a week to keep this place going for when my Charlie gets out and I ain't got money to throw about,' she said, and walked out of the bedroom, huffing as she went.

Robbie drained the last dregs of his tea. He was still penniless but at least he had a roof over his head for a few days.

Eileen poked her head back into the room. 'I've got to go. If you want something to eat you'll have to make yourself some toast, assuming you can manage that.'

'Thanks.' He paused. 'I've got to go out for a couple of hours. Have you got a spare key?'

'Yeah, there's one on the hall table. Bloody hell, I must be mad,' she said, her parting shot as the front door closed behind her.

Robbie pursed his lips. Now that he had opened up to her, Eileen wasn't being quite as friendly. Not that he was bothered. He had other things on his mind, starting with a visit to Adrian's. He needed some clothes, and his record player might earn him some money from the pawnshop, enough to at least offer Brian a couple of quid.

Malcolm climbed into the cab of his truck feeling unusually refreshed. For the first time in a long while, he'd slept the whole night through, and hadn't been plagued by nightmares about Robbie Ferguson. It'd be a long time before he lost any more sleep over that scumbag, he thought, and turned the key in the ignition.

Malcolm was happy whistling a Sinatra tune as he drove through the streets of Battersea on his way to Tooting to do his first pick-up of the day. Though his job was mostly solitary, he enjoyed it, and thought Adrian was a terrific boss. Even so, there was no guarantee Adrian would agree to Nelly cutting her hours, or even continuing to work once the baby was born.

He was a bit worried about the future and wanted to know how they would stand financially. The sooner his wife told Dorothy, the better, and with it out in the open Nelly would be able to sort things out with Adrian. He'd have a word with her tonight, see if he couldn't persuade her to get a move on.

He chuckled to himself. Blimey, he thought, it wasn't like Nelly to keep her mouth quiet about anything!

Dorothy took Rosie up to her dad's room. She'd normally put her in her cot, but she had no intention of leaving her alone for even a minute.

'Morning, Dad. I'm just going to lay Rosie here next to you for a minute whilst I pop back downstairs to get your breakfast. You OK keeping an eye on her? She normally dozes off at this time,' Dorothy said as she tucked Rosie in next to him.

'Vonnie . . . baby . . .'

'Yes, Dad,' she said, pleased to see the beaming smile on his face. He had loved Yvonne and now seemed equally enamoured with her baby. He reached out his hand and Rosie clasped his finger, happily gurgling.

Satisfied they were both comfortable, Dorothy dashed downstairs to the kitchen. It had been a difficult day yesterday, and she'd worried that all the noise had upset her father. He must have heard Robbie shouting, but thankfully he'd seemed unaffected by it and this morning he looked alert and happy.

Dorothy took a bowl of beef dripping from the larder, and noticed how empty the shelves were. She'd have to do some shopping later, which meant she'd need to ask Mrs Hart to come round to keep an eye on her dad. It wasn't ideal, but she had little choice.

As she lathered two slices of bread, her nose wrinkled. She hated the smell of beef dripping, and she wouldn't normally give it to him for breakfast, but it was quick to make and one of her dad's favourites.

She put the plate on a tray with a cup of tea, and, hoping that her dad was still all right with Rosie, she hurried up to his room. She missed Yvonne terribly and hadn't realised how much she'd come to rely on the girl. Maybe it was time to admit defeat and allow Adrian to hire some help.

If there was one thing that Cynthia detested, it was shopping, especially with the hangover from hell. She was out of tea and milk so missed her usual morning cuppa, something she'd kill for now, she thought as she trudged along the High Street.

She'd wrapped a scarf around her head to hide her unkempt hair, and donned a fashionable pair of dark sunglasses to cover her bleary eyes. It wasn't often she ventured out before eleven in the morning, and she was just thinking that there ought to be a bloody law against it when, to her horror, she saw Robbie coming towards her. She darted into the butcher's, hoping he hadn't seen her, and looked through the window, hoping he'd pass by.

'Morning, missus, what can I get for you?'

Cynthia spun round to be greeted by a counter displaying cuts of raw meat. Her stomach churned at the sight and she felt like throwing up on the sawdust-covered floor. Bile rose in her throat and, quickly flinging open the door, she stumbled outside. Closing her eyes, she leaned against the doorframe and breathed in gulps of fresh air that instantly made her feel better.

'Hello, Cynthia, fancy seeing you here,' Robbie said.

Her heart sank. She didn't want to be seen talking to him, so without saying a word she quickly walked away.

'Cynthia, what's up? Hang on, slow down.'

She picked up her pace, wanting to get as far away from Robbie as possible. There had been rumours about him flying around the pub last night. A bloke at the bar had heard it from his mate, who had heard it from his sister, who had heard it from her mate who lived in the same road as Robbie. It didn't take long for word to spread, and everyone had been disgusted to hear that Robbie had been involved in some sort of seedy scam to sell his own daughter, and when Cynthia had heard it, she'd cringed and wished for the pub floor to open up and swallow her.

News travelled fast, so without doubt most of Battersea knew by now and Cynthia deeply regretted taking Robbie to Jack's Yard.

He hadn't told her the full story, but even so, if anyone found out that she was implicated in any way she'd be ostracised and unable to walk into any pub in the area again.

Robbie didn't seem to be giving up easily, and, wheels spinning, he continued to follow her along the High Street. 'Cynthia, why are you trying to run away from me?'

Cynthia realised that she wasn't going to get rid of him, and turned to face him. She quickly looked around to make sure nobody was in earshot and then hissed, 'Leave me alone, Robbie. I don't want anything to do with you now. The cat's out of the bag. Everyone's saying you was going to sell your baby to a perv and they reckon you must be one too. Just piss off and keep me out of it.' With that, she turned and ran back towards home, forgetting all about the tea and milk, and not looking back to give Robbie so much as a second glance.

Stupid old cow, thought Robbie as he watched Cynthia race away from him. She was nothing more than a washed-up old tart. So what if people were talking, they couldn't prove a thing, and, as it happened, he hadn't done anything.

Now he had all the more reason to be nervous though. It wouldn't just be Brian's heavies vying for his blood, so would half the blokes in Battersea. They didn't take well to men they thought were kiddie-fiddlers, and from what Cynthia had said it appeared that's how he had now been branded.

How ridiculous, he thought; he'd never touch a child. The trouble was, he wouldn't be given the chance to explain his defence, not once the local hard nuts heard about him.

He looked around nervously and decided to forget his clothes and the record player. He would have to keep his head down and go straight back to Eileen's instead. No one knew he was there and he felt it would be safe, but by the time he arrived the muscles in his arms were screaming. He was worn out and sweaty, and, as Eileen was still at work, he cursed as he struggled to get his chair over the front step.

He finally managed it and wheeled himself into Eileen's living room, but, now exhausted, he slumped in his chair. With little rest the night before, and waking early that morning, Robbie closed his eyes and drifted off to sleep.

'Wake up, you bastard!'

Robbie woke with a start to see Eileen hovering over him, a snarl on her face. He was still half asleep and his throat dry as he croaked, 'What's up?'

'What's up?' she yelled. 'I'll tell you what's up. You failed to tell me that you were thrown out of your brother's 'cos you was gonna sell their kid to some . . . some . . . Gawd, I can't even bring meself to say it!'

Shocked that the gossip had already travelled this far, he blustered, 'It isn't true, I swear,' and reached out to grab her hand.

She jerked it away and slapped him hard across his face. 'I'm not listening to any more of your lies. Get out of my flat, Robbie. I just hope nobody knew you were here, because, inside or not, if my Charlie hears about what you've been up to your life won't be worth living, and nor will mine. Go on, sling your dirty hook,' Eileen snapped.

Robbie could see that he wouldn't be able to make her change her mind, but didn't want to venture outside, not with everyone talking about him and many probably out to get him.

'Did you hear me, or are you deaf as well? I said get out. Your sort ain't welcome here!' she spat. She walked behind the chair, pushed him to the front door and opened it.

'Hold on,' he appealed, but to no avail as he was shoved roughly over the step.

As the door slammed, the nerves immediately set in, and Robbie looked around, convinced that someone would leap out to give him a good hiding. He pushed himself down the street, frantically trying to think of somewhere he could go to hide out. A car came around the corner and as it slowed down Robbie's heart hammered in his chest. With his hands on his wheels, he froze, but thankfully it passed, though he was sure the man driving it had looked at him intently.

He set off again, but his paranoia was at a new height. Even an old woman washing her front window seemed to look at him with a wary eye. His fear continued to grow as he pushed himself through the streets, unable to think of anywhere to go that would offer him a safe haven. The streets he had grown up in and loved so much were no longer a safe place for him. His family had disowned him, and Cynthia, his only real friend, had cut him out of her life. He had nothing but the clothes on his back, and had never felt so alone and dejected.

Chapter 59

It hadn't taken Dorothy long to get used to Mrs Willis coming in every morning. She soon realised the benefits of having someone to help her, especially as it gave her more time with Rosie.

Her father was much happier downstairs in his own sitting room again, and he had taken to Mrs Willis. Dorothy would often find them playing cards together, or, when the weather permitted, having a natter in the garden. He also thrived on having Rosie around and, though he might never be the man he once was, she had seen a vast improvement in him.

Mrs Willis left at one, and Dorothy sat down to give Rosie her bottle. She had a joint of pork ready to go in the oven later as Adrian was bringing Nelly and Malcolm home with him after work. It wasn't Sunday but she knew that Nelly loved a roast dinner, and apparently they had something they wished to discuss.

Dorothy locked eyes with Rosie. 'I'm not blind and I can guess what they want to talk about,' she cooed. 'Nelly's going to tell me she's having a baby, so you, my little darling, will have a new best friend.'

Rosie never took a whole bottle, and it wasn't long before Dottie saw her eyes begin to droop. She lifted her up to place her in the pram and began to rock her to sleep, her thoughts drifting. Three weeks had passed since Adrian had thrown Robbie out, but she was still nervous about leaving the baby unattended. Her fears were slowly abating, but she was sickened by what he'd intended to do. It was impossible now to fathom how she'd ever fallen in love with him. They say love is blind, but she must have been blind, deaf and bloody stupid to have not seen what Robbie was really like.

Dorothy pottered around doing some housework and checked on her dad, but then heard Rosie crying. She lifted her out of the pram, holding her close to soothe her, and with a burp Rosie brought up some sour-smelling milk that went down the front of Dorothy's dress. 'Oh dear, Rosie . . .' she said, ineffectually trying to wipe it off.

She changed Rosie's nappy and then carried her upstairs. She'd seen there was no point in trying to sponge down her dress so decided to get changed, and after placing Rosie in her cot she took off her soiled garment and rummaged through her wardrobe for something else to wear. 'This will do,' she said out loud as she pulled out a white blouse and blue skirt, but as she slipped on the skirt and pulled up the zip, she noticed that the waistband was a little tight. 'Well, Rosie, I know for a fact that I'm not pregnant so I'm going to have to stay away from those cream buns.'

Rosie gurgled, little arms waving as though in agreement. Dorothy picked her up again and held her close.

Rosie had brought so much joy into her life and, as she held her, she was thankful that Robbie's plan hadn't succeeded.

Hours later, Dorothy checked on her meal. The pork was cooked perfectly with crispy crackling on top, and the roast potatoes were nicely browning. It was almost ready to go. She'd opened up the drop-leaf mahogany table and set it for four, and a bottle of wine had been decanted. She didn't normally drink wine during the week, saving the treat for weekends, but with Nelly's impending news, tonight was going to be a special celebration.

Right on time, Adrian pulled up outside and Dorothy went to the door to greet everyone. It wasn't long before the dinner plates were cleaned and Dorothy was receiving compliments on her finely prepared roast.

'Nelly, if you want a pudding, you've got to tell me what it is you want to discuss,' Dorothy said across the table.

She saw her friend glimpse nervously at Malcolm.

'OK . . . me and Malcolm . . . we're . . . I'm going—' Nelly said, but was interrupted.

'You're going to have a baby,' Dorothy finished for her.

Nelly's eyes widened in surprise. 'Yes, but how do you know?'

'We've been friends for years, Nelly, and I didn't think your increasing girth was due to putting on more weight.'

'I've been putting off telling you,' Nelly said, blushing. 'I wasn't sure how you'd take it, you know, what with you wanting a baby so much.'

'I'm over the moon for you both, really I am. Anyway, I've got a baby now,' Dorothy said, and, loving Rosie as much as she did, she meant every word. 'How far gone are you?'

'Nearly four months.'

'Goodness, you really have taken your time to tell me, but it's wonderful, Nelly. Rosie will have a new playmate and, like us, they'll grow up being the best of friends.'

'I'm just glad I haven't upset you.'

'But you've upset me,' said Adrian. 'I'm going to lose my secretary.'

'Well, funny you should mention that,' Nelly said and once again gave Malcolm a nervous look before she continued. 'To be honest, we can't really afford a baby right now, what with paying our rent and Malcolm's mum's too. I know it isn't conventional for married women to work, especially with a baby, but I'd love to stay on. If you'd agree to it, maybe I could cut my hours or do three days a week.'

Dorothy looked at her husband, who appeared almost gobsmacked. He was quite an old-fashioned sort of chap and she wasn't sure he'd agree to it. However, for Nelly's sake she hoped he would.

'I don't see why not,' he finally answered.

'What will you do with the baby when you're at work, Nel?' Dorothy asked.

'Before you offer, our Linda has already insisted on looking after it. I'll pay her, so she's more than happy. You know how hard up they always are.'

'Oh, so before you asked me if I'll be willing to let you work part-time, you'd already made these arrangements with your sister,' Adrian said.

'Err . . . well . . . yes,' Nelly said, looking sheepish, 'but I would have had to tell my sister it was a no go if you didn't agree.'

Dorothy hid a smile. Adrian had no chance against Nelly's wily ways. She said, 'Come on, don't you think it's time to toast the lovely news?'

Adrian poured the wine, and it turned into a jolly evening. It felt good to be free of living under the shadow of Robbie, and Dorothy fell to sleep that night happy, albeit a bit dozy from the wine.

Chapter 60

Robbie had lost track of days and weeks passing and his mind was muddled. At night he foraged in bins for food and had spent a fretful night hiding under the railway arches near the gasworks. He'd tried to sleep, but every noise had him jumping in fear, convinced that someone was about to attack him. The morning sun didn't bring him any peace either and, though he was cold and hungry, he was reluctant to leave the relative safety of the dark arch.

This was useless, he thought to himself. He couldn't stay here for ever. With trepidation he slowly began to wheel himself out of the shadows. Then he suddenly stopped in his tracks as he could hear the sound of men speaking. He pricked his ears. It sounded like there were at least two men, possibly three, and they were heading his way.

He quickly turned his wheelchair and darted back to the corner of the arch where he hunched down in the dimness, hoping not to be seen. He squinted towards the light as two men in flat caps came into view. To his dismay, one of them spotted him.

'Hey, lad, are you all right in there?' the man asked.

Robbie's stomach churned in dread. They'd found him. He didn't know if these men worked for Brian or if they were just a couple of blokes who'd heard about him being a so-called pervert, but either way he guessed his time was up.

Then Robbie heard the man say, 'He don't look too clever, Arthur. Do you think we should get him some help?'

'Nah, we ain't got time to hang about. Come on, leave the poor bugger be,' the other man replied.

Robbie watched as they carried on past the arch, but his heart was racing. He felt convinced they were going to fetch others.

In a panic, he wheeled himself out of the arch and fled along the road. He noticed a group of schoolchildren walking towards him. They seemed to be pointing at him and whispering. They know, thought Robbie, they know I'm a marked man.

He turned down the next street, heading towards the train station. Maybe he'd have a stroke of luck and be able to beg a free ride with the train guard. Then he stopped again. What was he thinking? He couldn't risk being seen in such a public place.

Robbie flicked his head from left to right, scanning the street for his potential killers. His breathing was rapid and sweat dripped from his brow. Never had he felt such despair.

He saw a young couple turn the corner. They were marching straight for him. For a moment, Robbie thought of turning his chair to flee, but then decided it would be pointless. His arms ached and his energy was low. It wouldn't take much for the young man to give chase and catch up with him.

The couple were just steps away and Robbie braced

himself. Thoughts of his own demise flashed through his head. Would they stab him? Would it be with a gunshot? He just hoped it would be quick.

He watched in horror as the couple stopped next to his chair and the man reached into his inside jacket pocket.

'I didn't do it . . . I swear. Please don't kill me . . .' Robbie cried.

He saw the man and woman exchange a strange look.

'I don't know what you're on about, mate. I only wanted a light,' the man said, bemused. Then he turned to his girlfriend and said, 'Come on, love, the bloke's a bloody nutter.'

Robbie's head dropped in relief, but then snapped back up. What if it was just a ruse and they planned to jump him from behind? He didn't dare look over his shoulder and instead mustered all the strength he had and pushed hard on his wheels in a bid to escape.

He inadvertently turned into a busy main road, only to find a sea of faces who were all staring intently at him. Anxiety coursed through his veins as the mob of people seemed to be closing in on him. He saw someone out of the corner of his eye. Was it Brian? He was sure the man was in the crowd.

'I'm innocent!' Robbie shouted. 'Why won't you listen to me?'

Then his body jerked in fright as he felt someone place a hand on his shoulder. He apprehensively turned his head, expecting to see Brian. Instead, it was a policeman with a colleague, which gave Robbie some small amount of comfort.

He frantically grabbed at the policeman's arm. 'Officer,

they're going to kill me . . . you've got to help me!' he said.

'It's all right, son, calm down. Who's going to kill you?'

'Them! All of them . . . Look . . .' Robbie answered, pointing to the people in the street.

'They're not out to hurt you, son. They're just everyday folk doing their shopping. What's your name?'

'You don't understand . . . they want me dead, all of them!'

Then a thought occurred to Robbie. If he 'fessed up to the jewellery shop robbery, he'd be taken into custody and thrown into prison. At least he would be safe there, and fed and watered. It was a better option than living in fear on the streets, or, worse still, living in a care home for the crippled.

'You have to arrest me. I robbed a jewellery shop in Knightsbridge . . . go on, take me in, I'm guilty.'

'Whoa, one thing at a time. So, no one's out to kill you, but now you're saying you did a robbery? How did you do this then, son?'

'I got up on the roof and through a skylight. I cleaned out the safe.'

The look Robbie saw pass between the policemen told him that they weren't taking him seriously. He felt frantic.

'That isn't all. I jumped a bloke and threatened him with a gun then stole his car too. I did a wages snatch as well, and robbed a pub. See, I'm bad . . . You have to lock me up,' he said in desperation.

'I don't think he's right in the head,' the first officer said to his colleague. 'I think we'd better take him in to see the doc.'

At last, thought Robbie, I'm going to be out of harm's way.

Adrian tiptoed down the stairs. It was unusual for Dottie not to be up, but he knew the wine the night before had gone to her head. He made himself some breakfast and then quietly left for work, sure that very shortly Rosie would begin exercising her lungs and his wife's lie-in would be over.

When he arrived at the office and got out of his car, he was surprised to see the door ajar. Either Nelly had bedbugs and was in the office early, or he'd been burgled. He walked up the few wooden steps that led to the door, but noticed something wasn't right. The door looked as if it had been forced open. His immediate thought was Robbie, but then he realised Robbie couldn't have got up the steps in his wheelchair. Fearfully he pushed the door and peeped inside.

'Mr Ferguson,' a man said in a very gruff, croaky voice. 'Come in. I've been waiting for you.'

The man was sitting behind Adrian's desk, but he didn't recognise him.

'Please, take a seat,' the man ordered.

He didn't like the man's tone, or that he was treating the place as his own, but seeing the two huge, thuggish men standing each side of him, Adrian decided that self-preservation was the best option. He sat down and looked uneasily at the man, wondering what this was about.

'I'm Brian,' the man croaked, 'and there's something you should know about me. I'm not a nice man. In fact, some would say I'm their worst nightmare. I don't know if I'd go that far, well, not unless someone fails to repay a loan. Ain't that right, boys?'

Adrian knew this was something to do with Robbie and this was confirmed when the man spoke again. 'So your little brother . . . where is he?'

'I . . . I . . . honestly don't know,' Adrian told him.

'I had a feeling you might say that. I could have my boys here put a bit of pressure on you and see if we can't get an address off you, but I think you might be telling me the truth. From what I've heard, the shitbag tried to stitch you and your missus up too.'

Adrian nodded, thankful that Brian believed him. He'd hate to think what the man might have done if he hadn't.

'Now personally I don't give a shit about what Robbie did to you and yours, but I do care about the money he owes me and I want it back. Now you're a sensible man. You've got a good little business here, and a nice home. Don't look so surprised, I know all about your house and your wife – Dorothy, I believe? Pretty little baby girl too. You wouldn't want them to come to any harm, would you?'

Adrian was fuming inside, but shook his head. He could put up with picking up the pieces from Robbie, but drew the line at veiled threats to his family.

'I thought not, so I'll tell you what I want. You pay me two hundred quid in cash, and we'll call it quits. I'll make sure nothing untoward happens to your business, home, wife or baby. How about that? Do we have a deal?'

Adrian found his voice, and, though he was afraid, he spoke up. 'I'll give you the money, but leave my family out of this. Stay away from them, or else! I know what my brother is like and this isn't the first time I've had to bail him out of trouble. You'll have your money.'

'Ha, so you ain't a wimp. Good, I like it. A man should protect his own, not try and sell them like your brother was going to do. Unless you've got the cash now, Big John will be here at five to pick it up. Don't let me down.'

'Fine, and I take it that'll be the last of it?' Adrian asked.

'I said so, didn't I? A deal's a deal. You pay me my dues, and you'll never see me again. I'm not a man to break his word.' He scraped the chair back and stood up. 'Nice to have met you,' he said, before leaving the office, followed by Big John and the other man.

Adrian went to stand up too, but his legs had gone quivery. He didn't know why Robbie owed Brian money, but assumed he had run up gambling debts again. He doubted it was two hundred pounds' worth, but he didn't care, just as long as Dorothy and Rosie were safe.

Chapter 61

Robbie shook his head, trying to clear the fuzziness. He remembered being taken to the police station and becoming upset when no one seemed to believe him. Then he recalled a man in a suit injecting something in his arm. Now he was in the back of an ambulance.

'What's going on?' he asked, his voice barely more than a whisper.

He heard the ambulance man call out, 'He's coming round, Ted.'

The ambulance came to a stop, and Robbie was wheeled out. He stared in disbelief at the imposing double doors in front of him. The stonework above was etched with the words 'Lambeth Asylum'.

'No . . . no . . . you can't take me in there . . . no . . . I'm not mad,' Robbie said, but his voice was just a mumble.

'That's what they all say,' the ambulanceman said, and once the doors were unlocked he proceeded to push Robbie through.

Although Robbie wasn't thinking clearly, he knew he couldn't let them take him into the asylum – he'd never come back out. He wished he could have jumped from his chair and run away, but he was completely at their mercy.

A nurse approached, wearing a stiffly starched uniform and an equally stiff expression on her face.

'I take it this is Robert Ferguson?' she asked the ambulance man.

'Yes, this is him. It's all in the file here. The police managed to trace his brother but the brother reckons Robert is a danger so he wants nothing to do with him. By all accounts, he was in a state of hysteria at the station. They called in the doctor, who sedated him. The doctor's authorised sectioning him. His initial diagnosis is paranoid disorder, but this will need confirming.'

'Right, you can leave him with me. Thank you, gentlemen,' the nurse said, and signalled to two orderlies to approach.

'He's all yours,' the ambulanceman said to the orderlies and left.

Robbie's thoughts were very muddled, yet even in his confusion he knew he didn't belong here.

'Wait, nurse, there's been a terrible mistake . . .' he said weakly.

'We'll see about that,' the nurse replied, then said to the orderlies, 'Take him through.'

Robbie wanted to protest further, but was struggling to focus. He felt dizzy and his vision was distorted. It must be the drugs, thought Robbie, remembering the injection.

One of the orderlies took a key from a large bunch chained to a belt around his waist and opened a door. Immediately Robbie could hear a cacophony of cries, moans and wailing. He wanted to fight and to scream out his sanity, but his subdued body wouldn't respond.

As the orderly pushed him through the doorway,

Robbie noticed a young man in tatty pyjamas edging along the corridor wall towards them. The man was repeatedly punching the side of his own head and had dried vomit spilt on his top.

'Get back, Terry. You know what'll happen if you don't,' the orderly warned.

Terry dropped to his knees and hunched down, covering his head with his arms.

'NOOOOOOOO . . . No stick! No stick!' he screamed.

'Do as you're told and I'll spare you the stick,' the orderly said.

Robbie looked again at the orderly and noticed the man had a truncheon attached to his belt next to the chain of keys. Terry scuttled along the corridor and disappeared into a side room.

The wailing continued to echo through the corridor. Robbie covered his ears in an attempt to block out the awful noise and concentrate his muddled thoughts. They passed a door. It was open. He glanced inside and what he saw chilled him to the bone. A bed with restraints and wires and a machine with lots of knobs. Oh, God, he thought, please don't let them do that to me. He'd heard about electroshock treatment for the mad and the thought of it scared the life out of him.

A little further down the corridor, they came to a stop and the orderly unlocked another door.

'Welcome to your new home for the next few years,' he said, then wheeled Robbie into the stinking room.

Robbie slowly turned his head from left to right as he scanned the large ward. There were rows of beds along each side of the room with little more than standing space between them. At a glance, he guessed there must be at least seventy beds, if not more. He saw some men tied to the beds with bandages, others sitting and rocking with blank expressions. One man was running around and dancing like a ballerina; another appeared to be arguing with a wall.

An old man limped towards him. 'Have you seen my Betty?' the man asked.

Robbie shook his head.

'Have you seen my Betty?' the old man asked again.

'No,' Robbie managed to answer.

'Have you seen my Betty?'

'Betty's dead. She's been dead ten years. Get back to your bed,' the orderly said.

'Have you seen my Betty?' the old man asked over and over as he wandered off.

Robbie looked around again, trying to take it all in, but it was almost surreal and for a moment he wondered if he was asleep and having some strange nightmare. He noticed the windows were barred and none of the residents were wearing shoes. He saw a man lying under one of the beds, drooling and touching himself inappropriately, and another with blood oozing from his arm where he was incessantly scratching it. A deathly pale-faced, extremely thin man leaped onto a bed and began loudly shouting to everyone to repent their sins. This seemed to upset people. Some appeared scared and began screaming or crying, others became excited and jumped around howling.

The orderly blew a whistle, and its piercing screech seemed to calm the men. Then he held his truncheon up menacingly and waved it in the air.

'Any more of this and you'll all get it! Now shut up and get back to bed.'

Most of the residents did as instructed, apart from those who looked too out of it to understand.

The orderly wheeled Robbie further up the ward and then stopped at a vacant bare bed.

'This is your place. You'll be issued with a set of pyjamas, one blanket, one flannel, a bar of soap and a toothbrush. We'll be back to collect you tomorrow to see the doctor. Enjoy your stay.'

Robbie felt himself falling forward as the orderly tipped up his chair and he landed in a heap face-down on the bed. He immediately noticed it stank of urine and turned his head in disgust. To his horror, he watched as the two orderlies left the ward and took his wheelchair with them.

As the sedative he'd been given earlier was wearing off, his mind began to clear and the horror of his situation started to sink in.

The overwhelming noise in the ward drowned out his own as he lay back on the stinking bed and screamed until his throat hurt. Bereft, Robbie wept and thought to himself, if hell really exists, then this is it.

Dorothy had been shocked when the police had called to talk to Adrian about Robbie, but after what he'd done to Yvonne and in trying to kidnap Rosie, she agreed that he was dangerous. Adrian had disowned him, wanting nothing more to do with his brother, and she felt the same; any feelings she had felt for Robbie were well and truly dead. He was in custody now so at last she could relax, safe in the knowledge that there was no danger of him trying to kidnap Rosie again. That evening, Dorothy dished up two more dinners as Adrian came through the door. She had already taken a tray to her father and now decided that she and Adrian would eat off their laps today as Rosie seemed to be content kicking her legs out on a blanket in the middle of the lounge.

'Hello, love,' Adrian said, kissing his wife on the cheek.

'Sit yourself down in the living room. Rosie will be pleased to see you and I'll bring your dinner through.'

'It looks lovely,' Adrian said as he watched her spoon dollops of creamy mashed potatoes onto his plate.

'Did you have a good day?' Dorothy asked soon after, as they tucked into their meal.

'Much the same as usual. Nelly seems a bit distracted at times and complaining that her clothes are getting a bit tight. Still, at least she doesn't seem to suffer from morning sickness, or if she does it's over with before she comes to work.'

Dorothy held her knife and fork still and gazed across the room as she thought about what he had just said. 'I'm so excited about Nelly's baby. I hope she has a girl.'

Adrian finished chewing his sausage before asking, 'Why a girl?'

Dorothy thought for a minute, then said, 'I just think it would be lovely. Rosie and Nelly's baby would grow up together and be the best of friends.'

Adrian put his plate on the side table.

'I agree, but it would be equally nice if she had a boy,' he said.

'I suppose so,' Dorothy said. 'He would be like a brother to Rosie and look out for her. I've almost given up believing that we'll ever be able to give her a brother or sister.'

'Maybe, but we have Rosie, and whether Nelly's baby is a boy or a girl, one thing's for sure – I won't allow our

Rosie to go dating with boys, not until she's at least twenty-one.'

'Oh, Adrian, you are funny! You talk about Rosie as if she's your real daughter. It's so nice to hear you being all fatherly and protective.'

'She is my real daughter, and yours. We're her parents now.'

Dorothy stood up from the sofa and sat on the arm of Adrian's armchair. 'I never thought this would happen . . . I can't believe it. Adrian, we really do have a baby!' she squealed ecstatically. 'I think it's only just sinking in. Rosie is *our* daughter!'

Adrian stood up to join his wife and gathered her in his arms.

'Yes, she certainly is, and I couldn't be happier.'

As Dottie looked up into Adrian's eyes and held his gaze, she suddenly realised that she loved him. What an idiot she'd been. She'd wasted so much time lavishing her affections on the wrong brother, but now she whispered the words she knew her husband had been longing to hear. 'Adrian, I love you.'

He looked ecstatic for a moment, but then his eyes clouded with doubt. 'Do you, Dottie? Do you really love me?'

'Yes . . . yes, I do. I love you so much, Adrian, and I think I have for a long time. It's just taken me until now to realise it.'

'Oh, darling, I love you too,' Adrian said, holding her tightly to him.

As their lips met, Dottie knew that Robbie would become nothing more than a distant memory. What she felt for Adrian was real love, lasting love, and she felt truly blessed. They had a child to love and nurture, and as Adrian stood back to look at Rosie with a look of wonderment on his face, she knew that this was a moment she would cherish for ever.

The End

The hardest choice she'll ever make...

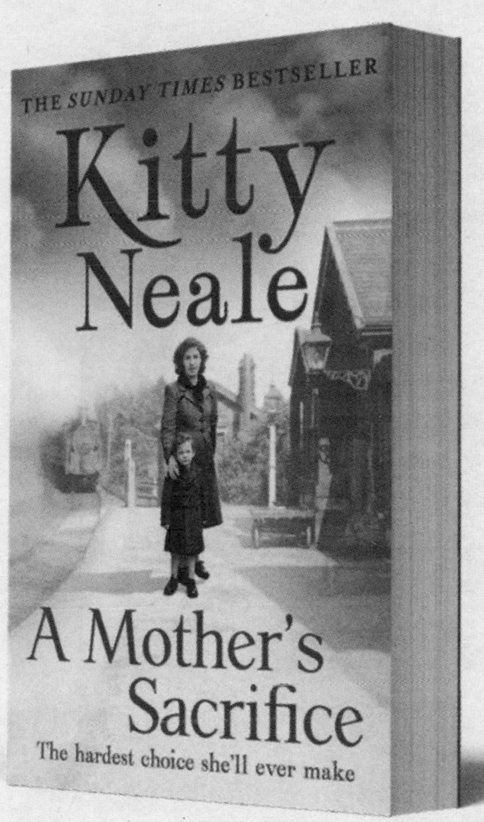

A heart-rending drama perfect for fans of Katie Flynn and Nadine Dorries.

You can never leave a bad man behind . . .

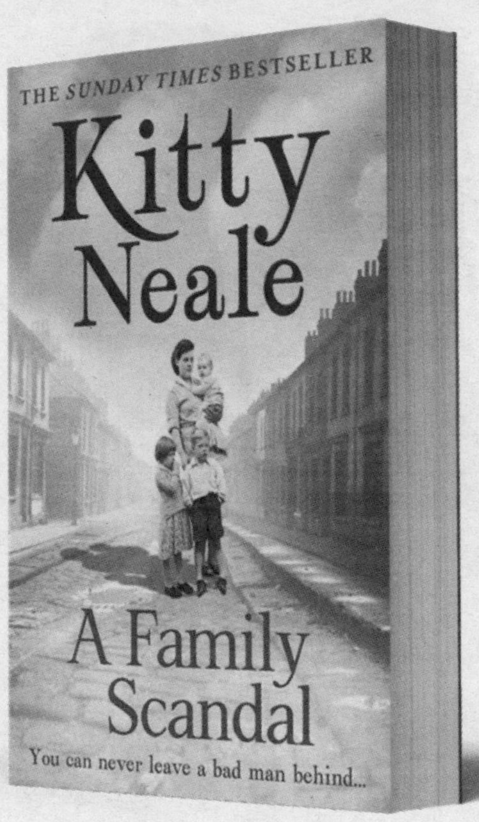

A gritty and emotional family drama from the *Sunday Times* bestseller. *A Family Scandal* is your next must-read!

How far would you go to find happiness?

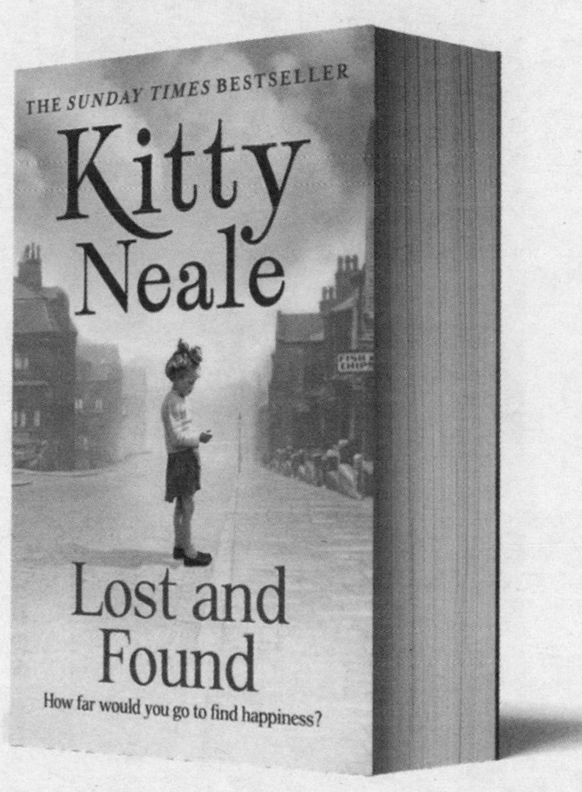

Bullied by everyone around her for years, has Mavis Jackson finally found happiness? Or has she jumped straight from the frying pan into the fire?

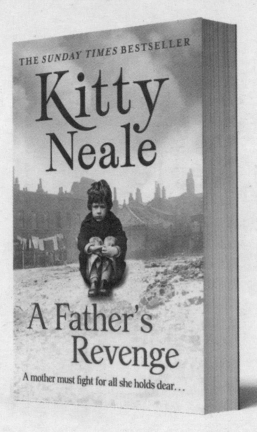

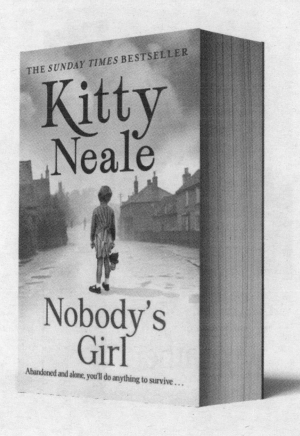

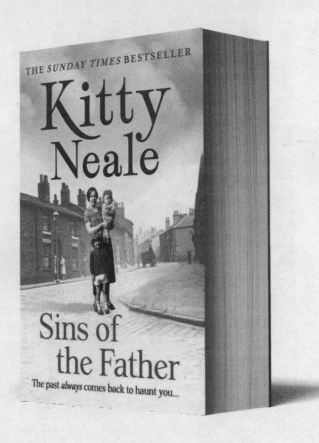